BIRTH
OF THE
DEFENDER

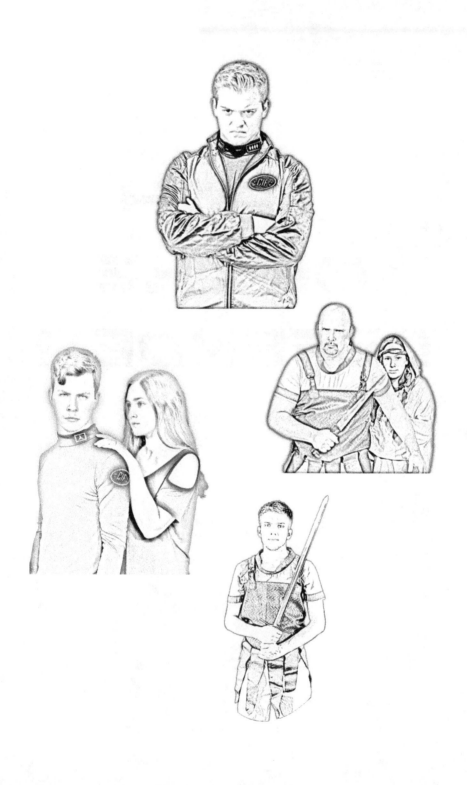

BIRTH OF THE DEFENDER

DEFENDER SERIES PREQUEL

BOOK 0.5

REGGI BROACH

DEFENDER CHRISTIAN
PUBLICATIONS

For I know the plans I have for you, declares the Lord, plans to prosper you and not to harm you, plans to give you hope and a future.

Jeremiah 29:11 NIV

TABLE OF CONTENTS

ACKNOWLEDGMENTS

The Lord has prospered me and given me hope and a future like Jeremiah 29:11 says. He has given me so many amazing tools to get me to that future and a point of prosperity. Before I started writing *Birth of the Defender*, I was new to the writing community. I had just finished writing *Birth of a Revolution*, introducing Tristan Alexander as David's father, and was exploring where to go next. Some of the other writers were talking about doing NaNoWriMo. I wasn't familiar with it and thought I would ride it out to see what all the fuss was about. A couple of days before it began, the idea for *Birth of the Defender* came to mind in amazing clarity. I had to do it. I joined the NaNo and went to town.

This book has awed me from the moment the idea came to me. It is representative of the birth of Christ and John the Baptist, only the order is slightly reversed. God's hand moves in so many ways and we can never see them all. I am so grateful to God for the ideas, thoughts, and dreams he has given me.

I'm thankful for the advice I received from David Stevens, author of the *Fuzed Trilogy*, to get in touch with the writing community. I have learned so much from my fellow authors in Realm Makers Consortium and Iron Sharpening Iron: Christian Speculative Fiction Authors.

This year has had extra blessings as the Lord provided a way for my husband to quit working outside the home and devote more time to helping me publish. *Happy Dance* As a result, Ron has incorporated some great new things into this book. I've been so excited yet nervous because this book is a "little different." I say that about every book, but this one really is different. The chapters go back and forth between one planet and another. I was afraid it would be confusing, but my wonderful husband added some graphic artistry at the beginning of each chapter to help the transitions.

I want to give a great big thanks to my cover models and graphic art models, Jake Wallin, Tommy and Alea Greene, Anna Frazier, Jason Dasher, and Matthew Frazier. I'm thankful these folks sacrificed an afternoon to stand still and make faces at a camera. They all did an amazing job.

Thank you, Annie Douglass Lima, for spending time during quarantine editing. I greatly appreciate your help.

I am very thankful for those who take time to read my books, and who put reviews for them on Amazon or Goodreads. Someone recently said their goal in writing Christian Fiction is to Entertain, Educate, and Evangelize. That really sums up my goals as well. I hope you are entertained, educated, and blessed by what you read.

THE PROMISED ONE

"Help me, please," the young woman cried out as she approached a small lean-to hut and campfire. She didn't know whose camp she was entering, but surely it couldn't be worse than what she was running from. Hearing a rustling, she looked behind her and ran faster toward the small shelter ahead. Not watching her own path, she ran straight into a shadowy hooded figure. The figure grabbed onto her tightly, preventing her from tripping into the fire. The scared young woman's perception was skewed. For a second, she believed the figure was attempting to throw her into the fire. Her instincts took over, and she inhaled sharply to scream.

A soft elderly voice stopped her short of announcing her presence to anyone within hearing distance. "Please don't cry out, young lady. I won't hurt you."

The young woman's eyes focused on the face of an old woman. A single tear slipped down the girl's face as she saw only compassion in the older face. "Please help me."

The woman's grip softened around her. She stroked the young woman's arm gently. "I'll help you. What do you need?"

The girl looked over her shoulder into the dark night. "There are men looking for me." She shivered and sniffed. "They're trying to kill me."

The woman released her grip on the girl. "Why are they tryin' to kill you? What are you? Fifteen? Sixteen? What did you do that was so terrible?"

Without realizing what she was revealing, the young woman absently touched her belly. "I didn't do anything. They think I did, though."

"I see," said the wise old woman. Her weathered skin made her appear older than she was. "What's your name?"

"Slaina."

"My name is Halyn. I am a healer. I travel great distances because I am the only healer around. I teach the women wherever I go about healin' because the day will come when I get too old to travel anymore. How old are you, Slaina?"

"My mother said I was sixteen in the spring."

"Well, Slaina, you look hungry. Let me get you somethin' to eat, and I'll find a place to hide you. Come sit down. I have a nice stew brewin' on the fire. It's more food than I can eat, and I would hate to waste it." Halyn bustled about spryly like a mother hen.

Now that she was feeling more at ease, Slaina's blustery personality started to emerge. The older woman was moving about easily and energetically. Slaina recalled her strong grip on her moments ago. This woman looked to be nearly eighty, judging by her dry, wrinkled face and arms. "How old are you?" Slaina asked without reservation.

The elderly woman had been leaning over the kettle, dipping some stew for her young guest. "What?"

"How old are you?" She asked again.

"Why do you want to know?" Halyn's eyes peered into the young girl's soul.

"Your skin is old, but you're still strong and active," the young woman brazenly answered.

Eyes filled with mirth, the old woman straightened up. She handed the bowl of stew to Slaina and smiled. "You might make a good healer. You're very observant and aren't afraid to speak your mind. I'm sixty-three summers old. I've spent most of my years outside in the sun, and my skin tells the tale. Now eat, while I find a place to hide you. If they aren't far behind you, they'll be here soon."

Halyn went into her lean-to shelter and began rearranging things. Slaina felt guilty about letting the old woman, who wasn't as old as she originally thought, work alone. She had to admit she was exhausted, and the food felt good in her belly. Slaina emptied her bowl quickly, then went to see if she could help.

Halyn was moving sandbags around inside and shoving the canopy over a ditch around the outside of the shelter. Slaina walked up to her. "Halyn, what are you doing? How can I help?"

"Finished eating so soon?"

"Yes, ma'am. It was delicious. Thank you for sharing it with me." Slaina had not forgotten her manners.

"Go fill your bowl again and bring it in here to eat," the woman ordered. "I'll have a place for you to hide momentarily."

When Slaina re-entered the shelter, Halyn had her sit in the ditch just inside the edge of the tent. "Eat quickly," she instructed.

Slaina shoveled her food down and handed the bowl to Halyn. Halyn took the bowl and poured her a cup of water. "Has your stomach been bothering you in the mornings? Perhaps more than just the morning?"

Slaina suddenly looked distrustful. Fearing her secret might have been discovered, she answered hesitantly. "What makes you ask such a question?"

Halyn smiled gently. "I saw you rubbing your belly as though it were botherin' you, and I can't guarantee my cookin' is the best. I'm good at mixin' medicines and potions, not so good at cookin'. I have an herb that will help your stomach. I can add it to the water if you would like."

Slaina looked at the medication—she was having trouble. Her recent fear had temporarily settled her stomach, but she worried it would soon come back, slowing her escape from those pursuing her. Slaina decided the chase was nearing an end. Either they would catch her or they wouldn't, and whatever she did at this point would be meaningless. She slowly nodded her approval to the woman.

Halyn stirred a spoonful of herbs into the water. She handed the girl the cup and instructed her to drink all of it. Slaina drank every drop despite its slightly bitter taste and handed the cup back.

"Slaina, you need to trust me. I will protect you. Lie down. I need to cover you to hide you. No matter what you hear, no matter how frightened you might be, don't make a sound. Don't cry out, not even a whimper. Don't even breathe loudly. The medicine I gave you will make you very sleepy in a few minutes. Don't be afraid to sleep."

Slaina's exhaustion and full belly were taking their toll on her. The medication hadn't started to work, but it wouldn't take long for it to add to the numbness she was already feeling. Slaina did as she was told. The ditch was just wide enough and deep enough to keep her form level with the ground.

Halyn pushed the edge of the lean-to canvas to the far side of the channel. She placed wicker mats over the girl, then moved a row of thin sandbags around the top and outer edges of the mats. She talked to Slaina as she worked, trying to keep her calm and to give her an understanding of what she was doing. "I'm goin' to put down my straw mattress on top of the mats. I'm puttin' my blankets over top of that, so you probably won't be able to see or hear much anymore. As soon as I think it's safe, I'll get you out of there, I promise. Go to sleep if you can."

Halyn heard Slaina respond with a muffled and drowsy, "Yes, ma'am." She smiled to herself. Something was special about this young woman, and she was glad to help her.

Halyn fixed herself a bowl of stew and ate quickly. Halfway through the bowl, she stopped eating and grabbed a shovel and a hoe. She moved to the outside of the shelter. The trough Slaina was lying in was meant to protect the shelter from runoff water. If anyone examined the area, they would see the shelter protected on the back and far side. An experienced traveler would know there should be a ditch on the near side as well. Halyn built up the sod barrier above Slaina's head, then redirected the trench down the new outer edge of the shelter. She was working feverishly to complete the task when she heard riders approach from behind her. She stopped working and turned to see her newest guests.

Six riders surrounded her camp. "Old woman, why are you out here all alone?" The leader addressed her gruffly.

"I am a healer and travel this route regularly. I used to travel with my husband, but Pateras took him two winters ago. Are you ill or injured? Do you need my services?" Halyn offered as she wiped sweat from her brow.

"No, we're all fine. We're looking for a girl who escaped from a city east of here. She has committed crimes against her family, her fiancé's family, and against Pateras. We need to take her back to answer for her crimes. Have you seen anyone pass through here this evening?" The man answered in the same hateful tone.

"No, I haven't seen any children since I made camp this evening," Halyn replied.

"This is a young woman, not a child." The leader corrected.

"You said a girl. I took that to mean a child. I wondered why you'd be pursuin' a child so voraciously." Halyn shook her head. "I've been alone most of the evenin' until now." Halyn looked around as though she were searching for something. "Have you seen a cat around here?"

One of the other men called out to her. "Old woman, you haven't finished your meal? What's distracted you from it?"

The leader added, "you were working very hard when we arrived. What's so urgent?"

"My bones are achin', and…" Halyn sniffed the air, licked one of her index fingers, and held it up. "…there's rain comin'. I haven't finished diggin' my trenches to protect my shelter. I can eat my stew after the rain starts. I prefer not to dig trenches in the rain." Halyn looked around and called out, "Here, kitty, kitty. Come inside before you get wet."

The leader was growing annoyed. "Let me know if you see the young woman I mentioned. She might need a healer. She's with child, a child that doesn't belong to her betrothed."

"I will gladly see that the young woman receives whatever she deserves. I don't suppose you kind gentlemen would care to help me dig my trench, would you?" Halyn knew these men would want to move on quickly to avoid the rain and find their prey.

"Sorry, Healer. We need to find this girl before the rain obscures her trail. We know she came this way, but the ground is rocky, and with the sun long gone, finding her is getting harder. I'm sure we're close, though. Forgive us, Healer, but we don't have time to help you dig your trench. May we light our torches with your fire, though?"

"Of course you may. Perhaps you should've lit them sooner. You may have missed something in the darkness already," Halyn chided. "May the light of Pateras guide you on your quest for justice."

The leader dismounted and carried his torch forward. He glanced into the woman's shelter, looking for anything that appeared out of place. Seeing nothing, he lit his torch and climbed into his saddle. He shared the flame with his men.

Turning to Halyn, he addressed her again. "I didn't get your name, Healer."

"Nor I yours, enforcer of the laws of Pateras," Halyn challenged.

"I am Nasha of the city of Somi. The governor of Somi has sent me to find this girl because she has embarrassed his household. His nephew was the one she was engaged to marry when it was learned that she was with child. The child is obviously not his. The governor wishes to make an example of her. The governor has taught her parents a lesson they won't soon forget about raising children. It devastated his nephew."

Before he could continue his tale, one of his men interrupted him, "Sir, we need to move on. The wind's picking up and I smell the rain."

The man nodded. "Spread out and move toward the river. She may try to lose us in the water."

The group rode off quickly, without another word. Halyn wisely completed her trench. She was done in a few minutes and added more warm stew to her half-eaten bowl. Putting a lid on her kettle, she sat down in her shelter to wait for the rain and stared into the darkness. She was fairly certain one man from the group of soldiers was still watching her.

The woman finished her stew, drank some water, then placed a bucket outside to collect the rainwater when it fell. She called out a couple more times. "Here, Kitty, come on in before you get wet." Halyn had traveled with a cat in previous years, but the cat died the year before her husband. She smiled at her own cleverness because she had not lied to the men. She merely suggested that if they heard Slaina make any small noises or movements, it might have been a daft old woman's missing cat. Her promise to see that the young woman got the justice she deserved didn't mean she would turn her over to them. She felt certain that justice was not what these men were offering.

Just as the rain started, Halyn pulled the final flap of her shelter over the opening and secured it with more sandbags. As she closed the flap, she caught sight of the one remaining horseman behind a brief line of trees. The man turned and rode away. The sound of the hoofbeats confirmed what her eyes perceived.

Halyn finished securing herself from the weather and rearranged the inside of the shelter. She scooted the mats and straw mattress off her new ward and covered her with a warm blanket. Halyn placed extra sandbags around the sleeping girl to be certain the rain didn't reach her.

Before she settled in, Halyn cast her eyes upward and asked, "Pateras, why have you brought this child into my life? There is something special about her. What do you expect from me?"

Halyn heard nothing but the rain falling.

Early the next morning, the air was fresh and clean. The birds were singing chipper songs as Halyn packed her belongings. She waited until the last moment to wake Slaina, knowing the young woman was still exhausted from her escape. She placed the items strategically in her wagon to create a compartment to conceal the young woman.

As the sun and the noise of Halyn loading the wagon disturbed Slaina, she crawled out of bed. She moved slowly at first, then as growing nausea and the desire to relieve herself overcame her, Slaina darted behind the nearest cover. She returned shortly, looking rather peaked.

Halyn handed her another cup of water laced with herbs. "I didn't put as many herbs in this cup. You needed the rest last night. Today you just need to settle your stomach."

Slaina sipped the liquid cautiously. She was uncertain if it would stay down this time. A few minutes later, her stomach was feeling better, so Halyn provided her with some bread and cheese. Slaina nibbled it slowly as Halyn finished loading her belongings and hitched her nearby horses to the wagon.

Slaina looked up sorrowfully. "I'm sorry. I should be helping you. I've just been so sick lately."

Halyn helped Slaina into the space she had carved out for her in the wagon. She covered the girl with the poles from the lean-to, then threw the canopy over the entire wagon and fastened it down.

The two talked idly for the first part of their journey. Once Slaina's stomach settled and she had eaten the bread and cheese, Halyn got pragmatic with the girl. "Slaina, do you know why your stomach has been so upset recently?"

"No, am I sick, or is it because everyone is so upset with me?"

"It's because of the child you carry," Halyn explained.

"But why would he make me sick?" Slaina asked innocently.

"He? Do you mean the baby's father?" Halyn asked.

"No, I mean the baby. He wouldn't do that to me, would he?" Slaina wished she could see Halyn's face.

"Being with child will sometimes make one sick," Halyn explained.

Slaina grew silent. After a long period of quiet, Halyn finally asked, "So, you believe you're carrying a boy?"

"I was told I would have a son. His name is going to be Arni," Slaina responded.

"Told? By whom?" Halyn queried.

"I don't think I want to talk about this anymore." Slaina knew this was the part where she had gotten into trouble at home.

"All right then, we can talk about something else. Did you hear the men who were looking for you come to my camp last night?"

Halyn couldn't see it, but Slaina's eyes grew wide with fear. Halyn went on, "They told me about your situation."

Again, the girl didn't respond.

"Slaina, what did they do to your parents?" Halyn asked. She wasn't sure if the girl knew, but perhaps she could get her to talk more this way.

Tears slipped down her face. "Halyn, please don't make me talk about this," Slaina begged, her voice clearly broken.

"I'm sorry, girl. I didn't mean to upset you, but I know Pateras sent you to me for a reason—but I don't know what that reason is," Halyn lamented.

Slaina wiggled out of her niche. She pushed the poles aside and pulled the canopy back as far as she could. With the sides tied down, she couldn't move it very far. "Pateras sent me to you? How do you know this?"

Halyn smiled. Now they were getting somewhere. "Pateras does all things with a purpose. He doesn't make mistakes or have accidents. I travel this route every year, but this year I'm two weeks early, and of all the campsites in the countryside, why did you end up in mine? It had to be Pateras."

"Please don't think I am lying or crazy," Slaina begged. "I am neither."

Halyn stopped the wagon by a stream to allow the horses to drink. She helped Slaina get out of the wagon to stretch her legs. She fixed the girl another cup of herbs and a small snack. As they sat down to eat, Halyn told the girl bluntly, "Never lie to me, and you will have my trust and my help."

"I won't lie to you, but please understand. What is happening to me is hard for even me to believe. My parents didn't believe me at first. My fiancé doesn't believe me, and his uncle is livid."

Halyn nodded. "The things Pateras does can be very unbelievable. Has he done something like that in your life?"

Slaina nodded nervously. She had told this story three times before, and things went very wrong afterward. "P-Pateras sent a messenger, unlike any man I have ever seen. He told me I would have a son. He's the one who told me to name him Arni. He is the son of Pateras. No man has ever touched me. I swear it." Slaina watched Halyn's reaction.

Halyn wasn't ready to form an opinion, and her face testified to that fact.

Slaina went on slowly. "I told my parents what the messenger said. My father was angry. He demanded to know what man had touched me. I told him no one had. My mother cried a lot. They watched me carefully every day. I was never allowed to go anywhere alone. Then I started getting sick. My father had a dream. The messenger who spoke to me told him I spoke the truth. My father went to my fiancé and tried to end the marriage quietly. He planned to move us away from Somi. My fiancé came to me after that day and spoke harshly to me. I told him what happened. He didn't believe me either. I went out of the city gates to visit my cousin. She is a strong follower of Pateras. She believed me. As I came inside the gates, there was a crowd gathering in the town square. My parents were being flogged publicly. The soldiers demanded to know where I was. All of my brothers and sisters, even the little ones, were forced to stand there and watch. My mother saw me. She waited until the noise died down, then screamed out my name and told me to run. I slipped slowly and quietly out of the gate and ran to my cousin's home. I told her what happened. She got on a donkey and took me as far as she dared, then headed back to her home. I've been running for four days. I don't even know exactly where I am now. I've tried staying off the road, but I keep getting lost."

For once, there were no tears in her eyes. She was prepared for Halyn to reject her as everyone else had. Halyn stared at the ground for a moment, then looked up seriously. "I have been taught that Pateras would send his one Promised Son in this way. I believe you."

UNDERCOVER MISSION

Meanwhile, ninety-eight light-years away on the advanced Commonwealth world known as Juranta, a handsome, young undercover officer's life is about to take an unexpected turn.

"Chief Warrant Officer Tristan Alexander reporting as ordered, ma'am."

"At ease. Have a seat, Chief."

"Yes ma'am." The dedicated young officer sat as ordered. He wondered why he had been called into his lieutenant's office. He didn't recall screwing anything up. The only complaints against him came from criminals he arrested, and those were based on their anger at getting caught. He wanted very much to jump the gun and ask what the problem was, but he reined his anxiety in.

Lt. Esmé Rhys peered over some files in front of her. A frown seemed to be permanently etched into her face. She finally looked at the warrant officer in front of her. "I suppose you're wondering why I called you in here."

"Yes ma'am, I am." Tristan's response was blunt but genuine. There was no humor or insubordination in his tone.

"I called you in because you were recommended and approved for a long-term, deep-cover mission, if you're interested," Lt. Rhys began.

Tristan leaned forward. Deep-cover missions were dangerous and exciting. He was definitely interested. He realized his lieutenant was still frowning, so Tristan proceeded cautiously. "You have my attention, but I need some information before committing to anything. You seem concerned."

"I'm not used to seeing missions like this. It smells of something from a deep government covert ops department. You know, like one of those departments that doesn't actually exist." The lieutenant was worried about what wasn't being said in the files.

"What sort of mission is it?" Tristan asked. He was getting more curious by the moment.

"Your mission is to establish a relationship with a young woman in college. Get to know her and her family. This says that additional orders will be supplied if the relationship is firmly established." Esmé continued to study the file as though she would find something she had missed.

"My mission is to establish a dating relationship with a college co-ed? For what purpose? Am I looking for illegal activity, or am I using her to get to someone else?"

Esmé finally stopped searching the files. She pressed a button on her desk and raised the privacy screens in her office. The walls turned a milky white and prevented anyone from seeing into the room. Tristan's concerns rose with the privacy screens.

She sat back in her seat and folded her arms across her chest. "Permission to speak freely is granted because it's what I'm going to do. This mission looks almost surreal. The parameters given are to meet this young woman, establish a dating relationship with her, get to know her family and... marry her."

"Marry her? Seriously? You want me to marry a total stranger?" Tristan balked.

The lieutenant sat there, waiting for his emotions to peak and settle out before telling him the rest. She bit her lip as she watched and waited for a moment.

Tristan began to pace. Why was he wanted for this mission, and what was the part he wasn't being told? He realized his superior was watching him closely. He stopped pacing and asked, "Is she pretty?" That wasn't the only question on his mind, but it seemed like a good place to start.

Esmé put the young woman's picture on the screen. She was an attractive woman. The picture was replaced with a surveillance video of his target laughing and enjoying the company of her friends.

Tristan sat down gingerly in his seat. "Ok, she's attractive and has a cute laugh. That's a plus, but marriage? You said I was recommended and approved for this mission. Who recommended me and who approved me?"

Esmé looked around at the blank walls guiltily. "I recommended you, but that was before I knew about the marriage part. It will be a short-term marriage contract and the government reserves the right to revoke the contract at any time without any penalty to you. You'll use your own identity, and from what I read in the file, you'll get some serious perks from this job. If you get her to accept your marriage proposal, you will be advanced in rank to a second lieutenant. You will still be a Commonwealth officer as your cover, but you are going in as a white-collar crime investigator."

"White-collar, like tax evasion or embezzling? That's not exactly my strong suit."

"Apparently, they've already got that covered. You're going to college to take some accounting classes, and your target, Jessica Deacons, will be assigned as your tutor," Lt. Rhys explained.

"I'm supposed to sweep a woman off her feet who's going to immediately think I'm an idiot because I don't comprehend accounting? Whose idea was this?"

Esmé shook her head. "Somebody above my paygrade. Just convince her you are ambitious about your job and impressing your superiors. Tell her you wanted to hire a tutor before you got into trouble. She won't look at you as an idiot. She'll see you as passionate."

"And we don't know what I'm looking at her family for?" Tristan really didn't like going into a situation blind.

"Apparently the orders say if Miss Deacons isn't attracted to you, the advanced information is top secret and you won't need it if you can't get close to her."

"How long is this assignment supposed to last?" Tristan was still suspicious about this task.

"It says the mission, if successful, is a two to five-year minimum with an option for being longer." Esmé watched Tristan's emotions subtly spike again. She had two more vital pieces of information to share with him, if he handled the rest well enough.

"Why so long? Wait. There's more, isn't there?" The urge to pace again rose. He pushed himself further back in his chair and looked at the face on the video screen. The image had frozen on a close-up of Jessica's smile. She did appeal to him. Tristan pulled his eyes from the image as Esmé filled him in on the next information pertinent to the mission.

"You—uh—you have to start a family with her. The government will pay any child support required after the marriage ends, so you will NOT lose any pay. I told you there were some serious perks. The file also says as soon as the mission is complete, you will advance another full rank. If the mission surpasses time and grade, you will be advanced in rank during the mission and a second rank will be awarded at the end of the mission, even if sufficient time has not elapsed. Tristan, is this bothering you as much as it is me?"

Tristan sighed. "My mission is to get married and have kids. Yeah, not what I expected when I walked in here at all. Why did you recommend me for this?"

"You're young, handsome, and personable, which is what this job calls for. I didn't know about this other stuff until now. There's one more thing. You are cautioned not to get emotionally attached to your new family and to be prepared to use extreme measures if necessary."

Tristan's heart skipped a beat. Extreme measures? There was more to this than met the eye, for certain. Maybe there was something here to sink his teeth into. "Make sure I understand this correctly—I get to keep my day job—I just have to have a wife and kids on the side? I can't stay in the department, can I?"

"No, you'll be transferred to the Government Financial Oversight Division. You will still have some minimal street assignments. In order for your cover to be believable, your job will mostly be a desk job. You have to go home at night to keep an eye on your... family. Your new supervisor knows how much you enjoy getting out in the trenches, and he's willing to give you the leeway you want, to get your hands a little dirty. If you take this assignment, though, you cannot take on any high-profile cases unless they fall under the auspices of Financial Oversight."

Lt. Rhys continued to study the young man carefully. It was obvious he was giving the assignment serious consideration. He was ambitious and a good officer. She was seriously regretting her recommendation. She hated to lose him from her department. She fully expected him to advance through the ranks rapidly. "There's one more perk I failed to mention."

Tristan cocked his head sideways. Another perk? "What is it?"

"Since you'll only have the one major assignment, you'll be free to use your desk job time to pursue whatever additional training you want. You can get additional training in hand-to-hand combat, weapons tech, ordinance disposal, forensic accounting, field medic... whatever you want."

Tristan's eyes lit up. Unlimited training? By the time his five years elapsed, he could have enough training behind him to take on any assignment he wanted.

Esmé shook her head. "I knew that last item would do it for you. Tristan, I'm going to be straight with you. This assignment sounds... off. It worries me. Keep in mind, things aren't always what they seem to be. I'm giving you a copy of this file. Take a couple of days off to review it and get back to me with your decision." Esmé copied the information onto a data crystal and handed it to him across her desk.

Tristan stood, sensing their time was at an end. "Yes ma'am. You don't want me to take it, though, do you?"

"My opinion isn't relevant. This is your decision."

"I understand that. You know me and what I'm capable of. If you don't think I'm capable of doing this job, then that's relevant to my choice."

Esmé smiled at the brash young man's way of twisting things to his advantage. "You're well-trained and have great instincts, but you're still young and inexperienced. You are a valuable asset to the department, and I don't want to lose you. That being said, this assignment is either going to be a glorified babysitting job, which is a waste of your talents—or there is something really nasty going on and you could find yourself in a situation you won't be able to escape."

"Understood. Thank you, ma'am. Is there anything else?"

"This is need-to-know only. You and I are the only ones who need to know anything about this. As far as the rest of the department is concerned, you are considering a transfer to GFOD. I need your decision before the end of the week. One more thing you should know: my superiors said I should push you to take this assignment. I trust I have said all the right things, even if you choose not to take it?"

"Yes ma'am. You were very convincing. If I decide against it, it will be after much personal deliberation. Will it hurt my chances for advancement if I don't take it?" Tristan's brow furrowed.

Lt. Rhys scowled. "Not as far as I'm concerned." Her tone indicated there was a reason to have doubts. She looked around at the blank white walls and followed up softly. "Someone higher in the chain-of-command may have different ideas. I've gotten messages from several levels up the chain expressing opinions about the matter."

"It sounds like unless I want to ruin my career, I'm taking this mission," Tristan griped.

"Take the time, as I suggested. You never know, that young woman may not even like you. You might come up with some other options. Don't make a hasty decision." Esmé stood and offered her hand to the junior officer. "I wish you the best."

"Thank you, ma'am." Tristan shook her hand, then stepped back and saluted.

Esmé turned off the privacy screen and dismissed the young man. She worried about what would happen to him. She knew what choice he would make even before he did.

Tristan headed to his sparsely decorated apartment. His job was his life, not this apartment. He wondered what he would do with a wife… and kids? Maybe a wife could make his apartment actually look lived in. There were certain niceties he had denied himself. He hadn't really given much thought to settling down. He expected he might take a wife once his career was firmly established, ten years down the road. Ten years? In ten years, he would be thirty-three. That was a little late to start having kids. Some started families later, but they always seem to regret waiting that long.

The longer he mulled the idea around in his head, the less he wanted to delay starting a family. The warning about extreme measures kept returning to haunt him. Would he possibly have to arrest his own future wife and the mother of his future children? "Extreme measures" was a term one didn't hear very often. It could mean arrest, detention, or… or… no, it couldn't possibly include that.

Something about this assignment was definitely disturbing. Could it really affect his career if he didn't take the mission?

Tristan sat on the sofa and set the data crystal Lt. Rhys had given him on the coffee table in front of him. He stared at the crystal as though he could read the files with his naked eye.

The concerned young officer finally stood, shoved the crystal into his pocket, and walked out the door. He jumped onto the closest public transport and rode to the nearest park. He got off and found a bench facing a playground to sit on. It took him a good five minutes of deep thought to even realize there was a playground in front of him. His eyes focused on the children running around chasing each other and shrieking excitedly. He saw one child fall and skin his knee and a worried mother hurry to his side. Tristan smiled as the mother treated the knee, dusted her son off, and sent him back to play.

The words "extreme measures" popped into his head again. His smile disappeared. Why was this bothering him so much?

"Are you mad?" a voice asked.

Tristan looked around to locate who had spoken to him. He spotted a little girl propping on the end of the bench he was sitting on. "I'm sorry. What did you say?"

"ARE… YOU… MAD?" she yelled.

Tristan scowled. "No. Why are you yelling at me?"

"Because you didn't hear me the FIRST TIME. I have to yell at my Pappaw, too." The little girl bounced back and forth on the bench.

Tristan sat upright and turned to talk to the child. "I don't have a hearing problem. I have a listening problem. You just have to make sure I'm listening before you ask me something. And no, I'm not mad. What makes you think I'm mad?"

The little girl continued to wiggle around on the end of the bench as she talked. "Your face thinks you're mad. It's frowning. My momma bangs things when she looks like that."

Tristan smiled. The little girl looked to be about four or five years old. Light brown braids with stray hairs poking out of each braid hung down the back of each side of her head. She had big blue eyes. Her observations were intriguing.

Tristan leaned forward. "I'm thinking really hard, but I'm not mad. Maybe I should let my face know?"

The little girl wrinkled her nose. "Yeah, maybe you should. Does it hurt when you think that hard?"

"No. Why do you ask?"

"'Cause your forehead gets wrinkled like you gotta headache," the little girl explained.

A voice called out across the playground. "Tessa! Go play and leave that man alone!"

"YES, DADDY! I gotta go." The little girl skipped toward the playground.

"Tessa... thank you for the words of wisdom. I enjoyed talking to you." Tristan smiled at the little girl.

The girl stopped skipping as he spoke and turned to face him. She tipped her head to one side and wrinkled her nose again. "Glad I could help!" she chirped, then trotted off.

Tristan smiled. This was why he had chosen the career he had. He was doing this job to protect the innocent and the helpless. Perhaps he had been looking at this new assignment wrong. Maybe Jessica Deacons was a victim instead of a criminal hiding something. Was she some rich guy's daughter who refused protection because she was oblivious to the danger she might be in? Were the extreme measures for her protection? Did they tell him not to get attached to his potential new family because if she found out he was there to protect her, she might throw him out? A family had a way of making a person take safety more seriously.

Tristan watched Tessa play for another few minutes. Kids could be fun.

Tristan suddenly felt the eyes of Tessa's protective father on him. He realized he had been paying an inordinate amount of attention to the little girl, and it was making her father uneasy. He decided to put the man's concerns to rest. Tristan walked directly over to the man. "You have a beautiful little girl, and smart, too."

"Thanks," the man replied suspiciously. Tristan's CIF uniform was the only thing that eased his concerns.

"She helped me make up my mind. I've decided to propose to a particular young woman." Tristan smiled and walked away, feeling the man's eyes on him as he left the park.

Thirty minutes later, he found himself wandering around the college campus where Jessica Deacons was a student. He located an information kiosk and reviewed the layout of the campus. The surveillance video he had seen was taken in an outdoor café. According to the map, there were three such places on campus. From what he remembered of the video and the building layout, he located the café.

He entered the cafe, ordered a coffee, and sat near the table he had seen Jessica and her friends using. Tristan glanced around at the sun. He hadn't seen a time and date stamp on the video. The video could have been from the last week or a year ago for all he knew. This might not be a regular hangout for her.

While he waited, he accessed the computer built into the table and started reviewing the academic calendar and class schedules. He decided if he was going to take this mission, he should go ahead and enroll in the school. He input his information, but the computer rejected his application, insisting it was a duplication. He pulled up the duplicate and discovered he was already registered, and his classes were scheduled for next semester. Classes were to begin in three weeks. Somebody really wanted him to take this assignment.

Tristan scowled. He picked up his coffee and tried to take a swig from his empty cup. He hastily shut the computer interface and took his cup to get a refill. Turning abruptly toward the dispensers, he ran straight into someone coming from the other direction. It was two young women who were talking excitedly about the posting of their recent grades.

Tristan steadied the young woman he had knocked off balance and apologized quickly for bumping into her. He took a step back and blinked. It was Jessica Deacons. She was prettier than the video representation. He quickly apologized a second time. "Can I get you a coffee to make up for my clumsiness?"

Jessica smiled for a second, then politely declined. She smiled again as though she couldn't help herself, but her eyes kept falling on his uniform.

Tristan hadn't changed clothes since leaving the base. He discerned this was a problem of some sort. He knew he was going to have to figure out what the issue was and how to get past it. Tristan moved on to refill his coffee. It was his job to be observant, but today he was only hitting it about fifty percent of the time. He had been oblivious to the little girl in the park. He accidentally bumped into the woman he was being assigned to on this mission. What else was he missing? Tristan thought back to the video. Yes, that was it. Part of the conversation included idle chatter about what each of the girls had been drinking. Jessica had mentioned the café had the best peach tea.

Tristan ordered a peach tea, then refilled his coffee cup while he waited. In a moment, the drink was ready. He delivered it to Jessica, who was caught completely off guard. "Here you go. Maybe this will make up for my clumsiness. After you declined the coffee, I figured maybe you were more into fruit tea or something. I went with peach—hope that's okay. I'm sorry again. I'll be more careful next time." Tristan nodded to her friend, then excused himself and moved back to the table he had previously occupied. He pulled up his class schedule and the layout of the campus. He peered at it, trying to memorize his way around.

His focus was more on the girls at the next table than it was on the information in front of him. The girl with Jessica giggled and whispered to her. Jessica pushed her away. The girl finally got exasperated with her friend. "Jess, what's wrong with you? He's cute and he likes you."

"He's in the military. After Robbie joined the Brigade, Mom and Dad had a fit. I don't dare bring a guy home who's in the military. It would break my mom and dad's hearts," Jessica explained loudly enough that Tristan could barely pick it up.

So that was the issue. Tristan wondered how he could get around the problem, short of changing his cover story. Maybe he could get her to fall in love with him before she even realized it, then she wouldn't care what her parents thought. He decided right then, the first step was to dress in civilian attire any time he was around her. It wouldn't change who or what he was, but it would keep his job from being blatantly paraded in front of her.

The next morning, Tristan arrived in Lt. Rhys' office. "Lieutenant, is there any way at all to find out what this is about?"

"No, I've tried."

"I did a little investigating of my own. Military men turn Jessica Deacons off because her brother joined the Space Brigade. I think we can get past that, but…"

"You did what? Chief, you weren't authorized for that!" Esmé realized her voice had carried outside of her office. Several curious glances came from nearby stations. She angrily stabbed at the security protocol controls. The door secured, and the walls turned milky white. "Tell me exactly what you did."

"I went to the university to look around. I was strongly leaning toward taking the assignment, so I started to apply for entrance into the university. I discovered someone had already registered me for classes next semester. I also accidentally bumped into the subject. I managed to make a positive impression, but I learned she has an aversion to military men. I might be able to work around that, though. Lieutenant, I don't know what's going on, but somebody is pretty sure I'm taking this mission." Tristan waited for Esmé's reaction.

Esmé shook her head in frustration. "Chief, have you come to a decision?"

Tristan knew she didn't want to hear his answer. "Yes ma'am. I need to find out what's going on. I want to take the assignment."

Lt. Rhys took a deep breath. "All right, I'll make the arrangements. Tell your coworkers at your leisure that you've chosen to transfer, and it will happen in the next week or two. Expect them to have the usual farewell parties and such. Play along. You are officially undercover. You'll have a preliminary meeting with your new supervisor next week. Make sure your reports and cases are closed out or handed off."

"I'm sorry if I've disappointed you. As soon as this is over, I would like to transfer back. As you said yesterday, there's a chance she might not even like me. I have to try this, though." Tristan admired his supervisor. She trusted him and gave him more latitude than older, more experienced field agents.

"I'm not sure you had a choice in the matter. It's been an honor working with you, Chief. I look forward to having you back in the department." Lt. Rhys was fairly certain she would never work with the young man again. Something about this assignment had an air of finality.

After another few minutes of farewell chatter, the chief left the office strangely excited by this new mission. Esmé sat down and stared at her blank screen as she attempted to gather her thoughts. Another officer poked his head into her open office door. "You all right, Lt. Rhys?"

Esmé shifted in her chair. "Yes, I'm fine. Did you need something?"

"Not really. I just wondered what was up. Chief Alexander seems as though he's in an unusually good mood, and you seem distracted."

Esmé grimaced. Here we go, she thought. "The chief has requested a transfer. I approved it. He'll be moving to GFOD in the next couple of weeks."

"Alexander? GFOD? You're joking. That is not where I pictured him landing. What brought this on?" The young officer looked as though he had swallowed an insect.

Lt. Rhys began to build on the story. "He didn't give me a lot of information, but I got the feeling he has his eye on a lady friend."

"A girl? I never pictured him settling down. He always struck me as a use 'em and lose 'em type guy."

Lt. Rhys added a word of warning. "Well, don't go spreading that around, because he never mentioned being in a relationship. I'm just guessing, okay?"

"Yes ma'am," the young man answered, then went in search of Chief Alexander.

IN PLAIN SIGHT

"Halyn, where are you taking me?" a weary Slaina asked softly from her hiding place in the wagon.

"Eventually, to my home. We're only a few days' ride from there, but I have to stop along the way. I have patients to see," Halyn explained. When Slaina didn't respond, Halyn said, "You're safe, Slaina. What's got you worried?"

Slaina looked around at the confines of her cramped hiding place, searching for answers that weren't there. "Why do we have to stop? I want to get far away as fast as I can." Slaina's eyes filled with tears. Every minute this wagon was taking her further from her family and the only life she had ever known. She was torn between the desire to run home and run away. Why were these terrible things happening to her and her family? She was doing what Pateras had asked of her. Slaina reached down and touched the slight bulge in her belly. She hoped this tiny baby was worth all of this. It had cost her everything.

"I wish I could push these horses as fast and as hard as I could, to get you back to my home. But if I did that, it would raise questions among the locals that would point those soldiers directly at us. If they come after me, they will find you. Girl, do you understand the importance of that baby you're carryin'?"

Slaina wiped away her tears again. "I know the Ancient Texts speak of a Promised One who will come to rescue us from the Reckoning. This baby is the one promised in the Ancient Text prophecies. He is to be the beacon for all of mankind to guide them and rule all of creation."

"Do you know what that means?" Halyn pressed.

"Only a little of it. I really don't know why this is happening to me. I'm nobody. My family isn't important or wealthy. Why did Pateras choose me?"

"Perhaps he saw somethin' in you that you can't see in yourself. We don't have to understand why Pateras does things. We do need to listen to him and obey him," Halyn gently explained.

"You seem to know a lot about Pateras. Does he talk to you?"

"Sometimes. I think I spend more time talkin' to him than he does to me. There are times when I have to remind myself to let him talk too. I get to thinkin' the weight I carry on my shoulders is more important than the weight he carries on his."

The conversation was keeping Slaina's mind off her hot, cramped hiding place and the waves of nausea that threatened to return. "How did you learn so much about Pateras?"

"My husband had a copy of the Ancient Texts. He used to read them to me every night before we went to bed. We would talk about them for hours, or even days." Halyn's eyes grew misty as she reminisced about those precious moments with her beloved husband, moments she would never again have.

"I wish someone could read them to me. If I'm to raise the son of Pateras alone, I need to know everything I can about him. A boy needs to know about his father, and this child more so than any other." Slaina thought if she could somehow be reunited with her own family, her father could read the Ancient Texts to them.

Halyn again anticipated Slaina's thoughts. "Child, you know you can't go home. You and that baby are in danger. If you rejoin your family, it would put them in danger as well. The Dark Lord doesn't want that child to be born. He doesn't want him to grow up and die for the crimes of humanity. If you and that baby die now, no one will ever know who he is or why he came."

"If this baby is so important, why isn't Pateras protecting us?" Slaina complained.

Halyn got quiet for a moment. "Slaina, those soldiers are sitting at the top of the rise ahead. Don't make a sound, no matter how scared you are."

"Yes, ma'am," the girl whispered. Her heart was pounding so loudly she was certain they would hear it as they passed by.

"Pateras, guard us and keep us safe. Don't let them find that girl." Halyn spoke with more confidence than she felt.

The soldiers waved for Halyn to halt her wagon when they reached the top of the rise. Halyn pounced on the reason for them stopping her before they could ask. "Did you find that girl you were lookin' for yet?"

The leader had intended to take an intimidating lead in the conversation. He scowled at the woman's quick question. "No. I don't suppose you've seen her since we last spoke."

"I haven't seen any new faces since you gentlemen left me alone to dig my ditch last night," Halyn snapped.

"We're sorry, Healer. We had to try to locate that girl before the rain. We meant no disrespect. The governor of Somi is anxious to put this matter to rest. Why are you so angry? Surely we haven't provoked you." The leader knew better than to offend a healer. If one needed her services and had caused offense, he might well remain in need, or her services could cost him dearly.

"My bones were achin' from the rain. I spent the last hour of the day diggin' a trench that would have taken you and your men five minutes to dig. My stew got cold and I'm gettin' too old to be sleepin' on the ground. I ache all over. I'm eager to get to my home and settle in before winter gets here. Is that sufficient reason to be angry?" Halyn spat.

"I suppose it is, old woman. Please forgive us, but this situation is of the utmost importance. Here's a coin to pay for the inconvenience we have caused you. Perhaps you can stop in the next town and get a hot bath and a soft bed to rest your weary bones."

Halyn looked at the coin suspiciously. She decided she should take it and offer a small amount of forgiveness to him. "Perhaps I misjudged you, young man. How is it you can perform such a harsh job with a kind heart beating in your chest?"

The man looked at her suspiciously. What was she trying to say? "I am doing what Pateras has asked of me."

One of the soldier's men seemed ambitious and continued to look for ways to impress his leader and improve his station. "Healer, who were you speaking to on the road? We heard your voice before you came up the hill. Do you have a passenger in your wagon?" The younger man challenged.

The leader suspected the same thing, but a voice in his head quietly cautioned him not to pursue this. "Did you find your cat, Healer?"

Halyn looked at the leader and smiled gratefully. "No, my kitty didn't come home last night. It's okay, though. We've traveled this route for years. He knows his way home."

"You didn't answer my question, woman. Who were you talking to?" The younger soldier interrupted again.

Halyn turned her gaze to the usurper. "You're a brazen young man. I was speakin' to Pateras. Why don't you be silent and let the adults talk?"

The man's face flushed bright red. He was nearly thirty winters old. How could she possibly suggest he was a child? He drew his sword. "Maybe we should search your wagon, old woman."

The leader knew his authority was in danger of being lost to the younger man. "Marek! Stand down. Did no one ever teach you that it is unwise to anger a healer? As a boy, I was taught never to anger a sorcerer, a politician, my father, or a healer. If she is committing any wrong, you had better have proof before drawing a sword. Right now, Pateras is her judge. If she's hiding the young woman we seek, and we find out, then we will punish her to the fullest extent of the law. But we cannot interfere with a healer without just cause! Now put that sword away before I do it for you! Remember your place!"

Marek slowly sheathed his sword, glaring at the old woman the entire time. Halyn met the man's glare with equal venom. The leader spoke again from the opposite side of the wagon: "Dismissed, soldier!"

Marek pushed his horse around behind the group of soldiers, waiting for orders from their leader. He had no desire to look any of the men in the eye right now.

"Healer, forgive us. Go about your business. Listen carefully to the words of Pateras. I know his words tell us to obey the authorities he has set over us. Perhaps there are some here today who need to be reminded of that."

The leader glanced at his brash, now embarrassed, zealot. His eyes landed on the elderly woman with an equal amount of meaning. He knew she was hiding the young woman, but without more than a gut feeling, it could be detrimental to him to accuse her without reason. Out here, away from the populated cities and townships, he could easily slay her and throw her body in the river. No one would know for certain who had done it, and if the young woman were in the wagon, she would be easy enough to find. If the young woman weren't in the wagon as he suspected, suspicions surrounding the old woman's death and who had done it would cause other healers to avoid the province. No, it was never wise to provoke a healer.

Halyn returned the man's meaningful gaze and softly replied, "I have chosen to obey Pateras first and foremost. He places those in authority over us, and they are expected to obey him as well. If they rebel against Pateras, they will face his wrath. I will obey those authorities until such a time that they prove disobedient to him. I pray Pateras gives you all the knowledge that you need to find the young woman you seek." The blessing was meant to make the kindhearted soldier think long and hard about the task assigned to him. Halyn chirruped to her horses and slapped the reins gently, urging them to move on down the road.

One of the other soldiers glanced at his buddies and quipped, "You would think a healer could heal herself from being in a foul mood."

Without turning around, Halyn loudly answered the man's wisecrack. "I'm old, not deaf. There's no cure for old."

The young men snickered softly, except for the one who was still trying to quell his damaged ego.

Their leader waited patiently for the old woman to get out of sight down the road. His second in command was the brash young warrior who had challenged the old woman moments ago. The old woman's impudence continued to eat away at the younger man. When he could stand it no longer, he moved over to speak to his commander. "Nasha, you know she's hiding that girl. She has to be in her wagon. Why did you let her go?"

"I told you why. You never interfere with a healer without being sure of it. Let's head back to her campsite and see what we can find," Nasha ordered calmly.

"Shouldn't one of us follow her? The girl could escape," Marek argued.

Nasha glared at the impudent young warrior. "I doubt that. If she's with the Healer now, it's because she has placed the young woman under her care and protection. She won't abandon her. She'll keep her close by. Second, she'll drop her guard if she thinks we no longer suspect her. The last thing, and this is the most important thing you need to realize, is that the old woman believes Pateras is protecting the girl. If she's right, it doesn't matter what we do. We will not be able to catch her, and we certainly won't be able to kill her."

Marek was taken aback by the man's last conclusions. The girl was a criminal. Why would Pateras protect her? "What are we going to do, then? Wait a day, then follow them?"

Nasha shook his head. "No, I want to take another look at her campsite. If two people were there, we might find some evidence of it. Let's get moving." Nasha steered his horse in the direction they had come and ordered over his shoulder, "Let's go!" The men took off at a moderate pace but rode hard for the next couple of hours to get back to the old woman's campsite.

Nasha stopped short of the area. He sent one man to take the horses to the river to feed and water the weary animals. The other men spread out and inspected the area. One man yelled out, "Sir, I may have something!"

Nasha and Marek moved cautiously over to the man's location. "Sir, I found some smaller, less indented footprints here behind the bushes. It could be the girl's, and someone threw up."

Marek pushed again. "Now can we go after her?"

"No, not yet. It only indicates they took a similar path. It doesn't mean the healer knew the girl was here. She could have arrived after the healer left or before she set up camp. Keep looking."

The men returned to their search pattern. Nasha stood still and played the events of the previous evening over in his mind.

He stared at the ground where the lean-to had been. The ditches ran up the right side of the shelter, across the back, then forked off into two distinct ditches down the left side. Nasha moved to the top of the inner channel and squatted. He picked up a long brown hair matching Slaina's. The inner channel was dry, but the outer channel, although now mostly dry, showed signs of recently having been rained on.

The old woman had concealed the girl inside her shelter. Nasha pondered the reasons for it. It was clear the woman had openly defied them. This was more than a case of pitying a poor, lost waif. This old woman was far wiser than that.

Marek approached his leader. "What did you find, sir?" Marek saw the same things Nasha was seeing, but it seemed more prudent to ask what his superior was thinking than to make an unwarranted assumption.

Nasha pointed at the extra ditch and held up the lost hair strand. "This ditch and strand of hair are the proof we need to pursue her. We still need to proceed cautiously, though. By now she's entered the next township. We don't have enough men to search the entire city without risking losing her completely. Give me a few minutes to consider our best chances for catching them. The horses need to rest a little longer, too. Let's head to the river."

They sat at the river's edge and ate while Nasha sat alone with his thoughts. He really needed to talk privately to the healer. There was something definitely off about this situation.

Halyn drove into the next town, as expected. Merchants and townspeople greeted her cheerfully as she passed by. She pulled her wagon into a large stable. "Joren, where are you, boy?"

A teenage boy slightly older than Slaina came trotting out of a horse stall carrying a pitchfork. Leaning it against a wall, he responded, "I'm here, Healer Halyn. What can I do for you?"

"Bring me a handcart. I'm going to put my supplies on it. When I get it loaded, take it to the meetin' house for me. Feed and water my horses, and they could use a good brushin' too. I'm going to need your help with some other things, but I'll tell you about those later."

"Yes, ma'am. The cart is right outside." The young man trotted out and returned momentarily.

Halyn selectively unloaded her wagon onto the cart.

Joren pushed the supplies to the meeting house as requested. While he was gone, Halyn released Slaina from her hiding place and sent her to the loft of the stable. She hoisted a few supplies to the loft to keep Slaina comfortable for a few days. Halyn climbed into the loft to see that the frightened young woman was properly situated out of sight. She peered out a window to see Joren unloading her supplies in the meeting house.

Slaina could already see what was about to happen. "Halyn, please don't leave me alone. I'm afraid."

"I'm just goin' to be up the hill there. Look out this window. See where Joren is? That's where I'll be. I can't take you there, because no one can see you. If those soldiers come this direction, anybody who's seen you could tell them you're here. It's safer this way. You aren't goin' to be alone. Joren will be with you. He'll keep you hidden and safe. He and I will be the only ones who know you're here."

Halyn saw the girl fighting back tears again. She wrapped her arms around her and hugged her tightly. "Trust Pateras—he's bigger than those soldiers. He'll keep you safe. Just stay up here and stay quiet. I'm leaving you some of the herbs to help your stomach, one pinch in one cup of water. One more thing before I leave: Pateras trusts you with his only son. That's reason to be joyful, not sorrowful. He has every reason to take care of you. You are highly favored, and I am honored to be of service to you."

Slaina blinked in surprise. She was nothing special. Why would a healer revere her like this? She would have to ponder this thought for a time. Halyn was simply glad to give her something positive to hold on to. It seemed the girl didn't grasp the fullness of what was upon her.

Joren returned as Halyn was cleaning out the other supplies from her wagon and stacking them in an empty stall. Joren looked perplexed. "Healer, what are you doing?"

If the soldiers happened to find her wagon, they might have been able to determine she had arranged the items in it to hide the young woman. Halyn wanted to pull everything out of the wagon to remove the hiding place. She continued to work as she explained to the boy, "Storm came through last night. I want to get everything out so it will have time to dry before I leave here. I also need my wagon swept out. Can you do that for me?"

"Yes, ma'am. Anything else?" Something about the healer seemed different today.

"Yes, young man, there is somethin' else. I placed some personal items in the loft. I need you to keep them safe. Somebody's likely to come lookin' for my personal stuff. If you stay out of the loft, you can honestly say you haven't seen anything they're lookin' for. Do you understand? Don't go up there even if you hear noises," Halyn warned.

Joren glanced at the loft. "Did you put a goat or something up there? A goat's gonna need water. I could put a fresh bucket of well water up there every morning and if I find any other buckets by the door, I could empty them."

Halyn smiled. The boy had always adored her. She treated him like a relative and not just a stable boy. "Thank you, Joren. I will owe you a great deal after this one."

"Healer, I have only one request. Take me with you when you leave this time."

Halyn sighed. "Take you where? What would you do? I am a poor woman. I can't afford to pay you."

"I'll make my own way, but I can't do that here. No one will ever see me as more than a stable boy. Give me a place to stay, and I'll earn my keep. I promise." Joren's eyes weren't pleading. They were determined. Something told Halyn that if she didn't find a way to take him with her this time, he'd follow her anyway.

"I'll see what I can do," Halyn promised. "Pack your things and have them ready to go at a moment's notice."

"Yes, ma'am. Shall I do that now, or does your... goat need water first?" The young man didn't know for certain what or who was in the loft, but he was determined to look after it.

"The... goat or whatever else is residing up there is fine for now. Take care of your normal duties first and pack your things later tonight. I would prefer not to draw any unnecessary attention."

"Yes, ma'am. I'll get your horses fed and watered and your wagon cleaned right away." The excitement was evident in his voice.

Halyn headed up the hill to the meeting house. It was a town hall of sorts, and when she came to town, it was hers to use as she pleased. She set aside one area as living space and set up another portion of the building to treat patients. She meticulously arranged her supplies to find what she needed easily. Word got out quickly that she had arrived, despite being a little early this year. A few people came that evening, bringing small ailments for her to treat and gifts of appreciation. The town kept a bed for her in the meeting house that was far more comfortable than the straw mats on the ground. As Halyn closed her eyes to rest, she kept a candle burning in an open window facing the stable so Slaina could see where she was. She couldn't see Halyn herself, but she would at least know where the woman was if she needed her.

Halyn rose early the next morning and went to check on Slaina. She brought her something to eat and gave her a project to do. "Slaina, I assume your mother has taught you how to make clothing?"

"Yes, she has. I made the tunic I'm wearing." She proudly displayed the ornate stitching on the sleeves and collar.

"You do good work, girl. I brought you some cloth. You need to make some clothes and diapers. Time will get away from you before you know it and that baby will be here. We'll also be staying in town a few days, and you'll need something to occupy your time. Here's a diaper I borrowed from a local woman and a baby gown to use as a guide. Only make two or three gowns. Use the rest of the material to make diapers."

Being the oldest of several siblings, Slaina had washed and changed her fair share of diapers. She knew how often a baby would need changing. The thought of changing so many diapers and washing that much laundry was suddenly very unappealing. Looking at the tiny baby gown softened her thoughts again. She was about to be a mother. She was going to have a baby of her own.

Slaina worked diligently until she heard a lot of noise below her. Several riders entered. "Stable boy! Where are you?"

Joren came rushing from a nearby stall. "Yes, sir? What can I do for you?"

"Feed and water the horses and point us to the nearest tavern where we can get some food and lodging."

The voices sounded familiar. Slaina crept to a crack in the walls of the loft to peek between the slats. Her eyes grew wide as she recognized the soldiers who had been chasing her for days. She inched her way to the corner furthest from the ladder into the loft.

Nasha was addressing the stable hand. A creak and a gentle rustling sound reached his ears as Joren took the horses' reins from the soldiers. Nasha's eyes followed the sound. A small spray of dust and hay drifted down from a crevice in the slats of the loft.

The men headed toward the door of the stable, except for Nasha, who looked back at the young man. "Which way to the tavern, boy?"

Joren stopped leading the horses. "Follow the main road up the hill. Go past the meeting house, and it's a few more buildings down on the right."

Joren got busy with the horses, trying to keep things caught up as he had promised Halyn.

Nasha stepped outside to join his men. He took a few steps, then stopped. "You fellows go on—I'll be along in a while. I want to pay the stable boy in case we have to leave quickly to catch that girl. I'm also going to grab some more food supplies from the market we passed. Rent me a room on the top floor facing the sunrise. Try not to get drunk. The day is still young."

Nasha knew his weak admonition would only serve to make them drunk faster. Marek wasn't with the other men because Nasha had sent him to request additional troops from the governor. This township was too big to search, and both Nasha and Marek knew it. If the soldiers took the time to eat and drink, Halyn would have no reason to believe they were watching her.

Nasha went back inside the stable. He walked into the stall where Joren was unbridling the horses. "Boy, I need some information. Do you have any horses for sale? I need a fast one."

"Yes, sir, there's four horses in the corral for sale. The bay one is the fastest of the four. He's not worth as much, though. He's not good for plowing or pulling heavy wagons."

"How much?"

Joren looked around to make sure no one was near enough to hear him. "The stable master said to ask fifteen coins for him, but he said he'd take less. Sir, I was planning on using my earnings to buy that one for myself."

"How much did the stable master say he would take for the horse?" Nasha pushed.

"Twelve," Joren grudgingly replied.

"Do you have all the coins you need to purchase the horse?" Nasha asked.

"No, not yet. I'm a little short still."

"I believe I only need the horse for a short time. When I finish my business here, I could sell him back to you. Here are fifteen coins for the horse and one for the care of our other horses. When your master comes to collect, give him the twelve coins he needs, plus the one for boarding ours. When I am done with the horse, I will sell him to you. Do we have a deal?" Nasha was attempting to buy some goodwill with the young man in addition to the horse.

"What about the other three coins? What did you want me to do with those?" Joren sensed there was more to this deal than he could identify.

"Fifteen is a fair price for the horse. I am willing to pay it, but I see that you need a few extra coins to buy the horse yourself. This helps you buy the horse, and it helps me as well. Essentially, I will only pay rent on the horse because I will sell it to you for whatever you can pay me." Nasha hoped this would be enough of an explanation because he had work to do.

Joren still looked concerned. "Even with the coins you allow me to keep, I will still be two coins short. I could only give you ten coins for the horse."

"It will be enough. Do we have a deal?" Nasha pressed.

"Yes, sir," Joren answered quickly.

Nasha started to turn and walk away, then stopped again to ask another question. "Is there a healer in the town? I've ridden that horse so long I have a boil that needs lancing and maybe a poultice."

"Yes, sir, the healer Halyn is in the meeting house, up the hill," Joren answered.

Nasha smiled disarmingly. "Halyn? Is her companion with her?"

Joren's eyes jumped to the loft for a split second, then came back to Nasha. "Companion? Halyn's been alone since her husband died a while back."

Nasha's smile faded. He had seen what he needed to from the young man. Hiding his newfound knowledge, the man frowned. "I'm sorry to hear of her husband's death. I'll be careful what I say to her."

Joren's face relaxed. Nasha added one last thing before he walked away from the boy. "I will also need to borrow a saddle for that horse. Do you own a saddle?"

"Yes, sir. It's nothing fancy, though."

"Perhaps since I'm giving you three coins you won't mind if I borrow that saddle too."

"Of course not. Do you need the horse saddled right now?"

"No, I'll let you know when I'm ready for it." Nasha walked away. He noticed a wagon covered by a canopy. He pulled the canopy off. It was the healer's rig, but all of her things were missing.

Joren walked out of the stall in time to see Nasha snooping. "Sir, that's the healer's. I cleaned it for her. The storm had it all mucked up. I put that over it to keep it from getting mucked up again."

"I thought it was Halyn's wagon. What happened to her belongings?"

Joren pointed inside the stall next to the wagon. "I've got them spread out in here. The storm left everything damp. She was afraid it would get mildewed if it wasn't aired out properly."

"She's quite right. Halyn is a wise woman. I—I—" Nasha suddenly swayed and fell to the ground.

Joren stood still in shock, then dropped to his knees and shook the man. Nasha didn't respond. Joren jumped-and raced out of the stable toward the meeting house.

The second the young man was gone, Nasha rolled to his feet and ascended the ladder to the loft. Reaching the upper level, he pulled his sword from its scabbard and walked around stacked sheaves of hay and a loose haystack. He found Slaina curled up in the corner clutching several scraps of cloth. She knew she couldn't escape this large, muscular soldier without help. He had her cornered. She uttered the only words she could. "Pateras, please help me."

"Why would Pateras help you?" Nasha's question was less rhetorical and more genuine than it seemed. "You are guilty of the crime of fornication."

Slaina slowly uncurled and stood before the large man with a new courage. "No, I'm not guilty of fornication. No man has ever touched me."

"You're with child. It doesn't happen any other way, young woman. Has some man lied to you? Taken advantage of your innocence? Name him, and we will punish him. You shouldn't die for the crimes of another."

"No man has touched me, in any way, ever." This time there was fire in her eyes. "A messenger from Pateras came to me. He told me, according to the prophecies from the Ancient Texts, the Neumatos would come upon me and I would have a son. I am to name him Arni. He is to be the sacrifice to free his people."

Her explanation was not what one would expect of a woman caught in fornication. "What did this messenger look like?" Nasha questioned.

"He was frightening to see. His face and his clothes were whiter than the sun shining on the snow in winter." A faraway look crossed Slaina's face as she spoke. When she finished her description of the messenger and the events, she grew quiet and waited for Nasha to decide her fate.

Nasha squinted at her. "There's only one problem. There's no proof your story is true."

A voice from behind Nasha calmly spoke. "Pateras, please protect her. Nasha serves you. Give him the proof he needs to know this child is the Promised One."

A brilliant flash of light engulfed the loft. A booming voice proclaimed, "This maiden carries my own beloved son. My delight is in him. Do not harm her." The brilliance vanished, and for a moment, no one could see anything.

As his vision cleared, Nasha sheathed his sword. He turned to face Halyn. "Healer, you and I need to talk."

THE COVER STORY

Tristan arrived at his new post two weeks later and reported to his superior officer, Capt. Leland Barrett. Tristan arrived in uniform, fifteen minutes early, and waited in the reception area for his appointment time. At one minute prior, he approached the man's office door and signaled his presence.

The door slid open, admitting him. Tristan walked in, officially reporting to his new commanding officer. He snapped to attention, announced himself, and saluted.

Capt. Barrett was in his forties, slim but sturdy, with dark blond close-cut hair, and wore civilian business attire. Capt. Barrett glanced up from his computer at Tristan, who remained at attention, holding his salute in place. When he finished perusing the files, he finally acknowledged Tristan's presence. "You trying to impress somebody? Take a seat."

"Yes sir." Tristan wasn't trying to impress the man. He was just following protocol. Before he could offer his explanation, Capt. Barrett moved on. "So, you're Chief Warrant Officer Tristan Liam Alexander?"

"Yes sir."

"I've been briefed on your assignment and I'm not buying this bunch of garbage. I don't want any loose cannons in my outfit."

"I don't think I understand, Captain." Tristan shifted in his seat.

"I want to know who's pulling strings for you," the man challenged again.

Tristan sat up straighter. "I believe I would like some answers along those lines myself. I wasn't really given a choice in this assignment."

"Are you trying to tell me this isn't some cushy assignment for you and your girlfriend to get married and start a family?" Capt. Barrett leaned forward. He wasn't happy to have this brash young man come into his department and play house.

"This girl is an undercover assignment. I looked into the mission, and I've already met her once. Although I have to admit she's attractive, and this gives the impression that this will be a pleasant assignment. I don't really know the woman, and I didn't ask for this assignment. I was quite happy in Covert Ops. I will do the job I was assigned, whether I like it or not."

Leland stared at him for a moment. "You expect me to believe you had nothing to do with this?"

"Whether or not you believe me is entirely up to you. I will follow my orders. If my assignment bothers you, take it up with someone with a higher pay grade than mine," Tristan snapped. He realized he could be making a mistake by addressing a superior officer in such a tone, but he felt it was important to make his position clear.

Leland continued to eye the chief, waiting for whatever else he might add. Tristan finally asked, "Do you know why I'm supposed to enter into a relationship with this woman?" He prepared to ask more questions concerning the potential use of extreme measures. It suddenly dawned on him that his new supervisor knew no more than his last one had.

Capt. Barrett had an epiphany of his own when he learned this young man didn't even know the woman he was assigned to. He got out of his chair and moved around to lean on the edge of his desk. "No, I don't know anything more. I thought you or the young lady had some ties from higher up and that you were jumping ahead of more qualified agents to work in this department."

"No sir, I prefer fieldwork. I was told I could do some occasional low-profile work in the field on this assignment," Tristan ventured cautiously.

"My orders say not just low profile, but you aren't to take on anything that could put your own life at risk. I guess we're supposed to turn you into a family man, from what I can piece together." Leland was talking a little more freely now that he knew this was a genuine assignment and not a luxury posting. "Exactly what do you know about this assignment?"

Tristan relayed everything he had been briefed on, along with the things he had learned from his accidental meeting with Jessica.

Capt. Barrett folded his arms across his chest. "Well, you may be in luck. Our division operates under a special dispensation because of our work with other governmental agencies. You have to maintain military grooming standards and health requirements, but we only wear uniforms when dealing with other military agencies in an official capacity. You can break her in to the military idea slowly. I'll assign you an office. You'll be operating fairly autonomously, but I'll check in on you periodically. Submit your reports to me. I'll give you the occasional cursory assignment after you've completed your courses at the university, to help sell your cover. I'll inform the other officers in the department the minimum they need to know, which is pretty close to what the two of us already know."

"Is that wise?" Tristan was a minimalist where information was concerned. Having others know too much could get one killed.

"These guys are five to ten years older than you are. They're going to think the same things I did about you if I don't set the record straight. That could put your cover in jeopardy if your new bride comes to see you at work. It could make being in the building uncomfortable for you if these officers don't trust you. Your cover is, you transferred in here as an intern to learn from your classes and the guys in the department. You need to get to know these people personally. It'll help sell your cover if Miss Deacons hears you talk about your coworkers. Are we clear on everything?"

"I believe so, sir." Tristan was feeling better about the man. His initial impression had been more than a little distasteful.

"Good. Let's go introduce you to the department."

Capt. Barrett led the way to a conference room, where a meeting was already in progress. The officer leading the meeting hesitated as the two entered, but continued when Capt. Barrett didn't step forward to take over. When the woman reached the end of her presentation, she stepped aside and offered the floor to her superior.

Leland moved to the front of the room and activated the privacy and security protocols. The clear walls turned the familiar white and an electronic barrier stopped all sounds and electronic signals from leaving the room. Leland eyed each man and woman to be certain there were no outsiders present.

"Ladies and gentlemen, I would like to introduce CWO Tristan Alexander to you. He is transferring into the department as an intern. This comes from somewhere far above my pay grade, so I need your full cooperation in acclimating this young man. Based on his age and the lack of interns we have in this department, you might have guessed he's not an intern, but he also isn't Internal Affairs. His assignment is outside the department. This department is his cover, and now every one of you is a part of that cover. You are to treat him as a real employee and a genuine co-worker. You may not see a lot of him to begin with, because he's being assigned to study accounting at the university. He needs to look and act like one of us, so take him under your wings and teach him. You blow his cover story, you will get shipped to the most remote outpost I can find, and it will be an arctic planet.

"I've just spent a few minutes getting to know him. He's genuine and straightforward. I think most of you will get along with him. There are a couple of you that don't get along with any of us, so I don't expect you to get along with him either. Any questions?"

Other than a few snickers, there were plenty of questions, although none were voiced. "Mr. Alexander, care to greet your new coworkers?"

Tristan stepped forward, knowing he was not going to be well received. "Thank you sir. Hello everyone. I look forward to getting to know you. I apologize if my presence causes you any difficulty. I'll do my best to keep out of your way. This—uh—assignment is not my preferred area of law enforcement, so try to overlook my rough edges. I am looking forward to doing my fair share. Nice to meet you."

Tristan turned his attention to his supervisor. Leland nodded to the woman who had been conducting the initial briefing. "I meant what I said about helping him fit in. I'm going to show him around the department. Carry on."

Leland escorted him around and introduced him to the few who were not in the staff meeting. Lastly, he showed Tristan to his office. There were two or three empty rooms, but Leland chose a small one in the middle of a row of offices. Tristan had noticed the location of the empty spaces. When he saw which one Capt. Barrett assigned him to, he was quietly impressed. He expected the man to shove him off into a corner somewhere.

Leland scrutinized the young man's reactions. "I trust this office meets with your approval?"

"Yes sir. It's perfect."

"I worked Covert Ops for a couple of years—couldn't stomach it. I transferred a couple of times before I landed here. These are good people, but they may have trouble with you. Nobody gets in here at your age." Leland continued to watch the young man. His early days in Covert Ops had never completely left him.

"If that's the case, let them give me a hard time. I can handle it. If they think I have some connections higher up, then that's what an outsider will need to see. Even an outsider can tell I'm the youngest man in the building. It will add to my cover story of needing a tutor to impress my new boss." Tristan watched Capt. Barrett for a reaction. Knowing what the man thought when he first walked in, he hoped this was a topic fully put to rest.

The muscles in Leland's cheeks flexed a time or two, then relaxed. "Sorry I gave you a hard time about this. It just looked very suspicious."

"It's understandable, especially if they didn't give you any more information than what I've gotten."

Capt. Barrett nodded, then placed his hand on the I.D. panel on the door. "Computer, program office identity protocols to CWO Tristan Alexander."

The computer replied, "Identity protocols now recognize CWO Tristan Alexander as primary user. CWO Alexander, please confirm identity."

Tristan placed his hand on the computer terminal on the desk. "This is CWO Tristan Alexander. Serial number 771XSTU340."

The computer droned on, "Voiceprint, handprint, and biometrics scan confirmed. Access granted. Would you like to add retinal scan and passcode protection protocols?"

Tristan pulled his hand off the computer terminal. "Maybe later," he droned.

"What are your plans now that you're settled in here?" A part of Leland enjoyed his Covert Ops days, but the good never outweighed the bad.

"My classes don't begin for three more days, so I'm going to study up on Miss Deacons and basic accounting, and get to know the people around the office. Let them take out any grudges or frustrations now. Get it out of their systems. I'm also picking some higher-level self-defense training courses. If it's okay with you, boss, I'm gonna skip out early to go to class," Tristan grinned.

Leland stopped a smile from forming on his face. He was starting to like this intelligent and calculating young man. "You skip out early on your first day at work, and they may not put their grudges behind them very quickly."

"You may be right. I'll skip today's class and pick up tomorrow." Tristan had seen the hint of amusement on his supervisor's serious face. He was going to have to watch this man closely to know what he was thinking.

Tristan did exactly what he told his new boss he would. He knew so little about accounting, he had better start studying.

Three weeks later, after his first test in accounting, on which he scored well but not exceptionally, Tristan requested a tutor.

While preparing dinner alone in his apartment, the computer chirped, alerting him to an incoming communication. Recognizing who the call was from, he walked into the kitchen and pulled his food off the heating surface. Still stirring it briskly to prevent it from sticking to the pan, he called out, "Computer, accept incoming transmission."

An uncertain voice called out from the computer terminal, "Hello? Is someone there?"

Tristan hollered across the room, "Hang on, I'm coming." He continued stirring the mixture in the pan until he was sure it was cool enough to set down. He sat down in front of the computer. Being unsure when her call would come, she caught him wearing casual slacks and a tight-fitting undershirt that defined his moderately muscular physique. He wasn't a body-builder, but he was clearly not soft either. His line of work required a sturdy yet athletic build. Tristan watched Jessica get momentarily distracted by his form. Inside, he celebrated his first victory. He smiled casually at her. "Hey, I'm Tristan Alexander."

Jessica cleared her throat and smiled pleasantly back at him. "H-Hi, I'm—My name is Jessica Deacons. I understand you've requested a tutor for beginning accounting?"

"Yes ma'am, I did. Are you my tutor?" Tristan asked, flashing a boyish grin.

Jessica tried to distance herself from him when she realized she had seen him before. "Do I know you, Mr. Alexander?"

Tristan leaned back casually in his chair as if to think about it for a moment. He suddenly sat forward again. "Oh yeah, we did meet, sort of. I accidentally bumped into you the day I came by to register for classes. I bought you some tea. Was it good?"

Jessica blinked nervously at the friendly young man. "Yes, thank you."

Tristan sighed a sigh of relief. "Oh, great. I was worried about that."

"Worried? Why?"

"First impressions are important. I would hate to make a bad first impression on someone who's going to hold my life in the palm of her hands."

"Your life? Mr. Alexander, I'm not your instructor, just your tutor. I don't think your life is in my hands."

Tristan flashed another grin at her. "Sure it is. I need to pass this class and all my others with flying colors, or I could lose my new job faster than I got it. If you can't help me stay on top of this, I'll get mediocre grades. They'll give my position to someone more deserving, and I'll end up writing driving citations and maybe get hit by a moving vehicle. You're saving my life."

"I haven't agreed to be your tutor yet," Jessica argued. She remembered his uniform and feeling attracted to him despite wanting to steer clear of a military man.

"Sure, you did." Tristan leaned in and propped his elbows on the desk.

"No, I didn't," she protested.

"You said you weren't my instructor, just my tutor," Tristan quipped.

Jessica glanced at his physique again and decided to change the subject. "Did I call you at a bad time? I can contact you again later if I need to."

Tristan looked over the screen toward the kitchen. "No, I was just cooking myself some dinner. The cheese sauce likes to stick to the pan if you don't keep stirring it. It's turned off now."

"You like to cook?" Jessica was getting more curious about this new person in her life.

"Sure. I'm no gourmet chef or anything. I'm more likely to screw up a meal than produce one that's edible, but I keep trying anyway." Tristan smiled less flirtatiously. He leaned back again. "Listen, I really need some stellar scores in my accounting classes. I'm a new intern in the Commonwealth Interstellar Force's Government Financial Oversight Division. I know that sounds like an impressive position, but... well, it is impressive, but only if I can keep the job. There's a lot of competition for these jobs. I'm looking to move up in life—I don't want to be some expendable ground trooper in the trenches. I want to make something of myself. I don't know why I'm telling you this— maybe I'm hoping you'll have mercy on me. I've even been thinking about someday getting married and starting a family. I don't want to get myself killed in the line of duty and leave behind a widow and fatherless children."

Jessica's eyes widened as he spoke. She stared at Tristan, not sure what to say to his admission.

Tristan moved around the room, still within sight of the computer screen. He rubbed his face with his hand. "I suppose you would never guess I used to be a Covert Ops officer. I really spilled my guts to you. I'm sorry. If you aren't comfortable tutoring me, I understand. Just let me know what you decide. I'll be studying after class at that café where we bumped into each other. If you decide to take on this hard-luck case, that's where you can find me. It was nice meeting you, Miss Deacons." He cut the comm off before she could respond, leaving her with the impression he was embarrassed by his admission.

Tristan promptly re-addressed the computer. "Computer, access the comm records of Jessica Deacons." The recent details of who she had contacted appeared on his screen. He had already programmed the computer to label each one as a friend, family, or business associate. He waited and watched to see who she might call next. If she called the University's tutoring office, he would know she had rejected him. If she called him back, that would mean she had pity on him, but only pity. If she called a girlfriend, it would mean she was excited at the prospect. If she called her family, it would mean she was attracted to him, and it made her very nervous. No calls meant she was thinking it over.

Thirty minutes later, she still had made no calls. Tristan smiled to himself. He'd never attempted to win a girl's heart before, only the chance for a fleeting moment of passion.

Weeks later, Jessica and Tristan were sitting together in the same café, waiting for final grades to be posted. The two had maintained a professional relationship, although there were moments of flirtation. Tristan discovered he was slightly distracted by her even when she wasn't around. He mentally kicked himself periodically to remember that she was his assignment, not a real romantic interest.

Tristan saw several girls wander in. Some stopped long enough to greet them but moved on, while others smiled slyly at the couple and kept their distance. Everyone seemed to know there was something between them except for Jessica and Tristan.

The upper-division grades were posted first. Although Jessica was younger, because of Tristan's military career, she was the more advanced student. When the grades showed up as being available to view, Jessica clenched her fists and took a deep breath.

Tristan leaned forward, grabbed her wrists. "Jessica, it's okay. I'm sure your grades are fine. Relax." He gently pried her fists open and gave her hands a reassuring squeeze.

Jessica sighed again. "You're probably right. I worry too much. I get this way every semester." She looked down and realized she was enjoying holding Tristan's hands for far too long. She gingerly extricated her hands from his and pressed the buttons on the computer necessary to view her grades. It took less than a second for the scores to be revealed. To Jessica, the time was interminable.

Her results displayed the proof of her academic prowess. Jessica jumped excitedly as she saw her grades. "Yes! I passed!"

Tristan looked at the scores in front of them. "Jessica? You did more than pass. You aced everything. Why were you so worried?"

Jessica smiled and sat down to wait with Tristan for his own scores. "You want to know the truth?"

"Sure."

"I was more interested in engineering than accounting, but my parents didn't think engineering was a good idea. My mother said it's a struggle for women in astrophysical engineering. I have to work to understand accounting, too. I started tutoring to improve my understanding of it," Jessica confessed.

Tristan smiled. She had confided something personal to him. Mentally, he placed another hashmark on his scoreboard. So far, he hadn't pushed, and the hash marks were few and far between.

A notification popped up on the computer screen: Tristan's grades were ready to be viewed. He looked Jessica in the eye. "Well, win or lose, thanks for tutoring me."

Jessica smiled. "You're welcome. Now push the button! I'm dying to see how you did."

Tristan waved his hand above the control theatrically, teasing his companion. Jessica finally grabbed his hand and forced it onto the computer screen.

The computer recognized his fingerprints and revealed the scores. Tristan had scored excellent marks as well.

"Yes! We did it!" Jessica squealed excitedly. Several other people were giving similar exuberant utterances throughout the café, so hers blended in. She grabbed Tristan and gave him a congratulatory hug.

Tristan returned the hug but didn't withdraw until he felt her pull back. When she pulled away, he grabbed her arms. "We need to celebrate. Miss Deacons, may I buy you dinner? It would be my way of saying thanks for all the help."

"I thought you enjoyed cooking," Jessica said, then blushed at the suggestion she had just made.

Tristan quickly rescued her from her embarrassment. "I do, but I also said it's only edible half the time. I'm trying to pay you back, and my cooking seems like a poor thank you for all that you've done to help me."

"Okay, sure. I think it would be okay this one time. I—I'm not allowed to date students that I'm tutoring." Jessica wasn't sure if she was trying to excuse her willingness to go out with him or give credence to why she hadn't done so earlier.

Tristan smiled. "Great. I'll meet you here at… six?" Again, he was being careful not to push by meeting at either her residence or his.

The two returned to their respective homes to get ready. Tristan hastily straightened his apartment, just in case. He dressed up enough to impress, without overdoing it.

Jessica wasn't sure what to wear. Her roommate helped her go through every outfit in her closet before deciding on something appropriately attractive yet not provocative. "Maddy, I don't know why I'm so nervous about this."

"Oh, come on. You and that hunk have had a thing for each other from the day you met in the café. I'm glad you're finally doing something about it."

"Don't get your hopes up. It's just a thank-you dinner," Jessica chided.

"I'm not the one who's excited. You are."

Jessica held up two different outfits, trying to decide which one to wear. She looked at Maddy and whined, "I know I am, and I shouldn't be. He's military. I can't get involved with a military guy."

"Wear the blue one. It's subtle but attractive. Who says you can't get involved with a military guy? Military guys need a life too. Your parents have already pushed you away from engineering like you wanted. You deserve to get something you want. Not everything is about pleasing them."

"You know what? You're right. I'm going to see what happens tonight. I need to get this place cleaned up, just in case." Jessica began grabbing the clothes strewn around the room.

Maddy jumped to help. "You get dressed. I'll put these away. It's nearly five already."

Jessica looked at the clock and panicked. After thanking her roommate for her help, she jumped into the shower.

Tristan arrived at the café fifteen minutes early and grabbed a cup of coffee to drink while he waited for his date to arrive. When the waitress handed him the cup, he took a large swig and burned his mouth on it. He swallowed the hot liquid quickly, then regretted not spitting it out. The waitress, seeing his error, quickly handed him a small glass of water. Tristan thanked the woman for her thoughtfulness and sat down to wait. He wasn't prone to making such stupid errors in judgment. He wondered why he was so distracted and how Jessica had gotten to him like this.

Jessica arrived precisely at six. Seeing the cup of coffee in his hand, she asked, "Am I late?"

"No, you're right on time. I was early. It's a character flaw on my part. Are you ready to go?" Tristan was both nervous and excited about this near first date. He wasn't sure if this counted or not, since it was a thank-you dinner.

The two left the café and went to a moderate level restaurant. As much as he would love to take her to the nicest restaurant in the city, he was afraid of scaring her away.

They enjoyed a very long dinner, laughing and talking. When they felt they had tied up the table for far too long, they grudgingly left the restaurant. As they exited the building, Tristan pulled Jessica in the opposite direction from home.

"Where are we going?" she asked.

"I thought we could go for a walk by the riverfront." Tristan smiled.

Jessica was still uncertain about him, but her roommate's admonition to have something she wanted, and not what her parents wanted, spurred her forward. "Sure, that sounds nice."

The two walked and talked for a few minutes. They eventually stopped under a streetlight. Leaning on the pier railing, they watched the dark water flowing past them. Tristan turned toward her. "Jessica?"

The nervous young woman turned toward him slightly. She knew she needed to decide whether to stop this here and now or move ahead. She looked into his eyes and forgot why she was supposed to put a stop to it. "Yes, Tristan?"

"I don't think I've told you, and I don't know if I'm being inappropriate considering our—professional relationship—but you look beautiful." Tristan reached out and took one of her hands in his. "I'd really like for this not to be our only—date."

Jessica smiled and squeezed his hand. "Why did you ask for a tutor? You were doing well without me."

"I told you. I needed to make stellar grades, not just above average. Why? Have I given you some reason to doubt me?" Tristan wondered if he had slipped up somewhere.

"No, but I can't be your tutor next semester." Jessica's hands started feeling sweaty. She was really about to step into the unknown and the uncertain.

"But why? I need you." Tristan was having trouble deciphering the look on her face.

Jessica took a deep breath. "I—I can't date a student I'm tutoring."

Tristan stared at her for a moment until the full implication of what she was saying sank in. He grinned mischievously, "Does that mean we'll have to settle for being study buddies?"

Jessica jerked her hand out of his and shoved him playfully. "Yeah, that's exactly what that means."

A voice behind Jessica interrupted their romantic moment when it had barely started. "Well, well, who do we have here?"

Tristan tore his eyes from Jessica's face and turned to the three men approaching them. He had observed them coming around a corner, but he was distracted enough that they had gotten close without his noticing. Tristan realized these three were from his old Covert Ops team. He wasn't sure what they were up to or how he should play this. Were they here by chance, or was this a purposeful visit?

He didn't acknowledge knowing them yet. "Do you mind? We were trying to have a private moment here."

The three surrounded them, leaving them loosely pinned against the pier railing. "What's the matter, Chief? Don't want to associate with your old buddies now that you've got that fancy new job?"

Tristan glanced around at the three men. At this point, they were giving the appearance of being drunk. The three smelled of alcohol. They wove and staggered the last few steps, and the one who had spoken was using slightly slurred speech. When he had seen them at a distance, they were walking straight and purposefully.

Tristan decided to try to blow them off. "Guys, really, we're on a first date here. Why don't you move along? Give me a yell sometime, and we'll go out for drinks or something."

The one who had been doing all the talking moved uncomfortably close to Jessica. "Aren't you going to introduce us to your lady friend?"

Tristan got a bad feeling in relation to what was about to transpire. He stepped firmly between the two of them. "Nick, go home. You're drunk, and in the morning you'll probably be glad I didn't properly introduce you."

Nick stepped back and looked at his companions. "You hear that, fellas? He's too good for us now, and so is his lady friend."

The one closest to Jessica pulled at a loose strand of her hair. Jessica jerked away from the man's unwanted attention. She put herself firmly behind Tristan.

The man tried to reach for Jessica again to bring her closer to him. Tristan caught his arm forcefully. "Vince, back off!"

The third man, Connor, spoke up. "Or what, tough guy? You took a desk job. The only muscle you've been exercising is your brain. You gonna think your way out of a three-against-one situation?"

Nick laughed robustly. "You've gone soft! You know, kid, I used to think you had potential in Covert Ops. Maybe we need to show you just how soft you've gotten."

Tristan was still in a one-armed power struggle with Vince, who finally jerked his arm from Tristan's grasp. "Are you sure you want to show out in front of the young lady? For being Covert Ops, you guys aren't paying much attention. The lady obviously doesn't like you. Her opinion of you is not likely to improve at this point," Tristan snapped.

Tristan kept his hands down at his sides. He really wanted this problem to go away peacefully.

Jessica had moved away from Vince's reach, but her move placed her easily within Connor's. Connor grabbed the young woman, pulled her close to him, and wrapped his arms around her. Jessica shrieked. Before Tristan could react, the other two were on him, pinning him against the railing. They landed several debilitating blows to his abdomen, causing him to collapse on the ground. Tristan rolled back and forth, working hard to catch his breath and clear his head. Through the haze, he heard Jessica calling his name. Nick and Vince moved in around her, stealing unwanted kisses and touching her inappropriately.

Tristan worked his way onto his knees and managed to collect a good deep breath. "NICK! Back off!"

Nick stopped his advances toward Jessica and looked at Tristan. "Stay down if you know what's good for you."

Tristan struggled to his feet, taking another deep breath. His lungs stopped burning, and his head was clearing. "I decide what's good for me, not you. Let her go—NOW!"

Tristan inhaled again and shook his head. He changed his posture to a defensive stance and raised his fists.

Nick turned his attention to the belligerent young man. He tapped Vince on the arm. "Looks like he didn't get enough. Let's make sure he understands this time."

Jessica screamed outright. Nick looked behind him at Connor. "Keep her quiet. We don't need anybody investigating her screams."

Connor covered Jessica's mouth and pulled her away from the impending scuffle. The two men charged their adversary, pushing him further from Jessica. Tristan dodged Vince and tossed him expertly to the ground. Nick wasn't as easy to dodge. The two exchanged swings and blows, putting even more distance between them and Jessica. Tristan twisted to avoid one of Nick's swings, then caught him in a brief headlock with their backs to Jessica. Tristan cussed softly. "What are you doing here?"

Nick was heavier and shoved Tristan into the railing again, breaking his grip. He pinned Tristan against the railing and landed a pulled punch to Tristan's abdomen. Tristan reacted as though the blow were real. Nick grabbed Tristan's shirt and smiled sadistically. "Orders are orders," he explained.

Tristan head-butted the man, freeing himself from Nick's grip. The two circled each other. Vince attempted to intervene, but Nick waved him off. "He's mine!"

As Tristan circled, he glanced at Jessica, who was safe but crying as Connor gripped her. When he had his back to her again, he softly asked, "Why are you doing this? You certainly aren't drunk."

Nick swung at Tristan a couple more times. "Apparently, the brass think you're moving too slowly. They wanted to give you a boost."

Tristan dodged the swings and countered—neither one landed a blow. Tristan swung again, but Nick caught him and put him on the ground. Tristan kicked his opponent and rolled to his feet. He glared, more at the orders behind this attack than at his opponent. They watched each other's moves carefully and circled again. "You know, I was about to kiss her for the first time when you goons interfered." Tristan was ready to be rid of this annoyance.

Nick faked left then popped Tristan squarely in the mouth, busting his lip. "Now she can kiss it and make it better," Nick jeered.

Tristan wiped a spot of blood from his lip with the back of his hand. "I'm through playing. Let's finish this so I can get my job done."

"Fine. I'm afraid you aren't going to like the ending," Nick warned.

Tristan definitely didn't like the sound of that. He took a deep breath, then yelled, "JESSICA! BITE HIM!"

Before Connor could react, Jessica bit into the hand Connor had covered her mouth with. Connor released his grip on her and pushed her away from him. With her mouth now free, Jessica screamed loudly and long. Her scream got the attention of two couples coming out of a nearby bar. The two young men left the women in the doorway and raced toward the noise.

Seeing their tussle was at an end, Vince jumped into the fray. They had been ordered to rough up the young man, and neither he nor Nick felt as though they had sufficiently achieved their task. Tristan's recent classes in hand-to-hand combat sharpened his skills enough that he could hold his own despite being outnumbered and outweighed. He wasn't about to let some bureaucrat pull his strings like this.

As the two men got close to the skirmish, Connor yelled at his buddies, "It's getting crowded. We gotta GO!" Connor grabbed Jessica again and shoved her toward the two rescuers. They caught her to keep her from falling. Connor ran from the two men and ducked into an alley.

Tristan took another swing at Vince and heard Nick behind him. "Sorry about this, my friend." He felt a sharp pain on the back of his head slightly above and behind his ear. The last sounds he heard before losing consciousness were of glass shattering and Jessica screaming again.

Tristan woke to find himself lying on the ground. Jessica was holding his head in her lap, gingerly pressing a rag filled with ice from the bar against the lump on his skull. He groaned and reached up to touch the painful spot. He pushed the icepack gently aside, then pulled his hand back. Even in the dim lighting, the blood was clear to see. He groaned again and started to get up.

One of the men who had come to join his cause squatted beside him. "Hey, buddy, take it easy. We've got medics on the way."

Tristan had trouble focusing on the man's face. It seemed to keep jumping. "No, I need to sit up. Jessica?"

"I'm right here, Tristan. Lie still. I've got you."

Tristan managed to sit up on his own. A wave of nausea washed over him and his head throbbed twice as hard in this position, making him rethink his decision to sit up. He looked over at Jessica. "Are you okay? Did they hurt you?"

"I'm fine, just a couple bruises."

Tristan looked at her lap where she had been cradling his head. His blood had stained her outfit. "Oh no, I ruined your clothes."

Jessica shook her head at him. "They're just clothes. I have more." She smiled at him.

Tristan tried to smile at her, but his swollen lip protested. "But you looked so beautiful in these."

Jessica blushed slightly, although the darkness made it impossible to see. "Since this was our first date, I saved the prettier ones for later."

"Really?" Energized by her comment, Tristan tried to get up. The ground spun wildly, and his head throbbed even harder. "Oh, bad idea. Where did those guys go?"

Jessica guided his head into her lap again.

The rescuer still squatting beside them answered, "They took off. We didn't go after them because we wanted to make sure you and your lady were all right."

"That's okay, I know where to find them. Thanks for your help."

Several hours later, Tristan was released from the emergency treatment facility and sent home. His concussion and bruises were healed, but he was still sore and exhausted. Jessica insisted on seeing him home and caring for him.

His apartment was a one-room studio with the sleeping area sectioned off by a half-wall. Jessica went in, pulled the covers down on the bed, and ordered him to lie down and get some rest. As she tucked him in, Tristan grabbed her hand. Jessica sat down beside him. She wasn't ready to consummate their relationship, so being in this position made her slightly nervous. She had just reconciled herself to admitting being interested in him.

Tristan knew her concerns and hesitations. He took great pains to move slowly. He looked into her eyes. "Jessica, I'm sorry our date turned out so badly."

Jessica smiled. "It was going fine until those goons interrupted."

"Are you okay? I mean really okay, not just bruised?"

"I'm a little rattled. I'm glad you're okay. Are you going to press charges against them?"

"No, I'm going to have a word with their supervisor, though. I guess now you have an idea why I transferred out."

"Yes, I do. If you had stayed, you might've become like one of them." Jessica shivered at the thought.

Tristan sat up in the bed and wrapped his arms around her. He whispered softly, "I'll never be like one of them." His conscience jabbed him sharply. He was exactly like them.

Jessica gripped him tightly and cried tears of relief from her stressful night. Tristan held her and rocked her for several minutes until her tears subsided. Jessica pulled back and whispered, "You need to rest."

Tristan cradled her face in his hand. He whispered back, "Our date isn't over yet."

Jessica looked at the empty side of the double bed nervously. "Tristan, I don't think…"

He slid his thumb across her lips, stopping her objection. "I haven't given you a goodnight kiss." Leaning forward, he kissed her lightly, then lay down.

Jessica curled up on the couch. She woke to find Tristan cooking breakfast in the late morning. When she returned to her apartment early that afternoon, Maddy grilled her for details about her "date."

ESCAPE

Marek entered the city gates of Somi shortly after midnight. He rode straight to the governor to request the additional troops needed to search the Helian city.

He raced to the provincial governor's home and beat on the large wooden door repeatedly until a servant finally answered. A woman wearing her dressing gown cracked the door and held up a candle to see who was disturbing the household. Glaring through the narrow opening, the woman rebuked the soldier. "It's late. The master has gone to bed. Go away!"

"I need to see the governor right away! It's urgent!"

The woman looked more annoyed. It appeared the young man had no intention of leaving. She slowly opened the door to allow him entrance. "This had better be worth waking him. He's likely to have you flogged if it's not."

Marek could see the thought of having him flogged was appealing to her. "I just hope he doesn't flog you for the delay in waking him over this urgent matter."

The woman glared at him again. "Wait here!" She disappeared into the dark house. Moments later, Marek heard indistinct raised voices. The woman returned quickly, lighting candles as she came into the ornately decorated entry hall. "The master will be with you momentarily."

The governor came barreling into the room. He was a large man. The shadowy room and his angry dispensation made him seem even bigger. "What is it, soldier? This had better be important!"

Marek suddenly doubted the wisdom of his current situation. "I believe it is, Governor Pravin. Capt. Nasha believes he knows where the girl you seek is. He doesn't know her exact location, but the Healer, Halyn, is helping her. Nasha sent me to bring more troops to search the city of Helia and prevent her from escaping."

"You could have gotten the troops without me. Why did you find it necessary to disturb me as I was falling asleep?"

"I have two concerns. The first is that it seems a lot to go through to bring one wayward woman to justice for fornication. I know she was pledged to your nephew, but why pursue this so hard?" Marek knew he was treading in dangerous territory.

"What is your other concern?" Governor Pravin wasn't overly inclined to dignify the young man's question with an answer.

"My other concern is that Nasha sent me away to keep me occupied. He has seemed unwilling to challenge the healer. I'm sure the girl was hiding in the healer's wagon, but Nasha refused to search it. He said it wasn't wise to challenge a healer without more proof. We went back to her campsite and found proof. That's when he sent me away to get more troops. I suspect he is buying time to allow her to escape us. If they get outside this province, how far should I go to stop them?"

Despite the dim lighting, Marek could see Pravin's face grow beet red. He stepped closer to Marek. "You want to know why that girl must be stopped? That child she carries may be the one promised in the prophecies. The Promised One will reign supreme. He will usurp my throne and take control from me. I may not live long enough for him to be a threat to me personally, but what of my son and my family? It's my job to protect them. She and her baby have to die."

"What if she isn't... the one?" Marek was overzealous, but he tried to channel his zeal to appropriate causes.

"Many signs indicate that she is. I can't take chances. It would be unfortunate if she isn't." The man turned away, but in a second, the hint of regret was gone, and his resolve returned. He turned around hastily. "Your name is Marek, isn't it?"

"Yes, my lord."

"Are you a follower of Pateras?" He watched Marek's response closely.

"No, I pursue my own paths. I don't have time for religious rhetoric." Marek sneered at the thought of wasting time studying ancient laws and prophecies and saying prayers to invisible gods.

"Then you won't have any trouble destroying that girl and anyone who tries to help her?"

Marek stepped closer to the large man. "Including a healer and Nasha?" he asked guardedly.

"Especially a healer and Nasha. Personally, I could care less who they worship or what religion they practice, except when it interferes with me. I know Nasha serves Pateras, and until now that has worked to my advantage. Pateras requires his people to do their best at whatever they do, to be honest, and to obey the authorities over them. If he is no longer obeying me, he is a traitor to his own god and must be punished. Take as many men as you require. Bring me the bodies of that young woman, the healer, and Nasha. I will put them on display for all to see what happens to those who cross me."

"I have one more question. What if they've gotten into the Nazar Province?"

The large man got uncomfortably close to Marek. "Do what you have to and whatever you think you can get away with. Just don't start a war with Nazar."

"Yes, Governor. I will return within three days and I'll bring whatever bodies I need to." Marek took his leave to collect soldiers and a fresh horse for himself.

With Marek on his way, the governor started back to his bedchamber. A noise stopped him. "Who's there?"

Pravin turned around to see his powerful, dark ally emerge from the shadows.

"It's me, Luciano. If your soldiers don't bring her body back, you only have one other recourse," the dark figure whispered.

"What's that?"

"Tell your nephew you were wrong about the girl. She wasn't touched by another man. She is carrying the Promised One. Send him to her quietly, to consummate their marriage."

"Are you kidding me? If he is the Promised One, how is that supposed to help?"

The figure smiled evilly. "The prophecies say the Promised One will come from one who has been untouched. If Jedrek goes to Slaina, if he consummates their marriage, the prophecy will be thwarted."

Pravin's smile grew to match Luciano's. "Tell me again why you're helping me?"

"Because I know more about this prophecy than anyone, and I know what the Promised One intends to do to me. I can not let that happen."

Marek charged into the barracks and ordered a large contingent of troops. While the ranking officer rallied the men and had them pack the needed supplies, Marek took a brief nap. He knew Nasha would not expect him back for another full day, so he wouldn't rush too quickly. Marek didn't intend to allow that full day to pass, so a four-hour nap was all he would allow himself.

Just before sunrise, the troops and Marek were ready to head out. With a fresh horse and restocked supplies, Marek gave the troops their instructions, but avoided naming Nasha as a potential traitor. "Anyone, and I mean anyone, who aids this healer and the young woman will pay for their treachery with their lives. This order comes directly from Governor Pravin. If you decide to have pity on this waif, your lives will be forfeit! Are we clear?"

"Yes sir!" came the resounding cry.

Nasha looked at the frightened young woman still grasping the tiny infant clothes. "Your life is safe. I will not harm you."

Slaina looked at the spot where the messenger had stood moments before. As much as his appearance frightened her, his absence was even more frightening. Her knees grew weak, and she sat down to keep from falling. She looked at Halyn. Joren had been right behind her the entire time. He saw the same things they all had. His eyes were wide in disbelief.

Nasha turned to Halyn. "Healer, we have to get her out of here. It's barely a two-day journey to Somi and back. If I know my second-in-command, he'll push hard to be back by late tomorrow morning. We have to get her out of here tonight and outside the Somian's reach."

"I can't pack up until after dark, or it'll get the attention of the townfolk, and word could get back to your men. I could stay here, and Joren could get Slaina out," Halyn suggested.

"No, you need to go as well. My second knows you've helped the girl. He'll go to the local magistrate to get you arrested." Nasha knew Halyn's life was already forfeit.

"My home is across the river. If we can get there, it's outside of the Somi Province. I can go to the town council and warn them about this. They'll protect us."

"Let me go to the tavern and buy a round or two of drinks to make sure my men are too drunk to know what we're doing. After they go off to bed, I'll take Slaina outside the city on a horse I've rented. I'll get her as close to the bridge as I can, then come back here in time to organize a search of the town. You slip out during the night to meet her." Nasha knew he could ride hard and fast and get the young woman out quicker than Halyn's wagon. "You could leave your things behind and ride your horses straight out of here."

"What about me?" Joren queried. None of these ideas had mentioned him at all.

Nasha quickly added, "You will have to help the healer get her things together if she decides she can't leave without them."

Nasha knew the boy wanted the horse, but he didn't comprehend why. Halyn knew what the young man was asking. "I promised the boy he could leave with me this time."

The seasoned soldier wanted to order the young man to stand down, but realized it would do no good. Halyn took charge of the situation. "Joren, start puttin' my wagon back together. Crisscross the poles in the back and put all the supplies on the outer edges. Leave the center empty enough for someone to lie down in it. You can put a mat down to soften it. Make sure the horses are fed and watered. After dark, bring the wagon to the meeting house late tonight. Help me get loaded, then come back to the stable. I'll give you a couple extra cloaks to wear. You and Slaina put them on, take that extra horse, and ride out of here by the northern gate, then head west. Take the mountain pass. The river is shallow up that way. After you get across, head south to the township. I'll meet you at the town hall. If anyone questions you, tell them I sent you. Tell the Town Council to send troops to meet me at the bridge."

"What if you get there before we do?" Joren worried.

"That's highly doubtful. I will be drivin' slowly, deliberately. I usually spend a week or two here, and I'm leavin' after one night. That's gonna get a lot of people's attention. I want them comin' after me, not after you."

Nasha folded his arms across his chest. "And what is my part in all of this?"

"Can you help them get to the mountain pass, then do whatever you normally would? I don't want to get you into trouble." Halyn appreciated the man's help, but if his collusion was discovered, he would get arrested at worst or could never go home again at best.

"No, Healer, I will take them all the way to the township in Nazar. As soon as I know they are safe, I'll lead the Nazaran troops back to find you. I know you, old woman. You'll get yourself into trouble." Nasha wasn't about to sit back and do nothing. He was a strong follower of Pateras, and seeing Pateras' messenger had assured him of the importance of protecting this girl.

Halyn bowed her head in deference to him. "If that is your desire, soldier. I am grateful for the help. I need to get back to my patients before they come looking for me. Joren, tend to your duties. If you have time, take a nap. You'll be riding all night. Slaina, put away the sewing and take a nap as well."

With a plan in place, they all went about their assigned tasks. Nasha went off to get his fellow soldiers drunk, being careful to drink as little as possible himself. Slaina found that napping, something she wasn't accustomed to doing, came more easily than she expected. Joren wasn't accustomed to it either, and he had lots of chores to attend to. He finally got a brief nap after the dinner hour.

Another rainstorm came through in the afternoon, which thinned out the crowd of people waiting to see the healer. Halyn closed her doors early and got some rest while she waited for nightfall and Joren to come. She smiled as she rested on her bed. Pateras had sent the rain to slow the approaching soldiers and to give her a much-needed rest before her tedious journey.

Joren got up and drove Halyn's wagon to the meeting hall while Nasha saddled his horse and the bay one he had bought from the stable master. Slaina watched out the window until she saw Joren returning. She was still slightly nervous being near Nasha, but he stayed on the floor of the stable and left her alone in the loft.

Once she saw Joren heading toward the stable, she climbed down. She put on the cloak Halyn had left for her, then Nasha hoisted her easily into the saddle of the bay horse. Joren raced in and threw his own robe on. Nasha had a robe to wear for cold or wet weather and wrapped himself in it. Joren climbed onto the horse. The saddle was already weighed down with what few possessions he could call his own. A bedroll, a couple of clothing changes, a knife, a sharpening stone, a couple of dishes, and cooking utensils were all he had. Slaina had only the clothes she wore and a second tunic she had worn to her cousin's house before she ran away.

The three rode slowly and quietly through the dark, dreary streets until they left through the city gates. They continued straight north until they were out of view of the city. The three picked up their pace as fast as they dared and headed for the mountain pass.

Meanwhile, Halyn grabbed the last of her things and climbed slowly into her wagon. She drove through the streets, and even after passing through the city gates, she kept her pace.

Nasha, Joren, and Slaina had been riding for three hours. The herbs Halyn had given Slaina to take as she traveled were only slightly helpful, and the long ride and the lateness of the hour were keeping her stomach unsettled. The men had to stop for her about once every hour. After the third stop, she shivered violently as she tried to settle back into the saddle behind Joren.

"You okay?" He had easily noticed her shivering.

"I'm c-cold." She shivered again.

Joren shifted in his saddle and loosened his robe. "Pull the back of my robe up over your head and scoot as close to me as you can. It will help keep you warmer."

Slaina did as Joren instructed. It didn't exactly seem warm, just less cold.

It stopped raining, but their clothes were still damp. A chilly wind blew through the mountain pass.

Nasha had ridden ahead to explore the path for potential difficulties. When the two didn't catch up, he returned to see what was holding them up. In the dark, Nasha didn't immediately see Slaina hunkered down under Joren's cloak. "Where's Slaina?"

Joren twisted slightly and looked over his shoulder at the lump behind him. "She's here. She's getting chilled. Do you know how much further it is?"

Nasha wasn't familiar with this territory. He could do little more than guess. "I think we'll clear the mountain pass in another hour, maybe more, if we have to keep stopping. The town is an hour or so beyond that. We should be able to pick up our pace when we get out in the open."

"Do you think Halyn got out all right?" Joren worried about the kind elderly woman.

"I'm sure she's fine. She'll probably arrive before we will. Let's get moving."

They cleared the pass more than an hour later, but Slaina got sick twice more. Joren helped her onto the horse and pushed to catch Nasha, who now wore a frustrated look. This trip should not be taking this long.

Nasha could clearly see hypothermia, dehydration, and exhaustion creeping up on Slaina. A few minutes later, Joren felt Slaina's hands and arms go limp from around his waist. With one hand, he pulled on the reins to stop the horse. With his other hand, he reached back to stabilize her. His quick reaction kept her from falling off the horse. "Nasha!" Joren called.

Hearing the alarm in his voice, Nasha whipped his horse around and galloped back. "What's wrong?"

"I think Slaina's passed out."

Nasha dismounted and pulled Slaina out from under Joren's cloak. The girl was barely conscious. Joren scrambled off his horse as well. Feeling her cold, clammy skin, Nasha reacted quickly. "Joren, pull out the bedrolls and blankets."

Joren grabbed both his and Nasha's and tossed the bedrolls on top of each other on the ground. Nasha gently laid the girl on them. He removed her wet cloak and covered her with the blankets. Nasha sent Joren to collect enough firewood for a small fire. While he was gone, Nasha retrieved the herbs Slaina was using to settle her stomach. He put double the dose he had seen her using on herself into a cup of water, then retrieved a bag from his own saddle. After digging in the bag, he finally found a small skin containing a thick liquid.

Joren came running back with kindling and arranged it on the ground. Using a flint, he got a small stack of pine needles and twigs and tried to start the fire. He watched Nasha mix the ingredients of the drink for Slaina. "What did you add to her herbs?"

"Honey. She needs it to give her the strength to try to keep herself warm." Nasha moved to Slaina's side and gently slapped her cheeks. "Slaina! Slaina, wake up! I need you to drink this."

Slaina moaned and tried to push him away. Nasha set the cup down and shook her shoulders. "Slaina! Drink this!"

Slaina took a sip or two, then lost interest. Nasha slapped her cheek again with more force this time. "Slaina, stay awake! Drink this!"

The girl roused enough to finish the cup. She shivered again, then closed her eyes. Nasha looked at Joren, who was still struggling with the damp kindling. "Joren, the fire's taking too long. Let it go. We have to get her into town as fast as we can. I'm going to put her on the horse with me. We have to move faster. Can you keep up?"

"With the cloud cover, it's too dark to see. The horses could be injured if we move too fast."

The wind suddenly picked up. Nasha looked at the skies. An opening was forming in the clouds, revealing a full moon. Nasha smiled. "Pateras provides what we need even before we ask."

Joren marveled at the miracle unfolding in front of him. The full moon wasn't due for two weeks. He smiled. "I can keep up. My horse is faster than yours."

Nasha wrapped Slaina securely in the blankets and lifted the petite young woman onto his shoulder. He mounted his horse and settled her in his arms in front of him, then raced for the city. Joren grabbed the bedrolls and hastily tied them both to his saddle. He mounted his own steed and pushed to catch Nasha. The closer they got to the town, the firmer and more dedicated the roads became. The last few minutes of the trip, the two raced at a hard gallop for the city.

At the northern gate, a sentry harshly greeted them. "You there! Halt! Identify yourselves and state the nature of your business in Nazar."

Nasha answered for them. "We're here to see Halyn. She told us to meet her here. This young woman's life is in danger, and she is ill. She needs to be warmed up right away."

The sentry responded, "The healer isn't due here for several weeks."

Nasha cast a concerned glance at Joren. "Did the healer not return by one of your gates this very night? She was taking another route to get here."

"I got reports from the other gates less than an hour ago. No one has entered this night."

"Then I need to speak with your magistrate. If the healer has not arrived, she may also be in danger. Please allow us entry." Nasha was ready for action.

The sentry yelled to another, "Open the gate. Admission is granted." He dispatched one man to the other gates, warning the other posts to be on the lookout for the healer and informing them of the admission of the three strangers. He sent another to escort their guests to the nearest inn and tend to their needs. A third he sent to fetch the magistrate as requested.

The sentry roused the innkeeper, who opened the door to them. Nasha carried Slaina into the inn and laid her on the floor near the hearth. The fire was nearly dead.

The innkeeper balked. "We have rooms upstairs. Don't put her here."

Nasha whipped around to face Joren. "Get that fire going again." He cast a cold, hard look at the innkeeper. "Do you have a room that is already warm with a roaring fire going?"

The innkeeper sputtered, "Well, no. I would have to start a fire in one of the rooms."

Nasha gave the man a look that told him he wasn't about to accept any excuses or disagreeable treatment. "If you want her moved to another room, then prepare one. She's chilled to the bone. We've come through a rainstorm and traveled through the mountain pass. She needs a hot meal, dry clothes, and blankets, quickly. Do you have a woman who can attend to her?"

The innkeeper stuttered. "I-I'll get my w-wife and daughter to come attend t-to her. I'll start a fire in one of our best rooms and get it ready for you."

The man trotted off to wake his household. He sent a teenage boy to get a fire going in an upstairs room. His wife and daughter grabbed blankets and clothing for the girl. Joren got the fire roaring with wood that was actually dry. The women hung blankets for privacy as they changed Slaina out of her cold, damp garments and into warm, dry ones. They covered her with warm blankets and left the additional blankets hanging to keep the warmth in a confined space.

Nasha paced nervously as he awaited the magistrate. The man arrived accompanied by a sentry.

The magistrate looked at the strange mixture of late-night, or now early morning visitors. Nasha explained only the most basic information to the provincial leader about their situation. He expressed his concerns for the healer's safety. He doubted the man would handle it well if he told him the incredible story about the visit from Pateras' messenger.

The magistrate paced the floor. "You want me to send my troops outside the city before dawn on the word of a man I know nothing about? I do not know you, sir. You are obviously a soldier. I can only assume you are from the Somian Province. We've been at peace with Somi for several years. How do I know the Somians aren't seeking to restart a war with us? Your story doesn't hold water. The healer isn't even due here for at least two weeks. She comes just after the full moon."

Nasha got an odd look on his face. He raced to the door of the inn and stepped outside. He looked into the sky. The moon was still as full as it had been an hour ago. He looked at the magistrate. "And when is the next full moon?"

The magistrate walked toward the door. "It's not due for two... weeks." His words dropped off as he saw the biggest, brightest full moon he had ever seen. He mumbled, "I don't understand. How can this be?"

Nasha confided, "I believe Pateras changed the moon to help us get here and get Slaina the help she needed. Perhaps he has left it full so that we can see to get to the healer before the Somian soldiers reach her."

The magistrate still hesitated to trust this stranger. Nasha was losing patience. "Magistrate, you can send troops with me or not, but I'm going after her. Halyn believes that girl carries the Promised One of Pateras. She must be protected. I can't let

Halyn pay for protecting the girl by losing her own life. I have to go help her."

"All right, I will send a dozen men out with you. I will also put patrols outside. If you have lied to me, you and your friends will be the first ones to pay for your deception," the magistrate promised. He summoned the sentry and ordered him to call out troops to go with Nasha and to patrol the outside of the city.

It took less than an hour to rouse the troops and get them armed and on saddled horses. Nasha was hard to keep calm during the wait. The commander of the Nazaran troops separated the two contingents of soldiers. He addressed those going with Nasha first. "Listen up! This man is Nasha. He will lead you in an attempt to rescue the healer, Halyn. You will obey him. If he leads you into a trap or is guilty of any treachery, see that he dies first. Until he shows himself to be untrustworthy, follow him. Keep your eyes open and bring the healer back here alive and well. Dismissed."

Nasha cast a frustrated glance at the commander. "Nice way to inspire them with confidence."

"I'm confident they will follow their orders and that you will think twice about betraying them," the commander replied smugly.

Nasha mounted a fresh horse and rode toward the southern gate. As soon as they cleared the gate, Nasha ordered the men to spread out, taking various routes toward the bridge crossing, and pick up the pace. If someone were watching them from a distance, they wouldn't know how many troops were heading toward them.

The innkeeper's wife and Joren used a pan of hot coals to warm the sheets in a room and then carried Slaina there. By then, she was awake and sipping the broth voluntarily. She was still shivering but able to talk.

The innkeeper's wife got her settled in bed with a warm, hearty stew. "Young man, would you like me to leave you alone with your wife now?"

Joren looked alarmed. "Uh—she's not my wife. The healer brought her into town day before yesterday. I only just met her."

The woman looked confused. "Is she the wife of the soldier you were traveling with?"

"Uh—no, he's just met her as well. I don't think she's got a husband." Joren didn't realize he should have remained quiet on the matter.

"But she's with child. Is she an adulteress? We can't keep her here. We'd be disgraced. This is a reputable establishment. The town council could shut us down."

"No, she's no adulteress. She carries the one promised by Pateras in the Ancient Texts. I heard the messenger say it himself. I will never forget that messenger." Joren recalled the exciting moment. His eyes sparkled brightly, even in the dim light. "Halyn knew it was true even before the messenger told us. Nasha had come to—to, uh, kill her. I saw him. He had his sword drawn. He was ready to punish her for being a fornicator. Halyn prayed to Pateras, and the messenger stopped him. I will never ever forget that."

The woman watched Slaina as she sat in the bed, thinking she was barely more than a child.

Slaina slowly ate her stew, her face reflecting the anticipation of being rejected as so many others had.

"Halyn believes this is true?" the woman asked.

Slaina nodded.

The three riding into town were an odd group, to say the least. Something was certainly unusual about the situation. The woman put her hands on her hips. Whatever the issue was, she decided to accept it—for now. "In that case, young man, you're going to need a room of your own. You can't stay in here. I'll send my daughter to stay with her. Let's get a fire started in a second room."

MEETING THE FAMILY

"Jess?" Tristan waited for her response. "Jessica? Are you okay?"

"Oh, I'm sorry, Tristan. I was thinking about something."

"Yes, I was quite aware of that—the silence was deafening. What's on your mind? Because it certainly isn't the study material for your test." Tristan looked at the blank screen she was staring at.

Jessica scowled at the tattletale screen that was forcing her hand, then looked around the room and sighed deeply.

"Do you want to talk about it, or is it something you'd rather not discuss?" Tristan pried gently.

The two were sitting together on a sofa in their favorite café, preparing for this semester's final exams. Jessica set her datapad down and twisted in her seat to face the handsome man who had kept her attention for several months now. She was being extremely careful in their relationship because she knew her parents wouldn't approve. She smiled. Tristan was respecting her slow pace, and she appreciated it. She also wondered why he put up with her reluctance. She cocked her head slightly. "Tristan, why are you so patient with me?"

Tristan returned the smile. She was beautiful, fun to be around, intelligent, and cautious. Most men wouldn't have cared about the last two characteristics, but he admired a woman who had brains and knew how to use them. "Patient? In what regard?"

"Our relationship."

"I'm still not sure I'm following you." Most couples, by this point, were actively involved sexually. Jessica and Tristan were not. Tristan wondered if this was what she was referring to. He wanted to be careful not to make any wrong assumptions and put pressure on her.

"I know I've kept our relationship moving slowly, and I have my reasons, but you haven't pushed. You haven't met my family, and we haven't… you know. Why do you put up with me and my strange ideas?"

Tristan sensed they were at a juncture in their relationship. "I like you." Putting his datapad down, he grasped both her hands in his. "To be perfectly honest, I think… I think I'm falling in love with you."

Jessica blushed and squeezed his hands. "I think I might be falling in love with you, too. Are you ready to test those feelings?"

Tristan scowled. This didn't sound as though the test would include physical intimacy. Although he was more than ready, he accepted she wasn't. "Test? How?"

"My brother has made the rank of Lieutenant Commander in the CIF Brigade. He's about to be deployed on a ship. There's a big party and a formal celebration this weekend."

"So… you want to see if I can stand up to your brother's scrutiny?" Tristan grinned. There was ongoing rivalry between the Brigade and the Infantry Divisions. He knew he had better brush up on his banter.

"Not just my brother—my parents will be there too. I've been wondering if I should invite you or not. If we're going to have any sort of future together, you either have to meet my family… eventually, or we'll have to run off and disappear on the opposite end of the galaxy." Jessica looked as though she were seriously considering the latter.

"I'm good with either one, so long as I'm with you." Tristan's face clouded. "No, I'm not. I want to meet your family. If we can't get along, or they really do hate me, then we can run away and disappear. I want to try to win their favor first, though."

Jessica smiled. "I don't know how they'll take it, but if you really want to pursue our relationship, it's got to happen sooner or later."

"Do you want me in civilian attire or my dress uniform? We can take this slowly and introduce them to me first and my career later," Tristan offered. "Or we could get it over with in one big bang. I don't know which way I'm more comfortable."

Jessica chewed on her lower lip. "I can handle whichever you choose."

Tristan stood up and bowed whimsically in front of her. "Your wish is my command, my lady." He picked up one of her hands again and kissed it gently.

Jessica giggled, then pulled at his arm. His display, although humorous, was getting the attention of nearby students. She didn't care for being in the spotlight. "Tristan, stop. People are staring."

Tristan dropped onto one knee. "Let them stare! I have professed my love to you, and if any other knave were to seek your affections, I want it well known that the lady is mine!"

Jessica blushed again. She decided the only way to stop his embarrassing activity was to play into it. "If you don't sit down and behave yourself, I'll give the kiss I've been saving for you to someone else."

Tristan grabbed his chest. "My lady, thou dost wound me." Knowing he was pushing his luck, he returned to his seat beside her and smiled. "Now, about that kiss?"

Jessica leaned in and kissed him as passionately as she could in a public place. The fire of rebellion grew in her soul. "Full dress uniform," she whispered.

Tristan smiled. "As you wish. You have until one hour before the event to change your mind." Tristan's smile faded. He still didn't know what his objective was for this mission other than to get close to Jessica and her family. So far, he had only gotten close to Jessica. He decided to push a little harder for information from all sides. "Jess, I hope this isn't too personal, but why doesn't your family like the military? I thought maybe if I knew what bothered them, I could put their minds at ease about me."

Jessica looked at him suspiciously. Her history had always been shrouded in silence. Her family was forbidden from discussing the events of her younger days. The military had watched her family closely during her childhood, and the surveillance only seemed to relax as she became a teenager.

Something gnawed at her. Was this handsome young man assigned to watch her? She shivered and shook off the idea as paranoia. Jessica nervously realized she didn't have an answer for him. Considering what had happened to her as a child, she decided there must be an answer that would satisfy everyone. "I—uh—I had an older sister. She died as a result of a military action many years ago. My family doesn't talk about her—ever. It was—it was some kind of accident," Jessica lied, blinking back tears. Her hands trembled as she recalled that awful day when her sister was executed in front of her young eyes.

Any other man might have stopped her from saying any more, but Tristan really wanted the information. He turned and scooted closer to her. Putting his arm around her, he held both her trembling hands in one of his own. He kept silent to allow her to say whatever was on her mind.

Jessica wiped away her tears, then laid her head on Tristan's shoulder. Her voice was barely audible as she continued her tale. "I—I was only seven when it happened. My family was so devastated. It took a long time for us to get back to normal, and they stopped talking about—about Abigail." Jessica looked at Tristan and blinked back tears again. "Tristan, can you make me one promise?"

Tristan wasn't sure what she was about to ask, but he planned on doing his best. "I'll try. What is it you want?"

"I hope I'm not saying too much. I mean, I don't want to be presumptuous, but if we—oh, I'm not sure how to ask this."

"I promise not to jump to unnecessary conclusions. Tell me what you want, and I will do it if I can."

Jessica took a deep breath and squeezed his hand tightly. She knew her next words would determine whether this relationship would go forward or die. "If we ever decide…" Her words came slow and haltingly. "If we ever decide to get married and we have a baby girl, can we please name her Abigail?"

Being an adept student of human nature, Tristan knew what she was risking by asking such a question. If a woman discussed marriage to a man who wasn't ready, the man would typically run away as fast as possible. Tristan knew his mission was to get exactly that far. He couldn't display his own eagerness, but he could offer a compromised position. He squeezed Jessica's hand, then caressed her cheek. Smiling, he gave his word, "Jessica Deacons, you have my word of honor that if we reach that point, our first daughter will be named Abigail."

Jessica blushed again. This man certainly knew how to get her flustered.

The next morning, Tristan went to his office. He tried to spend some time chatting with his supposed co-workers. The women in the office seemed to accept him more readily than the men. Although most of the women in the office were older and in relationships, his youth and good looks earned him some attention. The men merely saw a swaggering usurper.

Following a department meeting, Capt. Barrett pulled Tristan aside. "Chief Alexander, I haven't had a chance to ask you, but how are you doing at fitting into the department?"

The meeting was still breaking up, and several members of the department hadn't left the room yet.

"All right, I suppose. I spend so much time in my classes, I haven't gotten to know people as well as I would like. Nobody's picked any fights with me or anything, so I suppose that's a good thing." Tristan glanced around at his coworkers. Some avoided his gaze, while others gave him polite and thankful glances for not ratting them out. They all knew he was an outsider, and they were treating him as such.

"Well, try harder. You had better not screw this assignment up, because this thing is deeper than anything I've ever seen. Bring pastries a couple times, and the women will love you forever. The men, that's a little harder. If you can make friends with Riley Hardin, he's the key to the department. He's all business, but if he decides he likes you, the others will let you in."

"Yes sir. Anything else?"

The last employee filed out. "How's it going with Miss Deacons?"

Tristan beamed. "It's going great. At this rate, I'd better start looking for an engagement ring soon. She's ready for me to meet her family, and she wants to go all in for this meeting—even asked me to wear my dress uniform. Jessica also divulged a family secret that explains why they hate the military. She had a sister who died as a result of some kind of military accident. She wants us to name a daughter after her sister."

"That does sound promising. I was worried when you told me she hadn't slept with you yet. It sounds like we're past that point. The Covert Ops department will cover the cost of the ring when you're ready. Keep it in line with what a chief's budget would purchase. Understand?"

Tristan didn't burden him with the news that he and Jessica were still celibate. "Yes sir. I'm meeting her family this weekend at a CIF promotions ball. Her brother recently made the rank of Lieutenant Commander."

Leland's face clouded. "You're going in uniform to a CIF brigade ball. Don't get into any fights with the space cadets. I mean it! No shoving matches, no insult exchanges, nothing!"

"Yes sir, I understand." Tristan did not want to make a bad impression on his new future in-laws. "Is there anything I should know before I meet the family?"

"I don't have any new information. Get me a formal report by this afternoon, and I'll run it up the chain and see if I can shake anything loose."

"Thank you, sir. It would be nice to know what I'm looking for... or looking out for." This was the one part of this assignment that was really annoying him.

The morning before the party, Tristan walked into Capt. Barrett's office. The urge to salute him welled up every time he walked in. It was clear the man deemed the protocol unnecessary in this setting. Tristan's hand twitched ever so slightly as he approached the desk.

Capt. Barrett again had his head buried in whatever he was working on. "You just can't shake it, can you?"

"Shake what, sir?"

"The urge to salute me when you walk in here." Leland stopped reviewing the reports in front of him to watch Tristan.

Tristan looked at his hand. He had felt the twitch and wondered if Capt. Barrett had also seen it. "Some habits are easier to break than others. I'll get there."

Leland was glad to see Tristan hadn't lied to him. These Covert Ops people could tell believable lies all day and never bat an eye. "If we're ever outside the office investigating one of the military facilities, we'll be in uniform, and all protocols will apply. In here, I couldn't care less. If you feel the need to salute, go ahead. Just don't expect me to counter it. Now, what can I do for you, Mr. Alexander?"

"I was wondering if you had heard anything about what I'm looking for?"

"No, not yet. I'll let you know the instant I do, though. Is that all?" Leland was ready to get back to the material in front of him.

"In case you're interested, I passed all my finals and got top scores in my classes."

Leland scowled. "Are you sure you should be scoring such high scores? Won't Jessica get suspicious about why you needed a tutor in the first place?"

"No, Jessica is tutoring me privately and off the record. I told her I needed a tutor to keep my scores above mediocre," Tristan explained. "She's really the only reason my scores are so good. I get the basics in accounting, but the finer points are lost on me… they were lost on me. I understand them now. Like it or not, you may get a decent forensic accountant out of this deal."

"I have to admit, you seem to know your stuff. I almost came unglued when I found out you didn't request a tutor this semester. Good work. I know I'm no longer a Covert Ops specialist, but even I can see you're good at what you do. Anything else?"

Tristan shook his head. "No sir. That's all. I do have one more question. How many more classes do I have to take? I know I'm not going for a degree in accounting, but when do I get to stop?"

"After she says, 'I do.' How's that for motivation?" Leland grinned sadistically.

"Okay, then. Game on." Tristan's eyes flashed. He loved a challenge.

The young soldier returned to his office again, making eye contact with anyone who glanced his way. He ran by the breakroom and dropped off a large box, then announced to anyone in earshot, "I passed my classes! There are celebration refreshments in the breakroom." More people chose to make eye contact and give him some appreciation this time. A couple of the women went out of their way to thank him.

Tristan sat at his desk and reviewed some of the basic notifications that went out to the entire division of items of financial interest. A few minutes into his perusal, two people, a man and a woman, appeared in his doorway. Tristan stood, sensing this was serious business. The visitors wore business attire but carried themselves like military personnel. "Come in. Have a seat. How may I help you?"

The two wore serious looks on their faces. "We need to speak to you privately. Would you mind closing the door and activating the privacy screen?"

Tristan nodded and pressed a couple of controls on his desk. The door slid shut, and the glass partitions went milky white. A less visible signal jammer was also activated as a standard protocol.

Before he could make any inquiries, one of the two strangers began asking questions. "Chief Alexander, what sort of progress are you making on your mission with Miss Deacons?"

Tristan didn't like this approach. Since they asked about his classified mission, they were probably legit, but he couldn't say that for certain. "I'm sorry. My relationship with Miss Deacons is personal and private. She is not a conquest to be bragged about, and she's of no concern to you." Tristan reached to release the security protocols.

The second visitor stood and stopped his hand from hitting the controls. "Chief Alexander, I apologize for my associate's bluntness. Here are our authorizations and identifications." The man held out a data crystal.

Tristan took the crystal and plugged it into his computer. He eased into his seat and reviewed the information, surreptitiously making two copies for himself. One he placed on his local computer station and the second he sent to himself as a cyber file with a delayed delivery time. These two were his official handlers. He had seen their names when he worked Covert Ops, but had never met them personally.

When he was satisfied, he closed the file and handed it back. "Nice to finally meet you, Agents Gershom and Wallace. In answer to your original question, I'm preparing to meet her family for the first time tonight, and it would be really helpful to know what I'm looking for."

Agent Gershom was slightly more congenial than his blunt partner. "This case is extremely sensitive, and we didn't want to give you any more information than we had to until it was clear you were making some forward progress. We know she's been reluctant to have any kind of relationship with you. We almost pulled you off this mission after that night on the Riverwalk."

"You two were responsible for that?" Tristan's eyes narrowed. "I had the situation completely under control. That stunt could have blown it. From now on, let me do my job, my way. If I think getting rousted will help, I'll arrange it myself."

"Settle down, chief. We fully expected the two of you to end up in bed together. When you didn't, we allowed you a few more days. When Miss Deacons continued her relationship with you, added to the conversations she had with her roommate, we decided the situation could still move forward."

"You've got my apartment monitored?" Tristan came out of his chair again angrily. "I think I better get some serious explanations and now!"

"Chief, I'm about to do that, if you will sit down. We aren't monitoring your apartment all the time, only when Miss Deacons is present," Agent Gershom explained.

Agent Wallace finally attempted to add to the conversation more gently than her initial attempt. "Chief Alexander, this young woman's parents are working on some very sensitive projects for tachyon-based engines. In the past, they have been... subversive in their activities. They appear to be past it, but this project is at an imperative juncture. We can't afford to have someone come in and convince them to sabotage the project or for those old feelings to re-emerge. Their children are grown now. There's less reason for them to keep working, and as soon as Jessica graduates from college, they won't need to keep this particular job. This job is paying for her education. These engines will cut space travel time in half! They have to finish this. After the engines are complete, they can do whatever they like."

Tristan was still unsettled, but eased into his seat again. "Does this have something to do with the death of Jessica's sister, Abigail?"

The two agents looked at each other, conveying an unspoken message. Agent Gershom picked up again. "It does. This was not the military's fault, but Jessica's father believes it was. It was a freak accident. The entire family saw it happen. The engine was being tested for some modifications. It had performed perfectly on every test run, so Saul Deacons took his family aboard a ship using the new tachyon drive technology. One of the conduits broke loose and… uh… slit the girl's throat. She died right in front of them." There was a small amount of truth in his explanation. The girl had died from having her throat slit, just not by accident.

Tristan felt almost ill. He shoved his feelings into a dark corner of his brain. "Exactly what is my job here? Intimidation? Observation?"

"Your job will not be intimidation. Don't do anything that even remotely appears intimidating. That's our job. You just be your sweet, lovable self." Agent Wallace's tone was syrupy.

Agent Gershom spoke up again. "You are to keep the family under surveillance for questionable behaviors. We have their homes and offices monitored. It's the other places we have trouble with. The walks in the park, dinner at the restaurant across town: those are the places we can't account for. That file you copied has a list of names on it. If you hear the family speak to any of them, notify us at once."

Tristan grimaced when he realized they had seen him copy the file.

Agent Wallace warned him, "Do not get emotionally attached to her or any children born out of this relationship. If the word comes down for you to take any of them out, can you do it?"

"Take them out? I'm not an assassin. I'm trained to kill, and I can do that if needed, but I still feel as though I'm missing some pieces here. This doesn't sound like sufficient cause for extreme measures of that nature," Tristan objected, then added, "I'm a soldier, and I will follow the orders I'm given, but there is clearly a hole here."

Agent Wallace came back coldly, "Of course there is, but as we mentioned earlier, this is on a need-to-know basis, and you don't need to know. Follow your orders."

Agent Gershom winced and shifted in his seat, while Agent Wallace's gaze remained nonplussed. Agent Gershom asked, "Do you have any other questions?"

"Yes, am I reporting directly to you now, or do I still file my reports with Capt. Barrett?"

Agent Wallace jumped in again. "Only inform him of items that directly require his actions. Most of this, he doesn't need to know. Report everything else from here on to us and only us. Our contact information is with the data files we gave you."

Tristan stood again. "Yes ma'am. Yes sir."

His visitors stood to leave. The less cold and hard agent added, "Chief Alexander, I've seen your… uh… kill record. I know what we're asking is unusual and not what you are accustomed to. I sincerely doubt it will come to this. It's possible arranging a conspicuous accident could send the appropriate messages. I also know we're asking you to get close to the young woman in numerous ways. If we reach this point and you can't complete the task, let us know. We'll bring a specialist in, and you can arrange to be somewhere else when it happens. I wanted to give you a warning about getting emotionally involved."

"I'll keep that in mind. You said you thought her parents' subversive activities were in the past. What sort of activities were they, and why do you think they would resurface now?" Tristan's attitude was professional and dispassionate. He didn't like not knowing what he was dealing with."

Agent Gershom explained, "There are two possibilities. Their children are grown, so the parents no longer have small children to worry about. The second issue may be with the children themselves. Their parents might have adversely affected them, and now that they're grown, they could act out. They were old enough to remember some of their parents' activities. We could be completely wrong about this, but we have to be prepared. The children could become stalwart Commonwealth citizens, which is what we were hoping for. Jessica's brother, Robert, is doing that."

Agent Gershom sighed. "To be perfectly honest, we're hoping that if Jessica enters into a relationship with you, it will discourage her parents from acting out. It's why we want your history as a CIF officer to remain as part of your cover. If she accepts you, it proves she is a loyal Commonwealth citizen."

Tristan scowled and shifted in his seat. They had not answered his first question. Agent Wallace noticed his discomfort. "The Deacons family was causing problems on a new Commonwealth admission. Jessica's parents were prominent astrophysicists. They were using their influence to fight joining the Commonwealth. The details of their activities and the world they came from are classified."

"Why weren't their memories wiped?" The chief had legitimate questions and concerns.

The two agents glanced at each other again, but their reactions were polar opposites. Agent Wallace wanted the officer to stop asking questions and do as he was told. Agent Gershom was favorably impressed by the young man. "Chief, you are very astute. We could use someone like you in our department someday. The reason their memories weren't erased is because of the tachyon project they're working on. We couldn't take a chance on losing their knowledge of tachyon engineering principles."

"That's understandable. I apologize for giving you the third degree. I prefer to know as much as I can about whatever case I'm working on. It avoids potential problems. I think I have sufficient information to work with now."

Agent Wallace added her own admonition. "Good, don't get so attached that when the order comes down that you think you can whisk your lady friend, wife, whoever, off and hide her somewhere. We will find her and finish the job, then we will deal with you. Are we clear?"

"Crystal," Tristan responded.

The two left his office and disappeared into the elevator. Tristan got a cup of coffee and returned to his office, intending to review the file they gave him. He stared at the list of names, attempting to burn them into his brain. But all he could see were Jessica's smile and himself trying to execute her. He replayed scenario after scenario through his mind. The only thing he did was cause himself to feel sick.

Tristan's attention was so riveted on what he was thinking that he never heard Riley Hardin walk into his office. Riley looked at the list in front of Tristan. "New case?"

"Hmm?"

"That list of names. Is that a new case?"

Tristan casually closed the file and took a sip of his coffee. "No, just a new aspect of the same old case. I think my brain is tired from my classes. I can't even process that file right now."

Riley sat down without being invited. "Changing the subject a little—I heard a rumor you planned on trying to use me to get in with the rest of the office staff."

Tristan started to respond, but Riley waved him off. "Let me finish. I kept expecting you to show up, asking for help you didn't need or just stopping in to say hello. You didn't do that. Why?"

"Using people was a way of life in my former job. Like it or not, you are my coworker, not a snitch or an asset. If I can't get in on my own, I don't deserve to be here."

Riley pondered the young man's attitude. "Son, most of us spent ten to fifteen years trying to get into this department. You're what? Three… four years out of the Academy?"

"Three."

"Uh-huh. We've worked hard to get here, and you waltz in here with no experience and no training and take a spot away from another deserving, well-trained applicant." Riley wasn't trying to make Tristan feel bad—he just wanted him to understand.

"I thoroughly understand that. Really, I do. Do you understand I didn't ask for this assignment? I got a very distinct impression that I didn't have a choice in whether or not I took this job. It really was an offer I couldn't refuse. I liked my work in Covert Ops. I was not even remotely interested in moving over here. This department is filled with desk jockeys. I'm not cut out for desk duty. I like the excitement of the front lines. I'll gladly do the dirty work for the department if it gets me off the desk." Tristan's tone grew more acidic as he spoke. Realizing what he had done, his tone softened. "I'm sorry. You didn't ask for that."

Riley smiled. "No, but it tells me a lot about you. I think I like you, kid. I'll see what I can do to help you out in more ways than you thought possible."

Tristan wasn't sure he deserved the help but decided to graciously accept it. "Thanks, I appreciate it. Let me know if I can ever help you with anything."

Riley's face changed. "Let me help you with one thing right now. I don't know what that list was all about, but I saw one name on it that I've seen before. It's Pateras El Liontari. I don't know who he is, but he's a ghost. That name has come up a time or two in my investigations. I never could find anything out on him. People associated with him are very driven, and strange things happen to his associates. I would steer clear of him. He makes me very nervous."

"From what my two visitors told me today, I really hope this Liontari character isn't an issue. If he is, I'll keep your warning in mind. Thanks for the help. Don't mention this to anyone else, either. It's highly classified. Those two would nail me to the wall if they knew you saw this."

Riley smiled. "We can't have that. The women in the department would never get any work done if they had your carcass staring at them from the wall."

Tristan laughed, then turned his attention back to his computer. He wanted one more look at that information before he met with Jessica this evening.

Tristan arrived at Jessica's apartment. He stopped at a mirror in the hallway to do one last check to be sure his uniform was perfect. Everything was exactly where it was supposed to be. He took a deep breath and let it out slowly. It suddenly dawned on him that he was nervous. Why was he so nervous? He had dealt with criminals of all calibers, fought his way through brawls and ambushes. Why was this a problem? Was it because of his conversation with the two agents in his office earlier? Or was it because he was meeting his future in-laws? He took another deep breath and forced himself to relax. These were ordinary people.

He went to the door and announced his presence. Presently, the most beautiful woman he had ever seen greeted him. Jessica's hair flowed softly down below her shoulders. Her gown was sleeveless and cut low in the back. The bodice was a shimmering gold lace laid over a fitted burgundy top which tapered into a smooth, long, rich burgundy skirt. The skirt was full enough to have body but heavy enough to flow down her body without clinging to her.

Tristan was caught off guard by her beauty and simply stood there at the door, staring at her. Jessica giggled, then laughed outright at him. "Are we hanging out in the hallway tonight, or would you like to go to a formal ball?"

"I'm sorry. You look—so—beautiful."

Jessica giggled again. She was equally nervous about her family meeting Tristan. "Did you say you're sorry that I look beautiful? Because I could change into something less attractive if you like."

Tristan shook off his stupor. "No, don't you dare. Please don't change anything."

He offered Jessica his arm. "Ready to go?" Jessica took his arm and smiled nervously as he escorted her to the car.

Tristan had hired a private car for the evening. It wasn't a fancy one, but it afforded them the luxury of not worrying about certain minute details and allowed them the opportunity to have a few private moments.

During the drive, the handsome young soldier alternated between staring at the beautiful woman sitting beside him and staring past her out the window at nothing. He wasn't the biggest talker, but he could carry his share of a conversation. Jessica finally asked, "Tristan, are you all right? You seem distracted."

He forced his gaze from the window to her concerned face. He stroked her cheek lightly. His eyes avoided hers for a moment as he confessed, "I—uh—I'm a little nervous."

Jessica was equally nervous. She fully comprehended her own anxiety, but Tristan's anxiety was less clear. Her eyes dropped to his uniform. "I know I'm nervous about my family finding out I'm dating a soldier. Why are you nervous?"

"Meeting the girlfriend's family is a big step. What if this starts a civil war in your family? Maybe I should change clothes and do this more slowly."

Jessica giggled. "It's a little late for that, isn't it?"

Tristan shook his head gravely. "No, I threw a change of clothes in the storage compartment. I can still change into civilian attire."

Jessica clasped his hands. "No, don't you dare. You look so handsome in your dress uniform. I want to get this out in the open. My mom knows I'm dating someone. She keeps asking a lot of questions, and I'm a little tired of dodging some of them."

"I don't want to create a rift between you and your family." Tristan felt himself pull away from her mentally. The second he did it, he realized if he didn't pursue this relationship, they would simply find someone else to do it. It might be someone who would have no compunctions about hurting her or her family. Perhaps he would be better suited to protecting her from herself, from her family if they rebelled, and from the powers above him.

Tristan stared out the window again, then turned his eyes back to Jessica, who was staring at him with a frown on her face. She knew the signs of separation.

"Jess, that didn't come out right. I'm sorry."

A notice flashed across a screen in the vehicle, indicating they were arriving at their destination. Tristan scowled. He quickly ordered the vehicle to continue circling the destination in a four-block radius until further notice.

Tears formed in Jessica's eyes. She was certain this evening had put too much strain on their relationship, and it was about to end.

Tristan grabbed Jessica's hands again. "What I meant was, I want to be a positive part of your life, not a source of contention. I want you to have a good relationship with your family. I want to build a good relationship with them, too. I choose to believe that they will accept me. Maybe not tonight, but someday. I meant that I don't want to be thought of as a troublemaker. I don't want to come between you and your family. I want to meet them, and I want them to like me."

Jessica jerked her hands away from Tristan and grabbed for a cloth to wipe the tears from her eyes. She smiled again as one small sob of relief escaped. "I want to hug you, but I don't want to get makeup on your uniform."

Tristan took the cloth she was using and spread it out on his shoulder, protecting the area. "How's that?"

Jessica threw herself into his arms and laid her face carefully on the place prepared for her. The two hugged tightly for a long moment. Jessica looked appreciatively into his eyes. Tristan expressed his true feelings by kissing her.

Jessica pulled back presently. "We're going to be late."

Tristan smiled. "We'll make a grand entrance."

The young woman withdrew even further. "Daddy doesn't approve of tardiness. If you want to make a good impression, we should get in there."

Tristan sighed. "Are you sure you don't want to take another few circles around?"

Jessica smiled. "We still have the trip back. I do need to fix my hair and makeup again. Tighten the radius on the circles, and I should be ready in one more lap."

Tristan cut the radius down to a single block. As soon as she was ready, he redirected the car to the front entrance.

A group of new lieutenant commanders stood together near the bar, celebrating their newest promotion. Lt. Commanders Miles Johnson, Edgardo Garcia, and Robert Deacons gathered around a high-top table waiting for the festivities to get started. This party was a post-promotion ceremony and ball. The evening began with a meet-and-greet to be followed by a brief ceremony introducing the new officers. After the ceremony, the actual ball would begin, filling the evening with food, dancing, and fun.

Miles looked around periodically at the crowd. "Hey, Robert, I thought your family was coming."

"They are. My parents are seated at the third table to the left of the dance floor."

Miles nearly gave himself whiplash as he twisted around to see his friend's parents sitting alone at the table. "Where's your sister? I thought she was coming."

Robert set his drink on the table and gave Miles a hard stare. "Why do you want to know about my sister? My parents were more than a little ticked off when I joined the Brigade. Do you really think they're going to let you anywhere near her? Do you think I'd let you anywhere near her?"

Miles leaned in. "Oh, come on. Your sister is hot!"

Robert winced at the thought and shoved his friend away. "No, just no."

Edgar was focusing on something at the entrance of the ballroom when Jessica and Tristan walked in. He picked up his glass and sipped it, smiling. "Isn't that your sister?"

Robert looked around but didn't spot her right away and lost interest quickly.

Miles craned his neck to see as well. "Wait, she's got a date?"

Robert's interest piqued again. "A date? It's probably a friend from school she conned into tagging along with her."

Edgar scoffed. "I don't think so. She's with a ground pounder."

Robert slammed his glass onto the table and tried again to see her. Tristan and Jessica were nearing the table where her parents were seated when he finally located the couple. Robert stared in disbelief. "You've got to be kidding me. He's CIF and a ground pounder. My parents are going to go ballistic. I've got to get down there." He raced across the room as carefully as he could, considering the large population of high-ranking officers, civilians, and other dignitaries.

Miles gave Edgar an amused look. "I've got to see this up close." He took off after Robert.

Edgar smiled. It might be fun to watch. Then again, if everyone behaved themselves, it might not be that much fun. He sighed, gulped down the rest of his drink, then headed after the other two.

Everyone reached the table at nearly the same time. Tristan and Jessica were technically first. Jessica's father and mother stood as the couple approached them. Her mother, Kay Deacons, hugged Jessica, but eyed Tristan suspiciously. Jessica's father, Saul Deacons, simply looked distressed. There was no anger in his eyes, only sadness.

Before Jessica got a chance to introduce Tristan, Robert was suddenly at her side, followed by Miles and Edgar. Jessica knew instantly what her brother was thinking, and she set the tone right away. "Robbie! Congratulations on your promotion."

Robert froze as his blood ran cold. Jessica knew he hated being called Robbie. It sounded childish in his own ears. She had demeaned him and congratulated him in one breath.

Jessica grabbed him and pulled him in for a hug. She was careful not to muss his uniform but got close enough to whisper, "Behave, or I will remember every embarrassing thing you've ever done, and I'll make sure your friends hear all about them." She planted a careful kiss on his cheek, then pulled away.

Robert was now doubly mortified, but he recovered and smiled. Jessica smiled with an equal amount of genuineness.

Robert's eyes moved off her and onto Tristan, who was patiently waiting to be introduced. "Jess, who's your - date?"

Jessica introduced Tristan to her parents, her brother, and finally his two friends. Everyone maintained their pasted smiles and polite demeanors as they gently probed the couple's history.

Robert was eager to get Tristan away from the others long enough to give him a big-brotherly admonition to stay away from his sister. He hoped Miles and Edgar would be there to emphasize his point. Saul Deacons wanted some time alone with the young man to determine his intentions. Kay wanted to pull her daughter aside and warn her about the new man in her life.

Fortunately, the program started, forcing everyone to take their seats. There would be no more discussion for a while.

As the dining portion of the evening began, Tristan and Jessica excused themselves to head for the buffet tables. Tristan's case of nerves hadn't resolved since the tension in the air remained so thick. He was also very distracted by Jessica. She had always been attractive. Tonight, she almost seemed to glow. He listened to her chatter about how smoothly things were going so far. By the time they reached the end of the buffet line, Tristan's plate looked quite sparse. Jessica hadn't overindulged, but her plate was fuller than his.

Edgar was enjoying watching his friend brood over his sister's choice in men. He continued to jab at his discomfort. The two were several yards behind the couple in the buffet line. "You know, if it were my sister, I would rather have her date Miles than a ground pounder."

Miles was on the opposite side of the buffet table. "Hey, I heard that. What's wrong with dating me?"

Edgar had more needling to do. "Shut up, Miles. Can't you see Robert's distraught?"

Robert glared at the two men and snapped, "I'm not distraught, I'm concerned."

"Look at the way he's looking at her. It's like he's undressing her with his eyes every time he looks at her," Edgar jabbed again.

Miles joined in. "You gonna let him get away with that?"

Robert dropped his plate unceremoniously onto the buffet table. He turned around to face his friends. "I can't touch him in front of Jessica, or she would hate me. I also can't touch him in front of my parents."

Robert left his half-filled plate on the table and walked back to the bar. He wasn't usually much of a drinker, but tonight was really sticking him in the gut. He stood alone at the high-top table, drinking, for the next hour.

Saul wondered where his son and the family's guest of honor had disappeared to. His eye caught Miles, who was sitting at another table. Miles saw the question on his face and looked toward the bar. Saul followed his gaze until he spotted Robert drowning his sorrows. He excused himself to talk to his wayward son.

Most of the guests were done eating, and the dancing had begun. Sensing the tension at the table, Tristan decided he and Jessica should step away for a few minutes, so he invited her to dance.

Kay watched her daughter dance out of the here-and-now and straight into a fairytale. The two clearly appeared to be in love. This was a moment she had dreaded for the last fifteen years. Somehow she had always held out hope that Pateras would one day take them home. She wanted to see her daughter married to a man from their homeworld. A man who followed Pateras. Quiet tears flowed down her face as she sat alone at their table.

Saul approached Robert cautiously. Considering how much he might have drunk on an empty stomach over the last hour, his disposition and reasoning were likely compromised. "Robert, is everything okay, son?"

Robert reluctantly set his glass down. He knew his father was about to impart some unwanted words of wisdom. His father was generally right, but he didn't want to hear it this evening. "No, Dad, everything is not all right. I know you are upset with me for joining the brigade, but - but you know why I did it. I did it to keep anybody from having the kind of power over me that those ground pounders had over you." The words tasted vile in his mouth.

"Son, I am not disappointed in you. I resented anything to do with the Commonwealth. I wanted to keep you away from them, and you seemed to run straight into their arms. I understand what you're trying to do, really I do. You can't escape feeling out of control. Somebody somewhere will always be a step above you."

"Dad, it was a ground pounder who killed Abigail," Robert responded, leaning in.

Saul responded with equal discretion. "It wasn't this one. He was your age when that happened. You can't hold that against him."

"Are you saying you're okay with this?" Robert's face flushed with anger.

"No, I have other reasons to worry about this. What if they're trying to insert someone into the family to make sure now that you kids are grown, we won't cause problems? What if he's here to spy on us or as an ever-present reminder to behave?" Saul's face looked weary.

"I'll find out. I'll go beat the truth out of him." Robert started toward the dance floor.

Saul grabbed him and hustled him out into the corridor. "Robert, before you do that, listen carefully to me."

Robert respected his father very much and didn't fight back when he yanked him into the hallway. It didn't diminish the desire to break the grip Saul had on him and go after Tristan.

"We don't know for certain that this is anything but an unhappy coincidence. You also don't want to do anything rash in front of your sister or your superiors. You harm him, Jessica will end up hating you. Something else to consider: you're drunk, he's not."

Saul felt the tension leave his son's body. Robert nodded. "What do you want me to do?"

"Tonight, be civil. Go get a small plate of food and pretend to enjoy yourself. We can talk more about it tomorrow. Please don't act out in there." Saul hoped that a good night's sleep would help Robert see things better.

Robert followed his father sullenly back to the buffet and prepared a plate of food for himself, then sat down with his parents to eat.

Tristan and Jessica returned from the dance floor, winded after a lively dance. Jessica drank heartily from her glass of water, then excused herself to find a restroom. Kay joined her daughter.

Tristan was left in the awkward company of one who obviously hated him and another who was uncomfortable with him. He decided to play the situation straight up. "Is this the point where Mrs. Deacons is pulling Jessica aside to discuss me, or the point where she's delaying Jessica's return to the table so you can warn me away?"

Saul knew Robert was in no position to talk reasonably, so he picked up the conversation. "Are you a student of human behavior?"

"Somewhat. Some of it is gut instinct, and some of it is learned."

Saul nodded thoughtfully. "What are your intentions with my daughter?"

Tristan shifted in his seat. This was the part where he had to lay on his cover story smoothly. "I'm not sure I had any specific intentions except to get top scores in accounting. Jessica was assigned as my tutor, and it worked. We seemed to enjoy each other's company, and things progressed from there. This past semester, we started dating. We're taking things slowly. I changed areas of law enforcement recently. I don't want to make too many changes too fast."

Saul had another question on his mind but didn't want to ask around Robert. Tristan suspected as much. "I think I need a cup of coffee. Lt. Commander, may I get you something?"

"No, I'm fine," Robert gruffly replied.

"Mr. Deacons?" Tristan offered.

"I'd like a cup too. Thank you."

Tristan stepped away. Saul glanced at Robert, who was picking at his food. "Robert, I'm going to get you a cup of coffee as well. The night's not half over, and you should take the opportunity to dance with your mother and your sister for at least one dance. In your current state, you'll end up tripping them or stepping on their toes. You should also listen to your sister and ask questions, not tell her what to do."

Saul followed Tristan over to the beverage station. "Chief Alexander."

"Yes sir?"

"Was there something else you wanted to say to me?"

Tristan set the coffee cups down and looked his future father-in-law in the eye. "Yes sir, I wanted to assure you I have acted honorably toward your daughter, and I will continue to do so. I wasn't sure the Lt. Commander was willing to accept that from me. I know there's a rivalry between the two branches of the military, but he seems to be taking it to extremes."

Saul avoided eye contact. "This is no excuse for his inappropriate behavior, but he had an unpleasant experience with the infantry a number of years ago. It isn't you personally. It's what you represent. He'll see things more clearly tomorrow. Son, I've got one word of warning for you. Don't hurt my daughter, because there are forces greater than you know at work, and they will see to it justice is served."

His statement puzzled Tristan—did her father somehow know about this being a mission for him? He decided to focus on the part he did understand. Despite the numerous lies he had already told this evening, this part he meant. "I promise you, I will never intentionally hurt her. At some point, I will probably screw up and hurt her unintentionally, but that is unavoidable. I will apologize the second I know I've done it, though," he added wryly.

Saul smiled at the young man's attempt at lightening the mood. "I suppose as a father, that's about the best I can ask for. Tell me about this career change."

The two picked up their coffees and headed to the table. It mildly distressed Saul to hear about Tristan's history with the Covert Ops Division. It occurred to him, though, if the young man were truly spying on them, he wouldn't have admitted to being Covert Ops.

In the restroom, Kay talked earnestly with her daughter. "Jessica, are you sure about this young man? He seems nice enough, but he wears the same uniform as the one who…" She couldn't bring herself to say the words.

A shocked, then hurt expression crossed Jessica's face. "Mom! That wasn't Tristan! He's not even old enough to—to," Jessica couldn't finish the sentence either. "Mom, he used to work in Covert Ops. He's not made any secret of that. He got out of that because he didn't like it. Tristan's a good man."

Kay stepped closer to her daughter and whispered, "Ask Pateras if he's the right one for you, before you're too emotionally involved."

"Mom, I'm not going to do that. He stopped listening to me a long time ago, or we wouldn't be here having this conversation."

"Jessica, that's not true. He knows what he's doing. Please talk to him, before you get into a lifetime commitment," Kay entreated.

"It's not a lifetime commitment, Mom. Marriages are contractual here. If we get tired of each other, we won't renew our marriage contracts," Jessica shot back.

Kay coldly responded, "That wasn't what he intended, and you know it."

"If he can show me he really is in control, then I'll consider talking to him again, but not until then."

"If you wait that long, it may be too late," Kay snapped. She realized there was every chance she was alienating her only living daughter. "Jess, I don't want you to make a mistake, and I don't want you to get hurt. I'm sorry if I'm being hard on you. He does seem like a nice young man. I just always pictured you marrying a Drean."

"We're never going to get back there, and we might as well be happy here. Mom, he makes me happy. For the first time, I feel safe."

"Those are two of the things I wanted for my children. Hopefully, all the others will follow soon enough," Kay mused.

"What other things did you want for us?" Jessica hoped the ugly part of the conversation was over.

"I wanted both of you to get back home and marry spouses from home. I wanted you to love Pateras the way your father and I do and I wanted all the other things a parent wishes for their child."

The two left the restroom and headed to the table. Jessica grinned. "I hope Daddy and Robbie weren't too hard on Tristan."

HALYN'S CAPTURE

Nasha pushed his steed and his men as fast as he could to get to the bridge. They reached the crossing at sunrise. Marek and some of his men met them on the other side of the river. Nasha and the man assigned to aid him, or dispatch him, accompanied him to meet Marek at the center of the bridge. Nasha glanced at the concerned man. He knew he wasn't supposed to cross the river into Somian territory. "Just follow my lead."

The man nodded. "For a time."

Nasha rode his horse slowly onto the bridge. Marek, unsure of the game Nasha was playing, had brought a second with him. "You made excellent time, Marek."

"Why are you out here and not in Helia? Where are the men?" Marek asked suspiciously.

Nasha allowed his face to cloud with anger and disgust. "They got drunk after I warned them not to and were of no use to me. I discovered the healer left the city last night and assumed she was headed to Nazar. I suppose my judgment may have been in error. During the night, I traveled through the mountain pass and spoke with the magistrate of Nazar. He agreed to help us locate the healer and see that justice is done. He has no desire for his city to become a home for criminals of the Somian Province. The magistrate sent these men with me to search for her."

Marek eyed Nasha suspiciously. "When you learned she left the city, why didn't you simply chase her down? Surely your horse is faster than her loaded wagon."

Nasha came at his subordinate harshly. "How dare you question me? Do you think I am a fool? I didn't find out she was gone until she was out of sight. The rain was heavy and washed her tracks away. These events have truly been strange. It's like she's being protected and hidden from us. If the girl really carries the Promised One, I doubt we'll ever get our hands on her. Pateras protects whomever he chooses." Nasha made certain his voice carried to Marek's men.

Marek humbled himself for the moment. "How do you propose we proceed from this point?"

"Did you leave some men outside of Helia to prevent the girl from leaving if she's still hidden in the city?"

"Yes, I left two soldiers outside each of the city gates."

"I trust you won't consider it an intrusion if the magistrate's men aid us in our search?" Nasha probed his second-in-command cautiously. If the young man objected, it would be clear that he suspected his superior of subversion. He might accept the help simply because he saw no good way to avoid it.

"I don't think it's my place to make such a call, sir. You are the superior officer here." Marek played the more subservient role to placate his superior until he knew for certain whose side his superior was on.

"Wise choice. Your decisions have been far too impetuous of late." Nasha turned to his new Nazaran companion. "With your permission, I'd like to leave two of your men here to watch the bridge from the Nazaran side. I guarantee your safety with my life in the Somian territory. Please join us in our search."

The man turned his horse about and rode back to give the orders. He didn't like this plan one bit, but he played along.

Nasha crossed the bridge with Marek and his companion close behind. Nasha hastily assigned four of the twelve men to spread out and ride slowly toward the city of Helia looking for any possible tracks leading to Halyn. He gave them strict orders to track and watch her. "Send word to me the second you locate her. Remember, the healer is secondary. The girl she's hiding is the target." He watched Marek squirm as his advantage decreased drastically. There were now ten Nazaran soldiers to his eight. Nasha split the others into four teams of five. He sent one team to follow the river north, and one team south. He sent the other two teams halfway between the road and the river. One went toward the north and the other to the south. Nasha knew he should be on one of those teams. The question was which one? He glanced at his companion. "North or south?"

The man glanced both directions. "North," was all he said. Nasha looked back and forth once more. North sounded good to him.

An hour later, their choice paid off. The group had searched three homesteads and were approaching a fourth. Nasha kept Marek with him. He was afraid of what might happen to Halyn if Marek found her first. The group reached the top of a rise and spotted Halyn's wagon outside a small farmhouse. Her horses were hitched, and the wagon appeared ready to go. The house was situated in a neat little cove surrounded by rolling hills with only one small dirt road leading in. Nasha sent his men to surround the farm. He dispatched Marek and his men to the far side. He positioned the Nazaran commander on the rise closest to the road.

The men were still getting into place when the homestead door opened. A man followed Halyn out to her wagon. Their voices echoed in the valley, and Nasha could hear the man thanking the healer for her help.

Nasha rolled his eyes. Now he knew why she didn't arrive at the expected time in the very early hours of the morning. He needed to warn her before the other men reached their assigned stations. Nasha dismounted and grabbed a rock. His eyes located the Somian men. None were looking his direction. He lobbed the rock as hard as he could. The stone fell short of hitting the wagon, but Halyn and the farmer looked at the rock, both wondering where it had come from. They searched the hillside and saw nothing until the reflection of the sun from Nasha's sword hit their eyes. Halyn swiveled around to see the tops of heads bouncing above the crest of the rise. She bid the young farmer a hasty farewell and climbed into the wagon faster than anyone knew she could.

Halyn gave the horses several hearty slaps with the reins and chirruped to them aggressively. The horses started out at a hasty gallop and finally progressed to the all-out run she wanted.

The soldiers gave chase. Marek ordered one man to stay behind and watch the house, in case the girl was hidden there.

Nasha and the Nazaran commander were the closest to Halyn as they gave chase. The Nazaran commander yelled to Nasha, "Are you certain she trusts you? She's running from you."

"I signaled her from the hilltop. She saw my warning and knew to run," Nasha yelled back. "I'll keep myself between her and Marek."

The two men continued to give the appearance of chasing her. They were, in fact, closing the gap between themselves and Halyn for her protection. Nasha glanced behind him. He yelled again to his companion, "Marek's catching up. We either have to stop Halyn or take Marek and those other two out."

"Which one do you want to do?" The commander asked.

"Let's stop Halyn and search her wagon. Maybe that will convince Marek to leave her alone." Nasha wasn't sure it would be enough for him to see the empty wagon. He hated to stop her so far from the bridge and reinforcements. The bridge was still four or five miles away.

Nasha rode even faster, as he got closer to the back of the wagon and called out, "Healer! Stop your wagon!"

Halyn continued to push her horses harder. She was fairly certain Nasha was still supporting her. It was clear he was under pressure from the other soldiers. If she stopped too easily, whatever charade he was playing at would be lost.

The bumps in the road rattled her frame. She was too old for this sort of rugged activity. She spread her feet apart and pushed firmly against the buckboard to prevent herself from getting bounced out of her seat. Her back and arms quickly complained about the rigid activity.

Something caught her eye on a rise ahead. Four more soldiers were barreling down the hill toward the road in front of her. Halyn scanned the surroundings to see if there was another route she could use to avoid them. The hills were steep enough to slow the wagon down.

Nasha and the Nazaran commander saw the soldiers almost as quickly as Halyn had. It didn't take long for them to reach her. Two stayed in her path, and two flanked her horses. Nasha and his companion flanked the wagon. The two pacing beside the horses reached out and grabbed onto her reins. They slowed the horses. Halyn stopped fighting and reined them in as well. Her arms and legs burned from the strain of bracing herself and controlling the horses. By the time Nasha reached her and helped her down from the wagon, she was visibly shaking. He helped her sit on the ground and offered her a drink from his waterskin. As soon as she was settled, Nasha turned to the four soldiers who had stopped the wagon.

"Thank you for your help. I sent you four back toward Helia to look for tracks. I assume your findings led you here?" Their reappearance at this location, even if they had discovered something, was suspect. Any clues they found should have placed them squarely behind them, not ahead of them.

The one leading the team glanced at Marek for guidance. Marek offered the man no help. The officer finally defended himself. "Marek ordered us to ride toward the city for half an hour, then return to the bridge and follow your tracks this way."

Nasha folded his arms across his chest. "So, Marek now outranks me?"

The soldier looked nervously at Marek again. Marek approached the two cautiously. "I'm sorry, Commander. You were right about the rain washing away the tracks. There was no clear way to know which direction the healer went. I thought perhaps your God, Pateras, was guiding you to her as you asked."

Nasha knew the man was lying. The odds were not in Nasha's favor and he had better act quickly to maintain control.

Nasha punched Marek squarely in the face, knocking him to the ground, then drew his sword and held it at the man's throat. "You ever countermand my orders again, you better be prepared to arrest me or kill me, because I will do either of those to you. I might even do both of them."

Marek was afraid to move. He hadn't expected this from Nasha. Followers of Pateras were typically very mild-mannered and submissive. "Forgive me. It won't happen again. I swear it." Beads of sweat now adorned his forehead.

"I will spare your life—this time. Don't make me regret it. Now, let's have a word with the healer." Nasha kept his sword out and approached Halyn. "Old woman, why did you run from us?"

Halyn leaned around to see Marek as he was pulling himself together. "Because of that one. He's determined to cause trouble for me, and I don't want any more trouble."

"You lied to us, healer. You said you hadn't seen the girl we were searching for the other night."

"I didn't lie to you. You heard only what you wanted to hear. I said I hadn't seen a child and that I would see to it the young woman got the justice she deserved. She carries the child of Pateras, the Promised One. She has committed no crimes, so there was no reason to report her presence to you."

Nasha squatted in front of her. His eyes conveyed the kindness his voice could not. "Where is the woman, Healer? Speak the truth, and I will allow you to go free."

"I left her in Helia, in the stables. The stable boy was watching out for her. I haven't seen her since yesterday afternoon."

Nasha frowned. "As much as I would like to believe you, I cannot."

Nasha sent three of the men back to the farm to meet with the one soldier who had been left behind. He ordered them to search the farmhouse and the barn for the young woman. "Be thorough, but do not be destructive in your search."

Most soldiers would knock things over and destroy anything in their path. Nasha had no problem being destructive where the guilty were concerned, but his sense of justice and fair play prevented him from destroying the lives of the innocent. Turning to Marek and the two remaining soldiers, he ordered, "Remove the tarp from her wagon and search it for the young woman. Do not tear it or break anything."

The three climbed onto her wagon and gently removed the covering. They unloaded enough to determine Slaina was not on the wagon. Sensing Nasha's demeanor, they placed the unloaded items on the wagon and covered it again with the tarp.

"Healer, I'm afraid you're going to accompany us to Helia. If the girl is found, you will be free to go. If the girl is not in the city, we'll have to find a way to learn the truth from you." Nasha's threat earned him a harsh look from the Nazaran commander. He hastily addressed the man's concerns to a degree. "Let's head to the bridge and regroup with our other search parties." Nasha assigned one man each to ride in the direction each team had gone and recall them. He turned his attention to Halyn. "I will allow you to drive your own wagon if you think you can behave."

Halyn eyed the man. "I cannot tell you where that young woman is. I left her behind, and I have not seen her since. Whether she left the city or is still there, I could not say for certain."

"That is not what I asked you, Healer. I asked if you could drive your own wagon without causing problems for me?"

"It's apparent my animals can't outrun yours, so if I tried to run away from you, what good would it do?" Halyn knew running was not a viable option yet, but he had to be putting her back on her own wagon for a reason.

"It would vex me to chase you again. Do not try my patience. My patience is nearing its limit for today."

"You have my word. My fate is now in the hands of Pateras and no other." Nasha helped the old woman to her feet and escorted her to her wagon.

The soldiers surrounded the wagon as they rode for the river crossing for the next half hour. Halyn's attempted escape had taken them back toward the bridge at a faster pace than the speed they used to reach the farmhouse. Halyn let the horses set the pace pulling the wagon. They knew their way home. She had worked them harder than usual during the chase, and they needed the rest.

The caravan stopped before reaching the bridge. Nasha helped Halyn down from her seat on the wagon. He ordered two of the men to water her animals and all the others. Nasha walked past the Nazaran commander and softly advised, "Keep your men close by on the bridge."

Nasha didn't want to leave any of the Nazaran troops at the mercy of the Somian Soldiers. The soldiers from Nazar outnumbered their counterparts on each search team, but when they all returned, the numbers would be equal.

The day was surprisingly warm, and the sun was still high. The group found some shade trees to rest and take their noon meal under. While they awaited the return of the other teams, some napped while a couple went down to the water to wash off and cool themselves. Although Marek would have loved to do either of those things, he preferred to remain battle ready.

Nasha sat down near Halyn. He stayed alert for any sounds of riders in the distance. He expected they would wait about an hour before the others returned. The team heading north along the river arrived first. They had been closest. The southeastern team arrived an hour later. With only one team remaining, Nasha whispered instructions to Halyn. "Get to your wagon. Make a secure place for yourself in the back of it. Getting you safely to Nazar is my only goal here. The Nazaran commander will see to your safety. Slaina is safe, but she needs your skills. She fell very ill going through the mountain pass."

As the soldiers returned, they naturally segregated themselves according to province. Nasha began making perfunctory rounds among the Nazaran soldiers, thanking them for their assistance. He reached their commander as Halyn reached the back of her wagon. One of the Somian soldiers tried to stop her from climbing into it. Halyn promptly scolded the man loudly.

Nasha took three broad steps toward them. "What's the problem, soldier?"

"The healer is trying to escape," he returned.

"From the back of the wagon? I seriously doubt that. The reins don't reach that far. Use your brain, if you've got one. Hold the horses if you're that worried about it." Nasha shook his head and turned his back on them. He walked to the group of Nazaran soldiers and their commander. Shaking their hands, he offered his appreciation to them, then quietly instructed. "Commander, Halyn is in the back of the wagon. When the last team returns, you drive her rig across the river and keep going all the way to the Nazaran township. The rest of you help me keep my men from crossing the bridge after them. I want to get Halyn safely inside the city. I'd like to get the rest of us there too if possible." He looked directly at the commander. "Are you comfortable with this plan?"

The man shook his head. "No, I'm not. I'll assign one of my younger men to drive the wagon. I'm staying with you."

Nasha was perplexed. He felt it would be best to have an experienced superior see to Halyn's safety. "Very well. They are your men. Commission them as you see fit. Just know that I will position myself in front of the bridge, and none of my men will be allowed to pass."

Marek watched Nasha's every move. Seeing him mingling with the Nazaran soldiers kept him alert. He knew his commanding officer would make a move to free the woman eventually.

Nasha moved away from the soldiers to check on the horses. When the last team finally arrived, Nasha gave them a break while he cared for their animals. He kept his attention shifting to track everyone's movements. Marek had moved around aimlessly during the three hours they had been waiting. When the last team finished their food, Nasha mounted his horse and nodded at the Nazarans. Glancing over at the wagon, he saw that Halyn appeared to be napping. "Listen up. Soldiers of Nazar, thank you again for your assistance. Please convey my thanks to your magistrate. I look forward to working with you again soon. Your service is at an end for now.

"Soldiers of Somi, Pateras has promised us that one will come to free us from the darkness. I have seen a messenger of Pateras myself. He came to me and commanded me not to harm the young woman sought by Governor Pravin. She does indeed carry the Promised One. The Healer has done right to help the young woman known as Slaina."

Nasha's speech was meant to slow the reactions of his own soldiers and buy time for the Nazarans to mount their horses and be ready to fight if needed. There was more to his dissertation, but Marek had had all he could take.

"What you mean to say is, you're freeing the healer, aren't you?" he demanded.

Nasha looked down at Marek from his horse. "Marek, I will not cross swords with Pateras. It is a battle I cannot win. You shouldn't either."

Nasha took his eyes off Marek to nod his approval to the Nazaran commander. The distraction was more than he could afford. Marek's sword flew out of its sheath and swung at Nasha. The Nazaran commander and his men were ready to move. The one assigned to Halyn's wagon spurred his horse toward the wagon before the Somian troops could react. He launched himself from the back of his own steed onto the front of the wagon. One of the Somian soldiers tried to stop him but received a painful kick to the face. A second Nazaran grabbed

the Somian's horse's reins and pulled the steed away from the
wagon. The rest of the Nazaran soldiers formed a line of
defense between the Somians and the bridge.

The wagon made a wide circle and raced for the bridge. The
Somians attempted to mount their own steeds and attack the
Nazarans. Half of the saddles on the Somian horses had been
loosened by Nasha as he wandered about earlier, and the men
fell to the ground, spooking some of their horses. Those who
had grabbed the reins first, then attempted to mount their
steeds, ended up without a horse. The ones who intended to
mount first, then untie the reins, only lost time as they picked
themselves off the ground and put their saddles tightly back into
place.

Marek's swing dislodged Nasha from his saddle and earned
the commander a gash in his side. Nasha had heard the sword
leave its sheath and attempted to dodge the blow. Despite the
searing pain, Nasha rolled to his feet and freed his own blade.
Keeping his back to the Nazaran defensive line, he stood his
ground against Marek. The two swords clashed as the men
battled for their lives.

For the next few minutes, nothing could be heard but the
sounds of a wagon riding away, steel crashing against steel, and
the occasional cries of a man or beast as they were injured or
forced into unwelcome closeness with a challenger.

As the two circled each other looking for an opening, Nasha
challenged Marek to a more personal arrangement. "Marek, you
and I should determine how this ends. Call off your men, and
I'll call off mine. If you win, take me back to the governor and
blame me for the girl's escape. If I win, you go back and still
blame me, but you tell him I took the girl and the healer to the
Northern Province. No one needs to die here today."

Marek glared at his traitorous former leader. He glanced over
Nasha's shoulder at the men who were outnumbered and getting
more so every moment as injuries were incurred. "You're wrong.
One must die today. My sword will decide it."

The two men backed away from each other and called out to
their men to stand down. It took several cries to end the conflict.
Marek's men pulled their injured warriors back and dressed their
wounds while they watched Marek and Nasha.

The two closed ranks and restarted their skirmish. The
swords struck each other several more times before Marek

received a glancing blow to his left shoulder. He pulled back momentarily to assess the damage. Nasha waited for him to decide it wasn't worth surrendering for.

Marek advanced again and Nasha swept low and made no contact. Marek's blade swept harmlessly over Nasha's head. He managed to plant his left elbow in Nasha's face, bloodying his nose. The two traded blows several more times before Nasha got the upper hand and took Marek to the ground. Marek's sword flew from his hand and landed out of reach.

Nasha held his blade above his opponent. "Do you yield?"

Marek glanced at his sword. There was no chance of retrieving it from his current position. His face fell in visible defeat. He grabbed at anything beneath him to brace himself. Defiance welled up within him. "I will never yield. Do what you must."

Nasha regretted the need for such an action. He pulled his blade back to run his opponent through. Before he could push the blade forward again, a blurred image flew toward his face. Nasha dodged enough for the object to miss his eyes, but it landed painfully on his temple. Marek's hand had found a rock and launched it at Nasha.

Marek twisted and swung his leg, taking Nasha's feet out from under him. Nasha rolled away from Marek to get his bearings. Marek retrieved his sword. The two went at each other again. This time, they added banter. "Nasha, why are you doing this? You're throwing your career away for a fornicator. You aren't even in love with her. Why do this?"

The two exchanged more blows before Nasha answered. "I serve Pateras first and Governor Pravin second. Pateras chose this woman for a reason, and he ordered me not to harm her."

"Then don't harm her. By helping her, you have made yourself a target of the governor. Walk away. Disappear." Marek had no desire to harm Nasha—he just wanted him out of the way.

Their swords clanged again. Nasha and Marek circled each other, looking for a weakness or an opening. Nasha should have had an easy victory. His strength, endurance, and experience easily outmatched Marek. Marek was no child, but he still had the strength, stamina, and drive of a young man.

Nasha heard a noise in the distance and caught sight of Halyn's wagon returning. Without dropping his guard, he made eye contact with the Nazaran commander, giving him a questioning look. The man rode out to meet the wagon. Nasha forced himself to stay focused on the man trying to kill him.

Marek worked hard to stay equally focused, but questions kept popping up. Nasha challenged him yet again. "Do you care about anything besides yourself?"

"If I don't take care of myself, who will?"

"Pateras will take better care of you than you ever could," Nasha yelled back. Their swords crossed again. The blades slid down to the hilt and caught the two men were in a battle of sheer strength. Their fellow soldiers were surprisingly quiet throughout the duel. They weren't sure whom they wanted to win. Nasha was pushing Marek with all his strength and holding his own. Marek equaled him. Nasha had both feet planted. He twisted and pulled one foot back. Altering his center of balance sent Marek flying. The brash young man landed face-first on the ground. This time, he managed to hang onto his sword.

Marek tried to roll away from where he thought Nasha was—a painful kick to the ribs promptly greeted him. In retaliation, he swung his sword. Nasha jumped back, but not quickly enough. He took another large laceration to his leg and staggered back to regain his footing. Marek took advantage of the lull and rolled away from Nasha to get to his feet again. Before the two could strike any further blows, a line of arrows hit the surrounding ground.

The two stopped to reassess their situation. A row of archers and the Nazaran magistrate lined the river bank on the Nazaran side. The magistrate called out across the river. "Soldiers of Somi, the healer Halyn and the mother of the Promised One of Pateras are under my protection. Unless you want war with Nazar, cease hostilities and leave here!"

The words "war with Nazar" rang familiar in Marek's ears. It was the one thing Governor Pravin had warned him not to cause. Nasha backed down as he awaited Marek's decision. Marek wasn't prepared to give up yet. "This is a personal matter between Somian soldiers on the Somian side of the river. It is no concern of yours. When this matter is settled, we will leave here."

The magistrate called, "I have granted the soldier known as Nasha honorary citizenship in the province of Nazar. He is under my protection. His battles are our battles."

A lone arrow punctuated the magistrate's announcement by planting itself neatly at Marek's feet. Nasha turned to Marek. "What's it going to be, Marek? Do we finish this here and now, or do you want to live to fight another day?"

Marek hissed, "We had an agreement to finish this!"

Nasha nodded. "Yes, we did, and I'll finish it if that's what you want. The magistrate was not privy to that agreement. If you best me, I dare say he and his men will best you and the others. If I win, the men will be free to leave, and they can bury your body in an unmarked grave along the roadside. I suggest you accept your losses and live to fight again. You can't win this one."

Marek decided he could not go back completely empty-handed. "You took the girl through the mountain pass to Nazar, didn't you?"

"You may as well tell the governor everything. The young woman is safely out of the Somian Province. Also, tell him this: If I hear that he has caused even the tiniest harm to Slaina's family, I will slip into the city and through the private entrances into his home, and I will wreak ten times the havoc on all that he cares most about. Remind him that I know a good many of his secrets."

"Swear by your god," Marek demanded. He believed Nasha, but he wanted sufficient cause for Governor Pravin to believe him. "Is she in Nazar?"

"I swear by Pateras, Slaina is in Nazar. I took her there myself."

Marek, still gripping his sword tightly, glanced back and forth between Nasha and the magistrate. If he gave in too quickly, they would know this wasn't over. If the governor wanted to pursue it, he would want the element of surprise. Marek slowly sheathed his sword. "All right, you win. This is over. Never plan on returning home to Somi, Nasha. Your life will be forfeit. Whatever holdings you possessed will be confiscated by Pravin."

"I had nothing that I cannot afford to lose. I had a small piece of property, a home I rarely lived in, and two hired servants to care for it." Nasha realized how empty his life had been. He cared little for the governor's dealings, and he had no one to go home to. He was an only child whose parents had passed away several years ago.

Nasha sheathed his own sword with a feeling of finality. He looked down at the arrow by Marek's feet. He raised his head again to meet Marek's eyes with a meaningful stare. "Don't trust Governor Pravin. He will use you until he no longer believes he can trust you. Pateras is the only one you can trust."

Nasha walked away from Marek, leaving his back exposed. He had made his point with Marek and knew the young man would no longer try to touch him. The Nazaran commander returned to escort his men and Nasha to the other side of the bridge. He announced loudly, "The Healer Halyn would like to offer her services to the men of Somi. You will be permitted to cross the bridge to her if you leave your weapons and armor on this side."

Marek looked at his wounded men and his own wounds. "Nasha! Nasha! How do we know we can trust her? We tried to arrest her."

Nasha mounted his horse wearily. He grinned as the sun illuminated the sweat on his brow. "THAT is why you never anger a healer."

GETTING SERIOUS

Jessica sat around with her friends drinking hot chocolate, talking, and giggling. They had one last semester before graduation. There would be little time to socialize once the semester started. The conversation naturally turned to the men in their lives. Maddy walked in late to the party. Natalie and Lesa welcomed her home. Lesa jabbed, "I see your man finally let you come home for a change. He's been taking all your time during the winter break."

Maddy made a face at her in return. "At least my man likes spending time with me instead of going to all the games with the guys."

Lesa's face clouded. Natalie laughed at the sparring match. "Oh, you did not say that."

"Yes, I did. She asked for it. How did you get away, Nat?"

Natalie smiled. "His family's in town. He wanted to spend time with them."

Lesa perked up again. "You haven't met his family yet, have you?" Her eyes grew wide as Natalie admitted she hadn't. "Nat, you need to lose him. You've been dating for this entire year, and he hasn't introduced you to his family? Something doesn't smell right with that. I bet he hasn't even told them he's dating anyone." Now it was Natalie's turn to frown.

Jessica had been conspicuously quiet. Maddy asked, "Jess, you and Tristan have been pretty tight. How did you get a night away from him?"

"I just told him I wanted to stay in tonight."

Lesa was determined to stir something up. "What did you have to give him in return?"

Jessica's face clouded. "Nothing. I asked him if he minded if I stayed in with the girls tonight. He said it was fine and he would try to find something to do but that he would miss me." The cloud dissolved into a goofy grin.

Maddy laughed. "Oh, she's got it bad for that man."

Lesa came at her again. "Have you met his family?"

Jessica frowned. "No, he hasn't mentioned any family. I was a little afraid to ask since he hasn't said anything about them. I wondered if something bad happened to them or if he was orphaned or something."

"Has he met your family?" Natalie wondered.

Maddy laughed sardonically. "Has he met her family? You didn't hear about that?"

Lesa jumped on what sounded like a juicy story. "What happened? Tell us about it."

Jessica gave Maddy a dirty look. She knew Lesa wouldn't take a brush off, so she tried to placate her by hitting the highlights. "Tristan is Infantry, Robbie is Brigade and a jerk."

Maddy buried her face in a throw pillow for a moment. She lowered the pillow, revealing her chagrin. "There was way more to it than that."

Natalie was more sympathetic than the others. "I'm guessing things didn't start out well. Have they gotten better?"

Jessica was peeved, and her face made her point quite clearly. "No, Robbie's still a jerk."

Maddy shook her head again. "Jess, you've got to tell them what happened."

Jessica shook her head. "No, I don't."

Lesa pressed her lips together, determined. She had to know the details. "C'mon, Jess, spill it."

Jessica was still mortified by the events. She got up and headed for the kitchen. "Let Maddy tell you. I don't want to relive it."

When Jessica disappeared into the other room, Maddy began her tale. "Jessica's brother got promoted and invited the family to the ball to celebrate. Jess walks in with an Infantry guy in full dress uniform in a room full of Brigade. Apparently, Robert was not happy. He got drunk and showed his true colors."

Natalie looked mortified on Jessica's behalf. "Oh no, what happened?"

Maddy wiggled excitedly in her seat. She kicked off her shoes and pulled her feet up. "Jessica's dad thought he had Robert settled down toward the end of the ball. Her mom and dad left, and Robert headed back to the bar. When the ball ended, Robert and two of his buddies cornered Tristan while Jessica was in the ladies' room. Tristan ran like a coward."

"Oh, you're kidding. Tristan? I'm having trouble seeing that." Lesa was sure there was more to this story.

Jessica re-entered the room too quickly. "That isn't the way it happened. Maddy, if you're going to tell something, tell it right."

Maddy waved her hand to yield the floor to Jessica. "Okay, you tell it, then." That was what she had wanted all along.

Jessica sat down with her fresh hot chocolate. She pulled her feet up and tucked her toes under a couch cushion. "Robbie and his friends surrounded Tristan and challenged him. I came out of the restroom and saw them together. I knew they were about to cause trouble. My mother had said some things that made me think about what kind of man Tristan really is. I thought if I could follow them and watch, I might put her fears to rest. I heard Tristan suggest taking it outside so none of them would get put on report by fighting in front of their superiors. They headed out to the parking area."

Jessica's eyes glazed as she thought back to that night two weeks ago.

Robert got in Tristan's face with Edgar and Miles at his side ready to back him up. "This is your first and last warning. Keep away from my sister. You're going to break up with her gently—tonight!" Robert poked Tristan roughly.

Tristan sighed. This was a tricky situation. "Lt. Cmdr. Deacons, I don't think I can do that. I'm—in love with Jessica."

"Then we're going to have to give you a little incentive," Robert slurred.

"Gentlemen, you are officers of the Brigade, and you are quite drunk. Perhaps you would like to sleep on it, and we could get together and discuss this using whatever method of communication you prefer tomorrow."

Robert shook his head. "No, we're going to settle this tonight."

Tristan nodded. "Very well then. There are a couple of things you should know first. If you pummel me into a puddle of goo, your sister will hate you and feel sorry for me, so that probably isn't the best approach. The second thing you need to know is, my boss ordered me not to get into any fights with the Brigade, and I don't know about you guys, but I follow orders."

Tristan's words rubbed all three the wrong way. They believed in obeying orders and were good soldiers. Edgar volunteered, "Hey Robert, he's got a point. We wouldn't want to be responsible for causing him to disobey a direct order. You also don't want to be the one to beat him up. Your sister would never forgive you."

Robert was seething by this point. "What do you suggest?"

Edgar smiled. "You hold him while Miles and I teach him a lesson. If he fights back, he's the one disobeying orders. We weren't ordered not to start any fights."

Tristan smiled and nodded. "Great idea. I hadn't thought of that one. I suppose I could stand here and let you hit me. That would completely take Lt. Cmdr. Deacons out of the hot seat."

Miles smiled. "Yeah, you do that."

Jessica concealed herself behind a nearby vehicle and listened to the conversation. She thought for a moment that her heart was going to stop. She remembered one of the remote access keys to their vehicle was in her purse. It wasn't right for her to interfere in this, but she didn't want any of them hurt. Jessica pressed the call button to get the vehicle headed her direction.

Tristan smiled again. "Let's go one better. You guys stand there, and I'll punch myself. That keeps you guys totally in the clear. How about that one?"

Robert was about to reach his limit. "No, it's my sister's honor at stake. I'm going to break you."

"As I mentioned earlier, you three are drunk, and I'm not. You want to beat the stuffing out of me? That's fine, but here's the deal. You have to catch me first." Tristan started running toward the upper levels of the parking garage. The three took off after him, calling him various unflattering names that all equated to coward.

The girls interrupted Jessica's tale. "Wait, he really ran like a coward?" Lesa had trouble believing it. Tristan seemed polite and pleasant with a deep, quiet, almost frightening something beneath the surface.

Jessica frowned. "Tristan's no coward. He didn't want to hurt Robert, or me. After that night on the riverfront..."

Lesa scowled. "What night on the riverfront?" Here was another story her friend obviously hadn't shared.

Maddy gave Lesa a frustrated look. "Where have you been? Some drunks attacked Tristan and Jessica the night they started dating. Her knight in shining armor defended her until one of them tried to smash Tristan's brains out with a bottle."

Jessica scowled. "Did you want to hear the rest of this or not?"

Natalie didn't view Tristan as a coward either. Running away didn't seem like him. She was glad to know there was more to the story. "Yes! Tell us what happened. Did Robert catch him?"

Jessica picked up her tale again.

The three men took off after Tristan. Since Jessica had been wearing shoes meant for dancing, not running, she couldn't keep up. She took her shoes off and gave chase until the car caught up to her. She jumped into it. Tristan carried the second remote access. Jessica programmed the vehicle to drive to Tristan's location. The car drove up several levels before passing Edgar, who stopped to throw up from the alcohol and the running. Next, it passed Miles, who was doing the same thing, only one level higher. Reaching the roof, she found Robert weaving dangerously as he bent over, trying to catch his breath and finish the job he set out to do. The car came to a stop beside the two men, and Jessica jumped out to rescue Tristan and berate her brother. Tristan bent over, catching his breath as well. The parking garage had eight levels, and the two of them had run up all eight.

Tristan caught enough air to laugh. "That was good. I thought you were too drunk to make it this far." Tristan took off his dress uniform jacket and tossed it to Jessica. "Here I am, Robert. I'm all yours. If you want to hurt me bad enough to chase me up eight levels, you've earned it. I won't fight back."

Robert caught his breath enough to speak. Taking off his own jacket, he tossed it to Jessica as well. He raised his hands to prepare to fight. "No, you're going to fight back."

Tristan kept his hands down at his sides, though it went against every instinct in his body. He felt himself tense up, but he knew if he tensed, any blows Robert landed would hurt worse. He pushed himself to relax.

Robert swung at Tristan. Jessica screamed, "Robert, stop!"

Tristan easily dodged the blow. He glanced at Jessica. "Get back in the car, Jess. Everything will be fine."

Jessica did as she was told, but kept the windows down. The night air had gotten cold. Between the chill in the air and her fear, she was shivering. Tears formed in her eyes as she feared for the safety of both men.

Robert swung a couple more times at Tristan, who neatly dodged him. Robert yelled, "Fight me, you coward!"

Tristan shook his head. "No, Robert, I won't fight you. I don't want to be your enemy. I want to be friends. I would like to get to know you and your family. I don't want to hurt you, and I don't want to hurt Jessica."

Tristan neatly dodged two more swings. Jessica continued to yell out the window for Robert to stop. After one more swing, Tristan caught Robert's arm and twisted it around behind Robert's back, shoved him against the car, and held him there.

Robert tried to fight back, to no avail. "Let go of me, you coward."

Tristan argued, "You're drunk. You don't know what you're doing. Listen, if you think I have wronged you or Jessica in some way, I'll be at the gym on 12th and Rawlings tomorrow at 1400 hours. Meet me there, and I'll even fight back if you really want me to. I'm no coward. I'm just not willing to take advantage of you while you're drunk. For tonight, I've beaten you. Tomorrow, you are welcome to try again."

Tristan released Robert's arm and backed away, but he stood ready in case the fight hadn't left his antagonist. Robert righted himself slowly. He caught sight of Jessica's frightened face and the tears in her eyes. Even if he needed to teach this intruder in their lives a lesson, the reality that it didn't need to happen in front of his sister sank in. He turned around to face Tristan, calm but still angry. "You'd better believe I'll be there. You had better be there, and don't be late."

Robert started to walk away. Tristan reached inside the window and took Robert's jacket from Jessica. He followed Robert a couple of steps and called out, "Robert, here's your jacket."

The man grudgingly turned and accepted the jacket back. Tristan said softly, "Robert, I'm formerly Covert Ops. You wouldn't survive five minutes in that world as a coward. I'll be in that gym tomorrow, like I said. I will be more disappointed if you show up than if you don't. If you want to talk, come by my office in a couple of days. I think you know the building."

"Tristan got into the car, and we drove away. End of story."

"Nuh-uh, what happened the next day? Did your brother meet Tristan at the gym?" Lesa wasn't about to let it go there.

"I don't think so. Tristan was there, but he said he never saw him. I begged him not to go. He said he had to, but he promised not to hurt Robert." Jessica smiled fondly as she remembered what else he had said. Tristan had put his arm around her and held her tightly. He whispered, "I won't hurt him, and I promise not to let him hurt me either."

"Are you sure he didn't show up? Have you seen your brother since then? Maybe Tristan trounced him, and he's too embarrassed to show his face." Lesa was determined to stir up trouble. "I bet Tristan didn't want to tell you what he did to your brother."

"Tristan wouldn't lie to me," Jessica replied defensively.

Maddy shook her head. "You are so naïve. Every man lies about something. For that matter, we lie to them too. Everybody lies."

"Oh, come on. I expect him to lie to me about liking my cooking, but not something like that," Jessica objected.

Lesa laughed so hard she rolled off her chair onto the carpeted floor. "Your boyfriend beats the stuffing out of your brother, and you expect him to confess it? Your brother is bound to be too embarrassed to let you know what happened, so he's keeping his distance until you forget about the whole thing."

The look on Jessica's face revealed her fear. She began to have doubts. Lesa was making sense.

Natalie threw a pillow at her. "Lesa, you are so mean. Why did you have to say that? Now you've upset Jessica."

Maddy scooted closer to Jessica on the sofa. She put a comforting hand on Jessica's knee. "I think if something like that happened, Tristan is the type to feel so bad he would have to confess it. I don't think Lesa is right."

"What if she's right? Men are funny about this kind of stuff. Do you think Robert and Tristan would really hide this?" Jessica was getting a sick feeling in the pit of her stomach.

Lesa was feeling bad about upsetting her friend. To make amends, she suggested, "Go to Tristan's office tomorrow and ask him point-blank. You'll catch him off guard. He won't be able to lie to you. Start out all smiles and tell him you missed him and wanted to see him. Trust me, you get him in a place he isn't expecting it, you can rattle him. Ask him point-blank if he beat up your brother and whether he would ever lie to you."

"That sounds like I'm trying to trap him." Jessica winced.

Lesa nodded. "That's exactly what you're doing, but if he lied to you, you're entitled to catch him in his lies."

"What if you're wrong? What if he told me the truth? Won't he get angry?" Jessica worried.

Maddy and Lesa looked at each other. The look was almost frightening. Maddy finally asked the one question both women were thinking. "Have you never seen him angry?"

"He was a little angry the night those men attacked us on the riverfront. He was angry at them, though, not me. Why?" Jessica had never been in a serious relationship. She wasn't sure what the significance was.

Even Natalie knew. "Jess, you can't get serious with a guy until you've seen him angry, particularly at you."

Jessica looked at her friends as though they had lost their minds. "Why?"

"Nobody likes to get angry. If he frightens you when he's angry, you have to end it." Natalie was very practical in these matters. Lesa and Maddy agreed. Letting Natalie say it made Jessica listen.

"Are you suggesting I do something to make him mad?" Jessica didn't really like that idea.

The girls looked at each other and shook their heads. "You shouldn't have to. I would have thought he would have gotten mad at some point when you've argued."

Jessica scowled. "We've never argued."

Maddy's mouth fell open in shock. "You've been dating for seven months. How could you have not argued?"

"We've only been dating for four months. I tutored him for the first three months, so we couldn't date."

Lesa looked at Jessica suspiciously. "You've been dating for four months. You haven't seen him angry, and you haven't argued. What else haven't you done?"

Maddy knew the answer to that question. She was afraid Jessica was about to be pushed too far. "Ok, Lesa, I think that's enough. We got together to have some fun, not to pick apart Jessica's dating life. If anybody needs their dating life picked apart, it's yours. How many guys have you dated this past semester?"

The next morning, Jessica went to the building where Tristan worked. She had seen it before, but had never been inside. She walked in nervously. Somehow, she suddenly wished she had made Maddy come with her. Her goal wasn't to make Tristan angry, but what if he did get angry?

Inside, a friendly security officer checked her in and greeted her. He notified Tristan that she was here to visit him.

Tristan came down to meet her. He smiled warmly, and his eyes seemed to sparkle when he looked at her. They made small talk until they got upstairs. The young woman's presence earned the couple several curious glances. Tristan showed her around briefly, then escorted her to his office.

"What brings you here?" he finally asked.

"I hope you won't get mad at me for asking this, but I haven't heard from Robbie since the ball. Are you sure he didn't show up at the gym? Would you tell me if he had?"

Tristan leaned forward. "Exactly what are you asking me?" His eyes showed concern and a flicker of something more.

Jessica got nervous. She stood and headed for the door. "Never mind. I shouldn't have come."

Tristan shut the door before Jessica could get out. She turned around, afraid her friends had been right. All she saw was concern in his eyes. "Jess, what is it you think I've done?"

"I—I know men have some ego issues. I know you didn't want to hurt me or hurt Robbie. Would you lie to me? Just to spare my feelings?" Her thoughts were jumbled.

Tristan frowned. "Let me get this straight. You think Robert met me in the gym and I bested him, but didn't tell you about it to avoid embarrassing him or hurting you?"

"I'm sorry. The girls had me doubting last night. I—I had to ask." Jessica felt sick. He really hadn't given her cause to doubt him.

Tristan rubbed his face with his hand. He knew he had better tread lightly here. "Jessica…" he started slowly. "What have I done to make you think I would lie to you? Yes, guys have ego issues, but I thought we were beyond that sort of pettiness. If Robert had shown up that day, I would have done my best to see that things ended in a stalemate, and I would have told you about it immediately. I'm not the type to play games. I thought you knew that."

Jessica sat there silently, wishing she had not stepped foot in his office. She glanced at the closed door, a tiny red light indicated it was locked. The fact that she couldn't leave was unnerving.

Tristan saw her worry grow. He reached down and pressed a button, releasing the lock. The light changed to a more pleasing green. "Jessica, what did I do wrong?"

Tears formed in her eyes as she jumped up to flee the tiny office. "Nothing, you did nothing. This was my fault. I'm sorry. I shouldn't have come here."

Tristan stood and moved around the end of his desk before she could make it out of the office. Jessica stood at the door, her hand poised to open it. "Jess, please don't leave. I love you. I don't want to ever do anything to hurt you. Please—explain this to me."

Jessica turned around to face him. She wanted more than anything to explain everything to him: how she came to be on Juranta, where her true homeworld was, and why the Commonwealth had killed her sister. But saying anything could get her or her family into trouble. The turmoil of emotions escalated her silent tears to bold sobs. Tristan closed the gap between them and hugged her tightly.

Her sobs finally slowed. Tristan pulled her over to the two guest chairs in his office. They sat facing each other. Tristan reached across the desk and engaged the privacy screen. "Does this have something to do with your sister or my former job?"

Jessica wiped more tears away. She nodded and tried to catch her breath. "My parents are worried that you've been assigned to keep an eye on us. They didn't handle what happened to Abigail well. They were in prison for a while. I'm not really supposed to talk about it. The authorities watched us closely for a long time. It finally stopped a few years ago. When my parents met you and found out you were Covert Ops..." Jessica left the implication hanging.

"Your parents were in prison?" Tristan already knew about it, but since this was the first time she had mentioned it, he had to act surprised.

Seeing his concern, Jessica quickly said, "They were cleared of any wrongdoing. It was some kind of political thing. I don't remember much about it. I was only seven when it happened."

Tristan stood and moved away from her. He kept his back turned as he planned his next moves carefully.

Feeling the sudden chill emanating from him, fear rose in Jessica. She wondered if her actions had taken their relationship beyond repair. "Tristan, I know I messed up. I'm sorry. Did I go too far?"

The young chief continued to play his part. He turned around slowly. Worry clouded his face. "Go too far? No, you didn't. I'm so sorry. I made this all about me."

"What do you mean?"

"I'm a law enforcement officer. Getting involved with even former criminals on a personal level could cost me promotions and advancement at best and my entire career at worst."

Fire ignited in Jessica's eyes. Her own temper flared. In a flash, she was into his personal space, slapping him hard.

Tristan saw it coming. He could have easily caught her hand and stopped her. Jessica attempted to turn and storm out of his office, but Tristan caught her arm and held it tightly.

The angry young woman tried to jerk free. "Let go of me!"

"No, not yet. There's something you don't understand."

Her anger mutated from fiery flames to ice in her veins. "My parents are not criminals!" She tried again to pull away from him.

"I know, Jess. I wasn't trying to say that they were. What I am saying is that I love you and I want to get to know your family better. I enjoyed meeting them. I'm saying there may come a point in time where my superiors look at your parents' history and question me. It's something that could ultimately affect both of us. I'm sorry I reacted badly. It took me by surprise. I didn't mean I couldn't deal with it."

"Deal with it? I'm not following." Jessica had been pulling away. Now her body began to relax again.

"If you and I were to go our separate ways, there would be—nothing to deal with. If we were to have a future together, being fired or denied a promotion could affect us and our—potential life together." Tristan hoped he wasn't moving too fast for her. Since she had held back from a sexual relationship, he wasn't certain how deep her feelings for him ran.

Tristan felt the last of her tension drain away. Fresh tears welled in her eyes. "After all I've done today, you still want to have a relationship with me and maybe a future?"

Tristan relaxed his grip on her arm and pulled her close to him. He grasped both of her upper arms gently. "Yes, I do. I love you."

Jessica threw herself into his arms again. Tristan held her tightly. When she seemed more at ease, he pulled back to clear the air a little further. "So, if I'm understanding things, you came in here today to accuse me of spying on your family, beating up your brother, and lying to you about it. Do you mind explaining how I came to be such an ogre?"

A laugh of relief escaped from Jessica. She wiped more tears away. "I know it sounds silly. I'm sorry I bothered you with it."

"Considering what your family probably went through years ago, it's not silly. Let's take this one point at a time. First of all, I haven't seen your brother since we left him in the parking garage.

Second, if I had seen him, I would have told you about it because it would have bothered me very much if he had shown up that day. I don't want to hurt your brother, and I certainly don't want to hurt you. Lying about it would only compound the problem."

"I know. Between the girls egging things on last night and my parents being so paranoid about being watched, I guess I got carried away." Jessica snuggled in and laid her head on his shoulder.

Tristan allowed her to settle in, then added, "One more thing. Your parents were worried about me spying on them. Jess, I hate to point out the obvious, but it isn't very covert to announce that you are, or were, a Covert Ops agent. Before you ask, yes, I may at some points in time lie to you, and I would be quite convincing. It would be related to my job and a case I would be working. It wouldn't be about personal issues. Even in my new job, there are things I can't tell you about in open investigations. I will do my best to protect you, particularly from my job. At some point, you'll have to decide whether or not to trust me, even knowing that lies are part of my job."

The two spent a moment in quiet embrace, then Tristan asked, "Jessica, do we still have a future together, or am I asking for too much trust?"

Jessica still had her head on his shoulder. She kept it down as she considered his question. He had as much as said he would lie to her. He had told her it wouldn't be about personal issues. This was an odd way to establish a relationship. What person would go into a relationship knowing lies were a part of it? Somehow, there was a sense of honesty about his profession of dishonesty.

She lifted her head to look him in the eye. "You would never lie to me about your feelings for me?"

"Just to be clear, any lies I tell you will definitely be related to my job. I will never lie to you about my feelings for you." Since seducing her into marrying him and starting a family was his job, he essentially excused himself from any lie he chose to tell her. Telling her he loved her was his job.

He made sure his eyes conveyed what his mouth was about to say. "Jessica, I love you very much, and I want us to have a future together. Is that okay with you?"

Jessica pulled a little further back and looked at him oddly. "You aren't asking me to marry you, are you?"

Tristan got an amused look on his face. "No, not yet, not officially. I need to make the appropriate purchase first, and I'd like to have my job secured before I make such an investment. You'd better make sure I pass all my classes so I can afford you."

Jessica smiled at him as her heart melted and became intertwined with his. Tristan refused to admit to himself that he felt more than a basic attraction to her. In truth, he was falling in love with her as much as she was falling in love with him. He sealed their reconciliation with a kiss. He had to admit, this was an enjoyable assignment.

His computer beeped at him, interrupting their intimate moment. He glanced down to see a notification from the security officer at the front desk. He scowled and extricated himself from Jessica's arms. Moving back behind his desk, he answered the message, turned off the privacy screen, and unlocked the door again.

Jessica watched him until he looked at her with an odd look on his face. "What is it, Tristan? Should I go?"

He gave her a confused look. "I don't know."

Tristan walked around his desk and stepped outside of the door. He looked toward the elevator in expectation. In a moment, the doors opened and Lt. Cmdr. Robert Deacons stepped off. As soon as he spotted Tristan, he approached him contritely. "Chief Alexander, you invited me to come talk with you. I know that was two weeks ago, but is that offer still open?"

"Of course, Lt. Commander, but there's something you should know." Tristan stepped out of the doorway, revealing to Robert that his sister was sitting in the office. Tristan smiled disarmingly. "I've never had visitors here before. Today, I seem to have an abundance of them. Please come in."

Robert hesitated. "I don't want to interrupt anything."

Tristan grinned mischievously. "To be honest, this is a rather auspicious occasion. I believe we've had our first fight, and it was about you."

A wave of panic and embarrassment caused Jessica's face to flush. "No, Tristan, please don't."

Robert wasn't sure whether he should ask any questions or leave the subject alone. The one thing he couldn't escape was that it concerned him. "I hope I haven't caused you both a problem. That's why I came here. I wanted to apologize to you for my actions. Jessica, I'm actually glad you're here too. I also needed to apologize to you. It's taken me two weeks to come to terms with this. I'm sorry for attacking you, Chief, and for hating you on general principles. Jess, I'm sorry for embarrassing you, myself, and the chief. I hope I didn't ruin your date, or your relationship, since I've apparently caused a recent—discussion."

Tristan invited the man into his office and closed the door to keep prying ears from hearing any more of the conversation. Robert sat down in the chair next to Jessica. Tristan sat on the wide arm of Jessica's chair. He reached for her hand and squeezed it gently.

"Lt. Commander, I'm glad you decided to come talk to me. Jessica is a beautiful, intelligent, and wonderful woman. I don't want to see her hurt in any way. This barrier between you and me is causing her distress. I would love to do whatever is necessary to fix this."

Robert stared at Jessica. Her feelings for Tristan were obvious in her eyes. He could clearly see warmth and affection with a twist of angst.

He looked back at Tristan. The war between Brigade and Infantry was now over. "Chief, I'm very sorry for all the grief I caused both of you that night. Part of it was seeing Jessica with a man, a stranger. Another part of it was that you are—again I apologize for being so petty—an Infantry officer."

Something flickered in Robert's eyes. Tristan was quick to notice. He didn't want to suggest that Jessica had told him about their past. "What else? It seems as though there's something else on your mind."

Robert shook his head and rubbed his face. He attempted to avoid eye contact with either of them, but had to face his rash and uncontrolled behavior. "No, there's nothing else. I was embarrassed about drinking so much and behaving so inappropriately."

Tristan looked down at Jessica, who was nervous about the topic of discussion. He didn't want to put her on the spot. "Forgive me, Lt. Commander, but…"

Seeing that this young man appeared to be in their midst for the long haul, Robert interrupted. "Chief, forgive me for stopping you. It appears you've already won my sister's heart, and if my apology is to be genuine, then please call me Robert. Why, may I ask, was I the source of your first argument, two weeks later?"

Tristan knew his question was being derailed. He was determined to get the conversation back to where it needed to be. "Jessica knew I challenged you to meet me in the gym the day after the ball. She hadn't heard from you since that night, and she thought perhaps the worst had happened. She thought you showed up…"

"Tristan, please don't," Jessica begged. She was embarrassed enough by the situation.

"Jessica, it was a legitimate concern. You shouldn't be embarrassed. I really think we need to get everything out in the open. I don't want to keep secrets from you or your family. Would you prefer to explain it?" If she put it into her own words, it might sound less ridiculous and more credible, at least in her own ears.

Jessica nodded. "Robbie, I waited for you to apologize. After I didn't hear from you for three days, I decided you must still be mad at me, so I tried to hail you to apologize for springing Tristan on you so suddenly. You never answered, and you never got back to me. Tristan said you never showed up at the gym, but some of my friends convinced me that maybe you had shown up and Tristan didn't want to tell me about it."

Robert knew what she was saying. For a moment, he avoided her gaze as he gathered the strength to tell her what had happened that day. He rubbed his face with his hand, trying to wipe away his own embarrassment. "Chief, I'm sorry for calling you a coward. If anybody is a coward here, it's me."

Tristan cocked his head curiously. "How so?"

"I came to the gym. I got there early, and I was going to teach you a lesson you wouldn't soon forget. You were already there warming up with the training bot. You've got some serious combat skills. I realized right then, you were not somebody I wanted to trifle with. I knew I was no match for you stone-cold sober. If you wanted to kill me on the night of the ball, you could have. You could have put all three of us down, but you didn't. You let us think you were a coward to avoid hurting us and Jessica." Robert was afraid to look either of them in the eye.

Jessica looked at Tristan and smiled warmly. "Thank you for swallowing your pride for me."

Tristan rubbed her back affectionately. "I wouldn't do that for just anybody."

"I'm grateful you didn't take advantage of our inebriated state. From what I saw in that gym, you could have handed us our heads on a platter. You've got the skills to bruise our egos without causing us any serious injury. I know we sorely deserved it, but why didn't you?"

Tristan's eyes landed on Jessica. He kept his gaze firmly on her as he answered Robert's question with the simplest of answers. "I didn't want to."

Robert's brow furrowed. "Surely that wasn't the only reason."

Tristan snapped back, "Surely being an infantryman wasn't your only reason for hating me. That seems really thin, and you're a deeper man than that."

Robert was getting annoyed. "You've just met me. How would you know how shallow or deep I am?"

Tristan smiled. "As a former Covert Ops officer, I had to be a student of human nature. Jessica has always spoken highly of you, and she's not shallow. It's clear she admires someone who's got depth. You're also a high-ranking officer. You don't get that high up by being shallow, and getting into a fight with an infantryman is pretty shallow. I would love to put your mind at ease about me, but I can't do that if I don't understand the problem."

Robert scowled. He couldn't discuss this with Tristan. He glanced at Jessica, who was unusually calm regarding the topic of discussion. It finally dawned on him. "Jess—you told him about Abigail?"

"O-only a little," she stammered.

Tristan put the pieces together. "Oh, now I see. The one who was responsible for her death was an infantry soldier. I think I understand now."

"Jess, why did you do that? That was a private matter. You don't know him well enough to talk to him about that. You know what could happen." Robert was caught between anger and fear.

"I'm not your enemy, and I'm no spy," Tristan lied easily again. "You don't have to talk to me about it, but from what little Jessica told me, you've been suppressing the emotions of a loss for a long time. If you want to talk to somebody about it sometime, I'm here for you, for both of you. At least I know it isn't me that you hate, just something I, or rather my uniform, represents."

Robert shifted uneasily in his seat. "No offense, Chief Alexander, but I don't know you. You earn trust in my book. I've never trusted anybody with the knowledge of what happened to my sister. You want that much trust, you'll have to earn it."

Tristan nodded. "Fair enough. Robert, I'm not asking you what happened. I'm just saying if you want to talk, I'll listen. Whether or not you ever discuss this with me, I hope you will at least be able to trust me to that degree someday."

Robert's eyes shifted to Jessica. "I see. Jess, do Mom and Dad know?"

Jessica looked confused. "Know what? That I talked to Tristan about Abigail?"

"No, not that specifically. Do they know how serious it's gotten between you and Tristan?"

Her face clouded. "No, I didn't say anything specific to them, but somehow I think Mom knows already."

Robert nodded. "You're probably right. I should leave you alone. Chief, again, I apologize for my actions, and I hope you can forgive me."

"It's Tristan, and it's forgiven. I was really impressed you made it to the top floor of that parking garage in your condition that night. I think you could give me a decent workout—sober."

Robert stood to leave. "Thank you. Perhaps we'll get a chance to do some sparring someday. Part of the reason I came to talk to you now is because I'm shipping out in two days. I don't know how soon we'll get back this way."

Jessica vaulted out of her chair and into Robert's arms. "Two days? Robbie, why didn't you say something sooner?"

Robert bristled. "It's Robert, not Robbie. I'm a Commonwealth officer, not a kid." He grudgingly returned her hug. "I was going to meet Mom and Dad tomorrow night for a farewell dinner. Can you and Tristan come?"

Tristan quickly backed out. "That is a family event. I shouldn't intrude."

Robert released his grip on Jessica but kept his arm across her shoulders. "I'm not sure that's going to matter soon."

Tristan grinned. "I'll consider it and talk to Jessica about it."

Robert pulled his arm off Jessica and offered his hand to Tristan. He smiled, despite his strong feeling that something was wrong. He was starting to feel manipulated. "Do you suppose you could walk me out? Jess, I'm going to try to talk some sense into this man regarding dinner tomorrow night."

Jessica heard loudly and clearly that she was being asked to stay behind and butt out. Her face clouded. "Robert, be nice!"

Robert smiled with the same polite but less than genuine smile. "Jessica, I already know he could mop the floor with me. How inappropriate could I be?"

Tristan looked over at Jessica. "We'll be back in a minute. It's just guy stuff. He has to order me not to hurt you. I have to promise him you mean the world to me, and I would give my life for you. We throw in a couple of threats, and we shake on it with our strongest handshake to prove our masculinity. It's no big deal."

Jessica winced and scowled. "If you say so. Just know this: I'll hurt either or both of you if you act up."

Tristan grinned and winked at Robert. Taking the hint, Robert joined Tristan in turning smartly and saluting the young woman. "Yes ma'am."

Tristan and Robert headed for the elevator. Jessica stood at the doorway, watching suspiciously. She hoped Tristan wouldn't escort him all the way to the lobby. The two stopped at the elevator doors.

Tristan waited for Robert to start the conversation. Glancing back at Jessica, they were careful to keep the looks on their face pleasant.

Robert cut to the point. "Have you touched my sister?"

Tristan's face reacted briefly, and he looked away from Jessica while he re-plastered the smile on his face. It only took a second to recover. "That's not your concern."

Robert glanced at Jessica again and smiled pleasantly. "We were not raised to indulge in intimacy prior to marriage, and marriage is not to be entered into lightly or as a temporary measure. I know that isn't the popular notion in this society, but it's what we believe. It's what she was taught. If you've pressured her or seduced her to abandon her beliefs…"

That explained a lot about Jessica's hesitations. Tristan realized Robert wasn't just being an overprotective sibling. "Robert, I'm sorry. I assumed you were being—a big brother. No, I haven't touched her. She hasn't wanted to, and I've respected her wishes. Consider it a sacrifice of love and dedication on my part, because I've wanted to, very much. She's a beautiful, intelligent woman."

Robert winced slightly. "Okay, you've said enough. As to whatever she told you about Abigail—tell no one. Yes, an infantryman killed her. I don't know how much Jess remembers, but there was a cover-up. If you tell anybody what happened, it could rattle the wrong cages, and you don't want to wake the beast." Robert turned to press the elevator call button, then stopped short. "Oh yes, I almost forgot to threaten you. I don't really know you, and for now, I do not trust you. If you hurt my sister, I don't care how good you are at hand-to-hand combat, I will see that you answer for it. Are we clear?"

Tristan laughed outright. "I was fairly certain you wouldn't waste a chance to threaten me. I understand perfectly. You seem to be a fairly good student of human nature as well. You understand about things that are spoken and things that can't be said. I do what I do to protect people, and Jessica is no different. I will protect her, even from myself. You have my word on that."

Robert nodded. Tristan's message seemed complex for such a simple concept. He would have to rethink it later. "I'm glad we understand each other—mostly." He added, "I'm serious though—please join us for dinner. I want you to come."

Tristan glanced at Jessica. "So long as Jessica wants me there, I'll be there. We did have our first fight, you know."

Robert nodded his understanding, then shook his head. "I hope she'll let you come. Life with you in the picture is going to be interesting. I can already see that."

Tristan smiled. "I hope that's a good thing."

Robert called the elevator, then answered more seriously. "I hope so too." The elevator arrived and Robert stepped into the car, leaving Tristan alone.

Tristan returned to Jessica's side and invited her to go to lunch with him. She gladly agreed. The two talked at length about their recent conversations and the upcoming dinner. Jessica was both nervous and excited at the prospect of having Tristan go with her, this time in civilian attire.

Capt. Barrett greeted Tristan when he returned. He had been notified when Tristan's visitors showed up. "Anything I need to know about?"

Tristan smiled. "Yeah, I was promised a promotion as soon as Jessica and I become engaged. I'll be putting in for that promotion soon."

Leland smiled and shook his head. "Man, you're good. Be careful to keep your emotions free of this one."

Tristan nodded knowingly. "Tell me about it. Those two agents who came to see me recently are into some serious business. Crossing them could have ugly consequences."

Leland agreed. "You're right about that. I felt the chill when they entered the building. I guess you have another report to draft?"

"Yes, I do, and I think I'd better word this one carefully, because somebody is lying to me."

Leland shook his head. "I don't want to know about it. Submit only what is necessary to me, and whatever you do, don't lie to those other goons."

"Yes sir." Tristan nodded and headed off to his office to carefully construct his latest report.

JEDREK

Governor Pravin was in his courtroom conducting business when Marek returned from the edge of the Nazaran Province. When the governor saw him enter with two of his men, each sporting visible battle wounds, he immediately cleared the room of everyone except the three men. "Did you bring me bodies to view?"

"No. Governor, I'm sorry. Nasha, Halyn, and Slaina reached the safety of the Nazaran Province," Marek explained. His sullen appearance was displayed in his tired eyes, sunken shoulders, and dirty attire.

"It appears you've been wounded in battle. Who inflicted your wounds?"

"Nasha did, Governor," Marek answered simply. He wasn't ready to volunteer too much information until he saw how the governor was going to react to the situation.

Pravin's face flushed. "Why then, do you not have a body for me? Why do you stand here still alive? One of you should be dead!"

Marek stepped forward, feigning more confidence than he actually felt. "One of us would have been if the Nazarans hadn't interfered. Their archers could have killed all of us where we stood, and they would have, if we hadn't backed down. We were outnumbered and had no chance against them. You ordered me not to start a war with them. May I start a war with them now?"

The color in Pravin's face returned to normal, and his eyes danced with glee at the young man's suggestion. He had spirit. Pravin pulled his robust frame off of his throne and paced as he considered the words of his benefactor, Luciano. "No, not yet. Take three days of rest, then return to me on the fourth day for your next assignment. Your men may rest as well."

"Yes, my lord. Governor, don't you want a full report on what happened?"

"I don't think that will be needed. All that matters now is that the girl is mostly out of our reach. I have other ideas for how to get to her. Be ready on the fourth day to redeem your failure. Don't mess this one up. You won't get another chance to prove your value to me," the governor warned.

"Yes, my lord. If I fail you, I assure you, I won't be alive to return," Marek promised.

Pravin smiled. "You had better not be, because you will pay for your next failure with your life one way or another."

"Governor, before I take my leave of you, Nasha sent you one message. He sent you a warning not to cause even the slightest harm to the girl's family or he would repay you tenfold. I don't believe he was bluffing."

Governor Pravin bristled. He knew Nasha meant it.

Marek left the governor's hall and took his two men with him, showing no sign of intimidation. One man finally asked, "Sir, doesn't it bother you? What the governor said?"

Marek shook his head. "No, if I let it bother me, it might distract me and cause me to fail. I will not fail this time. Whatever he has in mind, I'll take care of it or die trying."

As soon as Marek and his men were gone, Pravin called two of his guards forward. Addressing the first, he ordered, "Fetch my nephew, Jedrek." To the second he ordered, "Go to the barracks and have the battalion commander assign squads to watch Slaina's family discreetly from a distance. Don't detain them unless they attempt to leave the city. If they do, place them under house arrest and keep all guards inside their home and out of sight."

The two men moved quickly to complete their assigned tasks and return to their posts. The first man returned, bringing Jedrek with him.

"Uncle, what is so pressing that I had to leave my work?"

"I need to know how to proceed on a particular matter, and it is of the utmost importance."

Jedrek cocked his head sideways. "Uncle, I'm a builder, not a politician. What knowledge could I have that you would need?"

"Let's go for a walk in my gardens. This is not business. It is a private matter."

The two left the formal courtroom and went to a cool spot in the garden where a spring bubbled up from underground. They took a moment to quench their thirst and sat down on a shady bench to talk. "Jedrek, I have treated you as though you were one of my own sons, have I not?"

"Yes, Uncle, since the death of my father, I have looked to you as a father. What is troubling you? Have I done something wrong?"

"No, my boy, you have not. I'm afraid I might have done a wrong to you."

Jedrek gave his uncle a puzzled stare. "What do you mean?"

"Tell me honestly. Did you care for Slaina? I know I have pursued her ruthlessly to punish her for betraying your betrothal, but was I wrong? If you truly care for the girl, I should have sent the two of you away to be married quietly and brought you back after the child was born. If you didn't want to raise a child that was clearly not yours, we could have sent the child away to be raised by another. I think there are a lot of things that could have been handled more compassionately than the way I chose to handle them. Tell me, how do you feel about the girl?"

Jedrek stared at a row of ants crawling across the ground. His mind went back to the day he found out she was with child. She had told him bluntly, but the story she told him was incredulous. He hadn't believed her. His uncle's reaction was worse than his own. Fornication was a capital crime, although it was rarely carried to that point. His uncle intended to carry out the harsh sentence. Jedrek was angry and hurt. He had made no attempts to temper the man's sense of justice. It had made him ill to watch Slaina's parents publicly flogged for their failure in the matter.

"I don't know, Uncle—I cared very much for her. I'm not sure how I feel now."

"As I said, you are like one of my own sons. I want to put this right. Slaina is alive and well. She is in the Nazaran Province. I will pardon her crime if that is your wish. How you handle this situation is your choice. I think you should go to Nazar and talk to the young woman. If you both still desire to be joined, then be joined. Bring her here, and we will have a large joining ceremony. The entire province will celebrate with you. Consummate the marriage, and the child will be yours. Don't consummate the marriage and we will keep Slaina hidden until the child is born. We can take the child far away and give him to some couple who are barren. It would bring them great joy to have the child, and you would not have to raise one who isn't yours."

"Uncle, why have you had this change of heart? You never asked my feelings when this started." Jedrek remembered how violently his uncle had reacted. He had seen the man angry before. This surpassed anything he had ever seen. The massive search by the soldiers sent every young girl in the province into hiding.

Pravin stood and paced the stone path around the spring, being careful to keep his face turned away from Jedrek. His voice sounded apologetic. It did not match his true feelings. "After I had a few days to calm down, I realized I hadn't considered your feelings. I reacted out of my own embarrassment. My goal was not to alienate you or create a rift between us. I want to stop this now before I cause you any more pain."

Pravin turned to face his nephew and chose a very precise term of endearment. "Son, I want you to go to Nazar. Discover if your relationship is reparable. If you want to restore your relationship with her, then bring her here and marry her properly."

The idea appealed to Jedrek, but he was hesitant to try. "What if she doesn't want to return here? You've probably frightened her beyond belief."

"I know I have. Send her my most profound apology. Assure her she is quite safe if she returns as your wife. I cannot allow her to return to her home, though. That would clearly defy the law. If she is still afraid, then remain with her where she is.

Consummate your marriage quietly. I suggest you raise the child as your own. If she feels comfortable a year from now, then bring her back here. I would want to send a small party with you to assure your safety, but I'll keep it very small, maybe three or four men?"

Jedrek hesitated. When Pravin saw his uncertainty, he added, "Jedrek, why don't you sleep on it and let me know your answer in a couple days. It's kept me awake these last few nights thinking about what that girl must have been going through and what she's about to face."

"About to face? What are you talking about?" Jedrek was not a teenager any longer, but his naiveté still showed itself. Their marriage had been arranged, and they had a supervised courtship.

Pravin appealed to Jedrek's kind nature. "She's about to have a baby and raise the child without the benefit of a father. She and her child are likely to be outcasts because of her obvious crime. If they don't both die of starvation, it will be a miracle."

Pravin excused himself to attend to other affairs of state, leaving the young man alone to think. That evening, Jedrek joined his uncle at dinner. The shadow of their earlier discussion clouded his countenance. Pravin gleefully watched his nephew wrestle with his conscience. Jedrek ate very little. As the dinner came to an end and the family went various directions, he hung around to question his uncle further. "Uncle, if I bring Slaina here, won't the family and the people reject her, even as my wife?"

Pravin's face gave the appearance of being genuinely concerned. "It's possible, which is one reason I suggested remaining away for a year or so. It would give people a chance to forget what's happened. Another thing is that if you leave to be with her, most will assume it is a case of fornication, not adultery. I'm afraid it could cast you in an unfavorable light. It's why I asked what your feelings for the young woman are. If you care for her, you won't mind your reputation being questioned. For that matter, go to Nazar, make a fortune building for them, and bring your fortune, your wife, and your child, or should I say children, back with you. No one will dare question you, or her. If you consummate your marriage, it doesn't matter who sired that child. It will be yours, as is tradition."

The governor said the last part to be certain his nephew thwarted the prophecy. If the girl turned out not to be the one, at least her life would be spared, and whoever the father of the child was, he would have no hold on them. Keeping the girl away from whoever had fathered the child would also hopefully sever any emotional ties between the two. The only drawback of his entire plan was losing his nephew for a time. The young man was a profitable builder.

Jedrek continued to weigh the matter in his mind. He thanked his uncle for the wise advice and retired to his room to sleep on it. His attempt to rest was met with resistance as he tossed and turned for several hours before falling asleep.

Late the next morning, he returned to his uncle with his answer. "Uncle, I have determined that I have feelings for Slaina, but whether they are feelings of pity or love, I cannot tell. I think you're right. I should go to her and discover what it is I truly feel. If it is pity, I'll provide what I can for her needs and return to my life here. If I truly care for her, I will marry her, if she'll have me."

"I believe you are making a wise decision, son. Take two days to see that your business will be properly attended to and prepare what you'll need for either a long stay or a short one. I'll send four men with you. If you decide to remain with her, send one back to collect what you have prepared to take with you for a long stay."

Jedrek objected, "I think I can be ready to go tomorrow morning. I won't need to wait that long."

Pravin had put more trust in Marek and wanted him to have ample time to heal before sending him on another journey. He wouldn't be fully healed from his encounter with Nasha for a few more weeks, but he would at least be able to travel after a couple of days. "That may be, my favorite nephew, but I am having a gift made for your bride by a jeweler in the city, and it won't be ready for two days. It is my way of apologizing to the young woman and welcoming her to the family. I insist you take it with you. If you deem it appropriate, then give it to her. If you do not think it appropriate, sell it and give her the money to provide for her needs. I also believe the girl needs a little time to rest from the fear I provoked. She will be more receptive if she is no longer running for her life."

Jedrek's decision was now propelling him to leave the city and pursue the young woman he had cared about. He was eager to leave. Again, his uncle's words seemed wise. He decided perhaps he should come up with a few gifts of his own to take to his former fiancée. When her apparent fornication had become known, he had initially despised her for her infidelity to their engagement. As the pain of rejection and betrayal eased, they were replaced with a sense of loss, then the former feelings of affection slowly resurfaced. She had, to the best of his knowledge, betrayed his trust. What if it had been against her will? What if it was really the outrageous story she told him? He had naturally assumed the worst about her. If this had not been her fault, if she hadn't betrayed him, he would have to work to win back her love and trust.

The second Jedrek left to make his preparations to leave the city, Pravin summoned a jeweler. His favorite craftsman was brought before him.

"Governor Pravin, how may I be of service to you?"

"I need a small trinket or bauble made for a woman my nephew is pursuing. It needs to look impressive without costing a fortune. I need it to be ready tomorrow evening. Make sure it's unique, not something you sell to every other man on the street."

"That will not be a problem, my lord. I received a shipment of silver and jade from the mountains two days ago. I can have it ready for you this evening if you like," the man offered, thinking his diligence would build favor with the monarch.

"No! I don't want anyone to know it is ready until late tomorrow. If anyone asks, you worked long and hard on it and barely got it ready in time," the governor barked at the startled craftsman.

The jeweler didn't understand what game the governor was playing at, but he cooperated. "Yes, my lord. I will have it for you tomorrow evening, before the dinner hour."

The man turned to leave, and the governor called after him, "Remember... impressive looking... not an impressive cost."

The man nodded again and left to attend to his task.

The next evening, Pravin stayed late in his court attending to the business of preventing the fulfillment of the prophecy. He summoned Marek.

The ambitious soldier approached the governor as ordered. "Governor, what do you have for me to do?"

Pravin ordered all the other occupants of the room out, including his own bodyguards. "This is a very urgent and delicate assignment. You have some time to complete this assignment, but it must be completed before that woman gives birth to her child."

"Yes, my lord. What do you want me to do?"

"Are you fit for travel and anything else I ask of you?" Pravin didn't want to send him if he couldn't handle this task.

"My wounds were painful, but minor. I can go into battle if needed." Marek didn't appear to be bragging. His face reflected a certain simplicity.

"I hope battle will not be required." Governor Pravin proceeded to explain his plans to push his nephew to marry Slaina and consummate their marriage, thus thwarting the prophecy. He also explained his contingency plan, should his first plan fail.

Pravin finished briefing the eager young soldier by explaining, "As far as my nephew is concerned, you are there for his protection. Do you understand your assignment? All of it?"

"Yes, my lord." The young man never blinked or showed any signs of regret.

"Choose three more men to accompany you. Choose well. If you are found out, you may need to escape or fight your way out. You need men who will stand by you and keep their mouths shut," Pravin added harshly.

"Yes, my lord. I will do all that you have asked. I will seek out men who do not serve Pateras."

Early the next morning, Jedrek was eager to depart. His gifts and short-term belongings were loaded on a small, simple wagon. He chose a plain wagon instead of a carriage or packhorse. The wagon would be useful if he decided to stay in Nazar for the year his uncle had suggested. With his uncle's concerns for his safety, he decided the carriage might draw attention to him. Five men on horseback could give the appearance of being a team bent on assault. Jedrek hitched four horses to the wagon. Two of the guards took turns driving. Jedrek sat in the back with the supplies and spare saddles. Marek and one guard rode ahead of the wagon. The last rider followed behind them.

Pravin wasn't accustomed to rising early, but having his plans on the cusp of fruition motivated him to see the young man off. He approached Marek with the appearance of giving him a last-minute admonition to protect his nephew. His true intent was to admonish him to stay true to his assignment and keep him informed.

The trip took two days. The second night, Jedrek got the wagon and horses into the stable in Nazar, then he and his men made their way to the inn. After getting settled in three rooms, they headed down to get something to eat. Jedrek pulled the innkeeper's wife aside and quietly asked if she knew the healer known as Halyn.

The woman easily admitted to knowing Halyn. "Halyn delivered every one of my children. She's delivered nearly every person twenty years old and younger in the entire province. The only ones she didn't deliver were the ones who were born while she was away in the Somi Province every year."

Jedrek smiled politely as he waited for her to finish. Her answer wasn't terribly long, but his patience was short. He asked for directions to where he could find her, which the woman gladly provided. Then she asked, "Are you all right? You don't look sick."

"I'm fine. I'm looking for a young woman who was traveling with Halyn a few days ago. Her name is Slaina. She is—was my fiancée until we had a falling out." Jedrek's eagerness overrode his sense of discretion.

"A falling out?" The woman remembered her discussion with Joren and Slaina a few days ago. "Is this about the child she carries or the young man who was traveling with her?"

"Young man? What young man?" Jedrek felt his temper threaten to flare. She had said there was no other man. The child was the Promised One. Who was this other young man? Had she known him before she was found to be with child?

"You don't believe the child she carries is the Promised One, do you?" The woman surmised.

"I—I don't know. I thought we should at least discuss it again. I'm willing to listen this time."

"If you don't believe the young woman, perhaps you should ask the child's father for the truth," the woman advised.

"Where is this—young man?" Jedrek was distracted at the thought of his perceived rival.

"I wasn't speaking of the young man. If the young woman believes she carries the Promised One, the child of Pateras, then it is Pateras you should speak with. The young man who returned with Halyn cares about Slaina, but not as a man cares for a woman. He is awed by the child she carries." The innkeeper's wife gathered the dishes from the table in front of him and left him to think.

Jedrek stared at the fireplace across the room as he contemplated the situation from every angle. Despite his hostess' reassurances, he was beginning to again believe Slaina had lied to him.

Marek saw the anger building in him from across the room, and he knew Jedrek's youth and passion would cause him to do something rash. He approached cautiously. "Master Jedrek, may I join you?"

Jedrek pulled his eyes off the flames that were sucking him in. His gaze seemed to take an eternity to focus on Marek's face and his thoughts to process the question he asked. He nodded for Marek to sit with him.

"Master Jedrek, you were so excited, and you are now disturbed by something. Is there anything I can do to help?"

"No, it's a personal matter," Jedrek snapped.

"I am aware of all aspects of our journey. Your uncle was concerned about you and wanted me to understand the situation. What troubles you?"

Jedrek eyed the man angrily. He didn't like his personal matters being aired in front of subordinates. Since the damage was already done, he took advantage of having someone to confide in. "Do the others know why we are here?"

"No, I am the only one," Marek assured him.

"It's possible Slaina lied to me. The innkeeper's wife told me Halyn came here with Slaina and a young man. I think I made a mistake coming here. We should head back tomorrow morning," Jedrek groused.

"I understand. I can have the men ready to go in the morning if that's what you want. There is something you should know, though. I was with Nasha as we tracked the young woman out here. She was alone until she met up with the healer. I saw her tracks in the dirt myself. No man came with her. We met Halyn camping in the hills and, except for Slaina, she was alone. I don't know where this young man came from, but it's possible he is a friend of the healer and only recently met the young woman. Even your uncle is beginning to believe her story about carrying the Promised One of Pateras. Perhaps you should do as you intended and speak to the woman before determining whether to stay or to go. We're so close now, it would be a shame to head back without knowing all the facts." Marek knew the governor would be upset if the mission wasn't completed one way or another.

Jedrek continued to brood without answering. Seeing he wasn't inclined to discuss the matter any further, Marek stood to go. "I suggest you sleep on the matter and make your final decision in the morning. May I ask you one other question, Master Jedrek?"

Jedrek gave the man an annoyed stare. "What is your question?"

"Do you follow Pateras?"

"Yes, of course. Why does that matter?"

"If it is his child, perhaps he's the one you should question, not this unknown young man. If you are a devout and valued follower of Pateras, surely he will advise you on how to proceed." Marek was not a follower of Pateras, but his words had merit.

Jedrek slammed his cup on the table, splashing the remaining liquid out of the cup. He stormed out of the inn and went out into the cool night air. The leaves were beginning to change colors, but were no longer visible in the low light of the moon. Jedrek had no particular direction or destination in mind. He soon found himself at the outskirts of the city. He reached the top of a hill where he had a clear view of the entire area and a clear sky above him.

"Pateras, I mean no disrespect to you, but I need some answers. Was Slaina unfaithful to me? Is her baby truly the one you promised? What should I do? Please answer me. I need to know a clear answer to this."

He was greeted with nothing but the sounds of the night. In a few minutes, a calm settled on him, and the cold worked its way into his bones. Jedrek headed back to the inn purposefully and stoked the dying fire in his room to warm himself. Once the chill left him, he undressed and climbed into his bed, the very bed Slaina had lain in days ago as she recovered from the cold.

The interminable night was fraught with frustrations and eerie dreams. It seemed the entire province felt an odd spirit as a heavy cloud cover blew in, keeping the sun at bay for a time. The darkness kept the roosters from waking the local inhabitants until the morning was well upon them.

Jedrek and his men slowly moved to the dining room in the inn. None of them were quick to talk, as the eerie spirit from the night refused to release its grasp on them. Marek was the only one who seemed immune. He wasn't among the slow-moving soldiers coming from their rooms. He entered the dining room from outside.

Jedrek's mood was calm, yet distracted. He looked up as Marek joined them for breakfast. "Where have you been already this morning?"

"Forgive me if this is impertinent on my part, but I went to the stable and readied two horses. Your horse and mine are outside the door. I thought we should go out to the healer's home and talk to her before we decided whether to stay or to go."

Jedrek took a deep breath. "You made the right decision." A feeling of relief crept in to replace the tension from the previous night, though he was still nervous.

"Master Jedrek, something seems different about you this morning. You were angry last night. Did your sleep relieve yesterday's tensions?"

Jedrek paused over his food and contemplated how to answer the question. "Something is different. I did as you recommended. I asked Pateras for guidance. He didn't answer right away. He sent a messenger to me in my sleep last night. I'm ready to see Slaina now. I want to talk to her, and ask her to be my wife again. She may or may not accept me. I disappointed her by not standing up for her. She has no reason to accept me back, but I have to try."

Marek smiled. The first step in the governor's plan was in place. He hoped the next step would go according to plan. He didn't want to enact the governor's backup plans. Although he didn't choose to serve Pateras, he didn't care to cross swords with him.

The wind changed directions, and a strong, warm wind hit the door, slamming it open. The sun peeked through the clouds, and a warmer temperature took up arms against the chill in the air. One of the innkeeper's daughters jumped to shut the door more securely.

Marek looked at the door suspiciously. The timing of his thoughts and the strong wind was uncannily meaningful. Marek knew who Pateras was and what power he held. The things he had known of Pateras were subtle and nondescript. History taught him that Pateras was capable of astounding wonders. He may not choose to serve this powerful entity, but no, he didn't want to anger him. Angering any god was never wise.

Jedrek's thoughts came together as he ate his meal. By the time he finished, he was thoroughly energized and gulped his last few bites aggressively. The innkeeper's wife stopped by the table to see if he needed anything. Seeing his change in demeanor, she smiled. "I see Pateras has cleared your mind."

Jedrek looked at her oddly for a moment, then smiled. "I believe he has. I need to beg my lady's forgiveness for doubting her and for doubting Pateras."

"Listen carefully to what the young woman is saying to you," the woman advised, "and speak the truth plainly. Do not hide things from her. If there is something you don't understand, ask her for clarification. Don't make quick decisions. Wait for Pateras to tell you what to do. Situations are usually simpler than we try to make them."

"Yes, ma'am." Jedrek's mother had died when he was very young, and he barely remembered her. His aunt tried to fill the void her death left in him, but he still felt a hole where his parents should have been. He found himself drawn to those who treated him as a son.

Jedrek and Marek mounted their horses and rode out to Halyn's home. The two heard voices coming from the barn as they approached. They walked in to find Joren and Slaina cleaning the stalls. The horses belonging in those stalls were confined to a small corral outside the barn. Jedrek thought nothing of the situation. Marek was thankful the horses were safely out of reach. He strongly suspected the two might mount them and attempt to run. They meant the young woman no harm this time, but the two young people didn't know it.

Jedrek heard the couple laughing at something. He saw Joren working with his back to them. He and Marek walked past the first stall and found Slaina working in the second. Jedrek stepped into the doorway of the stall. "Slaina?"

Hearing his voice, she dropped her pitchfork and jumped against the far wall. "Jedrek! What are you doing here? What do you want?" Her eyes filled with fear, more at the sight of his companion than Jedrek himself.

Hearing the voices, Joren tightened the grip on his pitchfork. He raced out of his stall and rushed the two men, yelling, "Leave her alone!"

Marek side-stepped the tool turned weapon. He grabbed the instrument away from the inexperienced defender and gave him a couple of painful bruises for his trouble. Joren rolled painfully on the ground, trying desperately to get to his feet again. Marek squatted beside the young man. "Master Jedrek is only here to talk to Slaina. We aren't here to harm her."

Joren knew there was little he could do about it if they were intent on harming her. He stayed on the ground, trying to catch his breath, until Marek's attention was no longer on him.

Jedrek paused to survey the activity. Seeing Marek had things under control, he moved closer to Slaina, who was edging away from him. "Slaina, I'm not here to hurt you. I want to talk."

Slaina glanced at Marek nervously. She hadn't seen him close up and wasn't aware that he had been Nasha's aggressive sidekick outside the wagon days ago. Her only concern was that he was a Somian warrior.

Seeing her fear, Jedrek ordered, "Marek, get on your horse and ride to the top of the hill. You can see to my safety from there."

"Marek?!" A fresh wave of panic washed over Slaina. She had not seen Marek with Nasha, but she had heard his name. "He's the one who tried to kill us!"

Jedrek frowned. Marek spread his arms out and kept his hands open and clear of his weapons. He stepped forward slowly. "Mistress Slaina." He called her by name to be clear he knew exactly who she was. "I apologize for frightening you. My orders were from Governor Pravin, and they were to hunt you down and kill you. Those are no longer his orders to me. Unless Master Jedrek amends those orders himself, you have nothing to fear from me."

Seeing the responsibility now clearly laid at his own feet, Jedrek quickly handled it. "Slaina, I will not harm you. You have my word. I came here to apologize to you and to beg your forgiveness. I—can we talk privately?" Jedrek gave Marek a quick look of annoyance. Marek took the hint. Grabbing Joren by the back of his collar, Marek escorted him roughly from the barn.

Fearing for his safety, Slaina cried out, "Joren! Jedrek, please don't let Marek hurt him. He's been kind to me."

Jedrek took the opportunity to ask, "Who is he?"

Tears formed in her eyes. "I met him a few days ago in Helia. He was a stable boy there. He wants to make more of himself here in Nazar. He believes no one in Helia will see him as anything but a stable boy. Halyn was helping him get a fresh start. Please, Jedrek, don't let Marek hurt him."

Jedrek stepped outside and shouted, "Marek, see that the boy isn't harmed!"

Marek shouted back, "If I must!"

Jedrek rolled his eyes. Turning to Slaina, he offered his hand. "Slaina, please come sit here and talk with me." The young woman still hesitated, so Jedrek added, "I swear to Pateras, I am not here to harm you or your child."

She stepped toward him slowly but refused to take his hand. Her feelings for him had grown during their courtship, though the feelings of rejection still overshadowed them. She felt her fear slipping away.

Jedrek escorted her to a bench along the wall and sat beside her. "I'm not sure where to start."

"You rejected me and called me a liar and other not very nice things. Why don't you start there?" Slaina spat.

Jedrek slid off the bench and onto one knee. Taking both her hands in his, he said, "You're right. I was wrong. You didn't lie to me, I know that, and I know you didn't betray me, and you certainly didn't deserve to be treated the way I treated you. I am so sorry for that. I hope you can one day forgive me."

"I'll try, and I suppose I will forgive you, but it's going to take time. It's not easy for a person to get over being hunted like an animal." Slaina pulled her hands away from him.

Jedrek got off his knee and moved away from her. "I wasn't responsible for that. My uncle did that. He wishes to send you his apologies as well. He says he overreacted. We have his blessing to marry if that is our wish. He sent you a gift to express his sorrow over the pain he has caused you. I brought you some gifts as well."

"Exactly what were you responsible for, Jedrek?"

"I told my uncle what you told me. He believed, as I did, that you betrayed our engagement. He didn't believe you carried the child of Pateras, either. He didn't say much that evening, but two days later, he was angry. I don't think I've ever seen him that angry before. I planned to end our engagement quietly and let you join with the man you obviously cared more about than me. My uncle is the one who carried this to the extreme, and he's very sorry. He says no harm will come to you or your family if you return to the city as my wife. He said you can't return to your father's household, though. He doesn't want to be known for enforcing the laws on others and not on his own household."

"What is it you expect to achieve by coming here? Why did you come?" Slaina was no longer fearful of anything but his answer.

"Slaina, I asked Pateras to guide me, to tell me what to do. He sent a messenger to me in my dreams. He told me not to be afraid to marry you. Your child is the Promised One sent to protect all of creation from the Reckoning of Pateras. When he gave me this message, I knew I owed you a great apology."

Slaina placed her hands firmly on her hips. "Did you really expect me to accept you and agree to marry you?"

Jedrek gave her half a smile. "No, not really. Pateras' messenger said I should not be afraid to marry you. He never said you would agree to marry me. My uncle said we would not even need to return to Somi if you don't want to."

Slaina turned and walked away from him. "I don't want to hear this. I don't need to hear this. Goodbye, Jedrek."

Jedrek chased after her and caught her outside the barn. Grabbing her arm, he pleaded, "Slaina, please hear me out before you reject me. I know I deserve it for the way I treated you, and I'm sorry, really I am. I had every reason to believe you had rejected me first. I was wrong. My uncle had time to cool off. He's no longer angry, and he isn't trying to punish you. Slaina, I was falling in love with you, and it tore me up inside to think you had been with another man. You and I are ordinary people. Pateras doesn't call on ordinary people to—to raise his child."

"You aren't ordinary, Jedrek. You're the governor's nephew."

"I'm his half-sister's only son. I work hard like any other tradesman in Somi. I'm not a politician or a rich man."

Slaina took a moment to consider his point of view. He did have every right to think the worst. This was certainly not an everyday situation. She scowled. "Tell me plainly what you want from me, Jedrek."

"First, I want your forgiveness. Second, I want you to reconsider our relationship. Whether we marry and remain here or return to Somi is entirely up to you. I will be happy wherever we are, as long as I am with you." Jedrek walked over to his saddlebags and pulled several gifts out. He showed her the silver and jade bracelet from his uncle. He had purchased some personal items, such as an embroidered shawl and a decorated leather tie for her hair. He also revealed a silver water pitcher, a small bolt of cloth, and several other items.

Slaina handed them back to him. "Jedrek, I need to think about this for a while. Keep these until I make my decision."

"I have a better idea. Keep one of them. If I don't hear from you within three days, I will return and begin to court you from the beginning and bring a second gift. Three days after that, if I haven't heard from you again, I will again bring a gift. If you send me away at any point, I will send all the gifts to you and leave quietly."

"Why would you do that? Especially if I send you away?"

"Raising a son is difficult enough. Raising him alone and without your family will be nearly impossible. You can do what you like with the gifts. Sell them to provide for your son. It is my gift to you and to Pateras. He wanted me to be there for his child. If this is all you will allow me to do, then so be it." Jedrek touched her face gently and smiled. "I will await your message, or I will see you in three days."

Jedrek mounted his horse and grabbed the reins on Marek's horse to lead it back to him. Slaina grabbed Jedrek's reins. "You know we cannot do all that must be done between a husband and wife until after the child is born."

"I know, and I will wait." Jedrek smiled at her.

WAR OF GENERATIONS

"Hey, Mom."

"Robert, I'm glad you called. I wanted to know what I should fix for dinner tomorrow night. Since you're going to be gone for a while, I thought you should pick what we eat."

Robert's face had been serious when he hailed his parents' home. His face brightened at the thought of his mother's cooking. "It doesn't matter, Mom. I'll enjoy whatever you fix."

"What about dessert? Isn't there anything special you would like?" Kay persisted.

Robert smiled. "No, Mom, just don't experiment with something new. I want to enjoy your everyday home cooking. The stuff I'll be eating over the next few months won't compare to anything you cook."

Kay smiled mischievously. "If you insist, sardine sandwiches it is."

Robert turned three shades of green for a half-second until his mind processed his mother's humor. "Mom! YUCK! That's not funny."

Kay continued to grin. "Sure, it is. Replay the video on the call and watch the look on your own face. It was hilarious."

Robert's eyes narrowed as he hastily planned his retaliation. "If you want to serve that to all of your guests, well, that's your choice."

Kay didn't miss anything but Robert's hidden message. "Your dad loves sardines, and I love cooking to please your dad."

"What about everyone else?" Robert was still caught between gagging at the thought and warning his mother about the guests he had invited to dinner.

"Jessica gets her taste for sardines from her father. I don't like them, but I'll have a nice salad." Kay continued to tease her son.

Robert continued to push his point home. "But what about our other guests?"

Kay was suddenly serious. "What other guests?"

"That's what I called to tell you about. I stopped by to see Jessica's new boyfriend. I invited him to join us tomorrow night."

"Robert, I wish you hadn't done that. Your father and I wanted to have this one last night alone with the family. We wanted to talk with you privately. We knew when we met Tristan a couple weeks ago how grown you and your sister have gotten. Our days as a family are coming to an end."

"Mom, we'll always be a family. We're just getting a little larger. I was also thinking about bringing a date."

Kay grappled with her emotions as she felt her last opportunities to be alone with her children slipping through her fingers. A quiet presence slipped in and wrapped itself around her, giving her the courage to say what hurt the most but needed to be said. "Robert, I know we will always be family, but I thought we could have this one last memory of the four of us. I would be glad to have Tristan and your date visit with us."

Robert and his mother talked a few minutes more. Both realizing the conversation was strained, they finally ended the call and moved on to other things. Kay sat in her chair for another moment, wishing she could speak the name of the only one who could help her through this. Saul walked in to find his wife staring at an empty computer screen. The stunned look on her face said plenty. "Kay, what's wrong?"

Kay looked at her husband, then back at the computer. The device's silent presence seemed to mock her. "I think I need to go for a walk," she said dryly.

She and Saul had many such experiences. Any time they needed absolute privacy, they left anything familiar and routine, fearing they were still being monitored.

The two got into their private vehicle and drove to a riverfront walkway. They walked for several minutes, leaving all communication and electronic devices behind in their vehicle. They found a small restaurant playing soft romantic music. The two sat down on the riverfront patio. The air was quite cool and less inviting to most patrons. The patio was warmed by heating units with decorative flames. Their waiter kindly cranked the units and adjusted them to provide the couple with adequate heat. Since they were alone on the cool patio, the waiter was more than glad to watch from the nearest window to see if they needed anything and allow them plenty of privacy.

Kay finally unloaded her burden on her husband. She told him about the conversation with Robert before he had arrived. Her heart was heavy over the things they had lost and the things now quickly slipping from their grasp.

Sensing she had things she still wasn't comfortable saying, he took her hand and invited her to dance with him. Kay looked at him oddly, then agreed. The music was slow and soulful. They danced without speaking for a minute. The waiter noticed and turned the volume up on the patio. Saul caught the young man's eye and gave him an appreciative smile.

Saul finally whispered to Kay. "Say what you need to say. They can't hear us here."

Kay looked up with tears in her eyes. "Saul… I hate that name," she spat. "I hate calling my children Robert and Jessica instead of their given names."

Saul smiled at her. He whispered back, "I'll try not to take that personally, Tyra."

"We can't. They'll find out."

"What are they going to do about it? Our identities are our own. They can't change them. We aren't telling anyone else who we are. We aren't trying to get home. We're doing the work they wanted us to do. Our children have been raised inside the Commonwealth. What can they do to us?"

"They can still hurt our children." Kay was worried. "Elliot, I wanted to spend time with them this one last night to remind them... of him."

"I know. We have to trust him to reach them if we can't. He'll bring them back. I'm sure he has a plan."

"They've taken everything from us. Elliot, I'm so tired of not being able to call his name." Kay's tears soaked into Saul's shoulder. "What if our children never find P-Pateras again?"

Saying the name of Pateras aloud made her heart pound in fear. She needed to say it, though. She needed to hear herself say the one name that comforted her. Fifteen years ago, she almost abandoned him. They had spent those first few years after being relocated teaching Robert and Jessica their new names and suppressing the memories of their past. As the danger seemed to decrease and their comfort level increased, Saul and Kay slowly leaned once again on Pateras. They had no support for their actions, no Ancient Text copies to guide them. They had only their memories. Attempting to recreate the Ancient Texts from the passages they had memorized was impossible. They had learned their knowledge in Drean. To speak Drean aloud was forbidden, and speaking it even in the privacy of their own home resulted in being called in for a harsh compliance conference. Their first year after leaving the Maran prison, they had been confined to a military base until they were fluent in Intergalactic Standard, the adopted language of the Commonwealth.

Kay cried quietly, still whispering in fear. "They took our identities, our firstborn, our belief in the Timeless One, our home, our language, everything. I'm afraid this young man, Tristan, is taking our daughter from us. The CIF has already taken Robert. We have nothing left."

Elliot Paulson, not Saul Deacons, pulled back from Kay. He grabbed her upper arms firmly and gave her a gentle shake. "No, they have NOT taken Pateras from us. He's still in charge, not the Commonwealth. We may not be able to speak his name, but he hears our very thoughts. You cannot lose hope. Pateras is bigger than the Commonwealth. He'll get through to them. I don't know how, but he will. We have to continue looking for openings. Tomorrow isn't the opening we were looking for."

"Elliot, I'm afraid even Pateras no longer trusts us. We betrayed him because we loved our children more than him."

"Tyra, we made some mistakes, and yes, we rejected him to save our children's lives. You've asked his forgiveness, haven't you?"

"Yes, of course I have." Tyra nodded as the painful memories continued to flood her mind.

"The Ancient Texts assure us he will accept any who ask in earnest. We are Pateras' children. He feels the same way about us that we feel about Richard and Vanessa."

Kay settled into her husband's arms, and they resumed their minimalist attempt at dancing. The two danced in silence for a time. The waiter slipped onto the patio and placed their plates of food on the table, refilled their drinks, and quietly disappeared inside the main dining area. He didn't know the situation going on between the couple, but he knew his presence was a disturbance.

Kay finally looked at her husband. "I felt his presence today. He came to me while I was talking to Robert."

Saul smiled. "See, he hasn't abandoned us. Even if we never see home again, he hasn't left us. He's all that matters. He's the one thing they can't take from us."

Kay smiled at him. "We should eat before our food gets cold."

Elliot gave her one last smile. "I suppose you're right. It's time for Elliot and Tyra to retire for the evening and Saul and Kay to return."

Kay frowned. "I always hate it when they have to leave. I miss them."

Elliot looked into his wife's face and kissed her gently. "I'll see you later, Tyra. I promise."

Kay smiled at him. "I love you, Elliot."

The two sat down to eat and began discussing the menu for their family dinner tomorrow evening.

The next evening, Jessica and Tristan talked on their way to her parents' home. "Tristan, I have a strange request," Jessica said.

The mere suggestion gave Tristan an odd feeling. "Okay, what is it?"

"I need you to talk to my dad."

"About...?"

"Me... us, I mean. If you want to get married, you need to talk to my dad."

"You're a grown woman. Why do I need to talk to your dad about it?"

"It's kind of a cultural thing. When a man wants to marry a woman, he asks her father for his blessing or permission," Jessica explained nervously.

"I know I'm not from Juranta, but I've never heard of this—uh—custom. What if he says no?" Tristan looked at her oddly.

"The custom is actually from another world where my parents were from. My dad and mom used to tell us stories about Daddy asking my granddaddy for his blessing to marry my mom. You should get them to tell you the story sometime. It was hilarious. Daddy was so scared granddaddy was going to..." Jessica giggled. "You have to get him to tell it."

Tristan scowled. He sensed there was a script for this sort of scenario, but he had no idea what it might be. "Is tonight the right occasion for such a thing?"

Jessica frowned. "I suppose not unless the situation presents itself."

"Presents itself? Since I don't know this custom, how will I know it's time?"

Jessica wrapped her arms around one of Tristan's and rested her chin on his shoulder. "I suppose if the two of you end up alone and he asks what your intentions are with his daughter. That would be the opening."

Tristan twisted to look at her face. "Are there any other customs I should know about?"

Jessica blinked, then lied to him. "No, that's all."

Tristan recognized the lie. He started to let it pass and decided he needed to build some trust. "Jess, I sense there is something else. I hope you know you can trust me with anything. I want to make you happy."

"I know, but marriages there were... different. They were almost magical. It can't be that way here."

Tristan smiled at her almost childlike dreams. "Tell me about them. I will do whatever I can to make it happen for you."

"Marriages happened in beautiful buildings, not lawyers' offices, and vows were exchanged aloud so everyone present could hear them. It's been so long since I saw a marriage, I'm not sure I could remember what sort of vows they said. The couple are dressed in their fanciest clothes, standing in front of all their friends and family."

"Is it like the toast at a marriage announcement party?" Tristan was a clear product of the Commonwealth. He knew nothing of the lifelong commitment of a marriage or the covenant aspect.

Jessica could not explain the concept of a minister who performed a marriage ceremony. Tristan had no clue what a minister was. "A man or woman conducts the marriage ceremony and exchange of vows, then he pronounces the couple as married."

"You mean an attorney or legal assistant?"

"No, it's someone who cares for people." Jessica was getting uncomfortable with the conversation.

"Well, that certainly knocks the legal personnel out of the picture. I am really not sure who would fit that role, a doctor maybe?" Tristan offered.

"The planet where marriages were done like this had an entire profession of people whose sole job was to take care of people. It was a stupid idea, forget it," Jessica grumbled.

"It sounds like a special time. I want to make this special for you. It's our first marriage. It should be special. I will do whatever I can to make the contract signing day as magical as I can."

Jessica smiled. He was certainly a sweet, caring, compassionate man, even if he was in the dark on this concept. The two were silent as their car carried them to Jessica's parents' house.

As the car stopped in front of the house, Tristan turned to Jessica one last time before joining the others. "Jess, I have two questions. First, what's the most magical place you've ever seen?"

"There's an observatory on the northern continent, the Lachland Falls Park and Observatory. It has a beautiful view of the stars, and the inside of the observatory is full of plants, waterfalls, and winding paths. At night, the light displays are unbelievable. Why?"

"Wait, my second question is one I asked already. What do I do if your father says no?"

Jessica laughed outright. "He can't actually say no. I'm a grown woman. He can, however, give you a lecture on what he expects from the man who wants to marry his daughter."

"Expects? I'm not marrying your father. He doesn't have a part in our marriage, does he?"

Jessica jumped out of the car and giggled. "It will be fine. I promise." She took off running toward the house, daring him to catch her with a flirtatious look.

Tristan took the dare and chased her all the way to the front door. He caught her before she could barrel through the door unannounced. He wrapped his arms around her and kissed her between giggles. Softly he whispered, "What does your father expect from me?"

Jessica whispered back, "He'll have to tell you that."

Before the conversation could go any further, the front door opened to reveal Kay Deacons. "Oh, hello. I thought I heard someone out here." Kay saw the couple rapidly pull away from each other and realized she should have waited to open the door until she heard them requesting entry. Mentally she kicked herself for not viewing the external security monitors before opening the door. "Please come in. Welcome, Chief Alexander."

Tristan smiled politely. "Please, call me Tristan."

Kay escorted the young couple into the living room where Saul was waiting. In a minute, Kay excused herself to tend to the dinner preparations. Jessica glanced at Tristan and giggled. "Wait, Mom, I'll come with you to help."

Tristan quickly got even with her for what she was attempting to do. "Are you sure it's a good idea to let Jessica join you, Mrs. Deacons? She doesn't seem very comfortable with the idea of cooking." His comment earned him a dirty look from Jessica and a delighted smile from his hostess. Tristan quickly learned that his future mother-in-law appreciated humor.

Kay responded to his jest. "It's never too late to learn. At least I keep trying to teach her. Maybe you've finally given her a reason to learn."

With the two men standing alone in the living room, Tristan glanced nervously at the nearest clock. "I thought Lt. Cmdr.

Deacons would have been here by now. It's not like a space cadet to be outdone by a ground pounder."

Saul offered Tristan some coffee to ease his nerves. Nearly thirty seconds of heavy silence passed in preparing their coffee. Saul invited Tristan to sit on the sofa. They sat on opposite ends and Saul answered Tristan's question. "Robert was told the party starts a little later. I wanted a chance to talk to you before he and his date arrive."

Tristan shifted in his seat. He leaned forward and placed his coffee cup on the coffee table. "Did Jessica know you wanted to talk to me?"

"Not that I know of. Why?"

Tristan smiled. "She wanted me to talk to you as well. She suggested the opportunity might present itself this evening."

Saul already knew the answer to his next question, but he asked it anyway. "What did you need to discuss with me?"

"You arranged this time to talk. You should go first." Tristan wanted to put his strange task off as long as he could.

"On the night of the promotion ball, I asked you what your intentions were with my daughter. I suspect you have a firmer answer than you did that night." Saul watched Tristan carefully.

Tristan glanced at the door leading toward the kitchen then at the clock again. Taking a swift gulp of his coffee, he gathered his wits and responded. "Yes sir, I do. Jessica asked me to pursue a custom I am unfamiliar with. She wanted me to ask for your blessing or permission to marry her. I don't want to be a source of contention in the family, but I love her, and I would like to have your approval to ask her to marry me."

This time it was Saul's turn to fidget. "She knows you want to marry her, then?"

"Yes, she does. She also said you would have some expectations of me." Tristan was trying hard to get through this uncomfortable situation without feeling out of control.

Saul set his own cup of coffee down and leaned forward. "What I am about to say may not make a lot of sense to you, but I expect you to do the best you can with it. This family has been through some difficult times in the past. If you are here just to test her and her alliances, then bow out now. She doesn't need to be hurt. We've raised our children to be loyal Commonwealth citizens. Jessica remembers very little about our life before joining the Commonwealth."

Tristan scowled as he got up and walked around for a minute. He turned to Saul. "Mr. Deacons, I have no intention of hurting Jessica. I want to start a family with her someday. She's told me a tiny bit about her past, and personally, it could hurt my career to marry her. She told me you were in prison at one point, but that you were cleared of the charges. It's possible I could be denied promotions, or even lose my job based on your history, but I'm willing to risk it, for her."

Saul's face fell. "I actually hoped she had forgotten about that time."

"I don't know what she remembers and what she's forgotten, but she remembers her sister."

A look of fear now crossed his face. "Her mother and I hoped to spare her the pain of remembering that. We haven't talked about her since it happened." Saul glanced around the room, hoping the electronic devices weren't still actively monitoring their conversations. He pushed the conversation away from this dangerous place as quickly as possible. "My point is this. We made some mistakes in the past. I hope you won't punish my daughter for my mistakes."

Tristan also knew someone would actively monitor their conversations. "I don't know much about your past, and it isn't my concern. If you want to explain it to me at a later time, then you can do so. I don't intend to ask about it, and I'm not here to judge you. I love your daughter, and all I want is to make her happy. May I have your blessing to marry her?"

Saul seemed nearly relieved that the conversation went no further. "If you've told me the truth, then you have my blessing. If you have lied to me, I can't stop you. There is someone who can, and he will. He will know every lie you tell, and you will pay for every one of them. You will never see him, and you can't stop him. I don't care how well-trained you are."

Tristan stared at the man. Was he posturing to protect his daughter, or was he mentally unstable? He hoped it was simply posturing. "Mr. Deacons, if you believe nothing else I tell you, then believe this: I love Jessica. I will never hurt her, and I will never allow anyone else to hurt her either. You have my word."

Saul nodded. "I hope you're telling me the truth. I really do."

"Aside from not hurting your daughter, is there anything else you expect of me?" Tristan asked. He knew their time before Robert arrived would be short.

"I expect you to love my daughter and her alone. Always respect and care for her. Do the same with any children. My daughter has never experienced a marriage dissolution. If she marries you, she's expecting you to be there for more than a year or two. I know she's seen friends go through marriage dissolutions, but she's seen her mother and me remain strong and true to each other for her entire life. Don't go into this thinking it's short-term."

Tristan picked up his cup of coffee and stared into it for a moment. This was the strangest feeling he had ever had. Most people's marriages didn't last more than ten to fifteen years, and the average person married four times in their lives. He and Jessica would have an initial marriage contract agreement of one to two years by law. There was no way to get around that. He knew their marriage would not last a long time, and Mr. Deacons' ideas were strange. He pushed through the confusion in his own mind. "Mr. Deacons, I have to admit, I haven't been thinking in the long or short-term. I've just been thinking about how much I love her and want to start a family with her. The law requires that our initial marriage contract only be for one to two years. I can't change that. I guess I'm not sure what you're asking of me."

Saul leaned closer. "I'm saying if you marry my daughter, do it without expecting to get out of it. We can't change the law, but we can make a choice as to how we view marriage. Don't look at it as temporary, or the first time you have a fight, a wall will go up that will one day be too big to climb over. It will separate you permanently."

"Yes sir."

"Most people believe that once you're married, you're done. You've won the prize, and now you can relax and enjoy the spoils of war. That's not the way things are. When you marry, the war has only begun, and separation is the enemy. You have to win Jessica's heart all over again every single day. She has to do the same with you. Once you're married, you see the ugly sides of each other, and winning the heart is even more important. Can you do that?"

Tristan took another sip of his coffee as he weighed his answer. "Mr. Deacons, your family has some—uh—unusual ideas about things. I understand what you're saying, and I can't promise to do everything right. I can tell you that I will try. Jessica is worth the risk."

Saul sighed. Something told him this was the best he could hope for. "I somehow doubt you understand how sacred marriage is. I hope you do someday, before it's too late."

"Too late for what?" Tristan doubted he was talking about it being too late to save a marriage.

The front door opened, and Robert's voice called out, "Mom? Dad? We're here."

Saul excused himself to greet them. Robert escorted his date into the living room and robustly greeted Tristan in a jovial tone. "Trying to set the bar pretty high by arriving so early, aren't you, Ground Pounder?"

Tristan grinned. "I couldn't let a Space Cadet outdo me, now could I?"

"Oh, I let you have this one so you could impress my folks. I won't be quite so generous in the next round." Robert grinned mischievously.

"You're about to be gone for the next few months. I'll have plenty of time to impress them with the solidness of the Infantry," Tristan teased back.

Saul shook his head at the two. "Robbie, why don't you introduce us to your date?"

Robert winced as his dad reverted to his childhood moniker. "Oh, sorry, I got distracted by trying to make sure this ground pounder knew his place. Hannah Roshan, this is my father Saul Deacons, and this is my sister's boyfriend, Chief Warrant Officer Tristan Alexander."

Tristan smiled politely and waited for his turn to greet the young woman. "Nice to meet you, Hannah. Do I know you?"

Hannah gave him a brief uncomfortable stare, then smiled with the same polite façade Tristan had. "Yes, I work in the campus coffee shop where you hang out. You get black coffee, and your girlfriend gets the peach tea."

Tristan smiled the same, almost irritating smile again. "Oh yeah. That's right. You usually wear your hair pulled back, don't you?"

Hannah smiled again with a matching demeanor. "Yes, I do. Are you one of those guys that doesn't see waitstaff or janitors?"

"No… no, I knew I recognized you, I just wasn't sure where I knew you from. I suppose I am one of those who is confused by small changes, like hairstyles. I'm not a total lout, just a partial one." Tristan hoped he had backpedaled sufficiently to appease the young woman.

Jessica and Kay returned to the living room to meet the newest arrivals. Jessica remembered the young woman immediately.

The evening was pleasantly quiet. Jessica pushed her parents into telling the story of how they got engaged. Her request captured the interest of everyone present. They each knew it was just a matter of time until her engagement was announced.

As the evening drew to a close, Jessica went into the kitchen to help her mother clean up. "Mom, is everything okay? You seem kinda quiet."

"I've got several things on my mind."

"What is it?"

"I wanted to have one last night alone with the four of us before we started… branching out. I'm also concerned that your young man is one more way to keep us from remembering who we are and where we came from." Kay's face had appeared to age in the last few minutes.

"What makes you think Tristan would do that?" Jessica didn't want to dismiss her mother's concerns too lightly.

"He's a Covert Ops officer. You told us that yourself."

"He *was* a Covert Ops officer. He's not anymore. I worried about that myself. I told him a little bit about our history. Tristan said something that makes a lot of sense. He said it isn't very covert to use an agent to spy on someone and tell them he's a Covert Ops agent."

Kay nodded, but inside she knew he might still be an agent bent on controlling them. "I suppose he's right about that, but I worry he might be using you and his background to make a statement to your father and me."

Jessica teared up and slammed the plate she had been carrying on the counter. "Mom, stop it! I love him. He's not what you think. He's a good man. He could have hurt Robbie a couple weeks ago, but he didn't."

"What are you talking about? How could he have hurt your brother?" Kay was instantly afraid for her son.

Jessica suddenly regretted her outburst. She tried to carefully explain without stirring up more problems. "Robbie was drunk the night of the ball. After you and Dad left, he and two of his friends tried to pick a fight with Tristan. Tristan outsmarted them. Robbie saw Tristan working out later and realized he was no match for him."

"You saw it?"

"No, not all of it. Robbie came to Tristan's office the other day when I was there and told us about seeing Tristan sparring with a bot. I've seen Tristan fight. He knows what he's doing." Jessica hoped she wasn't getting Robert into more trouble.

"When did you see him fight?" Kay wasn't sure she wanted to know the answer to her question.

"Some jerks on the riverfront got drunk and harassed us the night we started dating. There were three of them. He kept them from hurting me until help arrived. He ended up going to the hospital, though." Jessica was proud of his heroic actions.

"Jessica... why didn't you tell us about this? You could have gotten hurt. Those men could have known him from one of his undercover jobs."

The two continued to argue, and those in the other room soon heard their voices. Robert and Saul excused themselves to see what was happening. Tristan chose this moment to quickly ask Hannah the one question that had been burning in his mind all night. "You know, when I saw you in the coffee shop, I knew you seemed familiar to me. You were a year behind me in the Academy. Are you watching Robert or Jessica, or perhaps me?"

"Mind your own business, Chief. You've got your job to do, and I have mine. Don't interfere with me," Hannah snapped.

Tristan walked away from her to refill his coffee. He listened to the hushed tones coming from the other room. "I don't plan on interfering with your mission. I don't want us to cause any problems for each other. We could help each other, but if I don't know what you're after, I can't help you."

Hannah headed toward the kitchen. Tristan reached out and grabbed her arm. "Just so you know, Lt. Cmdr. Deacons is not going to take to this tough-girl routine. You want to impress him, act more like his mother."

Hannah gave Tristan a disgusted look. "You want me to pretend to be his mother? That's crude. I know what I'm doing."

"Do you? A man is attracted to a woman who reminds him of his mother. It isn't a conscious thing. It just happens. A woman likes a man who reminds her of her father. You'd best alter your personality, and quickly, if you want to keep him interested." Hannah jerked free of him. As she left the room, she heard him softly call after her, "Study his mother!"

Hannah had taken the same classes Tristan had. She knew he was right, but she hated to admit it. She stopped in the doorway and twisted enough to see him. "Fine, I'll do this your way." She sloshed her coffee cup onto her dress and cried out, "Oh no!" She headed toward the kitchen. "Mrs. Deacons?"

Tristan heard the tone of the conversation change as Kay Deacons went into mothering and hostess mode. Jessica made a beeline to get away from the fiery darts coming from her parents. She tried to persuade Tristan to take her home, but he refused. She whispered desperately, "Tristan, please let's go."

"Jess, I want to stay and get to know your family better. I want them to know they can trust me. I love you, and I don't want to come between you and your family."

Seeing he had upset her, Tristan took her out onto the patio in the family's backyard. It was quite nippy outside, forcing Jessica to snuggle close to him. She finally looked at him to bluntly explain the situation. "My parents are still afraid you're using me to intimidate them."

"Intimidate them? To do what?" Tristan pulled back. The look of confusion on his face reinforced Jessica's comfort with him.

"They're working on developing tachyon-based engines and converting the currently used bradyon engines to use tachyons. It's not a classified project, just high-profile," Jessica explained.

"I'm afraid I don't understand the problem." Tristan's lack of knowledge from his superiors fueled his desire to know the full story.

"My parents were working for a non-Commonwealth world on this same project. They were hired to develop this technology before the Commonwealth knew it was possible. The world that hired them was considered a threat to the Commonwealth and placed under an embargo. My parents are—were suspected enemies of the state. The authorities cleared them, but they've always felt as though they were being watched. I saw them start but never finish numerous conversations, like they were afraid of something."

Robert's voice came from behind them. "They are afraid. There are still other people out there who truly are enemies of the state, and if they ever find us…"

Jessica jerked away from Tristan. "What? What could happen?"

"They could force Mom and Dad to come back to work for them. It's what really got Abigail killed. Jess, we can't talk about this. The CIF said so," Robert reminded her.

"Tristan is CIF, remember? It's what you all are afraid of, isn't it? Tristan, please take me home."

"All right, let's say our farewells. Robert, best of luck to you. I'll see you when you return." Tristan offered Robert his hand.

Robert looked at it for a moment, choosing to shake it as a symbol of the peace they were trying to build between them. "Take care of Jessica and my folks while I'm gone, okay?"

"Sure thing. I'll protect them with my life if necessary," Tristan promised.

Tristan and Jessica said an awkward goodnight to their hosts and slipped out quickly and quietly. The two said little to each other on the way home.

When the car came to a stop in front of Jessica's apartment, Jessica turned to Tristan and kissed him passionately. They settled into a firm embrace. Jessica pulled back slowly. A strange look crossed her face. "Tristan, why don't you come inside?"

Tristan was taken aback by the request. He knew she was reacting to the strain from her relationship with her parents. Tristan kissed her again before answering. "Jessica, as much as I would love to come with you, tonight isn't the night. If I did that, you might hate me in the morning. I don't think I could bear to have you hate me."

Jessica grabbed onto him. "No, I wouldn't. I swear I wouldn't."

"Jessica, get some sleep, and tomorrow, call your mom. If you still want me to come over tomorrow night, I will. If I join you tonight, you'll end up hating me or yourself. I don't want you hating either of us. I'll call you when I get home if you want me to." This one thing took more self-control than anything else he could ever remember.

Before Jessica could respond, Maddy was at the door to the car, tapping on the window. Tristan opened the door and stepped out. He gave Maddy an appreciative nod as he reached inside to help Jessica out of the car.

Maddy warmly explained, "Hey Jess, Tristan sent me a message telling me you had a rough night at your parents' house. Let's go in and fix some hot tea or something, and you can tell me all about it. Was your brother there?"

Jessica gave Tristan an annoyed look. Tristan winked at her. "Call me later if you need to."

"You won't like it if I do," she called over her shoulder as Maddy ushered her away from the car.

Tristan got back in the car and headed to his own apartment. He passed a bar on the way home, triggering a debate between a cold shower at home or the comfort of a one-night-stand. Tristan stopped at a second nearby bar. His handsome young physique got the attention of several women, but somehow, none of them appealed to him. He finally realized that if Jessica called, she would wonder why he wasn't at home. Tristan abandoned his ideas of temporary gratification and returned to his apartment. Once alone, he took a long, cold shower, wondering what he had gotten himself into. The bits and pieces of what he'd learned weren't adding up. Why were his superiors bringing a second agent in on this?

Tristan waited up, thinking Jessica might call him. When she didn't, he decided Maddy must have kept her sufficiently entertained. He slept fitfully that night.

THREE DAYS

Jedrek seemed more relaxed as he returned to the city, with Marek at his side. Marek finally questioned him about the matter. "Master Jedrek, the young woman sent us away, but you seem to be in a better mood. Is this a sense of relief, or is it something else?"

Jedrek smiled. "She's thinking about it. We will return in three days to see her again. I guess our courtship has begun anew."

"I suppose it's a good thing that she didn't say no outright. But what if you go back in three days and she says no?" Marek knew he was asking questions far above his station, but he hoped the young man needed a friend more than a subordinate. Knowing Jedrek was succeeding was pertinent to the task assigned to him by Governor Pravin.

Jedrek gave Marek an annoyed look. "Did you really have to ask that particular question? I was feeling good about the situation until now."

"I'm sorry, Master Jedrek. I didn't mean to cause you any distress. I'm sure she'll want to see you again and again, especially when it's time to change dirty diapers." Marek grinned at his superior.

Jedrek made a face, which gave Marek even more pleasure. The two rode toward the entrance into town. Instead of going back to the inn, Jedrek planned to seek out the magistrate. Marek wondered what his master was planning, but kept his questions to himself. He suspected the information would present itself soon enough. His expectation was accurate.

Jedrek made no attempt to hide his actions. If he had known the full extent of Governor Pravin's orders to Marek, he might have chosen a different soldier to accompany him.

The two were met by guards as they re-entered the city gates. The watch commander gave him an invitation he couldn't refuse. "The magistrate wishes to see you. These men will escort you to him."

Jedrek looked at the guards surrounding him and Marek. Marek's horse sensed her master's tension and shuffled restlessly. Marek reached down cautiously and patted the horse. "Easy, girl, easy."

Jedrek smiled. "Oh, good, I want to speak with him as well. Please take me to him."

The entourage proceeded to the magistrate's estate. Jedrek noticed his other three guards were corralled in the courtyard. Seeing a few bumps and bruises, he surmised they had resisted.

Jedrek entered the magistrate's residence, which also served as his office and courtroom. The man wasn't currently occupied and could see Jedrek immediately.

"Magistrate, I am Lord Jedrek of the Somian Province. I intended to seek an audience with you today. It is convenient that you also wished to speak with me. What can I do for you?"

"Tell me why you are here!" The man demanded sternly.

"Of course. I wish to seek a secondary residence here in Nazar and set up a business."

The magistrate was not amused. "We've had far too many encounters with Somians of late. Now would not be a good time for that. Perhaps in a year we will be on better terms with Somi."

"Please, Magistrate, there is a woman here whom I seek to marry. If she agrees to be my wife, may I stay then? If she asks it of me, I will renounce all ties with Somi, and this will become my home."

Red flags waved immediately in the magistrate's mind. "Who is the woman?"

"Her name is Slaina."

"Slaina? You do know whose child she carries, do you not?"

"Yes, I know."

"You understand the child will never be your son." The magistrate tested Jedrek.

"I know. The baby is the son of Pateras. I love Slaina, and I want to help her raise this child. She is considering whether to allow me back into her life. She will see me again in three days. I want plans in place so that she knows I intend to support her in any way possible."

"You seek a home, and you desire to start a business here. What if she refuses you?"

"Then I will conclude my business, sell my house, and return to Somi." Jedrek had no delusions about the situation.

"You also realize this young woman and her child are under my protection, and if anything at all were to happen to her, it would mean war." The magistrate was not taking the situation lightly and wanted to be sure the young man wasn't either. He walked directly to Marek. "This man knows this. He was told several days ago. I trust the injuries Nasha inflicted on you are healing well?"

"I'm fine," the rigid soldier said.

"I understand, Magistrate. We mean her no harm. My uncle reacted rashly and has repented for his actions." Jedrek's dream had put everything into perspective.

"I will speak with Halyn and others on the town council. You will have an answer from me by morning. Meet me tomorrow morning in the town hall."

Jedrek nodded. "Yes, my lord."

The magistrate took two guards with him and rode out to Halyn's home. Despite being one of the poorer people in the area, Halyn had one of the larger houses. Her home was constructed with numerous guest accommodations, so she could tend to the sick.

The magistrate knocked on Halyn's door. Joren admitted the man and led him to the kitchen, where he found Halyn and Slaina sitting at the table. The magistrate had known and respected Halyn all his life. She was the midwife who delivered him and his four children.

Halyn didn't stand on ceremony or formality. "Danyl, come in. Please join us. I think we could use another set of eyes on this problem."

Danyl sat down at the table. "I suspect your problem and mine are one and the same."

"Slaina, tell Danyl what you told me."

Slaina glanced nervously at the man. "Why would the magistrate care about this situation?"

Danyl smiled wryly. "Speak your mind, young woman. I have promised you my protection. If something threatens you, I need to know about it."

"The man I was betrothed to in Somi has come here to see me. He asked for my forgiveness and wants to renew our relationship." Slaina didn't blink or flinch. Her fear from days ago was slowly being replaced with a boldness only Pateras could provide. She was beginning to understand Pateras could and would protect the child. "He says I would be safe to return to Somi, or we could remain here."

"You aren't sure he's trustworthy. Is that the problem?" Danyl attempted to fill in the blanks.

"Jedrek has always been honest and straightforward with me. When he thought I had betrayed him, he made his opinions quite clear. He wasn't the one who reported me. Three days after I told him about the baby, he came to me and told me his uncle was furious. His uncle demanded to know why he had revoked our engagement. He warned me to leave the city. I left and went to visit my cousin. I trust Jedrek. It's his uncle I'm not sure about. He says his uncle has calmed down and thought the situation through. He will welcome us back if we want to return to Somi."

Danyl sat there thoughtfully. "Jedrek has asked my permission to start a homestead and to be allowed to conduct business here. Do you want him to stay? If you say no, I will refuse him without a second thought."

Halyn scowled. "Aren't you askin' a bit much from her? She's hardly more than a child, and she's had the weight of all creation placed upon her."

"No, Healer, she hasn't. That child will have all the weight of creation on him. All I want to know is, does she want this man to go away or not? Even if you don't want to resume your relationship with him, does it matter to you if he remains in the province? Can you stand seeing him around if you reject him?" Danyl persisted.

Slaina pondered her answer carefully. "I asked Jedrek to return in three days because I didn't have an answer for him. Do you need an answer right now?"

Danyl scowled. "I told him to return to me tomorrow, and I would tell him my decision about allowing him to purchase property and do business here."

"You could tell him he can look around, but whether he may make purchases of land and conduct business is contingent upon Slaina's decision," Halyn suggested.

"I don't like the idea of leaving this hanging. I prefer to give him a flat yes or no."

Slaina stared at nothing in particular for a moment. A realization struck her. "Magistrate, did he say what he would do if I rejected him?"

"He said he would sell his property, conclude his business, and return to Somi. He also offered to reject Somi completely if you agreed to marry him."

Halyn frowned again. "You aren't helping matters, Danyl. She's a girl who was in love. She was hurt by her betrothed, and now he wants her back. I think that young man is as confused as she is."

"No, he isn't." Slaina shifted on the bench. Her back was starting to ache. She wasn't accustomed to having backaches unless she had been pulling weeds from the garden all day.

"What do you mean, girl?" Halyn knew there was more to this story.

"Pateras sent a messenger to Jedrek in a dream. The messenger told him not to be afraid to marry me. Jedrek wants to put things right between us. At the very least, he wants me to forgive him. At best, he wants me to reconsider marrying him. I told him we can't do all that is done between a h-husband and wife." Slaina blushed as she tried to speak in mixed company about such a sensitive topic. "Until after the baby is born."

"What was Jedrek's response? How did he react?" The magistrate needed to know Jedrek's frame of mind.

"He—" Slaina blushed again. "He said he knew, and he w-would wait."

"I see." Danyl nodded his understanding, then stood to go. He gave Halyn a meaningful look as he moved toward the door. Halyn told Joren and Slaina to remain where they were. The two stepped outside and continued to talk. "Halyn, I need to meet with the town council to discuss Jedrek's request."

"You want us there to testify, don't you?"

"Can you and the girl handle it? She was quite sick when she came to town. Is she strong enough for this? If some of the council members dig their heels in, it could make for a long and difficult night for you and for her."

"Danyl, are you callin' me old and frail? The most troublesome part of this is goin' to be makin' those hard-headed know-it-alls listen to reason."

"No, Healer, you know I wouldn't risk my life by calling you old," the man teased. "The other members of the council, however, could tax the patience of a saint, which is my opinion of you, dear lady."

"Go gather your council, Magistrate. Have a copy of the Ancient Texts handy, in case we have to prove the girl is the one to carry the Promised One. I will have Slaina and Joren eat a hearty meal and drink plenty. I'll give Slaina some herbs to settle her stomach before we enter the town hall, so she can go several hours without getting ill. We will leave here and join you in about an hour." Halyn sounded as though the matter were completely decided. "By the way, you might want to have that soldier, Nasha, there. I know he's also a Somian, but he has testimony about this situation."

Danyl shook his head. "I can't bring Nasha into this. He's not available right now. The council wouldn't trust him any more than they trust Jedrek. Why do you want to bring the boy? What light can he shed on this?"

"The boy saw the messenger of Pateras. He's from Helia, not the city of Somi. He's too young to know politics. There will be no deceit in his words. There's a lot he can share."

The magistrate sighed. "So be it. Bring whomever you wish. I will have a copy of the texts available to search out the prophecies."

Halyn's smile grew even bigger. "You are a wise man, Magistrate."

Two hours later, the group assembled in the meeting hall as planned. It was the custom of their people when conducting important and potentially disagreeable business to go to the town hall. Once all parties were assembled, the doors would be locked from the outside. No one was allowed in or out until the matter was decided. They were given enough firewood in the stove to conduct a brief and civil meeting. If it took longer than that, they would get cold. In the summer, the stoves were not needed because the air itself would be hot and the windows were small. There was a chamber pot in one small side room to relieve themselves in, but the group would have no food or water until they came to an agreement. Eventually, each one had to decide: was his own physical discomfort worth his stubbornness?

The town council was assembled in the room at their usual meeting table. Halyn and her two charges entered last. It was the custom for men to sit on the front rows in the meeting hall and the women to sit behind them. Halyn took the appropriate place in the second row, but placed Slaina and Joren in the front row. The council members glowered at her and whispered angry objections to Danyl.

Danyl scowled at Halyn, knowing what she was doing. "Healer, you know it is not customary for a woman to sit equal to a man. Why have you placed Slaina beside Joren?"

Halyn's eyes twinkled. "The child she carries is a son and the Promised One of all creation. His place surpasses us all. How do you propose I separate him from his mother? He is the reason we're here, is he not? Pateras chose that girl himself. Which one of you wants to push aside one chosen by Pateras?"

Whether they believed any of this story was not the current issue. Halyn had dared them to cross Pateras by moving the girl back one row. Slaina was unfamiliar with the custom and sat where she was told. The council's angry stares were making her uncomfortable.

Danyl answered her, "You are a wise woman, although you bear more confidence than is advisable. This is a small matter, and we are few today. Halyn, you may as well join the two in the front row."

"If that is your wish, Magistrate. I am honored that you would make such an exception for me." Halyn moved to the bench beside Slaina.

The other members of the council did not appreciate the decision, but Danyl didn't give them time to object. He brought the matter at hand immediately to the table. "As many of you may have noticed, the number of Somians in our province has increased recently. I know we're only talking about a handful of people, but the importance of those who have joined, and those who desire to join our province, is the issue at hand."

Bassam, the Minister of Trade and Finance, leaned forward and rested his arms on the table in front of him. "Magistrate, why didn't you handle this? Why do you need the council for a few immigrants?"

"Forgive the breech in protocol. Introductions before business, Minister Bassam. Healer Halyn, you know each of the members of the council. Joren, Slaina, you are new here and have not met these men. The impatient voice belongs to Bassam, the Minister of Trade and Finance. To his right is Eliason, the Minister of Justice. To my left is Rubain, the Minister of the Farmlands. To his left is Aken, the Minister of the Township.

"Ministers, I present Joren of the town of Helia and Slaina of the capital city of Somi. Halyn has brought Joren here to start a new life for himself. Slaina has sought refuge here from the wrath of Governor Pravin."

Minister Eliason interrupted, "What did she do to earn his wrath, and why did you grant her sanctuary if she is a wanted criminal?"

Danyl sensed the meeting was going to spin out of control quickly if he didn't move faster to explain the situation. "The girl did nothing wrong. She is the chosen one of Pateras to bring forth the Promised One. The issue at hand is her former betrothed, Jedrek, who is the nephew of Governor Pravin. The governor believes Slaina has dishonored his nephew and his family."

Bassam jumped in again. "So, give Jedrek the girl and let him handle it how he wants. This isn't our concern. Making an enemy of Somi is bad for business."

Halyn shook her head. Already it was clear they weren't listening. She interrupted before the magistrate could respond. "Making an enemy of Pateras is worse for business than making an enemy of Governor Pravin."

Bassam winced. He didn't like what Halyn was suggesting, but wasn't sure how to rebut her statement.

Danyl took a firmer grasp on the meeting. "Gentlemen, please allow me to get to the crux of the matter before you offer your preconceived solutions. You can't help me if you don't understand the problem."

The magistrate paused and made eye contact with each member of the council before proceeding. "Jedrek has seen the truth and the error in his thinking. He now claims to believe Slaina carries the Promised One and has asked to be allowed to start a homestead here and begin conducting business. He told me his uncle reacted rashly and would welcome Slaina back in Somi."

Bassam shifted restlessly, waiting for the magistrate to get to his point. Danyl eyed him sternly, daring him to interrupt again. "The problem is this: the prophecies clearly indicate the Promised One would be the ruler of all, and that those who rule at the time of his birth would seek to destroy him. Governor Pravin already tried to kill Slaina and her child. Jedrek, to our knowledge, has not tried to harm them. He claims to want to marry her, and he is willing to reject his family and the Somian Province. He told me his uncle overreacted and has since calmed down."

"So, as I said before, let him take his bride and go home." Bassam was clearly impatient.

"Slaina has not agreed to return to him yet, and she certainly has not agreed to return to Somi. I have allowed Slaina to remain here, and I have also allowed Nasha and Joren to remain in Nazar. Do I also allow Jedrek to remain? Tensions between us and the Somians are already high. Allowing Slaina to remain has increased those tensions. I fear that Governor Pravin is using his own nephew to entice Slaina back to Somi. Once she is in Somi, he can rid himself of her and the baby."

Rubain chose this time to insert himself into the discussion. "Isn't he rid of her now? Why would he allow her back if he fears losing his rule over Somi?"

The magistrate pulled out a copy of the Ancient Texts and opened them to the passage about the rulership of the Promised One.

> The Promised One of Pateras will descend from a line of kings blessed by Pateras, a chosen lineage of united kingdoms. The Promised One will be born of one who has found the favor of Pateras and not the son of a man's will, a woman who has never been touched by a man. Many will seek to destroy the Promised One before his days are numbered and after his birth is made known. The lives of those on millions of worlds will be redeemed by the life, death, and life again of him who is born of Pateras. He will be born of a healer, but his healing will go beyond the healing of men. His words and his touch will bring the healing of body and soul. There will be none like him.

"Well, there you go. This girl isn't a healer," the previously silent Aken interjected.

Halyn stood slowly, knowing her comments would not be welcomed. "Master Aken, forgive me, but there's information you do not have as yet. As you know, my husband and I were never blessed with children. I have not had a daughter on whom to impart my skills as a healer. When Pateras brought this girl into my life, I knew she was the one I was to train to replace me. I'm not a young woman, and the end of my days is coming sooner than I care to admit. Slaina may not be a healer yet, but she will be soon enough. She has the instincts of a healer."

Eliason scowled. "That's rather convenient timing, don't you think?"

Joren jumped up. "Are you calling Halyn a liar? Halyn would never lie! I've known her since I was a boy. She's never lied to me!"

Bassam couldn't resist laughing heartily at the young man. "You're not much more than a boy now."

Danyl pounded his fist on the table. "Minister Bassam, there is no need to be rude or insulting. Joren is a man. He is young, but he is a man, nonetheless."

Bassam attempted unsuccessfully to wipe the grin from his face. "Forgive me, Master Joren. I meant no disrespect."

Minister Eliason was still skeptical. "How do we know this young man isn't the true father of Slaina's baby?"

Halyn rolled her eyes. "They met less than two weeks ago. I brought Slaina with me to Helia, which is where Joren is from. He'd never left Helia until Nasha brought him here."

Bassam couldn't resist another annoying question. "What if Governor Pravin wants to be rid of the young woman because the child is his? How do we know for certain she carries the child of Pateras?"

Slaina's face paled for a second, then turned green as the thought made her ill. Her color finally settled on red as she pushed aside the sickening thought and grew angry at the suggestion.

Halyn told them of seeing the messenger of Pateras vouch for the girl, even though she knew her testimony would not carry definitive proof. Joren and Slaina backed her up. Slaina gave her testimony of all that had transpired over the last four months. She explained to the council that her feelings for Jedrek were uncertain. She still cared for him, but he had refused to believe her and trust her.

The council discussed the risks of war with Somi and whether Slaina and Jedrek were worth such risks. When it appeared the consensus might go against them, Halyn added one last thing to the discussion. "Councilmen, there is one thing you must keep in mind. I have seen the messenger of Pateras myself. Slaina spoke the truth about the child she carries. If you demand that she leave the province, I will sell my property and go with her. I will not remain in Nazar, nor will I ever return."

At her announcement, the room grew deathly quiet. Then, as the group processed her words, an argument ensued. The disagreement continued for quite some time.

Jedrek was making plans in his room at the inn and finally came down to the dining room to get some dinner. He overheard two other patrons discussing the town council meeting.

"It looks as though they're going to be in there a while."

"What makes you say so?"

"I heard a lot of yelling going on in there."

The innkeeper's son refilled the men's cups with water and added his own take on the situation. "I hope they don't stay in there much longer, or that girl's gonna get cold again."

One of the men turned and grabbed the boy's arm. "What girl?"

"That girl stayin' with the healer. Her name's Slaina. I saw her, the healer, and that man Joren go in there just after lunch. They're gonna run out of firewood soon."

Jedrek stopped eating and turned quickly to the boy. "Are you certain you saw the healer and Slaina go into the town hall?"

The boy was beginning to think he was in trouble for something. "Y-yes, sir."

Jedrek looked around and spotted Marek sitting by the fire, sipping on a pint of ale. "Marek! Come with me!"

Marek dropped the ale hastily onto the hearth and wasted no time following Jedrek out of the inn. The two trotted to the town hall where they were stopped outside the doors by guards who refused them entry. They walked around the building while Jedrek considered his options. There were four entrances into the building, and each one was guarded. Jedrek could hear the men arguing inside. He wasn't certain he was the subject of their discussion, but chances were good that he was a major part of it. As the two men came around the corner to the entrance they started from, Jedrek said, "Marek, I need this man moved out of my way."

Marek knew not to cause the man any serious harm. He smiled and nodded at his master as they walked past the guard a second time. "Yes, sir." Marek turned and punched the man in the jaw, then ran from the town hall. The guard bounced off the door, then fell forward. He pulled himself off the ground, glanced at Jedrek, who seemed happy to stand there watching, then raced after Marek.

As the councilmen heard the clatter at the door, the arguing died down. All eyes glanced toward the sound, waiting for whatever might come next. The sounds of lumber being removed from outside the door reached their ears, followed by the obnoxious squeaking of the hinges. Jedrek stepped into the chamber, which was only slightly warmer than the chilly outdoors. He hastened to the center of the room and stood before the council. "Magistrate, forgive the intrusion, but I believe I should have been included in this. It is my fate that is being decided, is it not?"

A brief argument about his interruption ensued until the magistrate shut it down. "Master Jedrek is correct. This does concern him, and he should have been here. The fault is mine for not including him. Would you all care to concede to this one point, or would you like to argue a while longer?"

The council members' throats were now growing dry and hoarse from the lack of water, the dry air, and raised voices.

The magistrate attempted to cut to the heart of the matter. "Master Jedrek, whom do you believe is the father of the child Slaina carries?"

"It is Pateras. I did not believe it before, but I do now. Pateras sent a messenger to me in a dream. I believe Slaina, and I have asked her to forgive me for doubting."

Bassam balked once again. He coughed to clear his raw throat before expressing his objection. "The prophecies clearly state that the Promised One will be in the lineage of kings blessed by Pateras and a chosen lineage of united kingdoms. Your lineage is established, but she's clearly a peasant."

"She's no peasant. My uncle vetted her lineage personally. She is the descendant of royalty. Her great-great-grandmother was given to my uncle's great grandfather to unite Somi and Nazar and end the war between the two provinces. My mother was given to your magistrate's brother to help keep the peace. I was born here in Nazar. My parents died when raiders came from the skies. My nursemaid took me to Somi. I told you I would deny Somi. I am only half-Somian. I am also half-Nazaran."

Danyl stared at Jedrek. "You're my younger brother's son, Jedrek? That's not possible. He died when the raiders destroyed your home. How old were you when this happened?"

"I was four. I remember that day extremely clearly. The nursemaid had taken me outside to play when we heard the raiders in the skies. I had never seen birds like those before. They were dragons that breathed fire. My nursemaid kept me hidden in the bushes until the birds flew away. As soon as they were gone, she took me, and we headed to Somi. It seemed as though we traveled for days to get there. I have lived in Somi ever since."

The magistrate nodded. "It happened as you said. We never found you and assumed you died in the fire. It seems there is little else to discuss. If you are already a citizen of Nazar, you may buy, sell, and conduct business as any other citizen. Why didn't you mention this to me before?"

"Because I am also half-Somian and I have lived most of my life there. I wanted to have the full blessing of everyone involved."

Bassam and Aken attempted to object. Having little ground to stand on, their objections were quickly dispatched. The two grudgingly conceded. "Magistrate, you know the Somians may still take exception to this," Aken argued.

"They cannot if Jedrek is a Nazaran citizen. And if Slaina chooses to marry him, it ties her lineage once again to ours." Danyl was ready to finish this and reacquaint himself with his long-lost nephew. It was also growing quite frigid in the council hall. Danyl rang the bell, indicating they had completed their deliberations. The guards opened the doors to allow all to leave. The guard escorted Marek roughly into the building and demanded to know what to do with the ruffian. Jedrek apologized to all concerned and took responsibility for his guard's actions. The magistrate forgave his transgression and released Marek to Jedrek.

Slaina approached Jedrek quietly and asked. "Why did you come here tonight?"

"I knew what they were arguing about, and I didn't want you to get cold."

Slaina shivered. "Too late."

Jedrek looked at Halyn. "Come to the inn. Eat supper and warm yourselves before you return home. The cost will be mine for all three of you."

Halyn smiled. "Thank you, Jedrek."

The three ate a hearty meal at the inn before returning to Halyn's homestead. Jedrek helped Slaina into the wagon. Before releasing his arm, her eyes twinkling in the moonlight, Slaina smiled softly at him. "You don't need to wait three days."

Jedrek smiled at her. "I will come see you tomorrow."

ARRESTED!

"Tristan!" Jessica cried out over the computer hail. "Please help me!"

Tristan had just come from the gym. He was hot, sweaty and dressed in his workout clothes. "What's wrong?" He saw panic on her face.

"They've been arrested! You have to do something!"

"They... who?"

"My mom and dad. I hailed my mom this morning like you told me to, and while I was talking to them..." Jessica began to cry and look toward her own door as though she feared it was merely a matter of time until they came for her as well.

Tristan leaned in. "Jess, what happened?"

"Troops burst into the house and arrested them. What if they come for me next? Do you think Robbie is safe? Tristan, I don't know what to do." Jessica looked more frightened than she had the night they were attacked at the waterfront.

Tristan knew exactly what was happening, and he got more ticked off the longer he thought about it. He wanted to slam his fist on the desk, but knew it wasn't the right reaction. "Jessica, let me make a couple calls and see if I can find out which agency has them and where they're being held. What I need you to do is head to my office and wait for me there. I'll alert security to expect you. They'll escort you in and give you whatever you need. I'll get there as quickly as I can."

Jessica kept looking at the door to her apartment. She wasn't focusing on what Tristan was telling her. "Jessica? Jessica, did you hear me?"

Jessica wiped fresh tears away and looked back at the screen. "Y-yes, I think so."

"Is Maddy there?"

"N-no, sh-she already left."

"Jess, go to my office and wait for me. I'll be there as soon as I can. If they come for you, let them take you. Don't try to run. I'll get this fixed. I promise. Nod at me if you understand." It was a simple instruction, yet necessary to deal with her befuddled mind.

Jessica nodded. She grabbed her jacket and raced for the door, neglecting to shut down the computer or close the hail.

The second she was gone, Tristan slammed his fist on the desk. He hailed the security office in his building and warned them to expect her. Closing his hail, he looked around the room. Knowing they were listening to him, he said loudly, "I'm going to take a quick shower. Somebody had better have some answers for me in about fifteen minutes."

In exactly fifteen minutes, Agents Gershom and Wallace were at his door. Tristan was putting his uniform jacket on. The thing had been hanging in his closet untouched for the last few months. He decided he needed it today as a reminder to all parties of exactly who he was.

Agent Wallace came through his door first, and as expected, took the lead. "You've got a lot of nerve summoning us this way… Chief."

Agent Gershom stepped in behind her and added, "The uniform is a nice touch."

Tristan secured the door behind the two agents. "What did you do with Mr. and Mrs. Deacons? Why did you arrest them, and where are they being held?"

Agent Wallace made herself at home on his sofa and snidely asked, "What makes you think we had anything to do with this?"

"You're listening to everything they're saying and doing. You know Jessica's parents don't trust me, and you thought you would help me out by setting me up to be a hero. I get them out of jail and BOOM, they trust me."

Agent Wallace smiled sanctimoniously. "You can thank us later."

Tristan folded his arms across his chest and planted his feet. "Oh, you won't be getting any appreciation from me. You made my job harder. You proved their point. They now know I'm in their lives to spy on them or intimidate them or whatever it is you want from me."

The smile faded from Agent Wallace's face. "Apparently, you aren't a team player."

"Oh yes, I am a team player, but from the choices you're making, I think you're playing for the other team."

Agent Gershom could see the situation spiraling. He jumped in quickly. "Okay, maybe we chose poorly. How do we fix this? Claim it was all a mistake and say we arrested the wrong people?"

Tristan took his eyes off the annoying agent and looked at the more reasonable one. "Uh—no. You want me to play the hero? That's what I'll have to do. You aren't going to like it, though. It's going to cost you."

Agent Wallace leaned forward. "Are you threatening us?"

Tristan rolled his eyes. "No, I am not threatening you. I'm telling you there is only one way to salvage this situation. You can continue monitoring their comms and their home, but you're going to have to lose the trackers you planted on them. Why haven't you planted trackers on Jessica and Robert?"

Agent Gershom jumped in to diffuse the contention between the two. "Jessica and Robert are not the ones we need. Saul and Kay are. We're keeping an eye on their children to make sure they stay on task. We are so close to achieving our goals on this project, we can't afford to lose them."

Agent Wallace glared at Chief Alexander. "We're not taking those trackers out."

"You want my help? Those trackers have to come out, or they're going to know I am exactly what they think I am. What would have been the best for all concerned is if you had left that couple alone. Eventually, they would have gotten over their fear. Now you've just reinforced it."

"How are we going to be certain they don't attempt to escape?" Agent Wallace snapped at the brash young operative.

"They won't leave while Lt. Cmdr. Deacons is deployed, and they won't leave without Jessica. Jessica won't leave me unless you pull another stupid stunt like this one."

Gershom nodded. "You win. I'll arrange to get the trackers out of them."

"No, not until I make an appropriate scene at the precinct where they're being held. And as before, if you pull any more stunts like this, I'm out."

"You can't transfer out until we say so," Agent Wallace replied in her saucy tone.

"Maybe I can't, but I do know how to go off the grid long enough to cause you problems."

A troubled Agent Gershom jumped in again. "You would go AWOL and ruin your service record over this?"

"You two are already screwing things up. I don't think I want this case to even show up in my file."

"I told you he wasn't a team player," Wallace snapped again.

"Which part of the team was left uninformed of the game plan?" Tristan snapped back. "From now on, you run this stuff by me before you do it or I will find ways to screw your plans so bad that starting over would have to involve a time jump!"

Agent Wallace's face conveyed a myriad of emotions. Before any words came out of her mouth, Agent Gershom jumped in. "You have my word. We work this through as a team from here on out. No more surprises, I promise."

"Now, where do I find my future in-laws?"

"Are you really that close?" Agent Gershom asked.

"I was yesterday. We'll see if I still am after today."

"We're sorry. Okay? We're working with you from here on out. Mr. and Mrs. Deacons are being held in the Pacification Division of the CIF. You'll need to talk to Cmdr. Jeffrey Baxter."

Tristan repeated the instructions to be certain he had the name and location correct before informing the two he was headed to his office to get Jessica. Before he left his apartment, he heard Agent Gershom giving Cmdr. Baxter a warning about what was coming his way. Tristan stopped to add one more quick suggestion. "By the way, Hannah... is too harsh. She's not going to keep Lt. Cmdr. Deacons' attention until she learns to be a little softer. You might want to look into that."

Tristan bolted from the apartment, leaving the two agents to let themselves out. He heard a string of cursing coming from Agent Wallace as the door slid shut. He smiled to himself. Something about angering that woman seemed to give him a lot of pleasure.

Tristan caught quite a bit of attention as he walked into his office in uniform. The second he entered, Jessica jumped into his arms. Seeing his attire, she didn't stay in his arms long. "Tristan, why are you in uniform?"

"I'm sorry I didn't warn you about it. I want to make sure that when I approach the people holding your parents, they know I'm not some irate boyfriend. They need to know I am an officer of the law, and they can't give me some lame story to believe. When I get through with them, they're going to know I mean business."

Jessica still looked frightened. "Tristan, you're only a chief warrant officer. Lots of people outrank you."

"I know. I still know what buttons to push. Let's get moving." Tristan reached for her.

Jessica pulled back. "H-How do I know you aren't really taking me in?"

Tristan managed to appear wounded. "Jessica, are you serious? You asked me to help. Fine, stay here, go home. Run if that's what you think you need to do. I'm still going to go get your mom and dad out. Leave behind anything they can track if you decide to run."

Tristan turned to go. He hesitated in the doorway, then walked away from her. Jessica realized she had alienated him and perhaps judged him wrongly. She chased after him. She jumped onto the elevator before the doors closed and grabbed his hand. "I am so sorry. I didn't mean what I said. I'm just scared. My mom was worried they sent you to put pressure on them. I thought she was being paranoid, then this happened."

"You're right. It's incredibly suspicious, and I intend to find out what's going on." Tristan squeezed her hand. The elevator stopped on the bottom floor. Tristan ran into Capt. Barrett as he got off. Seeing the business dress uniform, the captain stopped him. "Chief Alexander, is there a problem?"

"Nothing I can't handle, sir." The look on his face told Capt. Barrett far more than he wanted to know.

"Report to my office when you're available," he snapped, and let the couple go on about their business.

The two rode public transit to the Pacification Division Office. The lobby was busy with security officers and receptionists. Tristan stopped inside the doorway and whispered to Jessica. "This may look like I'm bringing you in, but I promise you, I'm not. Please, please trust me."

Jessica's face was stone cold. "I don't care anymore. Do whatever you want."

Tristan gave her a quick, reassuring smile. "Trust me. It'll be fine."

Leading her over to the receptionist, he asked for directions to Cmdr. Jeffrey Baxter's office. The receptionist gave him a cold, forced smile, then asked, "Do you have an appointment?"

"No, but perhaps someone in his department can handle this. I have a material witness in a case he's working on."

The receptionist looked at Jessica's pale face and decided to let him through. "His department is on the twenty-second floor. There's another reception area as soon as you get off the elevator. They can direct you from there."

When the two were alone on the elevator, Jessica asked, "Are you doing something…" She glanced at the cameras in the elevator. "Something you shouldn't be doing?"

Tristan smiled gently at her. "Mm… no, not exactly. I may be bending the facts slightly and making inferences. The receptionist drew her own conclusions."

The elevator doors opened, and Tristan escorted Jessica to the receptionist's desk. "I need to see Cmdr. Jeffrey Baxter, please."

"Do you have an appointment?" the receptionist asked.

"No, I need to talk to him about a couple of detainees he has."

"I'm afraid he's busy right now. If you would like to wait, he may be available in a couple of hours." The young man wasn't being overly helpful.

"I don't have time to sit here and wait for him. Which way to interrogation? Send him my way the second he's available." Tristan started to walk away, then stopped and loudly ordered, "And don't let any of those reporters in here until I have spoken with the commander."

He cocked his head sideways and pointed down the hall. "Interrogation?"

The young man was suddenly busy hailing his superior. He shook his head and motioned in the opposite direction. Tristan nodded his thanks and pulled Jessica with him. The two headed down the hall briskly. Jessica only kept up with him because he was pulling her after him. "Tristan... Tristan..."

Tristan stopped. "What is it?" he asked softly.

"What reporters are you talking about? I haven't seen any reporters."

Tristan smiled again briefly. "You know, I didn't see any either. Maybe I should call some."

"I don't understand. What are you doing?" Jessica was unnerved at being in such a high-security area and walking around as though they owned the place.

"I'm laying the groundwork for getting your mom and dad out of here. Just stay with me."

Chief Alexander quickly found an empty observation room where he could access the surveillance feed in any of the interrogation rooms. He found the feed from Jessica's mother's interrogation and listened to the questions and the answers, despite Jessica's pleas to rescue her. Tristan finally grabbed her by the arms. Looking into her eyes, he moved her in front of a chair. "Jess, I need to focus. Please sit down and be quiet for a moment."

In a couple of minutes, he switched the feed over to Jessica's father's interrogation. Both interrogators asked the same questions. They wanted to know why the couple had gone off the grid the night before last, where they had gone, who they met, and what they discussed. Once Tristan learned what they were looking for, he sent a private message to both of the interrogating officers ordering them to report to Cmdr. Baxter's office. As soon as the two men left the rooms, Tristan glanced at

Jessica. "Stay put. If anyone finds you, tell them CWO Alexander ordered you to stay here. I'll be right back."

Jessica nodded. As Tristan left the room, he determined she was suffering from emotionally induced shock. He stepped into the room where Jessica's mother was being held. Kay seemed disappointed to see the young man. "Are you happy with yourself, Chief Alexander?"

"I had nothing to do with this, ma'am. I'm trying to get you out of here, but I need to know what they're looking for. I heard them asking why you went off the grid, where you went, who you met, and what you were doing. Please, give me the basic answer to what they were asking. Where did you go, and what were you doing?"

Kay glared at the young man. "What are you going to do if I don't? Are you going to hurt my daughter—or my son? Jessica said you could have hurt him a couple of weeks ago, but you didn't. Did you come in here to intimidate me?"

"No, Mrs. Deacons, I came to see what I could do to get you out of here. The man who was interrogating you is going to learn very quickly that I sent him on a fool's errand and he's going to come back here in a panic. I need to be gone before that happens. Please tell me where you went and why."

Kay sat there stubbornly, refusing to speak. A strange look crossed her face, and she finally answered. "Saul and I wanted a few minutes alone where we could say whatever we wanted without fear of being overheard. We walked along the riverfront. We stopped and ate dinner at a restaurant out on the patio. It was so cool outside, no one else wanted to sit out there. That's it. That's all. We just wanted some privacy. The waiter was the only one we spoke to."

Tristan smiled. "Thank you for trusting me. I'll be back as soon as I can—unless I get arrested, too."

Tristan slipped out of that room and into the next one. He quickly confirmed the story with Saul Deacons, then returned to the observation room.

Meanwhile, the two interrogation officers attempted to meet with Cmdr. Baxter and learned that he was on a conference call and had not summoned them at all. The two raced back to their respective rooms, fearing their prisoners had been freed. They were relieved to find their prisoners still present and secured to the table in front of them. A new litany of questions began.

Cmdr. Baxter, now fully aware that something odd was going on, excused himself from his call and made his way to the observation room. He walked in to find Tristan watching the display screens as Saul and Kay Deacons were being questioned. He glanced at the pale, frightened young woman sitting in a chair against the wall. Deciding she was not a viable threat, he questioned Tristan. "Who are you, and what are you doing in here?"

"CWO Tristan Alexander of the CIF Government Financial Oversight Division. I'm here to help you avoid some embarrassment. You need to release these people quickly and quietly."

"Why, in the name of Juranta, would I do that? They are known terrorists, and they went off the grid two nights ago."

Tristan planted his feet and folded his arms across his chest. "When and what was their last act of terrorism?"

"I don't answer to you, Chief Warrant Officer. I don't care who you work for."

Tristan leaned forward and pressed a button on the computer. He had hastily spliced Saul and Kay Deacons' answer to his questions of where they went and what they had done that night.

"Yeah, so? That's their cover story. There's more to it than that." Cmdr. Baxter wasn't ready to back down.

"No, here's where I save you and your department some embarrassment." Tristan pushed another button, and the security video from the restaurant pulled up. It was moving at an accelerated speed but distinctly showed the couple approaching the restaurant, standing outside to debate entrance into it, getting seated outside, ordering food, eating, dancing and speaking to the waiter.

"So maybe the waiter was their contact, or they met someone on the way to or from the restaurant," Cmdr. Baxter retorted.

"You are welcome to review the footage. I haven't had time to go through it completely, but from what I saw, Mr. and Mrs. Deacons just wanted to be alone."

"You are so naïve. There has to be more to it than that. They are planning new acts of terrorism now that their children are grown."

"Their son is in the CIF Brigade, and their daughter is about to finish school and start looking for a job. Why would they jeopardize their children? To my knowledge, they have been model Commonwealth citizens for the last twelve to fifteen years."

"So why go off the grid, then?"

"Are you married, Cmdr. Baxter?"

The man looked down at his hand. A brilliant new holographic tattoo glistened on his skin. Tristan smiled when he saw the mark. "A new contract or a renewal?"

The holographic tattoos were designed to be clearly visible in the beginning, and as the time for the marriage contract renewal approached, the image would slowly fade until the contract and the tattoo were renewed.

"Renewal," the man answered. He wondered why his private life mattered.

Tristan asked, "Do you enjoy having private conversations and moments with your wife?"

"Yeah."

"Ever talk about things you don't want anyone else to hear?" Tristan pushed.

"Sure, who doesn't?"

"That's exactly my point. This couple, because of their past, know they're being monitored. Sometimes you need a little privacy."

"I am not releasing them because you have a theory. My theory is much more viable and more dangerous," Cmdr. Baxter bellowed. "Get out of my department."

"Yes sir, I'll do that. I'll head straight to the nearest news agency and let them know that fine, upstanding citizens are being arrested for removing their electronic devices."

"No, they're not. We don't arrest random citizens." Cmdr. Baxter was getting red in the face.

"Mr. and Mrs. Deacons don't have any public arrest records before today. I checked. If they are terrorists, it's not documented, at least not under the names of Saul and Kay Deacons. If they were given new identities, though, perhaps someone might recognize them from the news and search them out. Someone from their past, perhaps? A real terrorist, maybe? You have no legitimate reason to hold them here. Release them, or so help me, I will get their names and faces spread across the entire galaxy along with your profile and your department. Can you imagine how that's going to look if a Financial Oversight Officer gets involved in this situation?"

By this time, the man's face was beet red. His heart pounded in his ears. This was a sensitive situation. He blustered for a moment until he managed to get a thought together. "Wait here."

Cmdr. Baxter headed down the hall to his office. It took a good thirty minutes until he returned, still as ruddy as when he left. Tristan briefly worried the man was about to have an aneurysm. "My superiors have authorized me to release them into your custody. We will give them a stern admonishment never to go off the grid again, then we'll release them to you."

Tristan shook his head. "No, you won't. You're going to bring them in here now and stop doing anything more than casual surveillance."

"That's not going to happen. They're working on a very sensitive project. We can't take the chances of them disappearing from us."

"And going where? The CIF Brigade has their son. I'm about to marry their daughter. Where can they go? Do you think they would risk the lives of their children? You give them some privacy, and they won't need to go off the grid."

Cmdr. Baxter continued to stew. "Fine! Take them and get out!" He leaned over to the computer and ordered the two interrogators to escort their prisoners to the observation room.

Jessica's parents were escorted in and their binders removed. The two interrogators stood by in case Cmdr. Baxter had further need for them. The irate officer waved them away. "Here you go, now leave!"

Tristan started to escort the family out, then stopped. "That was a little too easy."

Cmdr. Baxter looked alarmed, realizing this brash young insubordinate officer wasn't finished testing his limits.

"Computer, scan Saul and Kay Deacons for transmitters, trackers or recording devices."

The computer scanned the couple as ordered and displayed a flashing locator beacon on a silhouette of the couple. Tristan walked over to Saul Deacons and touched a spot near his ear. "Do you know how long you've had that nodule?"

"It's been there for years. I don't really know how long. I saw a doc about it once. They said it was nothing." Saul touched the familiar spot again. "This is a tracker?"

Tristan scowled. "It's not just a tracker. They heard everything you said the other night when you supposedly went off the grid. They didn't need to question you."

Tristan turned to Cmdr. Baxter, who was casting a guilty look toward Jessica. "Why were you..." An apparent look of realization formed on Tristan's face. He looked purposefully at Saul and Kay. "They were right. You're using me and my relationship with Jessica."

This time Tristan's face turned red. He looked like he was near losing control. Slamming his fist on the desk, his voice neared a low growl as he attempted to control his temper. "That stops now. Get those devices out of them."

"You don't have the authority to do that or to order me around. My superiors authorized me to release them to you. That's it."

"You get them out or I will. You know I have the resources to remove the trackers and help them disappear. I'm pretty sure your superiors don't want that to happen, now do they?"

All of the computer screens in the room lit up with the face of Agent Gershom. "Cmdr. Baxter, I apologize for interrupting. I've been monitoring the situation. Chief Alexander, we've had this situation under control for nearly fifteen years. What makes you think you can come in here and disrupt it this way?"

"I don't really know what happened fifteen years ago, and I'm not sure I care. I'm an officer of the law like you are. I checked their records. There is nothing on their files in the last fifteen years, and you've monitored them far more closely than even they knew. If they haven't caused you any problems before now, they aren't going to. Since nothing about their behavior has changed, I can only assume I'm the reason they're in here. I don't appreciate being used as a heavy without my knowledge."

"Mr. Alexander, I apologize if we have inconvenienced you. If you are willing to take personal responsibility for them, I'll authorize the removal of the transmitters."

"You're still going to make me the bad guy here?" Tristan griped.

"It's not without your knowledge or the knowledge of all parties concerned… this time," Agent Gershom replied in a syrupy tone.

Tristan stepped over to Mr. and Mrs. Deacons and continued his charade. "I would ask for a moment alone to discuss this with you, but considering the circumstances, it would be pointless. I know you worried that I was here to—to intimidate you or keep an eye on you or whatever. I'm afraid your fears have been actualized with or without my knowledge and consent. I'm so sorry. I really didn't mean for this to happen."

"What did you mean to happen?" Saul asked suspiciously.

"I meant to pass accounting with stellar grades," Tristan replied flatly. "Falling in love with Jessica wasn't on my radar." He cast a meaningful glance at the still frightened young woman.

Saul touched the device near his ear again. Glancing at Kay, he asked, "What do you want from us?"

"Your word you'll continue to behave as you have for the last few years," Tristan said. He had studied the couple carefully. If Saul gave his word, he meant it and Tristan trusted his word.

Saul looked down at his tired wife. It was not even lunchtime, but the situation had wearied her. Kay nodded her acceptance. Saul offered Tristan his hand. "You have our word."

Tristan shook Saul's hand, his eyes still reflecting anger and sorrow. Tristan stayed tapped into the anger he felt at the agents who nearly screwed up his mission. Inside, he gave a quiet sigh of relief as it seemed the situation could be salvaged. A sigh that he couldn't afford to indulge in the slightest.

Tristan turned to Cmdr. Baxter and the image of Agent Gershom. "I take full responsibility for them. Get those blasted devices out of them now."

Agent Gershom nodded to Cmdr. Baxter, who motioned the couple toward the door. As they were escorted from the room, Tristan turned to Cmdr. Baxter again. "Commander, don't think I won't scan them again for any foreign bodies."

Cmdr. Jeffrey Baxter scowled, then smiled when he heard Agent Gershom take up his cause. "Chief Alexander, I'm releasing them into your care, but don't think for one minute that we are going to cease monitoring them. Their home, office, vehicles, public transport, etc. are going to be watched like before."

"I think you're wasting your time and the taxpayers' money, but that's your business. No, wait, I believe that is now my business," Tristan snarked back.

"Don't threaten me, Mr. Alexander. You'll regret it," Agent Gershom postured.

"In the spirit of - cooperation, I will tell you this. I'm going to remove all surveillance devices from their bedroom, Jessica's, and my own. I will check those places regularly for those devices. Are we clear? No one should be afraid of their own bedroom."

"You really don't have sufficient leverage to stand on here. You're at your limit," Agent Gershom warned him.

Tristan returned a perfunctory salute. "Understood, sir!"

Ten minutes later, Tristan and the Deacons family left the building. Tristan summoned a private car to pick them up out front. He escorted the group back to the family home, but stayed outside as Jessica and her parents started toward the house. Jessica stopped and asked, "Aren't you coming in?"

"I—uh, need to go by my apartment and pick up a personal scanner. I want to scan your mom and dad's bedroom for surveillance devices. I also thought you might need some time alone."

Jessica looked at the house and envisioned every surveillance device in the building. "I'm not sure we'll ever be alone." She wrapped her arms around him. "Thank you for saving them."

Tristan returned the hug with less enthusiasm. "I'm not responsible for their freedom. I'm more responsible for getting them arrested. If I had jumped off the tallest building, they would have been released by nightfall. There's nothing to thank me for, except maybe getting the trackers out of them. I can take credit for that one."

"I don't understand." Jess pulled back and looked into his troubled face.

"They're using me to get to your parents." Tristan pulled away from her and paced outside the car.

"Get to my parents? I don't understand. Why now? What's changed? They haven't done anything different in the last fifteen years." Jessica pressed.

"I don't know. I can try to get ahold of the CIF surveillance data to see if I can figure out what. Somebody's worried about something." Tristan shook his head. He caressed Jessica's worried face. "Go take care of your family. I'll be back in a little while." He kissed her gently and started to get into the car.

"Tristan?"

"Yes?"

"You aren't going to ask me what I think they're worried about?" Jessica queried cautiously.

Tristan was curious but knew this wasn't the time. He hesitated, then shook his head. "No. If you think it's something I should know, you can tell me later. I don't want to know right now." He kissed her again, got into the car, and left.

Jessica went inside to talk to her parents.

Tristan got out of sight of the house and hailed Cmdr. Baxter. He apologized for his insubordination and informed the man of the progress they had made. He also inquired about what they were watching for with Mr. and Mrs. Deacons at this strange and apparently uneventful juncture in their lives.

Cmdr. Baxter was unable to give him any insight. He thanked the young man for his call and his apology. "You're an insolent little... well, let's just say you're... proficient at your job, and leave it there."

Tristan grinned at the man's restraint. "I appreciate the professional courtesy despite my earlier actions. I apologize for any difficulties I caused you."

Tristan informed the man he would be removing any surveillance devices from Saul and Kay Deacons' bedroom shortly and advised him to jack up the gain from devices in other rooms if he felt it necessary. After completing that call, he hailed Agent Gershom, and the two discussed the situation. Tristan informed the man that he would let him know in a day or two if the damage had been sufficiently repaired. If all was well, he would need an engagement ring and a lawyer to begin the legal preparations for his marriage to Jessica.

HOSTAGES

Bam! Bam! Bam! Bam! Danyl and his family were sitting down to dinner when the pounding at the door interrupted their personal time. Visitors this late in the day never brought good news.

Danyl smiled reassuringly. "Don't worry, it's probably somebody passing by and smelled your mother's delicious cooking. Go ahead and finish eating, but don't you boys eat everything before I get back. Save a little for me."

Opening the front door, he was greeted by a hooded figure. Danyl raised his candle higher. The added light revealed the troubled face of Nasha. The look confirmed Danyl's suspicions that the news was not good. "Nasha, come in. Warm yourself by the fire."

Danyl stepped over to the fireplace. He tossed two more small logs in and rearranged them to aerate the dying embers.

"Thank you, Magistrate. Winter is wasting no time in coming this year. I've not seen it get steadily colder in the fall like this before."

"You're right. It usually goes back and forth for a time before the cold sets in. It seems that each day has been getting a little colder than the one before."

The two men sat opposite each other where two benches in the room were angled in front of the fireplace. Assuming he had been traveling hard for an extended time to reach him, Danyl started to offer Nasha something to eat and drink. Before he could get the words out, Danyl's wife carried a tray into the room with two bowls of stew, bread, and two cups of tea. She quickly passed a warm, soothing bowl of stew and steaming cup of tea to their guest. Handing the second set to her husband, she politely joked, "If I hadn't brought these to you now, those boys would have downed the entire pot of stew."

Nasha thanked the woman for her kindness as she left them to their business. He paused a moment before taking the first bite.

Danyl smiled faintly with approval. "Please eat. Pateras has already blessed it."

Nasha's thankful smile was barely noticeable in the dim firelight. He gulped down three large bites before explaining the reason for his late visit. "Magistrate, I wasn't able to bring Slaina's family from Somi. They're being watched. I half expected they had been detained. Governor Pravin is still clearly interested in them. It's as though he's waiting for something. Since Slaina is here, I could only deduce that he's expecting some type of outcome here. Magistrate, has anything changed with Slaina? Has she had any visitors or have you seen anyone new in town?"

Danyl sat his food down and paced. Had Jedrek lied to him? He pondered the possibilities for a few minutes, then turned to answer Nasha. "Jedrek is here, along with four men who guard him."

"The governor's nephew? Why is he here? Does he know this is where Slaina is? Has he seen her?" Nasha was nearing the point of all-out alarm.

"Finish your stew. He knows she is here and has had interaction with her twice already. It appears they are attempting to put their relationship back together. I believe Pateras has touched Jedrek," Danyl was disturbed by Nasha's news, but not alarmed.

Nasha took two more large bites as he considered what this might mean. Just before the third bite went into his mouth, he asked, "Is Marek among Jedrek's guards?"

Danyl sighed. "Yes, he is. He seems to follow Jedrek's lead. He hasn't harmed or even attempted to harm Slaina."

Nasha looked at his half-eaten meal. He wanted to finish, but a new sense of urgency hit him. "Marek must have orders that Jedrek isn't aware of. I have to get to him immediately."

Danyl sat down and picked up his own bowl. "No. Marek thinks things are going according to plan right now. I need you to go to Somi and get her family out. It's possible Marek's given orders to the others to be followed if he were unable to complete his task. I'll see to her safety. Rest here tonight, and tomorrow morning I'll send four men with you to help get them out. You may have to resort to trickery to retrieve them. Have you warned her cousin's family?"

"I did, but they didn't want to leave until they knew the others were safe." Nasha finished his bowl of stew and sipped his tea.

The two continued to discuss ways to smuggle the family out of the city without being seen. An hour later, Danyl showed Nasha to a guest room. As Danyl walked away, a wave of doubt washed over him. He was taking a substantial risk in trusting Nasha. The man had done nothing to cause this doubt, but he was still a Somian, and he had little to go on but Nasha's word.

Danyl shook off the doubts. Halyn trusted him. There was little reason to question him.

Danyl hurried to tell his children goodnight. He hoped all questions and doubts would soon be laid to rest.

Early the next morning, Danyl ordered the troops and supplies he needed. He returned to his home as his family and Nasha were sitting down to breakfast. He sat quietly with them. The commotion of four boys and a three-year-old daughter served to only frustrate Danyl as he mulled over whether Nasha was trustworthy. A stern look from their father calmed the children quickly.

Danyl's doubts about Nasha's loyalties and devotion to Pateras reached a climax. He decided to put his fears to the test. "Nasha, would you do us the honor of asking Pateras to bless this meal and this day?"

Nasha nodded humbly. His face displayed both the honor he felt at being asked and his pleasure at the thought of entering the presence of one as magnificent as Pateras. The soldier in him felt undeserving of such an honor. The commander in him followed orders. He stood and extended his arms with his hands open over the table, as if to cover it with his words. He bowed his head in reverence to the greatness he was about to address. "Pateras, thank you for the many gifts and blessings you have given us, gifts we are undeserving of. Thank you for this food you have provided for us. May it strengthen and enable us as we serve you this day. Bless those who prepared it. Forgive yesterday's shortcomings and go with us this day as we seek to serve you with all our being. Pateras... we do not know why you have entrusted us with your Promised Son. We do not deserve this honor, but we vow to do all that we can to protect him and the family you have allowed him to be born into. Help us keep your will at the center of all that we do this day." A hint of emotion caused Nasha's voice to crack briefly as he spoke out of the fullness of his heart.

Danyl smiled as Nasha completed his prayer and blessing. His doubts melted away. No man could fake this emotion. It was nearly impossible to describe to someone who had not experienced the presence of Pateras. Reaching out and seeking favor from one so great yet so benevolent, knowing the magnitude of one's own failures produced an extraordinary mixture of undeserved love, gratitude, and sorrow. This was a thing so powerful it was capable of overwhelming the strongest of souls.

The family's breakfast reverted to business as usual for Danyl. He reminded his sons of the chores that needed to be done before leaving for school. Lilla interrupted. "Papa, I wanna go tuh 'cool too. When I be big enough for 'cool?"

Danyl finished his last bite, picked her up, and hugged her. "You're special, Lilla. You get to do all your learning here at home with Momma. The boys are the only ones who have to go to school. They have to share their teacher. You get Momma all to yourself."

"But I wanna go tuh 'cool too," the little girl whined.

"When you pray to Pateras, tell him about it. Maybe he can arrange for a school for girls," Danyl teased, thinking if he put her off on Pateras, he wouldn't have to deal with it again. Little did he know this subject was far from dead.

The little girl's brothers knew better than to tease her. They had paid for such trespasses numerous times. Previous transgressions had evoked an ear-piercing shriek from the child unmatched by any other, followed by swift punishment from either parent. They couldn't help but giggle and scoff at her suggestion. Hearing them, Danyl gave all four boys a scowl that quickly quieted them.

The boys headed off to tend to their chores, and Danyl's wife cleaned the breakfast dishes. Nasha thanked her for her hospitality and delicious meals.

Nasha followed Danyl to the town hall where they met with the wagon, troops, and supplies Danyl had prepared early that morning. Danyl briefed the group, then gave them a farewell blessing. "May Pateras go with you, keep you safe on your journey and fruitful on your mission."

The group rode out slowly until they passed through the city gates. Turning east, they picked up speed. They rode hard and set up camp late, while they were still a four-hour ride away from the city of Somi. The men sat around the campfire and discussed the plans for getting the family out of Somi unnoticed. They were uncertain about Nasha's plan and offered alternative ideas. Nasha assured the men it would work. "Trust Pateras and your own magistrate. This was his plan."

The men woke at sunrise and rode more casually around the south side of Somi to a recently burned-out home and barn. They stopped and looked around, uncertain why they were there. Nasha seemed unusually quiet as he looked around.

"Sir, what are we doing here?" Winton asked.

Nasha stuck two fingers in his mouth and whistled a loud, piercing tone, then waited and listened. The men scanned the area to see who or what Nasha was signaling, but they heard nothing more than the sounds of birds chirping, roosters crowing, and dogs barking. The barking grew louder. Bracken placed his hand on his dagger in case the animals were wild or dangerous. As the dogs came into view, the men could see there were two of them, and they were running as fast as they could at

Nasha. They were large herding dogs. They jumped onto Nasha, knocking him over. The men started to rescue their leader when they realized Nasha had done nothing to protect himself, and he was not fighting for his life but laughing and smiling. He was petting the animals, not fending off a vicious attack.

"What is this place?" Shula asked.

"This used to be mine. Governor Pravin apparently repaid my desertion by burning my home and my barn. I'm just glad the dogs weren't hurt. I had a caretaker that would come by and look after the place from time to time." Nasha dusted himself off and walked over to the wagon. He lowered the back and ordered the two dogs into it. The well-trained animals jumped in and lay down in the back.

"You brought us here to pick up your dogs?" Shula's irritation was evident on his face.

Nasha smiled. "We're going to need them."

"Two dogs? We need two dogs? Why?" the man groused again.

"You'll find out soon enough." Nasha closed the wagon. He swapped places with the wagon driver, who mounted Nasha's steed. "Give me an hour to get into the marketplace before you enter the city. Ask for directions to the best inn in town, the stable, the pubs, and the marketplace last. If anyone gets suspicious, they won't be surprised to find you in any of those places, and they won't know where to look for you first."

The men acknowledged their orders and followed Nasha until they reached the edge of a wooded area outside the city walls. They stopped at a stream, watered their horses, and refilled their canteens, while Nasha headed into the city alone.

As a soldier, Nasha had kept his face clean-shaven. Since he left Governor Pravin's employment, he had allowed his beard to grow. The magistrate of Nazar didn't require his troops to be clean-shaven. The guards at the gate could recognize him, as he used to command a good portion of the Somian troops, but he hoped his beard had grown enough to hide his face sufficiently.

Nasha pulled the hood of his robe over his head and stuck two wads of cloth scraps into his cheeks to change the shape of his face slightly. The cloth in his mouth would alter his speech patterns enough to hopefully make them unrecognizable.

His choices were prudent. Nasha recognized the soldier who greeted him at the gate. "Where are you from, and what is your business in Somi, friend?"

"I'm comin' to the market to sell the last of my harvest. Sold all I can in the countryside to the south. Thought I'd try sellin' what I got left here. It was a good harvest. Wudn't too hot, too dry, or even too wet this year. I could use another harvest like this one next year." Nasha droned on about the weather and his harvest until the guard got tired of listening, which took all of two more sentences.

The man walked around the wagon suspiciously. He grabbed the tarp covering the cargo area and flipped it back brusquely, only to be greeted by the two snarling dogs. The man jumped back three feet, drawing his sword.

Nasha turned around to calm the dogs. "Easy now. Settle down." He glanced at the unnerved guard. "I'm not as young as I used to be. I keep the pups around to protect my harvest. They're good guard dogs. I've had 'em since they were pups. Haven't had a bit o' trouble with thieves since I started bringin' em."

The guard attempted to derail Nasha's discourse. "Why do you have four horses for such a light load?"

"For one, the load wasn't this light when I started. I sold off a bunch to folks south of here. Second, I need to pick up a full load of wood on muh way back home. It's gonna take all four horses to haul that wood back. I need to build…"

"All right, go on about your business." The impatient guard waved Nasha on through. He didn't care for being startled. He thrust his sword into its sheath, then grabbed a drink of water from his canteen to settle his nerves.

Nasha pushed on through the gates and headed for the stables. He dropped off his wagon and the horses, but kept the dogs with him as he made his way to the market. It was the time of day when the women would be out doing their daily shopping. Nasha already knew where Slaina's home was and could recognize her family on sight. He had been one of those responsible for bringing the family in when Slaina's parents were publicly flogged. Nasha found a vantage point from which he could watch several things at once. The position he chose gave him a place where he could see the men who were surveilling Slaina's family, the road his own men were traveling to enter the market, and Slaina's home. Slaina's father, Garand, and oldest brother, Eston, worked at a construction site along the northern wall. They had to be at work already. Her eight-year-old brother, Orun, was in school. Luisa, Slaina's mother, and her two sisters, Faris and Irana, tended to their home.

Nasha saw many women in the market, but Slaina's mother had yet to appear. He began to worry they had been removed when her twelve-year-old sister stepped outside to dump out a chamber pot. The girl returned inside, calling out to someone in the house. Nasha wasn't certain who was still there, but he was relieved to know where part of the family was located. He glanced down at the marketplace in time to see his men enter the area. Pulling his dagger from under his robes, he reflected the sun's light, catching the eye of one of the men. He signaled one of them to meet him at the edge of the market. The others split up and meandered about, perusing the items for sale there.

Braken, the highest-ranking soldier of those traveling with Nasha, met with him. "Slaina's mother hasn't come down here yet," Nasha told him. "Most of the other women are already there. I saw one daughter, so I know some of the family are still in the home. One of you should stay with me. Send someone to the steward to arrange for a booth for us in the marketplace for the next three days. We need a space at the edge, so we can leave quickly. Get one of the others to book rooms at the inn for all of us."

Braken glanced around, making sure they weren't attracting any unwanted attention. "Where do you want the fourth man?"

Nasha glanced around as cautiously. "Keep him someplace close where he can watch and assist us if needed. Everyone will need to be where they can see Slaina's home when her father and brothers come home tonight. I want all four of you to be able to recognize them. If I'm spotted, I'll be arrested, so you will have to get Slaina's family out of here."

Braken surveyed the area and found a place to put his man. He returned to the other three and gave them each their assignments. He chose to stay with Nasha himself. The women of the city began leaving the marketplace. As the market became less crowded, Luisa and her two daughters emerged from their home. They chose a route that would afford them the option of avoiding their neighbors.

Nasha didn't move to intercept them. He waited and watched as the two men on a nearby rooftop moved to a position where they could continue to observe the mother and her daughters.

Braken looked back and forth between the family and Nasha. "When do you plan on making contact?"

Nasha shook his head. "I can't. Those two are watching her. They know me personally. They'll recognize me. You need to approach, casually. Don't give them any reason to think it is anything but chance. Tell her Slaina is safe and we're coming to get her and her family out tomorrow. Have her keep her younger son home from school and bring him to the market early tomorrow. The busier it is, the easier it will be to escape. Tell her you'll let her know where to go tomorrow morning. Assure her we'll get her husband and son out as well."

Braken nodded. He was as skeptical of trusting this Somian as Danyl had been. So far, everything he was doing made sense, but Braken preferred to do this his own way.

Nasha had taken the time to introduce his dogs to Braken and the other men. The dogs were familiar with their scents before any of them entered the city and knew their master trusted them. Nasha didn't typically bring the animals into town. Only a couple of people knew he owned the dogs.

Braken headed into the market ahead of Luisa, taking one of Nasha's furry companions with him. If anyone recognized the animal and questioned him, Braken knew to say the dog had wandered into his camp south of the city a couple of days ago. He moved past several booths, stopping at one selling fruits and vegetables adjacent to the one Luisa was currently doing business in. He couldn't make out exactly what was being said, but her voice was strained, and there was a look of pain on her face. The only thing he could make out was, "… but I don't have that much."

The vendor coldly took some of the food from her basket and returned it to its bin. "Sorry, I can't help you. That's all I can give you for that price."

Braken stayed close to the entrance and picked up two melons. One was clearly a good one, and the second was not. As Luisa left the vendor's tent, she turned toward home. Braken took a step toward her. "Excuse me, ma'am?"

Luisa looked up nervously. She glanced around, thinking the stranger must be talking to someone else. Seeing no one near them, she answered, "Yes?"

"I'm sorry to bother you. My wife usually picks out the melons for our family. I'm passing through, and I'm not sure which of these melons is the better one. Could you spare a moment to help me?"

The vendor came rushing to Braken's side. "I can help you with this. You don't want help from the likes of her."

Luisa's face fell. She reached down for her younger daughter's hand to make a hasty escape to protect her little one from a potential barrage of foul language and hateful insults.

Braken was nonplussed by the abrasive vendor. "Sir, unless you have tasted this woman's cooking and know it to be offensive to the palate, I would trust her to have more discriminating tastes as a patron than you. You seek to make a profit as a vendor. She seeks to please her family. If I don't care for her opinion, then I will ask for yours."

The man returned an angry glare. "Suit yourself," he muttered as he walked away.

Braken turned back to Luisa. "I apologize for his rudeness. Can you still help me?" He smiled gently at her.

Irana was enamored with the dog at his side. "Can I pet your dog?"

Braken knelt beside the dog. He hoped it wouldn't be a problem. Setting the melons on the ground, he petted the animal reassuringly and guided the girl to the dog. He showed her how to let the dog get her scent first, then showed her how to pet the dog gently.

Irana petted the animal gleefully, and the dog seemed to enjoy it. "What's his name?"

"Her name is Sash." Braken watched them interact for a moment before he picked up the melons again. He smiled at the little girl. "Do you like melons?"

"Yes. Momma, can we get a melon?" Irana pleaded. "We haven't had a melon in a lonnnnng time."

Luisa sighed. "Not today, Irana."

Braken stood and addressed Luisa again. "So, how do I determine what's a good melon and what isn't?"

Luisa instructed him on sniffing the melon and reviewing the texture and color on the outside. Braken put her teaching to the test and decided on three melons. He asked Luisa bluntly, "If you were purchasing a melon, would you buy these?"

"Yes, I believe you have chosen good melons." Luisa looked at two men who stood at a distance, watching her interactions. She knew they were looking for Slaina to return. What she didn't know was that they expected Nasha to return to liberate her family. She took comfort in their presence because she believed it meant her daughter was still alive and out of their grasp.

Braken turned to the vendor. "How much for three melons?"

The vendor was still glaring at Luisa. "Three bits."

"Three bits! I knew you weren't to be trusted," Braken complained.

The vendor came rushing out of his booth, ready to assault Luisa. "Just what did you tell this man?" He raised his hand to strike her.

Braken stepped between the two. His imposing physique stopped the man in his tracks.

"The woman hasn't said a word about you or your business. You've revealed yourself to be untrustworthy. She's told me nothing but how to pick out a melon. What has this woman done to harm you? You've done nothing but insult her from the moment you laid eyes on her."

Sash, sensing the tenseness of the situation, stood and faced the vendor, growling softly at him. She stepped closer to the now nervous vendor.

The man decided the melons and their price were not worth this much aggravation. "Two... two bits for three melons. It's my final offer."

Braken smiled. "So, you can be reasonable. Two bits for three melons and an apology to the lady and her daughters for your rudeness."

"But you don't know..."

Braken was still holding two melons in his arms and a third in his hand. He squeezed the one melon in his hand until it burst.

Seeing Braken easily crush the melon with one hand, the man envisioned what the brawny man might also do to him if he didn't comply. The merchant stepped back toward his booth. Sash barked loudly and growled again. The man looked over at Luisa. "Madam, mistresses, please forgive my rudeness. I apologize."

Luisa nodded. "I will forgive you if you will treat me fairly from this day forward. I have done nothing wrong. No matter what Governor Pravin believes, I raised my daughter properly. What happened to her was out of my control."

Braken looked at Luisa sharply, yet kept silent.

Something touched the vendor's heart. Sometimes parents could do everything right, and their children still chose to do wrong. "Forgive me. Perhaps I misjudged you." The man retreated to the rear of his booth and busied himself with organizing his already organized supplies.

Braken placed the two melons discreetly into Luisa's basket. He pulled the two bits from a pouch on his belt and laid them in the vendor's view on a counter, and nodded his thanks. He turned to Luisa and asked softly, "Do you believe Slaina carries the Promised One of Pateras, as she said? Do you think she dishonored her family?"

Luisa panicked. "Who are you? What are you doing?" This man's accent confirmed him to be a visitor to the region. How did he know Slaina?

Seeing she intended to run, Braken picked Irana up and held her. "Irana, tonight you get to eat melon. Eat as much as you can and don't let it go to waste."

Faris, now as frightened as her mother, spoke up. "Momma?"

Braken answered before Luisa could address Faris. "Faris, your sister Slaina is safe. I've come to take you to her. The trip will be dangerous. Luisa, come early to the market tomorrow and bring your son Orun with you, along with the girls. I have friends with me and one of us will tell you where to go. You must trust us. We serve Pateras, and we believe what Slaina has told us. Bring only what you absolutely have to. It must be carried in this basket or worn under your clothing. Anything else will look suspicious. The men who are watching you know someone is coming to free you. Don't give them reason to suspect anything."

Luisa wanted very much to look at the men she knew were watching her.. "How do I know you speak the truth?"

"I was hoping the gift of two melons, my declaration of dedication to Pateras, and my kindness to you would be sufficient. I'm not sure there is anything else I can do except to ask you to please trust me. The choice is yours. Those men aren't watching to see if Slaina returns. They're watching to see if a friend of ours is coming to help you. They know he betrayed the Somian army and helped your daughter escape. He saw the messenger of Pateras and has sworn to protect Slaina and your family with his very life if needed." Braken gently handed the child in his arms back to her mother. "Trust us. Trust Pateras. Eat well tonight. You will need your strength for tomorrow. Remember, come early to the market."

"A Somian soldier helped Slaina?" Luisa mentally rifled through the information this stranger was feeding her. She finally settled on the most important things. "I believe Slaina spoke the truth about the child she carries. How early do you need us here?"

"Just before the rush. The market needs to be busy if we are to escape unnoticed."

"What about my husband and our other son?"

"We will get them out another way. Trust us." Braken turned to leave her. After taking two steps, he stopped and held the broken melon up. "Thanks for your help with the melons. Could you also point me toward a good inn?" he called out.

Luisa pointed toward the largest inn in the city.

"Come, Sash!" Braken called, then walked away from the family. Knowing he couldn't turn back without being watched, he headed directly to the inn.

Along the way, he met Leesil returning from a meeting with the marketplace steward. He had secured them a spot at the northern side of the grounds. The two men headed to the inn and took a nap, knowing they would need the rest for later.

As the sun began to set, Leesil, Braken, and Wintin gathered at the edge of the marketplace. Shula stayed with Nasha after Braken left. Nasha and Shula met the other three near a fountain in the center of the market. Most of the merchants had closed and headed home. Only those intent on causing trouble would remain in the area. Sentries were moving through, lighting oil lamps. Nasha saw what appeared to be construction workers coming from the direction of the construction site.

"Gentlemen, get your wineskins and canteens out. Drink liberally from them. Act as though you're having a good time."

Shula looked up, confused. "You want us to act like we're drunk? On water?"

Nasha, perturbed by the young man's lack of understanding, explained, "Unless someone samples your canteen, they won't know it's water."

It took the younger men a minute to get into their roles. Nasha and Braken laughed loudly and drank deeply of their water-laden wineskins. Nasha helped the men get into character by telling them an amusing story from his past. In a few minutes, he had all of them exuding mirth.

Most of the men gave the group of rambunctious loiterers a wide berth. The last two to come through were Slaina's father and her oldest brother.

Nasha motioned to the others when he spotted the two. Garand and Eston tried to alter their route to avoid the noisy bunch. Nasha nodded at Braken, who was getting into the spirit of Nasha's plans. Braken stepped directly into the path of the two. He asked loudly in a drunken tone, "Why do all the men in this city seem to be avoiding us? Doesn't anyone want to relax after a hard day's work and enjoy some libations? Can you tell me why that is?" Braken grabbed the older man and pulled him into the circle.

Garand's face was clearly troubled. "Please… allow us to pass. We're late getting home. My wife and daughters are expecting us."

Nasha stepped close to the man. As the light hit his face, the man gasped fearfully as he recognized Nasha. "You—you're the one who…"

Nasha shoved his wineskin into the man's mouth. "Why don't you have a drink and loosen up?"

His expectation of wine caused him to gag and choke. As the taste of water pushed its way through the fear and worry, Garand stopped struggling. Nasha laughed loudly. "I think he likes his wine strong." The men around them joined the raucous laughter.

Nasha pulled Garand in closely. He softly ordered the man to drink slowly from the wineskin. Eston tried to push his way into the circle. He was a skinny fourteen-year-old boy and no match for the brutes rousting his father.

Seeing he wasn't in as much trouble as he thought, Garand pleaded with Nasha, "Sir, he's just a boy. Let me send him home to his mother."

Nasha nodded, grabbed the boy by the back of his neck, and placed him face-to-face with his father. Garand grabbed his son by the front of his tunic. "Eston, you must run straight home. Don't stop anywhere. Speak to no one. Do not come back here, no matter what. I'll be there as quickly as I can. Obey me, no matter what! Do you understand?"

"But Papa…"

"No! Do as I say and nothing else. Tell your mother only that I was delayed, and I will be home soon." Garand shook his son to enforce his point.

"Yes, Papa." The boy tried hard to control his emotions, but tears forced their way out of his eyes.

Braken leaned forward and spoke so softly that only Nasha, Garand, and Eston could hear. "Tell your mother that your father is with the man who gave her the melons. She will know he is safe. Obey your father, and he will only be a few minutes behind you."

Although he was terrified, Eston managed to nod his agreement. Nasha still had his hand on the back of the boy's neck. He shoved the young man out of the circle in the general direction of his home. Eston stumbled, then took off running.

Braken backed away and encouraged the others to keep laughing and talking loudly as Nasha filled Garand in on the plan to get his family to safety.

When he finished, Garand looked into the eyes of the man responsible for punishing him and his wife. "Why are you doing this?"

"I serve Pateras. I'm sorry for what I allowed to happen to you and your family. I helped Slaina escape. Governor Pravin will use you to hurt Slaina if I don't get you out. I owe you, her, and Pateras at least that much. Do not tell anyone you've seen me. If they know I'm in this city, they'll arrest your family again and hold you until they find me. Do you understand?"

Garand nodded nervously. "You'll take us to Slaina? You're certain she's safe?"

"She's safe for now. If we don't get you out of here, I can't guarantee her continued safety. Are you ready to go home now?"

Garand nodded.

"Oh, no! My wineskin is empty! We need to go back to the tavern! Besides, this man doesn't seem to enjoy our company." Nasha shoved the man roughly aside, and the group moved noisily through the streets. As they rounded the far side of the market, Braken circled back and got into a position where he could watch the family's house without getting the attention of the soldiers watching it.

Nasha called the men together and briefed them one last time. Tomorrow, everything would come together. If his plan worked, in two nights, they would all be home in Nazar. Nasha smiled to himself. Nazar—home. It was a comfortable thought.

Garand made his way home as quickly as he could. His wife and children were relieved to see him enter alone and unhurt. Their evening prayers to Pateras were filled with thankfulness and requests for safety.

Luisa and Garand had a lot to discuss that night.

DAMAGE CONTROL

Tristan stepped into his apartment and sighed with relief. He hoped the worst was over. He changed out of his uniform and grabbed his gear. Testing his scanner near his own bed, he found two listening devices, which he promptly removed while conveying a verbal message to whoever was listening. "Don't even try to replace these devices near my bed."

If something were to develop with Jessica, he wanted to know they were truly alone. Their relationship was already on display. Their intimate moments deserved at least a modicum of privacy. In keeping with that line of thinking, he disconnected the computer connections from his bedroom as well. Tristan moved to the living room and again sent a verbal message to those he knew were listening. "Agents Gershom and Wallace, I apologize if I seemed too pushy today. I was only trying to do what needed to be done. Forgive my impertinence, please."

As expected, a hail promptly appeared on his computer. Agent Gershom's face greeted Tristan on the screen. "Chief Alexander, please allow me to apologize again for making your job difficult. I promise we will do our best to stay together on this from now on. You really are good at your job."

"Thank you, Agent Gershom. I wish Agent Wallace shared your sentiments." Tristan watched Agent Gershom's eyes flick slightly off to the side, then instantly back to the center. Agent Wallace was obviously present, but out of sight. Tristan never flinched, so as not to reveal what he had learned. "I'm headed to the Deaconses' home to remove the surveillance devices. To avoid suspicion, I may have to remove some of the peripheral devices. You'll have to revert to using the computer connections to monitor them until you can replace them. Just remember, don't replace the ones in their bedroom. Are we clear on that point?"

Agent Gershom gave an annoyed, "Yes, we're clear. Are you certain it's safe to leave a dead zone in their home?"

"Yes, it's perfectly safe. Everyone needs a safe place to go where they can be themselves and be alone. Let them say what they want in there. They won't act on it as long as their children are at risk." Tristan kept his voice calm and confident, despite his anger and disgust.

The one thing he couldn't assure them was that Saul and Kay wouldn't take advantage of the lack of surveillance and indoctrinate their children about the tenets of the Ancient Texts and the following of Pateras. Tristan had no knowledge of Pateras or the dangers associated with that knowledge. Information about Pateras was strictly guarded, and someone well above him decided he didn't need to know anything about Pateras at this time.

Tristan concluded his business with Agent Gershom and jumped on the nearest public transport to travel to the Deaconses' home. He had released the private car upon returning to his apartment. He assumed he would either escort Jessica back to her own apartment or she might stay with her parents overnight. He wanted to be very certain he didn't give her the illusion of being alone, even in an automated private vehicle. He also didn't want her to make the mistake of becoming intimate with him for the wrong reasons. Tristan rubbed his face to try to erase the arousing thoughts from his mind. He wanted to be intimate with her, but somehow the timing was always wrong.

Tristan leaned back and felt the warm sun coming through the windows of the tram. The warmth and brightness transported him back to his youth when he would play an intricate strategy game opposite his caretaker in the sunroom of his group home. He had quit playing the game after he left and joined the Infantry. It had become more work than fun those last few years. Somehow, this assignment was beginning to resemble that game.

The tram stopped several blocks from the Deaconses' home, giving Tristan a little time to walk and think. Every step seemed heavier than the last. His thoughts were jumbled. He could sabotage this mission easily. They would never be able to prove what he had done. What would it cost him? Promotions? His job? A more important thought occurred to him. What would happen to Jessica and any children she had? Someone was using her and her children to keep Saul and Kay in line. From the pieces of the puzzle he had assembled so far, the couple's oldest daughter had been killed to secure their cooperation. Somebody considerably above his own pay grade had invested a lot in this mission. They were apparently willing to sacrifice more lives to accomplish their goals. If he didn't see this through, someone with no conscience would. He hated to admit it, but he cared for Jessica and her family. Would he still be able to pull this off? What if he had to take the family and disappear? It would take a lot of time to accumulate the money and resources to disappear. He didn't know how long this assignment would last.

Tristan stopped directly in front of the house. He stared at the pleasant, warm, inviting structure. In his mind's eye, two children chased each other about in the yard. He saw Jessica, Saul, and Kay sitting on the porch enjoying the sight. Then his vision took a sudden ugly turn. A mysterious dark stranger appeared from the bushes and shot the children. Tristan watched the imaginary children fall to the ground. He heard Jessica screaming hysterically as she raced to gather their lifeless bodies to her. The vision progressed in slow motion as though it wanted him to savor every second. He could feel the hearts of Saul and Kay break as they watched the drama unfold in front of them.

The images faded from his mind, and he shivered. He had to go through with this… for her. He hoped she would still have him.

Tristan caught sight of the curtains moving in the living room. In a moment, the front door opened, and Jessica walked slowly down the sidewalk toward him. "Tristan?" She stopped a few steps short, trying to make out the look on his face. "Why aren't you coming in?"

His gaze was still fixed on the house, a suburban family home. His eyes were stuck on the sight and everything it represented. He forced himself to look at Jessica's face and rode his emotions into her life. "I was afraid." His short, nondescript sentence spoke more than Jessica could understand.

Jessica took another step toward him. "Afraid? What are you afraid of?" The idea of anything frightening him was laughable to her, but the look on his face kept her from laughing.

Giving his emotions free rein for once, he let a single tear escape. "Afraid of losing you. Afraid I would no longer be welcome here—I don't want your parents seeing an enemy every time they look at me."

Jessica viewed him as her rescuer again today, not the cause of the day's troubles. She held her hand out to him. "Let's go inside and talk to them."

He looked down at her hand and wanted to take it, but something held him back. "Jessica, I promised your parents I would remove any surveillance devices, and I'll do that. The second they leave the house, the authorities can reinstall them. You can't expect to ever be free of this."

Jessica smiled weakly. "We know that. Tristan, I love you. Please take my hand. You're scaring me now."

Tristan took her hand and followed her into the house. He set to work removing the devices as promised and disconnected the computer accesses in the bedroom. He explained to Saul and Kay that they could no longer access the computer relays in that room, so if anyone tried to contact them during the night, they would have to leave the room to answer the hails. His face displayed defeat. "There are undoubtedly other devices in the rest of the house. I can remove them if you want, but they'll only replace them the second both of you are away from the house."

Saul and Kay exchanged knowing glances. "Leave the others in place. As you said, it would be pointless to remove them. Is there a way to be certain they haven't reconnected the computer access in the bedroom?"

Tristan showed them how to make sure it was disconnected. There was one quick and easy disconnect they could use at will if they desired.

Tristan finished and started to leave. Jessica grabbed onto him. "Mom, Dad, can we sit down with Tristan and talk? He thinks you hate him."

"Tristan, we don't hate you," Kay assured him.

Saul scowled. "I do think we need to talk. Let's go to the dining room. Kay, could you fix us some coffee?"

"I should go. I'm not sure there's anything to discuss. Every time you look at me, you're going to see an enemy. I love Jessica, but I can't come between you and her. I can't stay here knowing you think I'm spying on you or here to intimidate you," Tristan argued.

Saul folded his arms across his chest. "I don't think you can tell me what I do and do not think, young man. I think you owe me the chance to speak my own mind. I will allow you to do the same. Go sit down now."

Tristan's emotions peaked as he realized he had worked the situation around to a probable win. He forced himself to focus on the negative side of things to keep the downtrodden facade. He hesitated before moving to the dining room as ordered.

Saul left Jessica and Tristan alone while he went to help Kay with the coffee. She didn't need any help, but he wanted a moment alone with her. "Kay, I need to ask you what your thoughts about Tristan are before we go back in there."

"I don't know, exactly. He's extremely… I'm not sure how to describe it. He seems like he's got everything ordered in his life. This is the first time I've seen or heard about him having a bad day. He strikes me as being too together. Whether he's here to spy on us or not, I can't say for certain. It seems they've already been spying on us. Why would they even need him?"

"I agree. We haven't interacted with him that much. I think we need to get to know him a little better." Saul picked up the creamer and sugar and set it on the serving tray. He carried the tray into the dining room.

After the pleasantries of serving coffee were complete, Saul got to the point. "Chief Alexander, I do not know if you are here to cause problems for us or not. It would seem to be a bit of overkill, in my opinion, for someone to purposely place you in our lives. We appreciate your help in getting us out of that situation today and removing the surveillance devices. The issue that concerns us is that things with you have been too perfect."

Jessica jumped in. "Too perfect? You got arrested today! How is that perfect?"

Tristan responded, "I'm not sure I understand."

Kay tried to explain his statement. "I know we haven't spent very much time together, but you are too perfect. We have to ask ourselves why. We're not saying circumstances are perfect. Your actions today got us out of jail, but you're just a chief. How could you pull that off?"

Jessica became distraught. "Mom! Dad! He rescued you. Does it really matter how?"

Tristan listened carefully to their concerns. "Mr. and Mrs. Deacons, this is the kind of thing I'm worried about. I don't want to have to explain myself every time something goes wrong in your lives. I am a former Covert Ops officer. It's my job to be in control of my emotions and my situations at all times. I got you out of that situation because I manipulated those in charge. I took a little bit of knowledge and used it to my, or rather your, advantage."

"Mom, he's not perfect!"

Tristan glanced at Jessica with a perturbed look. "Thanks for that vote of confidence, Jess."

Jessica returned a reassuring smile. "What I mean is, he was really nervous about meeting you and talking to dad. He may seem like he's calm and in charge, but he does have emotions and fears." She squeezed his hand as she thought about their conversation outside the house an hour ago.

Saul asked bluntly, "Do you still intend to marry my daughter?"

A thick silence filled the room. "I want to marry her very much, but..." Tristan felt Jessica's grip tighten on his hand. "I don't want to cause a problem for the two of you. Sir, I may not understand these marital traditions Jessica told me about, but I do understand one thing now. I really need your blessing if we are to go any further."

Saul looked over at Kay, who could provide no proper answers for him. She finally plied him with one small piece of advice. "Saul, we know who is in charge. I say we take a step of faith here."

Saul knew she meant Pateras was in control, not the Commonwealth brass. She was advising him to leave it in Pateras' hands. Saul switched from rank to a more personal form of address. "Tristan, I choose to believe you aren't here to cause us any problems. You have our blessing to marry our daughter."

Tristan looked at Jessica and smiled. He squeezed her hand tightly. "Thank you, sir. I swear to you, I am not here to hurt you or her in any way."

Jessica leaned over and wrapped her arms around his neck and kissed him.

Tristan stood and pulled Jessica to him. His arms wrapped around her, and a multifaceted feeling of relief flooded his body. For a second, he thought he could protect her from anything. He gave her an impassioned kiss. Holding onto the feeling of relief, he smiled and whispered, "I love you."

Without completely releasing her, he turned to his future in-laws. "Thank you for trusting me and giving me your blessing." Tristan offered Saul his hand to shake.

Saul gave Tristan a hard look before shaking Tristan's. "Don't betray my trust. Earning it back is far more difficult."

"I understand, sir—I won't let you down, I promise." Tristan turned to Jessica. "I need to go to work. Are you staying here, or should I escort you back to your apartment first?"

"It's so late in the day, do you really need to go into work?" A soft whine permeated her voice.

Tristan pulled her close again and kissed her forehead. He smiled. "Jess, I know my job is more… lax than most other CIF posts, but technically, I'm AWOL. Do you remember Capt. Barrett asking me to stop by his office?"

The morning's terror made it difficult for her to remember even seeing the man, let alone remember what he said. "Are you going to get into trouble because of me?"

Tristan smiled reassuringly. "No, probably not. He'll want a full explanation, and he may even ream me out for not attempting to notify him, but I'd have to screw up much worse than this to get fired as an intern."

Jessica squeezed his hand. "I'm going to stay here with Mom and Dad for now."

"Tristan, we'd like the chance to get to know you better. Why don't you come back here for dinner this evening? You can escort her home after dinner." The things Kay had experienced fifteen years ago had toughened her. She wasn't nearly as upset by the events of the morning as Jessica was. She didn't need Jessica to stay with her as much as Jessica needed to remain with her own mother and father.

"Thank you, ma'am. I would love to join you for dinner. I'd like to spend some time getting to know you as well."

The four exchanged a few more pleasantries before Tristan excused himself to get back to his work.

An hour later, he found himself stepping into the office of a disgruntled Capt. Barrett. Knowing how he felt about the military pomp and circumstance, Tristan managed to avoid any attempt at saluting, yet he had to assume the posture of a soldier standing at ease. It was now only an hour before the end of the business day.

"Nice of you to show up today. I see you finally lost the desire to salute."

"It's a conscious effort, sir."

"The salute or showing up for work?" Leland groused.

"The salute, sir. I apologize for not giving you a heads-up about what was happening this morning. Someone decided I wasn't working fast enough and tried to give me a little push. They nearly screwed up my case." Tristan held his posture as Leland wasn't quick to offer him a seat. Tristan assumed his boss was trying to keep a degree of pressure on him. Unfortunately for Leland, Tristan's knowledge of power plays and human behavior kept the young man from feeling uncomfortable or even remotely rattled.

"Would you care to fill in the blanks?"

"Of course, sir." Tristan proceeded to report the entire chain of events to Capt. Barrett.

The more the young man told him, the more aghast Leland became. He slumped in his chair, feeling as though half the military was about to bang angrily on his door. "And you called back and apologized to everyone you... bullied?"

"Yes sir. I know I stepped on some toes. I wanted to make sure there were no hard feelings. Everyone else was doing their job the same as I was. I needed to come off looking like a hero to Jessica and her parents. Jessica wants to see me as the hero. Her parents aren't convinced that I'm not culpable in this situation, but they are voluntarily choosing to accept me at face value for Jessica's sake."

Leland rubbed his tired face. This young man and his case were going to be the death of him. "All right, take a seat. Is there anything I need to do at this point?"

Tristan sat down and grinned mischievously. "You're playing the part of the kind, understanding boss who gently reminds me to call in if I'm not showing up for work due to a family emergency."

Leland squinted and folded his arms across his chest. He regretted allowing the young man to sit so soon. "This wasn't your family."

Tristan continued to grin. "All I lack is the ring and a romantic dinner."

Leland still didn't like having this outsider in his department. Nevertheless, the young man's exciting success spilled over onto him. He futilely resisted the urge to smile. A crooked grin crept across his face. "I guess I need to put you in for that promotion, then."

"As much as I would like that, we'll need to time it right. I can't get a promotion that coincides with my engagement, wedding, or the birth of our children. That would look suspicious."

"You're scheduled to take one more semester of classes, then you'll be paired with a senior forensic accountant to complete your so-called internship. You'll have internal training to complete while you train with the senior accountant. I'm going to pair you with Riley for that. He actually seems to accept you. We could time your promotion to coincide with the completion of your external classes. That would give it the appropriate credibility. You could always ask her to marry you at that point."

Tristan nodded. "That works. I'm going to save some credits to see what I could reasonably afford. After I purchase the ring, I'll turn the receipt in to Agent Gershom for reimbursement into a private account. I wouldn't want my new wife finding my hidden stash."

Leland shook his head. "No wonder you're good at your job. You are so cold and calculating. If you ever have to investigate me, just tell me point blank. I'll confess and surrender on the spot."

"Duly noted, sir." Tristan grinned. All his superiors needed to believe he was not emotionally invested in this case, or they could pull him off it. Or they could feasibly leave him in place yet drop him out of the loop when things started going off script and enact those extreme sanctions. This case was going to be very involved. "If you don't need me any longer, I'll go get my official report done, then I'm having dinner with my future family."

"They aren't too stressed over the situation this morning to have dinner?"

Tristan got to his feet before answering. "No, they're made of some pretty stern stuff. Jessica's freaked out. I get the feeling she's got some post-trauma psychosis or something."

"From what?"

"There were some problems when she was seven years old. Her parents were arrested, and she had an older sister who was killed. I think today's situation reminded her too much of the past."

"Okay, do what you have to do and consider yourself verbally scourged for not telling your boss you had an emergency. Dismissed, Chief."

"Thank you, sir."

Tristan spent an hour filling out his report, including as many details as he could recall. He filed the report, then hailed Jessica to let her know he was heading back for dinner.

The group had a pleasant meal, and the events of that morning seemed to be behind them.

Tristan let his curiosity get the best of him. "Mr. Deacons, have you talked to your own supervisor at work? Did you tell him what happened?"

"I told him the authorities picked us up. I didn't give him the specifics, but I told him they were concerned about a potential security breach on the project. I assured him the matter had been cleared up. Kay and I are working on the same project from different departments. She told her supervisor the same things. I expect things will be tense for a few days at work, but they should be fine. The authorities will back us up on this one."

Jessica shook her head. "What happens after I graduate and get a common job? How do I explain this stuff to my employer if it happens again?"

Tristan reached over and squeezed Jessica's hand. "Tell them your parents are working on a government project and you were brought in for your own protection due to a security breach. The authorities will confirm your story."

Jessica shivered. "You said that far too easily. You told me if you ever lied to me, it would be believable, but I thought I could see through that kind of stuff."

"Jess, I told you. In my former occupation, if people could see through my lies, it could get me killed. I'm trained to be good at it. I'm also a law officer. I'm here to protect the innocent. That would be you. I'm not going to lie to you unless it involves a case I'm working on. I swear it." Tristan raised his hand as though he were taking an oath.

Saul and Kay exchanged worried looks. This man was making no bones about being able to lie, and he was apparently good at it. The story he proposed was believable. Should they trust him?

Tristan caught sight of their expressions. "I'm sorry if this worries you. Jessica and I have already had this discussion. If I'm investigating a case, I can't discuss the contents of that investigation. I'll be investigating corporate espionage, tax evasion, embezzlement, and other white-collar crimes. She'll be working in that area. What happens if I'm investigating the company she's working for? It's a clear conflict of interest. As a former Covert Ops officer, I'm practiced at lying, and it was part of the job. I gave her my word I wouldn't lie to her about my feelings for her. I also warned her I would lie to her if it involved my job." Tristan scowled. "I mean, if it involves a case. Speaking of which, I learned something today." Tristan's mood lightened suddenly, and his eyes danced. "After next semester, if I pass my classes, I'm getting my next promotion. I'll be working with a senior agent and completing my in-house training. I'm going to need that promotion... and pay raise."

Kay smiled. Her face gave way to a mischievous expression. She managed to wink at Tristan without Jessica seeing.

"Congratulations, Tristan. Were you planning on saving for something specific?"

Tristan grinned. "Oh yeah. I've had my eye on this fishing boat at the marina."

Jessica smiled in anticipation of his response, but those were not the words she expected to come out of his mouth. Her jaw dropped abruptly. "What? You are not!"

The three laughed playfully at her. Tristan grabbed her hand and kissed it gently. "You know I'm joking. My next large purchase will be for you and only you."

The rest of the evening went smoothly. Tristan called for a private car and gave Jessica a few minutes alone with her parents before escorting her to her apartment.

The car stopped in front of her building. They spent a few semi-intimate minutes in the back of the car. Tristan pulled back from their embrace and eyed Jessica skeptically. "You sent Maddy a message not to come down here, didn't you?"

Jessica bit on her lower lip. She nodded slowly.

Tristan grinned. This job was getting harder. He pulled her close again and kissed her passionately. "You little imp. You knew I asked her to meet us," he whispered.

Jessica giggled. "I think I'm ready now."

Tristan sighed. "Jess… not yet. Today you've been in freefall one minute, and seven G's the next. This is something I really want to be right. I want it to be on a day that's been nothing but pure joy. I'll walk you in, but I'm not coming inside. I need to go home and take a cold shower."

Jessica's face fell. "Tristan, don't you want to sleep with me?"

Tristan adjusted the temperature controls to a cooler setting in the vehicle and pulled his collar away from his neck. "Oh, definitely, I do." He stopped as he tried to explain his situation. "Do you remember when you asked me to ask your dad's permission to marry you?"

"Yes." Her tone had grown colder.

"You said he would give me a list of expectations."

"What did he say? Did he tell you not to sleep with me? As you pointed out, I'm a grown woman. I can make my own choices." Jessica looked as though she were ready to tear into somebody if she didn't get some suitable answers.

"No, not specifically. Your father asked me to respect you. I also promised your brother I would take care of you and your family while he's gone. Robert said you were raised with some expectations regarding marriage and… intimacy. He asked me to respect those expectations. Please, allow me to do this for you and your family." Tristan watched her face for a reaction. It was hard to make out what she might be thinking.

Jessica finally explained what was running through her mind. "I'm not sure whether to be flattered or angry. I'm also not sure who to be angry with, you, my dad, or my brother."

"If anger is the direction you're leaning, I vote for your dad or brother to be the cause. Unfortunately, I'm probably the true cause. I would really prefer that you be flattered. There's one more reason. Jessica, in my previous duty post, I did a lot of unpleasant things in the line of duty. Using women was part of the job. I don't want to be that man anymore, and I never want to look at you like one of them."

Jessica blinked back tears. Tristan was confused. Where were the tears coming from? "Jess, what did I do wrong?"

"My dad and my brother are right. I wasn't raised like the rest of the Commonwealth. My parents taught me to wait until after marriage to be intimate. You were right to respect that. I'm the one who's in the wrong here. I'm sorry for putting pressure on you. Thank you for your wisdom and your restraint." Jessica jerked the door handle and escaped from the car. She ran toward the door to her building.

Tristan caught her. "Jessica, please don't leave upset like this. I love you, and we will be together, just not yet. Let me walk you to the door… please?"

Jessica nodded. The lump in her throat wouldn't allow her to speak now. She was angry with herself for giving in to something she didn't believe in. The stress of the day was taking its toll on her.

Tristan touched his bracelet to signal Maddie again, then wrapped his arms around Jessica to comfort her. He escorted Jessica to the door and held her there for a few minutes whispering gentle reassurances to her. He promised to call her when he got home. Tristan opened the door and found Maddie waiting for them. He left her with the brief explanation that it had been a rough day. He knew if Jessica asked him one more time, he would indeed stay the night.

It was late when Tristan finished his cold shower and crawled into bed. He fell asleep quickly but was awakened two hours later by a persistent hail. Tristan tried to answer the hail from his bed, only to remember he had removed the computer link from the bedroom. Stumbling to the living room, he mumbled to himself, "This had better be important."

The hail opened to reveal the face of Lt. Cmdr. Robert Deacons. "Chief, I know it's late, and I apologize for waking you in the middle of the night, but I have to go on duty, and this is the only time I could talk. I spoke to Mom and Dad earlier. They told me what happened today. Thanks for taking care of them— I appreciate the help. I didn't expect a problem so quickly after I left."

Tristan wiped his eyes, trying to clear the cobwebs in his mind. He groaned as he tried to put his thoughts into words. "No problem. I'm sorry it happened. I want... I want you to know that I had nothing to do with them getting arrested. I rattled some cages today, and I don't think anyone will bother your parents again. I got the feeling they were using my relationship with your sister as leverage to remind your parents to stay on the straight and narrow path."

Robert looked away and spoke slowly. "Chief, I don't know if you're on the level or not. Dad said he was choosing to trust you. Maybe that's a mistake, but I'm going to make the same mistake. Nothing like this has happened in years. Why it started now is a mystery. I don't know the reason for it, but I doubt you're the one to blame."

Tristan scowled. "I just thought of something. What if they aren't trying to send a message to your parents? What if they're trying to send a message to you and Jessica? Your sister reminded me tonight that she's a grown woman and can make her own decisions. Maybe they're trying to keep you and Jessica from making poor choices."

Robert nodded. "I suppose that makes some sense. What I don't understand is, I'm a member of the CIF, and a lieutenant commander, no less. How is that making a bad decision? Jessica is dating you. That wouldn't be a bad decision either."

Tristan shook his head. "I don't know. I'm spit balling here. It's the middle of the night. Don't expect me to make too much sense. Everyone's been thinking this is about your parents. I just thought, what if this is about you and Jessica instead of your parents? "

"You said Jessica reminded you she's a grown woman. Did you two have another fight?"

Tristan rubbed his face again. "No, I wouldn't say we had another fight. We did disagree about something. She wanted me to spend the night with her. As you can see, I didn't do that. Today's events were very stressful, and I wasn't about to take advantage of her emotional situation. We left each other on good terms."

"It wasn't about me again, was it?"

Tristan smiled. "No, not directly. Although our discussion the other day did affect the conversation."

Robert rolled his eyes. "It's a good thing I'm gonna be gone for a while. I'm not sure your relationship could survive my hanging around."

"How long are you going to be gone?"

"I'm not sure, somewhere around six to nine months?" Robert knew he was keeping Tristan awake and proceeded to wrap things up. "Listen, Tristan, I wanted to thank you again for looking after my family. I guess you're one of us now, so whatever happens between you and Jessica is between you and Jessica. Welcome to the family."

"Thank you, Robert. Keep us posted on your itinerary. I'm hoping Jessica and I can be married while you're home on leave."

Robert smiled. "That's great. I look forward to meeting your family."

Tristan grinned sheepishly. "Unfortunately, I don't have a family to meet. Your family will be all that I have. I was raised in a children's home. I've never met my family."

Robert's face sobered. "I'm sorry, Tristan. I didn't know. Does Jessica know?"

Tristan nodded sleepily. "Yes, she knows. We don't talk about it much. I think she's afraid talking about it would be too painful for me. It's not. My parents died when I was an infant, and I was raised in a great home for kids. They encouraged us to excel in all areas of our lives and apply to advanced placement academies early on. I thought it was awesome at the time, but looking back on it, it took kids out of the welfare system and put them on the military budget. In any case, I'm making something good of myself and not living in the streets or being re-educated every year."

"You have an incredibly pragmatic view of things. I know I woke you, so I'm gonna let you go back to bed and I need to get a bite to eat before I go on duty. I look forward to talking to you again sometime. Goodnight, Tristan."

"Goodnight, Robert." Tristan wandered off to bed and hoped tomorrow would be a better day.

ESCAPE FROM SOMI

Early the next morning, Luisa headed to the market with her children in tow. The older children carried a basket and a bag each. No one noticed they were dressed more heavily than normal. They carried a few personal belongings in their bags and baskets. Luisa made sure the baskets appeared to be empty. She hated going to the market at this time of the morning. Those she had once considered friends and neighbors now treated her badly because of Slaina. The entire city's population had heard about Slaina's unborn child and believed Louisa and her husband to be unfit parents for allowing such a thing to happen. Louisa understood their thinking, but how they could be so cruel to her and her children, she didn't understand.

Going after the morning rush meant there was less chance of being mistreated. Today she was trying to get out there early. At such an early hour, she hoped she would be ahead of the other women of the city. A surge of adrenalin raced through her. Her children weren't fully awake yet. They had no idea what the day would hold. Luisa carried Irana on her hip and pulled Orun by the hand. As much as she wanted to run, she forced herself to stroll toward the market with her head down to avoid eye contact with others.

The two men assigned to keep watch over the family were unprepared for the premature departure. The night chill left them stiff and slow. They abandoned their uneaten morning rations to follow their charges. Luisa and the children were nearly out of sight before the two could follow them.

Wintin watched the family and their chaperons as Garand and Orun left their home to head to work. He was ready to move and tired of sitting still. Wintin followed behind the two guards from suspension bridges above the city, designed to allow pedestrians to cross the city more directly. He passed over the market and crossed to the northeast corner, descending from the overpass into the construction site.

The walls protecting the city were partially constructed from the outer walls of homes built atop each other, but Governor Pravin had learned there were better ways to build his walls. The construction sites were places where the governor was removing the living quarters and replacing them with more fortified barriers. Men were fortifying small sections of the wall at a time. Wintin had scouted the area out the day before and found an uninhabited section of the wall. He chose an empty home for them to make their escape from. Each of the homes was constructed with a small window in the wall big enough to allow a man through. There were also small windows facing the inside of the city. To discourage the construction workers from entering this particular apartment, Wintin poured a bucket of water on the steps leading to it. During the night, the water froze, leaving a treacherous path in the early morning hours. He expected the ice to melt around the middle of the day, and expected their rescue efforts would be complete long before that happened.

Garand and his son started their day as usual. He had been told which apartment they would escape through. As he worked, he kept one eye on his son and the other on their intended escape route. An hour into their day, he spotted Wintin.

To help guide Garand and his son across the icy path, Wintin strung a rope tied to the windows along the walkway. Wintin stepped into the apartment and looked out the outer window. Seeing his comrade on the ground below him, he stepped back outside the apartment and nodded to Garand.

Garand snatched some supplies he had prepared that morning and handed them to Eston. He told the boy to take the supplies to the man at the edge of the construction site.

Eston pulled back in fear. "But Papa, he's one of the men from last night."

Garand glanced at the men walking around him. "Eston, listen to me. That man did not harm me last night. None of them did. They are here to help us. Take these supplies up to him and stay with him. Hold on to the ropes along the walkway. There's ice on the steps. Do exactly as I say, and do it now!"

Eston nodded, feeling the stranger's eyes on his back. He turned around and climbed the steps to the apartment several levels up. Using the rope along the walkway as his father instructed, he stepped nervously into the empty habitation.

Wintin took the supplies from the boy. They included a rope, a hatchet, and a small tarp. Wintin handed one end of the rope to Eston. "Tie this end off around that support beam. Make it good and tight."

Eston took the rope and moved toward the beam. Not understanding the situation, he turned to confront the man working near the window. "Who are you, and what are you doing? Why should I do what you want?"

Wintin stopped what he was doing and stepped toward the young man. "Eston, I'm here to help you. I don't have time for long explanations, but I'm trying to get you out of the city and someplace safe. I'm sending you and your father out that window, so tie this off quickly and securely. I don't want that rope to slip and hurt you."

Eston wasn't entirely convinced. "Why did you harass my father last night?"

"They did it to keep us safe, Eston." Garand's voice came from the doorway.

Eston balked again. "But I don't understand. He tried to hurt you."

"He wasn't trying to hurt me. It was a distraction. Eston, the governor has guards watching our every move. If this man and his friends are caught, they can't help us."

"Why do we need help? Papa, I don't understand." Eston's voice got louder as he grew more upset.

Garand grabbed the boy and shook him. "Eston, Governor Pravin wants Slaina dead."

"It serves her right for what she did. She broke the law and her marriage engagement. She disgraced herself and us," Eston spat bitterly.

Garand's eyes grew large. He was at a loss as to how his own son could want his sister dead.

Seeing Garand paralyzed by shock, Wintin stepped in. "Your sister has done nothing wrong. Pateras chose her. Even her fiancé knows this. He is with her now, asking her for forgiveness. Whatever has made you angry over this, you need to let it go. Did Pateras teach you to withhold mercy and forgiveness?"

"No, but the law…"

"She never broke the law. It looks that way because Pateras has power we do not know and ways we don't understand. I believe she has spoken the truth, and I believe Pateras has seen the goodness in her heart and chosen to use her. She agreed to this, knowing what it could cost her. Your sister is a brave woman."

Garand recovered enough to speak again. "Governor Pravin wants Slaina dead, and he's not afraid to kill us to get to her. Son, your sister didn't break her vows or betray Jedrek. Whether you believe her or not, for our own safety we must leave right now! Do everything this man and his friends tell you. Your life is at stake, as are the lives of your mother, brother, and sisters… and mine. Do you want to see your family killed over this?" Garand wasn't as concerned with his own life, and he hesitated to mention it. It occurred to him that his son might need to hear exactly what was at stake. "Can you do what this man tells you?"

The boy had been angry and fearful before, but now the anger was replaced with a double portion of fear. He nodded to his father. "Yes, Papa." His anger at how people treated his parents after Slaina's situation was discovered, was no longer important now that he realized his sisters' and younger brother's lives were at stake. If anyone was innocent in this situation, they certainly were. The adults around him continually condemned his older sister and his parents, but his siblings were victims.

The boy picked up the rope and tied it off as instructed while Garand and Wintin formed a sling with the tarp and the rope. Wintin tested the length and strength of the rope. With the sling now attached, he tested it one more time by throwing the sling out the window. The length was perfect. The sling settled two feet off the ground.

Wintin turned to Garand. "You first."

"No, send my son first," he objected.

"Garand, it will take the boy and me together to lower you slowly and gently to the ground. I can lower the boy myself. I can't do that with you. He will be right behind you," Wintin argued. Every second the two were out of sight, the chances of someone raising an alarm increased.

Seeing the wisdom and feeling the time crunch, Garand got into the sling as Wintin took the hatchet and removed the wooden crossbars from the window. He hoped the nearby sounds of construction would mask the noise.

Garand climbed into the window. He looked at the ground five stories below him. Working as a builder, he was accustomed to heights, but this seemed different. He took one last look at his oldest son. "Eston, do as he says. Everything will be fine."

Wintin and Eston got a firm grip on the rope. Garand eased himself out the window. He felt the tension tighten on the rope. They lowered him slowly toward the ground. He looked down as a rider with a spare horse approached. The rider was one of the men who had accosted him the previous night. This time the look on his face was one of concern, not drunken tomfoolery. Garand searched the top of the wall above. Sentries passed by, watching the horizon. Garand muttered a quiet request: "Pateras, please don't let them look down."

The sling swayed gently and scraped against the wall as it descended. The longer it took for the thing to descend, the faster Garand's heart beat. To his relief, the rope finally stopped him slightly above the ground. Leesil was ready to help him out of the sling the second it came to a stop. Leesil signaled Wintin when Garand was on his feet. Wintin pulled the rope up quickly.

One of the sentries glanced down at the base of the wall and saw the two men and the sling. He pulled his bow from his back and expertly nocked an arrow. He didn't know who the men were, but he recognized suspicious behavior when he saw it. He fired, narrowly missing Garand.

Leesil grabbed Garand and shoved him toward the horse. "Head for those trees, fast. I'll be right behind you."

Garand heard shouts along the top of the wall. He hesitated. "My son?"

"Go! I'll get him out another way!" Wintin yelled.

Leesil jumped onto his horse as more arrows zipped past them. The two bolted for the wooded area a short distance away. As soon as they were out of range, Leesil led Garand on a northeasterly route, taking them further from Slaina.

Meanwhile, Wintin grabbed Eston and pulled him to the door. "We've got to go another way. If we get separated, head for the sheep pen in the marketplace. Run as fast as you can." Wintin pulled the sling inside and shoved it over Eston's head.

Eston gripped the ropes holding the sling tightly. His fears had stopped his ability to think beyond the moment.

Seeing the boy's white knuckles on the ropes, Wintin repeated his instructions to the boy. "As soon as I lower you down, get out of the sling and run for the sheep pen in the marketplace. Got it?"

The boy gave a dazed nod. Winton shook him. "Eston, repeat that back to me. Where are you going?"

The boy's eyes came to life. "When you lower me down, I run to the sheep pen in the market."

Wintin smiled and winked at him to lighten the mood. "Good boy. Don't look back and don't stop for anything." Wintin brought the boy outside and lowered him over the edge of the patio to the inner stairway below them. Seeing he could go further in the sling, Eston pushed himself off the second level of stairs. The rope took him down to a third, then a fourth level. Wintin smiled when he saw the boy was using his reasoning skills again. Seeing the boy's fear, he doubted Eston would respond well enough to get beyond the first level.

Fearing the rope wouldn't make the fifth stairway, Wintin stopped the boy from rappelling any further and waved him out of the sling. As soon as Eston was clear, Wintin grabbed the rope and rappelled down the wall. He heard the shouts of the soldiers above him, telling him to stop. The guards converged on the room where the three had been moments ago. One guard looked over the edge at Wintin as he lowered himself down the walls and steps toward the bottom. The guard smirked when Wintin glanced up to check on his pursuers' proximity. He pulled his sword and sadistically enjoyed watching the concern well up in Wintin as he anticipated his own impending doom. The guard swung his sword, cutting the rope Wintin was hanging from.

Seeing what was about to happen, Wintin had only a split second to reposition himself. He dropped his feet under him. The tension on the rope collapsed, and Wintin felt himself falling. He hit the steps on the level below, twisting his ankle painfully, bounced off the edge, and fell onto the next level down. The beginning of the next stairway wasn't far, so the fall was short but painful. He attempted to control his landing on the steps this time. He put a hand out to push himself away from the edge, thrusting his body toward the wall, but his own weight caused a painful wrenching sensation in his right arm. The edges of the steps pummeled his ribs, and his head hit the wall with a dizzying blow. Wintin, his head spinning, collapsed in a heap. He was still conscious, but for the moment, he wasn't able to see or hear much.

A second guard had attempted to stop the first man from cutting the rope. The instant the rope was sliced through, the second man gave the first an angry shove. "What did you do that for? Now we can't use the rope to follow him."

The first guard scowled. "Look at him. He's not going anywhere now. We can simply walk down and scrape whatever's left of him off the stairs." The man turned away from the edge and started down the steps. He got two steps down before the ice proved to be too much, and his feet flew out from under him. Having nothing to stop his momentum, he slid all the way to the bottom of the first flight, collecting bruises on his legs, back, and buttocks as he went. When he finally came to a stop, he was too rattled to move.

The second guard stood at the top of the stairs and commented, "You really need to think before you act. You didn't even give me a chance to warn you about the ice on the steps." He looked back to the spot where Wintin had landed. He was gone. The guard cussed under his breath as he tried to spot his escapee. He glanced at the rope along the windows going down the side of the icy stairway. Addressing the other soldiers who had followed him, he ordered, "You two, use that rope to get down the steps as quickly as you can, and find that man. The rest of you head up the steps to the swinging bridge. See if you can spot him from above." The men had not seen Eston, and weren't looking for him yet.

Wintin shook his head to clear it and took several painful, deep breaths. He knew they would come for him soon. He slid down a few more steps until he was sure he had his sense of balance back. He stood slowly and limped painfully down the steps, leaning against the wall for support until his strength returned. Reaching ground level, he turned toward the center of the construction site rather than staying near the perimeter. He removed the hooded cloak he was wearing. Grabbing a wheelbarrow, he tossed his cloak in it and limped slowly toward the market. As he walked, he grabbed a couple of sturdy posts from a stack of lumbar and tossed them in.

A construction supervisor caught sight of him and attempted to interfere. "Where are you going with that? Who are you? I don't know you! Are you trying to steal-?"

The man was promptly met with a couple of debilitating blows to his abdomen and back, putting him on the ground. The abrupt and forceful activity made Wintin's head spin. He stopped a moment to steady himself again, then abandoned the wheelbarrow. He grabbed his cloak and leaned on the post to help him walk. Wintin made his way around the corner outside the construction area and found Eston waiting for him.

Wintin scowled at the boy. "I thought I told you to head to the sheep pen if we got separated."

The boy was beginning to trust this stranger. Despite the warnings about not looking back, he had. He saw Wintin's fall and had come back to help. He was afraid to re-enter the construction area, so he waited close by for Wintin to reach him.

He pulled Wintin's free arm over his shoulders and put an arm around the man's waist to help him walk. The cloak dropped to the ground as the two hobbled as quickly as they could toward the marketplace.

Luisa wasn't sure where she was supposed to go, so she wandered about the market, imitating a shopper. Braken pulled his hood over his head and walked to a stack of melons among the fruits and vegetables near Luisa and her children. He didn't turn toward her to speak. "I hear melons are cheaper at the tent at the far end of the market." He turned and held a melon up. Looking the direction he indicated, Luisa saw another man waving. Setting down the fruit that she was scrutinizing, she took Orun's hand again and led the small group toward the tent.

Another shopper suddenly blocked Luisa's path. "What are you doing out so early, Luisa? I thought people like you and your family didn't come out until the sun went down."

"Please, Rubea, not in front of the children. Let me pass."

"I didn't think you believed in raising your children properly, Luisa. Isn't that why you were flogged in the town square?"

Luisa felt her face flush. "Rubea, please, let us pass."

Rubea started to lecture Luisa mercilessly. Braken walked past the women, then stopped and turned around. "Rubea? Is that you? It's been some time since I saw you. Are you still hanging out in the local pubs?"

Rubea stopped berating Luisa. Braken stopped behind the woman, forcing her to turn her back on Luisa. Rubea's face turned bright red. "See me? In the local pubs? What are you…? I don't…" the woman sputtered.

Luisa and her children slipped past and hurried away from her. Several bystanders enjoyed seeing the spiteful woman get a taste of her own medicine. As soon as Luisa was clear, Braken grabbed the woman's hand and kissed it firmly. He announced loudly, "Rubea, it was so nice to see you again. I'm sorry I missed you last night. We must have been in different pubs. Oh well, maybe next time."

Rubea pulled her hand roughly away from the large man. "I have never frequented a pub!"

A merchant who had long been a friend of Luisa's family responded, "So you only show up occasionally?"

The woman pulled an apple from her bag and threw it at the merchant, who caught it and took a bite out of it. "Thanks," he mumbled as he chewed. Rubea turned and stomped off.

Luisa rushed her children into the tent at the end of the marketplace. She was greeted by Shula, who pulled her to the wagon waiting at the back edge of the tent and helped her and the children in.

The crowded marketplace, as expected, made it easier for them to lose their guards. Braken made sure the guards weren't following, then helped load the wagon with the supplies they had come in with to obscure the family from sight.

Shouting from overhead attracted the attention of the patrons and shopkeepers and the Nazaran rescue party. Guards from the walls ran across the suspension bridges above them. Nasha took one look around and knew something had gone wrong. "Be ready to move when the dogs reach the wagon. Drive out of here slowly until you are out of sight of the city, then push the horses as hard as you can. Don't wait for the rest of us."

The two men finished loading the wagon, and Shula scrambled into the driver's seat. He waited and watched the surrounding activity anxiously.

Nasha kept his head down as he mounted his horse and raced for the sheep pen. The pen was large enough to be a clear meeting place, busy enough to stay hidden, and a great place to create a diversion. He ran straight into Winton and Eston. Seeing his companion's condition, he dismounted quickly. "How badly are you hurt?"

"I twisted my ankle, wrenched my arm, and I think I cracked some ribs."

"Can you ride?"

The man shook his head. "Not very far. I've got a nasty bump on the head, too."

Nasha sighed. It could have been worse. "Get on my horse, ride over to the wagon, and get in it. Leave the horse behind for me." Nasha helped the man into the saddle and practically tossed the boy on behind him. The two rode toward the tent.

Eston had seen Nasha when his parents were publicly flogged, but in the rush to get Winton back to the market he didn't realize who he was.

Nasha saw guards coming down a stairway from a platform at the center of the market where the swinging suspension bridges converged. More guards were coming from the construction area, checking everyone wearing hooded cloaks. Nasha smiled. This could take them a few minutes—the cold weather had brought out lots of cloaks.

Nasha's dogs were waiting patiently at the far side of the sheep pen. The sheep's owner was leaning against the gate, waiting for buyers. The man was the same height as Nasha, but he weighed a good deal more. Having no desire to harm the man or get himself hurt, Nasha said, "Excuse me, sir. I need to create a diversion so my friends can get out of the city unnoticed. Would it be all right if I turned your sheep loose in the market?"

The man stood upright. "You want to do what?"

Nasha smiled again. Now that the man was no longer leaning on the gate, he would be easier to move. "Thanks." He elbowed the man in the gut. Using the flat of his sword, he swept the man's legs, taking him to his knees.

Nasha sheathed his sword, threw open the gate, and whistled shrilly. The dogs barked and jumped into the rear of the pen. The sheep jumped back and forth for a moment, then flocked together and pushed their way out of the gate. They tried to stay together, but they were quickly channeled to whatever empty pathways they could find. The mayhem created by the frantic sheep and the crowded market clogged the walkways. The guards trying to reach them were facing the sheep head-on. Many tripped and fell as they tried wading through the mess.

Nasha navigated down a side aisle the sheep hadn't found and raced toward the tent. He ran straight into a soldier and former friend he had served with for many years. The man held him at bay with his sword. "Nasha, why did you come back here? You know there's a warrant out for your arrest."

Nasha backed away slowly. "I'm not here to hurt anyone. I'm here to save lives. Sometimes Pateras asks things of us that are beyond the ways of men. Let me pass, Asa."

"I can't do that. If your cause is as righteous as you claim, you will be cleared in a trial."

Nasha shook his head slowly. His attention was on a man standing behind Asa. Braken was bringing Nasha's horse to him. "Asa, if I'm arrested, I won't live to see a trial. Governor Pravin wants me dead for betraying him. I'm doing this to protect the Promised One of Pateras. The young woman who was betrothed to Pravin's nephew carries the one who will redeem us in the eyes of Pateras."

Asa shook his head. "The Promised One of Pateras? Tell Governor Pravin about this. Surely he would spare the woman's life."

Nasha kept his hands up in surrender as he stepped closer to his former friend. "He already knows. He wants her dead anyway."

Asa shook his head. "I know he doesn't serve Pateras, but he wouldn't dare cross him. He knows better."

Nasha inched forward until the point of his friend's blade was against his chest. "Something evil fuels him. He has never been a good man, but it's more than greed that now propels him. I will not let him hurt this woman. Do what you have to."

Nasha felt his friend's resolve falter when the blade twitched against his chest. Nasha slipped to the side of the blade. "Join us," he whispered as he stepped beside his friend.

Asa shook his head. "You ask too much. Go in peace."

Nasha placed his hand on the man's shoulder in appreciation. Asa lowered his sword and turned around to see that Braken, sword in hand stood a mere ten yards from him. Before Asa could express his gratitude, he heard Nasha's voice. "I'm sorry, my friend. This is for your own good." Nasha punched the man in the face busting his lip, then pulled his sword and knocked him on the head with the hilt. The man dropped to the ground. Nasha retrieved Asa's sword and nicked himself with the point. A smear of blood now adorned the blade.

Braken eyed him warily. Nasha dropped the blade on the ground and glanced around to be certain no one had seen the interaction.

Seeing Braken's skeptical look, Nasha explained, "At least it looks as though he tried."

They mounted their horses and rode for the western gate. The wagon was moving slowly and meticulously in the same direction. Nasha saw Wintin's horse following the wagon with Eston riding it. He turned sharply to Braken. "Why's the boy riding? He'll be seen."

"Wintin says they didn't see the boy escape, and the empty saddle would have gotten unwanted attention. It also keeps the weight down in the wagon in case they need to run. He's hoping they won't know the boy on sight. They've been warned to watch for the family as a whole."

Nasha looked at the increasing activity heading their way. He pulled a small dagger from his belt and pushed his horse beside Eston. He slipped the dagger to the boy, handle first. "Stick this in your belt. Go around the wagon and ride quickly to the gate. If they stop you and question you, tell them you're going spearfishing. You'll make your own spear when you get to the creek. You're in a hurry. The fish are biting. Smile and go!"

Eston recognized Nasha as the man who had arrested his parents a couple of weeks ago. He looked at the dagger fearfully.

Braken, who had helped Eston load Wintin into the wagon, rode up beside Nasha and nodded his approval. Eston's anger welled up again. He took the dagger and pointed it menacingly toward Nasha. "I should use this on you for what you did to my mother and father."

Nasha understood the boy's hatred. He grabbed Eston's tunic. "Listen, boy. I know you hate me, and you should, but if I don't get you out of this city, your father will hold me accountable. You keep that dagger with you and follow the western road past Helia and across the bridge into the Nazaran Province. If I make it there alive, feel free to seek whatever justice you believe you are entitled to. I won't fight back. Right now, you need to go. The guards are about to close the gates. Go NOW!" Nasha released Eston's tunic, then kicked the horse's rear to encourage it to pick up the pace.

Eston galloped ahead of the wagon and got to the gate. A guard stopped him and asked him where he was going.

"Fishing," came his curt reply.

"Where's your fishing pole, boy?"

"Going spearfishing, and I'll carve me a spear when I get there."

"You don't sound too happy about going. Is there a problem?"

"My friends left without me early this morning. We had a bet about who could get the most fish." Eston was a quick thinker.

The guard nodded. "I see, so they're probably way ahead of you by now. Well, hurry along then. If you win the bet, though, bring me a fish for my dinner."

Eston smiled. "Yes, sir!" He pushed his horse to a trot on the road, picking up speed as his path cleared.

The wagon was stopped right in the gate when a cry came from above: "Close the gate! Nobody gets out!"

Nasha looked over at Braken and said one word. "Bait!" He pulled his hood off and kicked his horse roughly.

The horse took off past the wagon. Nasha kicked the soldier who tried to stop him out of his way. Braken knew if he stayed behind the wagon, he might also be trapped inside the city, but he was hesitant to leave the wagon unprotected. Shula didn't attempt to move the wagon yet. He just turned around and appeared to watch the commotion.

The guards above them recognized Nasha and reiterated the call to close the gate. Braken took off after Nasha, knocking down the guard who was getting back on his feet.

Shula looked at the guard next to him. He was prepared to defend himself and the wagon if needed, but that would produce a chase he didn't want to be a part of. "Sir, should I move my wagon out of the way so you can close the gate?"

"Yes, go on and hurry!" the guard snapped.

Shula slapped the horses with the reins and got them moving. He stayed at a slower pace until he rounded a corner out of sight of the city walls. The second he was no longer visible, he yelled to his passengers, "Hold on! We're going to pick up some speed." He gave them a minute to steady themselves, especially Wintin, whose ribs hurt and whose sore arm and leg prevented him from bracing himself well.

Eston saw the wagon catching him and stopped to wait on it. They slowed to give the horses a chance to catch their breath. Luisa called out to Shula, "Sir, your friend needs tending to. I think he's lost consciousness."

Shula stopped the wagon. Wintin had been shaken so much that between his concussion, pain, and difficulty breathing, he had indeed passed out.

The family had been lying under the canopy with a layer of hay over them to hide their presence. Shula decided hiding them was less necessary now. He pulled the canopy out and repositioned the family on top of the hay for comfort. He and Eston laid Wintin out beside them. Shula handed Luisa some sticks and rags. "We have to get moving again. Try to splint his arm and leg, then cover him with the canopy to keep him warm. Keep the children covered as well. There's a skin of water back there. Get him to drink some if he wakes up."

Before Shula could get the wagon moving again, Eston stopped him. "Where's my father? He got out of the city before we did. Why haven't we caught up to him yet?"

His questions got Luisa's attention. She wanted to know where her husband was. Although the question was plaguing her mind, she knew she needed to tend to her children right now. Eventually, she would have an answer, and whether it was a good answer or a bad one wouldn't change what had to happen now.

Shula answered, "Leesil was instructed to lead any troops away from us if they were seen escaping. They are going to head due east for now. That will put them a long way behind us. They'll catch up, but it may take some time. We have to go."

Luisa kept silent, relieved to know her husband had gotten out of the city. Hopefully, she would see him again soon. She didn't want to face Slaina without him. Luisa watched the road behind them. Who would catch them first, Somi troops or the men protecting her husband?

ENGAGEMENT

The end of the semester was rolling around, and Jessica's graduation was drawing near. Tristan hadn't proposed formally to her yet, and she was growing antsy. The day of her graduation, Robert was unable to be there. Tristan hailed him and told him what the family's plans for the celebration were, along with his own intentions. He had the engagement ring in his pocket and planned to ask her to marry him that night in front of her parents. He wanted to time it so Robert could be available by computer hail at the same time.

As with all ceremonies, the graduation speeches droned on, and the ring was burning a hole in Tristan's pocket. He wiggled incessantly during the ceremony, earning him concerned looks from Saul and Kay.

He sat down to dinner that evening with Jessica and her parents to celebrate. The waiter refilled his water glass frequently, which led to several trips to the restroom.

Kay attempted to cover the awkward mood at the table caused by Tristan's case of nerves with polite conversation. "Tristan, how are your job and school going?"

Tristan took another sip of his water and cleared his throat. "Good—great, in fact. I'm done with my external classes. The rest of my internship, I'll be taking in-house training and working with a senior agent on my first actual cases. When I— uh—turned in my grades, they told me that in six more months when I finish my internship, I will—uh—earn my promotion to second lieutenant."

Jessica's face brightened. "Really?"

Saul cocked his head. "You don't need your degree in accounting?"

"No, I need a basic understanding of the principles, and the department teaches me the rest. Um, if you'll excuse me, I'll be right back." Tristan headed to the restroom for the third time since they had sat down.

Jessica watched him go. Fears crowded her thoughts and displayed themselves blatantly on her face. Kay broke the eerie silence. "Is he okay? I've never seen him like this."

Tears welled up in Jessica's eyes. "I don't know. Mom, he still hasn't proposed to me. What if he was using me to pass his classes, and now that he has…?" Her words trailed off, leaving the implication unspoken.

Saul shook his head. "No, I don't believe that. He truly cares about you. It's obvious in the way he looks at you and follows you with his eyes, even when you aren't looking."

A guilty look crossed Jessica's face. "If he loves me, why hasn't he proposed yet? And he hasn't even tried to… well, you know." She had tried to seduce him on more than one occasion, but he had gently declined.

"Saul, why don't you go check on him? Maybe he isn't feeling well, or something could be bothering him, and he doesn't want to spoil our celebration," Kay suggested.

Saul pulled his napkin from his lap and placed it on the table. "All right, give us a few minutes."

Saul walked into the restroom and found Tristan leaning over the sink mindlessly washing his hands with actual water. Most people used ion or chemical cleansers, but sometimes only water would do. Tristan stared at his own reflection as he performed the repetitive motion.

Saul stood in the doorway, watching the young man for a moment. Tristan's trance was broken as he noticed the figure standing behind him, staring at him. He took a deep breath and finished washing. He ran his hands through the hand dryer for the full three-second drying cycle. Turning, he confronted his stalker. "How long have you been standing there?"

"Long enough to see you've got something on your mind. Want to talk about it?" Saul offered.

Tristan looked around the room at nothing in particular. "I've uh—never been in a situation like this before."

"What sort of situation are you in?"

Tristan shook his head. "Maybe we should get back out there."

Saul stepped directly in front of him, blocking his way. "Not yet. You need to know a couple of things first. Jessica is worried and upset."

"Upset? About what?"

"You asked for my blessing to marry her, and you have yet to propose. She's finished school, and apparently, so have you. She's afraid you've gotten what you wanted, and now you're going to break up with her."

Tristan blinked in shock. He turned to pace, then whipped around to face Saul. "Are you serious?"

Saul moved out of the doorway. He folded his arms across his chest and leaned against a nearby wall. "I believe my daughter worries too much and sees problems where they don't exist. Am I wrong?"

Tristan rolled his eyes and shook his head. In a moment, his face brightened as he reached into his pocket and pulled out a small jewelry box. "You're not wrong. I'm not one to discuss my—feelings. I just handle it and move on. I have never been so nervous in my life." Tristan opened the box to show Saul the ring he had been carrying all day. "I wanted everything to be perfect. She deserves a memorable night."

Saul smiled at the sight. He was glad the young man was nervous. He was also relieved to see the ring. It told him the one thing he needed to know: Tristan loved Jessica and was taking the idea of marriage seriously. "Son, tell her what's in your heart. She'll never forget it, even if you get tongue-tied and stumble over the words. She's not going to care if you're getting rained on, if you tripped the waiter, or if you spilled food on your clothing. All she wants to know is that you love her and want to spend your life with her."

Tristan flinched at the last phrase. He decided Saul meant it metaphorically, since the likelihood of their marriage lasting the rest of their lives was fairly small. People just didn't do that. He refocused his attention on the earlier parts of what Saul was trying to tell him and nodded nervously again. "I've never asked a woman to marry me before. My last job, I had to uh—do a number of - unsavory things in the line of duty. Mr. Deacons, I think I'm more scared now than the time my cover got blown and I faced a dozen angry arms dealers."

Saul looked around momentarily as he formulated a plan to snap the young man out of his fear. "I think you should walk away now. Don't even say good-bye. Slip out of the restaurant and disappear."

Tristan's smile faded. "Excuse me?"

"If you're this afraid to ask her to marry you, then you must not care enough about her to make this marriage work. Walk away, right now."

Tristan shook his head. "I can't do that. Why would you suggest such a thing? You know how I feel about her." Some things that played into his nerves he couldn't discuss with Saul. A lot more than a marriage hung in the balance.

Tristan glanced at the bracelet on his arm. Every word the two were saying was being monitored. He wasn't sure where Saul's new attitude was coming from. "I love her. I want and need her in my life."

Saul smiled again. "Then what are you waiting for? Get out there and ask her to marry you."

"I can't, not yet."

"Why not?"

"I told you, I want it to be perfect. I'm waiting for Robert to hail. I told him what I was planning. He's going to hail me to congratulate her on her graduation. While he's still on, I'm going to propose so your whole family can be there."

"What are you going to do if something happens and he can't hail?"

Tristan froze. "I hadn't considered that possibility. I suppose I will give him until we finish dessert, then go on without him. If that happens, could you do me a favor and record it for him?"

Saul smiled. "Okay, I've got your back. Son, you do need to pull yourself together and do something to settle Jessica down."

"Yes sir. Go on out. I think I need to hit the latrine one more time. I'll be right there."

Saul went back to the table and sat down with the two women. He glanced at Tristan's water glass. The waiter had filled it again to capacity. Saul shook his head. The young man didn't need another glass.

Jessica and Kay looked at him expectantly. "He'll be back momentarily. I think his stomach is a little upset. Jess, see if you can get him to stop by a clinic and get checked out if his stomach is still upset after dessert."

Kay scowled. "Dessert? Is that a good idea?"

Saul took her hand and squeezed it before she could continue the thought.

As promised, Tristan returned momentarily and sat next to Jessica. Picking up her hand, he smiled and kissed it tenderly. "You are the most beautiful woman I have ever met. I hope you can forgive me for being so inattentive tonight."

"Tristan, are you okay? Dad said you weren't feeling well." Jessica's brow was still knit together.

"I'm feeling much better now. Your dad's a great doctor." Tristan squeezed her hand again. "Everybody ready for dessert? I know I am."

Kay gave Saul a suspicious look. Saul responded with a wink. They ordered dessert just in time for a hail to come in from Robert.

Jessica gave Tristan a confused look. "Why is Robert hailing you?"

Tristan responded to Jessica before answering the hail. "Why don't I take this and ask him?" Tristan transferred the hail to the holographic imager on the table so they could all see him. With the activation of the imager, a noise-dampening field activated around the table to prevent the call from disturbing the other patrons. "Hello, Robert. It's good to hear from you. What's up?"

"I wanted to congratulate Jessica on her graduation, and I thought you would know where to find her." Robert had an expectant grin on his face.

Jessica leaned in. "I'm here, Robbie."

His smile faded, and he cringed when Jessica called him "Robbie" again. But since this was a special day for her, he let the matter pass. "Hey, sis, congratulations on your graduation. I'm proud of you."

Seeing his reaction to her address, Jessica remembered his distaste for the pet name and attempted to keep her tongue in check. "Thank you, Robert. I wish you could have been there. I have a copy of the ceremony for you, though. I received a couple of academic awards, too. I hate that you couldn't see it in person."

"Oh, I don't. This way, I can fast forward through the boring speeches and see the important parts: you and your awards." Robert grinned mischievously.

Jessica sighed at her brother's wit. The speeches meant something to her, even if they didn't to him.

Tristan broke out in a sweat, knowing his moment was almost here. He wiped his sweaty palms on his napkin and placed it on the table, then reached into his pocket to retrieve the small but powerful box.

Robert kept glancing back and forth between Jessica and Tristan. He could see his future brother-in-law had a case of nerves.

Robert put aside his teasing. "Jess, I really am happy for you for graduating with honors. I do wish I was there to congratulate you in person and to give you a big hug for that and for what's next."

Jessica laughed. "Yeah, I know. Now I have to find a job. I've already been searching the job market. This is the fun part."

Saul reached over and grabbed Kay's hand. Kay suspected something was up, and Saul's repeated displays of affection reinforced her suspicions.

Robert smiled again. "I'm not talking about what happens tomorrow. I'm talking about what happens tonight."

Jessica blushed. "What happens tonight?"

Tristan stood then lowered himself to one knee, facing Jessica. He opened the small box and held it up for her to see. "Jessica Deacons, would you do me the honor of being my wife?"

The display caught the attention of several nearby patrons, who watched anxiously to see what the young woman would do. Jessica's eyes lit up, more at the sight of Tristan on his knee asking for her hand than at the sight of the ring. Happy tears slipped down her face. She reached out and hugged his neck tightly. "Yes! Yes! Of course I will! I love you so much!" She kissed him, then pulled back to actually look at the ring. "Oh, Tristan, it's beautiful." She stared at the ring in the tiny gift box.

"Would you like to put it on?" Tristan prodded.

"Yes!" She held out her hand, and Tristan slid the ring onto her finger. She admired its beauty for a moment, then grabbed Tristan's neck again.

The other nearby patrons applauded as they saw Jessica accept his proposal. Kay leaned over and whispered to Saul. "You knew about this, didn't you?"

"I found out a few minutes ago. It's why he was acting so squirrelly all day."

Robert smiled from ear to ear as he watched the events unfold. "Congratulations, sis. Congratulations, Tristan. Welcome to the family."

Tristan extricated himself from Jessica's grasp long enough to get off the floor. "Thank you, Robert. I'm glad you got to be here with us, at least in a way."

Kay moved around the table to see the ring and hug her ecstatic daughter. Saul reached across the table through the holographic image of his son and offered Tristan his hand. "Welcome to the family, son."

"Thanks, Mr. Deacons."

"Dad, you couldn't reach around the image instead of through it? You don't know what that does to the image on my screen when you reach through a hologram. I see a hand reaching out of nowhere. It's creepy," Robert complained.

Saul moved around the edge of the table. "Better?"

"Yes, thank you. Listen, I have to go. This is actually my lunch break. I'd like to cram a little food down before I have to go on duty again. Congrats sis, and you too, Tristan. Looking forward to being there for the wedding party. Mom, Dad, I love you."

———————————⬚⋈⬚———————————

Robert closed the hail and headed for the dining hall. He met his friend Lt. Cmdr. Miles Johnson. "Hey Deacons, putting in a quick call home on your lunch break?"

Robert smiled. "Yeah, Jessica graduated from school today, and she got engaged."

Miles looked pained. "Oh no, I was still hoping I had a shot at her. Who's she marrying?"

"Tristan Alexander."

"Wait. What? The ground pounder? And you're okay with this?"

"Yeah, I am. He's really not that bad. He's only made one mistake in his life, and that was joining the Infantry instead of the Brigade. He's making up for it by marrying into the family. I think he learned his lesson. Who knows, maybe I can talk him into transferring someday." Robert tried to downplay their previous rough start.

Miles continued to whine about losing the love of his life to a ground pounder. Robert gave his friend a painful jab in the arm and the ego. "I told you I wasn't going to let you date my sister. She's too good for you."

Two of the waitstaff watched the chain of events from a distance. "Man, your tip just went through the roof. Customers in a good mood always tip well."

"Are you sure? I bet that guy spent everything he had on that ring. He probably doesn't have anything left."

"Oh, I'm sure he kept enough back to impress that girl with more than the ring."

"I hope you're right. Do you suppose they still want their dessert?"

"You better ask if they want it for here or to go."

"You might be right."

The group talked for a while longer, then went their separate ways. Tristan escorted Jessica to her apartment and walked her all the way inside. He sat down in the living room as Jessica excitedly showed off her ring to Maddy. After a few excited minutes, Maddy started to slip out to leave the couple alone. Tristan stopped her. "Maddy, I think Jessica is going to be too wound up to sleep for a while. You might want to call some friends she can show her ring off to. I have an early morning meeting. I need to go home and get some sleep."

"What? You could stay here." Jessica suggested.

Tristan smiled and kissed her. "If I stay here, I won't sleep. I can't be falling asleep on the job. I've got six months left to earn that promotion. I can't blow it now. I'm too close. Want to walk me out?"

Jessica was growing accustomed to him putting her off. She walked to the door with him and stepped out into the hallway.

"Tristan, you said you wanted to wait for a special night. Tonight is special."

Tristan cupped her face in his hand. "Yes, it is. Jess, I want to wait until our wedding night."

"Did my family put you up to this?" she demanded.

Tristan's head bounced back and forth. "Not specifically. They told me that was how you were raised, and I want everything to be perfect. I don't want to interfere with that. Let me do this one thing right for you. Can we please agree on this?"

Jessica's face fell. "If that's what you want, then - I'll go along with it. Yes, I was raised that way, but the way we were raised is what got us into trouble many years ago. I don't want that to ever happen again. I suppose since I've waited this long, what's a few more months compared to a lifetime?"

Tristan's eyes widened. "You mean, you've never?"

Jessica shook her head. "No, I've behaved the way my parents taught me all my life. I just wanted to misbehave one time. They pushed me away from the career I wanted. They won't let me talk about Abigail."

Tristan pulled her close to him. He brushed a stray hair from her face. "After we're married, if you want to go back to school for a different career, I'll do whatever's needed to pay for it. I already agreed to name a daughter after Abigail. You can talk to me about her anytime you want to. How's that for misbehaving? Let's not misbehave on this one point. Can we agree on it?"

Jessica nodded. "Agreed." It seemed he wasn't about to compromise on this. She snuggled into his arms and put her head on his shoulder.

Tristan kissed her goodnight and headed to his apartment for yet another cold shower. He wondered why this was so important to him. This was his first marriage, but it wasn't his first sexual encounter by far. His job over the previous couple of years had opened the door for numerous meaningless encounters. Maybe the lack of meaning before brought him to a point where, for once, he wanted something with meaning.

Early next morning, Tristan was in a conference room in his office with Agents Gershom and Wallace, and Capt. Barrett.

Knowing about the tension between Agent Wallace and Chief Alexander, Agent Gershom took the lead in the meeting. "Chief Alexander, I understand congratulations are in order. Miss Deacons accepted your marriage proposal."

As much as Tristan wanted to throw in a smart remark, he kept himself in check. "Thank you, sir. I did my best."

"What are you planning next?"

"I'll set up an appointment with the lawyers to work out the marriage details. We haven't set a date for the celebration party, so Jessica and I will have to do that after our initial meeting with the lawyers. I plan to set up an immediate two-year contract."

Agent Wallace jumped on his admission. "Why a two-year contract, Mr. Alexander?" Her tone wasn't quite accusatory or snide, yet there was a hint of disapproval.

Tristan peered into her eyes, trying to see her motivation for the question. Unsure of what was fueling the inquiry, he answered plainly. "First of all, Miss Deacons and her family are starting to get past their fears about me. They have some—odd ideas about marriage. If I start the marriage with a one-year contract, it's going to put all of them into an alarm state. Second, you wanted me to saddle her with two children. Since I recently passed several accounting classes with flying colors, I'm pretty sure my math skills are fully functional. It's going to take at least two years to accomplish that. Third, I was told the government could annul my marriage at any time, so I lose nothing if the mission is canceled."

Agent Wallace crossed her arms. "Uh-huh."

Tristan felt the hackles on his neck stand up. He rubbed the back of his neck and forced himself to respond conservatively. "Are you concerned about something in particular, Agent Wallace?"

Seeing the tension mounting between the two, Agent Gershom intervened again. "There have been some—concerns expressed that you may be getting—too emotionally invested."

Tristan stood abruptly and paced around the room. If he got defensive, they would believe he was indeed too emotionally involved. He knew he was in truth quite emotionally invested.

The three watched him pace and waited for his response. Leland knew the conflicts Tristan was dealing with. "Chief, what's the problem?" He chose that particular question to guide the young man in for a safe landing.

Tristan stopped pacing and stared at Leland as he processed the question. His tone started more sharply than he intended, but calmed as he spoke. "The problem is, I'm both angry and frustrated. I've been working hard to complete this mission. You've thrown stumbling blocks at me on two occasions, and the second I get things under control and going the way they're supposed to go, you think I'm screwing up. I'm not sure I understand what the problem is. You wanted me to get her to fall in love with me and agree to marry me. I've done that. Are you asking me to walk away now?"

Agent Wallace reached over and activated a surveillance file of Tristan's talk with Saul Deacons in the restroom the previous evening. She smiled smugly. "You were rattled, Chief."

Tristan smiled just as smugly. He wasn't as prepared as Agent Wallace, but he had a response for her. "Computer, access my Deacons Surveillance Files. Load and play the file of Saul and Kay Deacons' discussion in the kitchen the evening after they were arrested."

The file revealed Kay's belief that Tristan was too perfect and too in control. Tristan raised his eyebrows and nodded at Agent Wallace. "Does that answer your question? You aren't the only one studying the surveillance footage. Agent Wallace, when I am working a case, I take a minor emotion and amplify it in my mind. I ride whatever tiny emotion is going on at the time to achieve the appropriate emotional display. Yes, I was nervous about asking her to marry me. I've never done that before, so I took that small amount of angst and combined it with a little more angst over making sure I reacted as an appropriately nervous boyfriend. It doesn't take any anxiety to drink a gallon of water, causing me to need to use the restroom. Tell me again how rattled I was."

Agent Wallace's eyes launched fiery darts at the young man she clearly despised. "You've got an answer for everything, haven't you?"

"Having answers keeps me alive! You seem to enjoy looking for problems where there aren't any," he retorted. His patience had reached its limit with the woman.

"Answer this one for me then." Agent Wallace played the discussion between Tristan and Jessica about why he was refusing to sleep with her. The tension in the room increased as everyone knew they were getting a theoretical glimpse into Chief

Alexander's sex life. As the last pertinent sentence played, Agent Wallace slammed her hand onto the table. "What's the real reason you haven't slept with her? You got a conscience, Chief? Some standards, maybe? You don't get paid to have those kinds of issues. You're out of control!"

Tristan laughed outright. "I have an easy sexual target, and I'm out of control by not taking advantage of it? Please feel free to check the water usage logs for my shower. Do you even want to know how many cold showers I've taken? Do you want to know why I haven't taken advantage of her?"

Agent Wallace's chilling voice answered, "Tell us it's not because you're in love with her."

"I don't have the file handy, but I'm sure you know where to find it if you want to verify what I'm saying. The night you sent those goons to rough us up, I told her I left Covert Ops because I didn't want to become like one of them. She hasn't asked much about my time in that department, but she knows the kinds of things I had to do. You can tell by the look on her face she knows I've slept with numerous women and I've hurt people. By my not sleeping with her, she knows what I told her about wanting to be a better person than the goons who attacked us is true."

"I want you to sleep with her—tonight," Agent Wallace demanded.

"No. It will ruin my credibility and damage my cover story. You know, we've put a lot into this mission, but I'm about ready to walk away and forget it. You think you know better how to handle this?"

Agent Gershom jumped in to defuse the situation. "Chief, we've looked at your history. You have killed in the line of duty, and you've done it in hand-to-hand combat as well as in firefights."

"Yeah, so?"

"This job calls for extreme measures. I ask you again: can you do that if needed?"

"I'm not sure I know what you're asking."

Agent Wallace displayed another file of a woman from a case Tristan had worked a year earlier. "This is—was Paula Phipps." Her face filled the main screen. "She was a known consort of the arms dealer, Sato Chao. According to the file, you used various methods of persuasion on her to find Sato. Ms. Phipps later died from her injuries."

Tristan paced again, keeping his face from full view. He finally stopped behind his own chair. Grasping both sides of the high-backed chair, he calmly responded, "Everything I did, I was authorized to do. I was well within my mandates as an officer of the CIF Covert Ops and the Principles of Operation."

Agent Wallace leaned forward. "Could you do the same things to your fiancée? Could you kill her if we asked you to?"

Tristan steadied himself, then folded his arms across his chest. "I would need an excessive force dispensation approval in my possession before I would consider such a thing. My records indicate I was transferred out of Covert Ops a year ago. I know I'm still an intern, but I don't think the Financial Oversight Division is authorized for those types of actions."

Leland grinned. "Good man. Always watch your backside."

Agent Wallace stood up and placed her hands firmly on the table. She leaned forward. "If we get the authorizations, COULD. YOU. KILL. HER?"

Tristan knew he would get into trouble if he agreed too quickly. "When I am in the field, I have to make choices, sometimes with only my gut to guide me. I'm no assassin. If you give me full disclosure, and I see her as a clear danger, then yes, I could do it. Under the current circumstances, no, I can't kill her. If she comes at me trying to kill me, I would certainly defend myself, but even then I would more likely arrest her. You want me to use extreme measures against her? Give me a reason. I am an officer of the law, not an assassin for hire."

Agent Wallace gave Agent Gershom a silent remark with nothing more than a look. Agent Gershom nodded, then addressed Tristan. "We will take your points into consideration. They are not unreasonable requests. Please keep in mind that if our superiors determine extreme measures are needed, they may arrange it with or without your cooperation."

"Understood. If you don't trust me with the information I need, don't expect me to help you." Tristan pulled his chair back and sat down again. He knew his file didn't indicate he was a cold-blooded killer. They would know he was lying if he blatantly insisted he could kill her. At this point, they were likely to believe whatever he told them. He knew Jessica wasn't entirely safe. If they wanted her dead today, they could send a trained assassin in to handle it and say nothing more to him. He also knew if they were still moving forward with his mission, they weren't planning to harm her anytime soon.

Leland moved to help the young man out again. "Chief Alexander was promised a promotion if he got the young woman to agree to marry him. I believe he's earned that promotion, although we'll have to handle this covertly."

"We can't authorize that. His girlfriend will get suspicious if he gets a promotion the second they got engaged," Agent Wallace said scornfully.

Capt. Barrett leaned forward and rested his arms on the table. "That's why I said it would have to be handled covertly. He's got a separate account set up to run reimbursements through. Until his promotion is official, put his pay raise through that account, so his future wife doesn't find it."

"Reimbursements? We aren't buying your dinner, Chief," Agent Wallace snapped.

"I'm expecting to get reimbursed for the ring, the lawyer's fees, and the cost of the honeymoon," Tristan coolly explained.

"Those are normal living expenses. Why would we pay for those?" Wallace snapped again.

"Because getting married and transferring out of Covert Ops wasn't my idea or a part of my plans. It was yours," Tristan snapped back. "I'm not asking you to pay for my house or utilities, just the things that are clearly your idea."

"Won't your wife get suspicious about where the money is coming from? She is an accountant now." Agent Wallace's acrid tone was not improving.

"She's not going to see it. It will be in an account she doesn't have access to, and I'm not planning on touching it until we go our separate ways. I took those accounting classes too," Tristan retorted.

Leland jumped in to stop the banter. "Agent Gershom, can you make the arrangements to give the young man the pay he's due for the change in rank and his required reimbursements?"

Agent Gershom nodded. Turning his gaze to his partner, he gave her a hard stare as he spoke to Tristan. "Congratulations on your engagement and promotion, Lt. Alexander. Get me the account information, and I'll see to the arrangements. Is there anything else we need to go over?"

Hearing nothing but silence, Agent Gershom dismissed the meeting. He thanked Capt. Barrett for his help and cooperation.

The privacy screen had been engaged during the meeting. Leland lowered the screen as the meeting broke up. The group was greeted with several curious glances as the milky white walls cleared.

Agent Gershom glanced around. He had hoped they would be done with their meeting well before the regular employees showed up. "Just out of curiosity, Capt. Barrett, how do you plan on explaining our presence to the others in this office?"

"I don't. They know he's been assigned here as a cover, and they won't question it."

"What?" Agent Wallace bellowed. With the privacy screen down, her voice carried through the glass walls. "This is classified! Why would you do that? Now you've blown his cover! We'll have to move him or get someone else to take his place."

"Don't be ridiculous. His cover isn't blown. This was the only way to keep his cover intact. When he walked in here, they looked at him as a spoiled rich kid who paid somebody off to get his foot in the door. They were ready to make his life a nightmare. I had to tell them to get them to accept him as part of the department. Your appearance here in this room cements what I told them, and they know better than to ask questions. They weren't about to treat him like he belonged. His cover is quite secure. You run your department your way and let me run mine my way."

"Exactly what did you tell them?" Agent Wallace demanded.

"I told them this job is his cover and he's to be treated like he belongs here. They know I will string up anyone who doesn't protect his cover. That's it! They have no idea what his job is. They do know he'll have to take an occasional case to support his story. This is all good."

Agent Wallace stormed out. If the door hadn't been automated, she would have slammed it angrily.

Agent Gershom pulled Tristan aside. "By the way, I wanted to let you know we did take your advice about Hannah Roshan. She's undergoing personality recalibration to make her more suitable to Robert Deacons. She's not happy right now, but she'll be better soon. She had several choice words she wanted us to give you. I'll spare you the particulars. I think you know what her message was."

Tristan shook his head. "She could have spared herself the discomfort if she'd used her instincts and adapted to her surroundings. I wasn't trying to get her reprogrammed."

"Just be careful where Agent Wallace is concerned. You don't want her pushing to get you reprogrammed to be a killer," he warned.

"If she starts pushing for that, you might want to let her know it could cause unfortunate accidents, and I could kill Jessica because of the programming. She could divorce me too soon if my personality is altered. I've worked hard to convince her I'm not one of those goons you hired to rough me up a few months ago."

"I'll remind her of that." Agent Gershom excused himself and followed after Agent Wallace.

Tristan glanced at Capt. Barrett. "I think I need some coffee and some fresh air for a few minutes. I'll be in the rooftop garden."

Leland nodded. "I'll join you, if that's all right."

The two walked to the break room, then to the garden. They stood there, sipping their coffee silently for a few minutes, before Tristan touched a button on his bracelet. "Did you have something you needed to say to me, sir? We've got about ten minutes before they discover the soundtrack is looping."

One of Leland's eyebrows lifted in amazement. "Sheesh, kid. You're so prepared for anything that you scare me sometimes."

"I can't afford to drop my guard. Sometimes I get tired, though. I feel like I'm working both sides against the middle this time. I'm afraid I'm going to miss something if I'm not careful."

"Just don't get emotionally involved, and you'll be fine."

Tristan looked away and sipped his coffee to keep Leland from seeing his face.

Realization struck Leland when Tristan didn't look at him. Leland cursed softly under his breath. "Son, you've got to distance yourself from this, or you'll get yourself killed and maybe that girl, too."

"I know. What can I do? I don't even know if I should trust you with this information, but I need to talk to somebody about it."

"I understand. You're lonely but never alone. I'm not on their payroll. Whatever you say to me stays with me."

Tristan didn't know if the man was being honest with him or not, but he decided to risk it. "Sir, since we are limited on time, I'll be blunt. I'm in love with Jessica, and I took this case to protect her before I fell in love with her. She seemed nice and innocent. I didn't trust anybody else to take care of her. Now I really don't trust anyone else."

"I figured as much. Listen, kid, I'll cover you as much as I can, but you really need to watch your step."

"One more thing you need to know. I didn't kill Paula Phipps. Sato's men did that. They found out she slept with me, then they beat her until she told them I was a cop. They continued to beat her and left her to die. I found her like that. That incident blew my cover. I called a rescue squad, but she didn't make it. I'm no killer, at least not that kind of killer." Tristan looked almost ill as the memory poked him uncomfortably.

"Cut the sound loop off," Leland ordered.

Tristan faded it out and sipped his coffee loudly as the sound file closed. "Kid, I know you're miffed about this case, and I don't blame you. You're trying to do your job and fighting your own people in the process. You could use a break, I think. I have a case that I could use your help with, and it supports your internship story. I know you have a wedding to plan, but this might do you both some good."

"How is this supposed to help?" Tristan could clearly see what Leland was doing, but he needed to carry on the conversation.

"This case is going to take you off-world for a couple of weeks. You won't have agents barking at your heels, no fiancée to keep up the charade with, just some peace and quiet, except for the case. You would still have to do the call home every night to talk to your so-called fiancée, but it's just a computer hail." Leland sipped his coffee to stay warm. He was anxious for this conversation to be finished.

Tristan smiled at his intuitive boss. "What kind of case? Am I stuck behind a desk, or will there be more to it than that?"

Leland smiled. "There's more to it than that. Let's go in and talk to Riley. It's his case. He's leaving day after tomorrow."

The two walked inside and continued their discussion in the warmth of the office.

SAFETY IN NAZAR

"Governor Pravin, I am sorry to be the bearer of bad news, but I have reason to believe Nasha has helped the family of the adulteress Slaina escape the city." Asa stood bravely before the governor, knowing his own life could be forfeit.

"Tell me what happened, Sergeant."

"I received reports from the soldiers atop the northeastern wall that two men escaped through a window in the wall at the edge of the construction site. Another man was injured while escaping inside the same area. One foreman reported Garand and his son as missing from the job site. There was a disturbance in the marketplace where Luisa and the rest of their children were lost. Nasha and another man were seen leaving the city on horseback. We think the family got out hidden in a wagon before Nasha was spotted."

Governor Pravin sat in his luxurious chair, pondering the circumstances. "How long ago did this happen?"

"An hour ago. Shall I pursue them?"

Pravin picked up a large wine-filled goblet from the table in front of him and sipped.

Before he could answer the question, Asa asked another, "Governor, I have heard a rumor that your nephew's fiancée may be the one who carries the Promised One. Is this true?"

Pravin took a deep breath and a large gulp of wine. He set the cup down gently. "There is reason to think what you say is not rumor, but truth. No, do not pursue them. The guards were only there to protect them. Did you send a contingent after Nasha?"

"Yes, my lord." Asa wasn't about to get caught totally unprepared.

"Good. Nasha betrayed me and our people. He deserves to be punished, even if he did it to protect Slaina from me. I can't allow him to set such a poor example for the men who served under him or the citizens of Somi. He could not have known the girl's importance. The girl and her family can go free. Nasha owes me a debt, though." Pravin stood slowly and walked around the large table. "Do you know what saddens me the most, Asa?"

"No, my lord."

"It saddens me that I reacted badly and now the Promised One will not be born here in Somi. It would have been an honor to host the King of all Creation." Pravin stepped over by a window overlooking the city and gazed at his citizens, who were like innocent lambs waiting to be shepherded.

"Yes, my lord, it would have been a great honor."

"Asa, let them all go free, even Nasha," Pravin finished meekly.

Asa acknowledged his orders and went to recall the soldiers. He chose his lightest soldier and the fastest horse to send after those chasing Nasha. Nothing pleased him more than allowing his friend to go free. The soldier was more than an hour behind those chasing Nasha, but he carried a horn which could be heard for miles around. He could hopefully reach them before they got too far away.

Nasha and Braken took the northern route to lead the troops away from the wagon. Several hours later, a familiar sound reached Nasha's ears. The lone rider sent by Asa to recall their troops was blowing his horn. The sound resonated throughout the valley. Nasha led Braken up the nearest ridge to get a better view of the soldiers. Their hunters came to a stop as the lone Somian rider closed the gap between them. The horses desperately needed to rest, so Nasha and Braken dismounted to give them time to recuperate. The two were also glad to get out of their saddles for a few minutes. The pursuing soldiers were equally glad to have a break. They kept their eyes trained on their prey standing on the ridge ahead of them. It appeared they had an unspoken agreement on a respite.

Nasha had no such thoughts. His thoughts were merely cold calculations of strategy. He wasn't about to take his eyes off the men until he knew where they were headed. If they turned south to intercept the wagon, he was prepared to match their course. If they returned to Somi, he planned to allow them, but he wanted to be certain of their intentions before taking a less aggressive ride back to Nazar.

Braken finally inquired, "What are they doing?"

Nasha squinted in concentration. "I don't know. That was a recall signal on the horn. I can only think of one reason why they would let us go and recall their troops."

Braken scowled. "I can think of two reasons. I'm hoping it's the second."

"What's the second reason?"

Braken winced at his thought before he spoke it. "Everyone got away, and they're giving up?" It was more of a hope than a valid conclusion.

The two watched the messenger reach the soldiers and convey his message. In a moment, the man blew a different tone. Braken glanced at Nasha. "What was that?"

"He wants a truce. I'll go talk to them. You keep your distance and make sure the soldiers don't circle around behind you or head toward the southern route to Nazar."

Braken wasn't keen on letting Nasha go alone, but he knew they couldn't both be taken. "Pateras be with you."

"Whether they take me or not, Pateras will be with me. May he also guide and protect you." Nasha rode until he was within a hundred yards of the troops.

The messenger wrapped a parchment around a bolt and fired it from his crossbow at a tree near Nasha. "Asa sends you a message, Nasha. You and those with you are free to go."

The messenger turned and followed the soldiers, who were already leaving the area at an easier pace. Nasha turned toward Braken, who was equally puzzled yet still vigilantly watching the departing soldiers.

Nasha retrieved the message and rode back to meet Braken. The two took their horses to a nearby creek to water them while Nasha opened the parchment. His brow furrowed as he read.

"What is it?" Braken didn't want to intrude if it was private, although he doubted that was the case.

"Asa says Governor Pravin has decided to let everyone go. He seems to have given up and expressed regrets about his actions." Nasha still scowled at the page.

"You aren't convinced this is over, are you?"

"No, I'm not. Asa gives no opinion of his own, only what he observed."

"His lack of opinion suggests he's not convinced either. If he were, he would say so. If he said anything to the contrary and someone read it, he could be arrested," Braken surmised. "What do you want to do?"

"Let's head northwest a little longer, then we can turn south and catch up to the others."

The two continued another hour, monitoring the route behind them before turning south. They rode hard toward the bridge across the river into Nazaran territory. Their northern trek put them far behind the wagon.

Leesil and Garand rode several hours eastward until they crossed out of Somian territory. The second they passed the borders, the two took a rest and ate some rations Leesil had brought. Garand wasn't able to stop for very long. He ate quickly so they could push on. Leesil knew they were in no position to help the rest of Garand's family. He indulged the man's desire to push on, for now. When it came time to stop for the night, that would be the time to disagree.

Shula breathed a deep sigh of relief when he drove the wagon across the bridge into the Nazaran Province the second night. The plan was for him to head for the capital city of Nazar. With Wintin still in pain, he opted to head directly to the healer's home. It had already been dark for a couple of hours, and it would take another couple of hours to reach their destination.

A little after midnight, the wagon pulled up outside the healer's home. "Halyn! Halyn!"

Luisa, Wintin, and the children were sleeping until the wagon stopped and Shula began shouting.

Shula sent Eston to pound on the elderly woman's door. Joren was the first one to the door. Shula jumped down from the wagon and called out to Joren, "I have Slaina's family in the wagon, and one of our men was injured as we attempted to escape. He needs the healer."

Halyn appeared from behind Joren. "Bring him and the family in. Joren, light the candles and oil lamps, then throw some wood on the fire." Halyn turned to see Slaina standing at a distance in the hallway. "Girl, greet your family, take them to two of the spare rooms and get them settled, then come help me tend this injured man."

Halyn stepped outside to find out how badly he was injured before moving him. Wintin took in a slow, deep breath and coughed painfully. "Halyn, I can walk with help. My ankle is swollen and stiff. My arm is hurt, but it still works. The bigger issues are my ribs and head. The cold air…" Wintin took another deep breath, coughed, and winced with pain.

"You've said enough. Shula, help him get in here." Halyn went inside and prepared to treat the man.

Slaina greeted her family warmly and showed them to their rooms. The two chambers shared a fireplace. Slaina quickly got a fire going. Eston was not quick to greet his sister and actively snubbed her. Slaina finally asked, "Momma, where's Papa?"

"He's probably dead, and it's your fault!" Eston snapped, leaving Slaina with a stricken look on her face. Luisa was unable even to speak as she realized how much pain her eldest son had been hiding. The younger children started to cry, thinking they would never see their papa again.

Halyn's patient didn't need her urgently, so the woman moved rapidly over to Eston and slapped his cheek. It left his face stinging, but it hurt his pride worse. "Boy, don't you ever contradict the will of Pateras like that, not in this house you don't. Your sister has bravely faced overwhelming odds and accepted in her life a task greater than any other. You apologize to her, or you'll be sleeping in the barn tonight. I've seen Pateras' messenger myself. No matter what your Governor Pravin believes and did to your family, your sister is innocent of any wrongdoing."

Shula interrupted and put one matter to rest, giving the boy a little more time to process Halyn's message. "Slaina, your father got separated from us and was forced to take a longer route. He should be here in a couple more days."

Eston finally gave a cold and limited apology. "I'm sorry. Papa was riding away from the city the last time I saw him. He wasn't hurt."

Halyn gave Eston a disgusted look. "Ah, not much of an apology for the horrible thing you said, but it's late, and I will take that into consideration. You had better be a lot more cordial tomorrow. Why don't you all get some sleep and we'll talk more in the morning?"

Luisa took the children into the two rooms and put them to bed. Halyn pulled Slaina over to Wintin and began to teach her how to examine his injuries, how to know when bones were broken, and how to treat them. Since it was the middle of the night and early in the education process, Halyn was careful not to go into too much detail. Part of her goal was to refocus Slaina's mind off her brother's cruel statement. She could have allowed the girl to go to bed, but it was obvious sending her to bed would not result in her getting rest.

Luisa tucked the last of her children into bed, then pulled her troubled oldest son aside. "Eston, I think you owe me an explanation, and you certainly owe Slaina a better apology than what you gave her."

"What's to explain? This whole mess we're in is her fault. I think she owes us an apology." Eston sat on the floor in front of the fire and stared into it.

Luisa sat next to him. "Your father heard from a messenger in his dreams. This child is the one sent by Pateras. Your sister has committed no crimes."

"Papa just had a dream. He wanted her to be a good girl and dreamed what he wanted to be true. There's no way to prove it. If she had done what's right, why would people be treating us so badly? Why did the soldiers hurt you and Papa? It's her fault they punished you! It's her fault our friends hate us now! It's her fault we had to leave and that the soldiers were chasing us! It's all

Slaina's fault!" Eston's voice got continually louder until it carried down the hall.

Slaina heard his accusing tone as she wrapped her patient's ankle with bandage strips. Wintin saw her fighting back the tears. He reached down and lifted her chin. "Mistress Slaina, he's a boy who's lost everything. He needs someone to blame. His conscience won't allow him to blame Pateras. In a few days, things will become clearer."

Halyn stopped working and added her own take on the matter. "Slaina, we know you did nothing wrong, and some very unfortunate things have happened. Your brother needs to place his anger on someone, and he's chosen you. Can you choose to be the focus of his anger?"

"Wh—what do you mean?"

Halyn's eyes twinkled in the dim light. "Let him be angry with you. Push him to be angry. If you push him hard enough, he'll eventually realize the error in his thinking. If you want to help him, make him think about what he's saying. Take a little pride in what you've done. You honored Pateras' wishes. Be proud of what you've done, not saddened by the damage done by Pateras' enemies."

Wintin took another slow, deep breath the way Halyn had instructed earlier. A couple of brief coughs punctuated his breath. "The healer is right. You chose to do the right things, and the Dark Lord will do all he can to stop you, including harm your family. Help your brother to see that it is the Dark Lord he should be angry with. Your mama and papa understand that. Eston needs time. Can you be strong?"

Slaina wiped away her tears and nodded. She continued her work. By the time she was done, she had found a strength to fuel her own anger at her brother's accusations.

Halyn dismissed the young woman to go to bed, knowing she would sleep. Her anger also fueled her strength, and she wrapped Wintin's ankle a little too tightly. Halyn loosened the wrapping and helped Wintin lie down to get some rest as well.

Shula left Nasha's dogs with Halyn and took the wagon into town. He deposited the wagon and horses in the stable, reported to the watch commander, and grabbed a bunk to get some sleep.

The next morning, Shula reported in to the magistrate. Danyl decided it might be prudent to set up an encampment near the bridge crossing the river into the province and a second one near the mountain pass. He sent troops in both directions and a handful to keep watch over Halyn's home from a discreet distance.

Halyn's household was late in rising. By the time Luisa and her children got up, Slaina and Halyn had prepared a hot breakfast. Joren came inside from tending to the farm animals. He carried an armload of firewood in and put it on the hearth.

The group sat at Halyn's large table for breakfast. Halyn thanked Pateras for the food and the safe return of Slaina's family. She asked his indulgence in returning the rest of the soldiers safely, along with Slaina's father.

Breakfast was filled with questions. The children wanted to know where their father was and if they were staying here, or if they had to get back in the wagon. Slaina's youngest sister, Irana, was excited to see her big sister again. She thought they had come to get Slaina and take her home. Luisa did her best to answer their questions, but she really had no answers to give them.

Halyn wisely put the entire crew to work. There were chamber pots to be emptied and cleaned, wood to be chopped as there were multiple fireplaces to fuel now, two horse stalls to be cleaned out, livestock to be fed, dishes to be washed, and many other chores to be done. Shula had left the remaining baskets of vegetables outside the door to Halyn's house, so Halyn sent Orun and Faris to carry them into the pantry.

Late that afternoon, Slaina sat at the table with her mother, Faris, and Halyn to work on sewing more clothes and diapers for her baby. Eston came in carrying another load of firewood. When he saw what the women were working on, he roughly tossed his load atop the existing pile of wood instead of stacking it neatly. He stomped from the room, slamming the door behind him. Joren carried in two buckets of water from the well for

Halyn. Seeing Eston's disgusted behavior, he cast a questioning glance at Halyn, who nodded. Slaina simply watched and waited. She was now filled with a justified amount of righteous indignation at her brother's behavior.

Eston chopped wood with far more gusto than he had previously. There was already sufficient wood chopped, but Joren helped him anyway. He gave Eston a minute to slow down before interrupting his thoughts. "Eston, why are you upset?"

"Why do you care?" Eston swung his ax. His swing, although forceful, was unfocused. The blade landed at an angle and bounced, doing little damage to the log.

"You're new here just like I am. I need to make new friends, and I thought you could use a friend too," Joren offered.

Eston rested the head of the ax on the ground while he caught his breath again. "Are you from Somi?" he asked suspiciously.

"I'm from Helia. It's in the Somian Province, but I've never been to the Somian capital. Never left Helia until Halyn brought me with her. This was a time I'll never forget. I always dreamed about being an important fellow that folks would look up to, but I never expected it to happen like this." Joren was young but wise. His distraction drew Eston in.

"Why are you important?" Eston was not convinced, but he was curious. Joren didn't look like much. His clothes were simple and not new. He seemed to be nothing more than a farmhand.

"I've seen a messenger of Pateras. I also helped the mother of the Promised One escape to Nazar."

Eston dropped the ax on the ground. "My sister is NOT the mother of the Promised One of Pateras. She's a fornicator. She betrayed her oath to her betrothed, and she's lying to protect her reputation!"

"That is not what Pateras' messenger said!" Joren retorted.

"It was a dream. It wasn't real!"

Joren grabbed Eston's tunic. "I wasn't sleeping!" He shoved Eston backward and walked away from the boy.

Nasha's dogs began to bark and took off running. Joren stopped to see what had their attention. The magistrate, Shula, Nasha, and Braken were riding toward Halyn's house. Joren bolted toward the front door to alert the others. Eston forgot his anger in favor of curiosity and followed Joren more slowly.

Halyn stepped out onto the porch as the riders reached the house. Joren was right behind her.

The men dismounted and greeted Halyn warmly. Slaina, Luisa, and the children stepped outside. Danyl dropped to one knee. "Mother of the Promised One, we are honored Pateras has brought you to us."

Slaina blushed with embarrassment. "Magistrate, please stand up. I'm just a normal girl. I don't know why he chose me. It's the baby who's special, not me."

Eston stared as the four men all knelt before his sister. The display disgusted him, and yet, at the same time, he was intrigued.

Danyl and the others stood as Slaina requested. "Is this your family?"

"Yes, Magistrate. This is my mother, Luisa. My sisters are Faris and Irana. This is my youngest brother, Orun, and that is my brother, Eston—if he still accepts me as his sister."

Danyl glanced at Eston. Shula had informed him of the tension between the two. "It is his loss if he chooses to abandon you. Nasha and the others tell me your father had to take a circuitous route to avoid the troops. I have placed my own troops at strategic places near the borders of Nazaran territory to help them if they run into trouble. I expect they will arrive in another day or two. Halyn, may the family remain with you until Slaina's father is found?"

"Sure, they can. I have a big house and nobody but me and the boy there. I would appreciate it if you could take your other soldier off my hands. He's doin' nothin' but lyin' in the bed all day." Halyn grinned as she spoke.

Wintin's voice came from inside. "I heard that. Magistrate, she nearly slapped me silly when I tried to get up this morning."

"He's well enough to travel, then?" Danyl was about to ask more about the man's condition, but Halyn beat him to it.

"He needs to take it easy for a few more days, but he can do that in his own home with his own wife tending to him."

"Healer, may we borrow your wagon and a couple of horses to get him home? I'll have Shula take him. He can pick up his horse when he returns the wagon." Danyl thanked the woman for caring for the soldier and paid her well for his care.

Halyn declined to allow Shula to take Wintin home. She assigned the task to Joren. Her request was merely her amusing way of informing the magistrate of the man's condition. Halyn sent Joren and Eston to the barn to hitch the horses. She told Wintin to stay where he was and sent Slaina inside to continue sewing.

"Danyl, how long are you goin' to keep that bunch of men campin' out on the rise?"

Danyl shook his head. "I was hoping you hadn't noticed that."

"At least let them set up camp in the barn to stay warm. They can take turns makin' rounds or standin' guard on the hill. This fall's goin' quick. My bones are tellin' me winter will be here soon." A stiff wind chose that moment to blow through, giving the older woman a chill.

Danyl rested his hand on Halyn's shoulder. "Healer, I will have the men move to the barn. I suggest you return to the warmth of your own home before you need a healer for yourself. Do you still intend to train Slaina as a healer?"

"If that's what the girl wants. She's got good instincts. I have no daughter to train. If I don't train somebody soon, there won't be a healer around for miles." For a second, Halyn lamented her inability to have children. She had delivered so many babies but had never had one of her own.

Pushing her regrets aside, she asked one other boon of Danyl. "Could you send Nasha with Joren and Eston to take Wintin home? Eston's havin' a difficult time with his circumstances. I suspect Nasha could shed some light on his situation."

Danyl nodded. "I will take care of it as soon as you get inside and get warm."

Halyn hurried into her home.

Danyl explained the situation to Nasha and told Joren and Eston to accompany the soldier to his home. Eston did as he was told. He owed the soldier his life and was not troubled by helping the man back to his home. He was, however, annoyed at his traveling companions. Eston and Nasha helped Wintin settle into the wagon and covered him with a blanket to keep him warm.

On the ride to Wintin's home, conversation was strained. After releasing Wintin into his family's care, Nasha rode with the two young men for a short distance until the road split. Before heading back to town, Nasha spoke plainly to Eston. "Young man, I am sorry for the harm that I allowed to happen to your family. I promised you we would settle this when we got you to safety. You are safe. Step out of the wagon and have whatever retribution you need."

Anger grew inside Eston as he stared at Nasha. The seasoned soldier dismounted and tied his horse to the wagon. Eston's mind flew back to the day his family was rousted out of their home. They were brought to the town square where he and his siblings were forced to watch his parents being punished for Slaina's crime. Eston saw Nasha there, overseeing the deed and giving the commands. He supposed Nasha was following the governor's orders. Eston stood slowly in the back of the wagon. He kept his eyes glued to Nasha. Climbing out of the wagon, he continued hurling daggers of hatred. He stood directly in front of the seasoned soldier. Nasha was several inches taller and far more muscular, not to mention he carried several weapons.

Nasha saw the boy eyeing the weapons. He slowly removed each of them and laid them in the back of the wagon. Joren watched wide-eyed. Nasha held his hands out to his sides. He motioned at the weapons. "Take them and use them if you feel the need."

Eston looked at the weapons, then back at Nasha suspiciously. "I'm no match for you, even if you are unarmed."

Nasha nodded. "I know. I told you I wouldn't fight back. Now is your chance to pay me back for what I did. Come on, strike me in any way that you choose."

"Were—were you following the governor's orders when you hurt my parents?"

"Yes, I was. It was an order I shouldn't have carried out. Your parents were innocent of any wrongdoing. The governor was using them to try to flush your sister out. He learned who she really is, and he's threatened by her child. He wants them dead. He was willing to turn her family against her to kill her and her baby."

"Why are you saying this? Why did you help us leave the city?" Eston's fists balled up as his anger grew.

"Because it's true. I saw the messenger of Pateras. He told us it was true. Joren can tell you. He was there, and so were Slaina and Halyn. I didn't believe it until then. I was seconds from killing your sister. My sword was in my hand. She was as close to me as you are when the messenger appeared and stopped me."

"No! Liar! You're both liars! This is all Slaina's fault! It's her fault they made you hurt Mama and Papa! It's her fault we had to leave! It's her fault people started hating us and my friends stopped talking to me!" Eston began throwing wild punches. The punches that landed bounced harmlessly off Nasha, who allowed the boy to vent. When his anger gave way to tears, and the venom sapped the strength of his punches, Nasha reached out and held the young man in a fatherly embrace until the anger drained away into sobs.

Eston's sobs slowed and faded, giving Nasha room to counsel the boy. "Son, this was the will of Pateras. Slaina didn't choose this for herself. She is willing to accept it, and she knows this will be a tough road. There are people even here in Nazar who may treat her poorly because they don't believe. It's the ones who don't believe who mistreated you in Somi. I was one of them. I treated your parents badly, and I nearly killed Slaina because I didn't believe. That has changed. It's why I came back to get you and your family out of the city. It's because I believe this is the will of Pateras."

Eston pushed back. "How do I know? How do I know for sure?"

"You can simply choose to accept your sister's word, or you can ask Pateras. I doubt he will send his messenger again, but surely he will find a way to tell you what you need to hear. Can you do either of those two? Can you ask Pateras to tell you?"

Eston wiped his face with his sleeve and nodded. "I'll try."

"Wise choice. Are we done here?"

Eston nodded again. "Why did you let me hit you?"

Nasha put his weapons back in their places. "Because I am a man of my word." He had other reasons. This one seemed sufficient.

FIRST MISSION

"So, when's the big day?" Capt. Barrett asked.

"We have a tentative date set for five months from now."

"Five months? Why so long?"

Tristan twisted in his chair. His superiors all felt he was taking too long, and he hated explaining his reasons for every decision, but he knew Leland wasn't being critical or demanding. "Robert will be back from his deep space mission a couple weeks before that, and Jessica wanted to have a job secured before we get married. She also thought it would be better for us financially if I had my promotion, too."

Leland leaned his chair back and pulled his right ankle onto his left knee. "Are you handling this low-key normal guy life okay? I don't mean to pry, but a year ago you were dodging bullets and taking bad guys down hard. This is a big change."

"I could use some excitement, that's for sure. I'm going to get soft if I don't get some action soon." Tristan shifted restlessly again. The thought that Agents Wallace and Gershom could use Capt. Barrett to keep tabs on his own mental state ran through his mind again. Talking to him plainly was a risk, and he knew the two agents were listening in to everything he said.

"That case you and Riley took a couple of weeks ago didn't help you any?"

"No, I'm afraid not. They tried to bully Riley for about five minutes, then when I walked in, it stopped. I got the feeling they knew I was more than another forensic accountant."

"I'll see what I can come up with. You really should be careful what you wish for. You never know if you might get it. Riley's current case is probably less exciting than the one you just completed. He's working on Lado Pharmaceuticals. There were some complaints against the company resulting from some botched assisted suicides."

"How is that a fiscal responsibility issue?" Tristan asked.

"The company is partially government subsidized, for the assisted suicides in particular. If they're botching the suicides, we have to find out if there's a misappropriation of government funds or simple clinical error."

"Simple clinical error? A botched suicide is not a simple issue. What sort of outcomes did they experience?"

"It varied. Some patients went to sleep for hours and never expired. Their families waited at their bedsides for the end, and when it didn't happen, they were not happy. Some were determined to be brain dead and took days to actually die. They died of dehydration. A few woke up in the morgue and started wandering around. These same patients had to be put down less humanely. The resulting litigation from irate families has the potential to blow back on the Commonwealth itself." Leland shifted uncomfortably in his own chair. "This department doesn't only investigate potential criminal activities. We also serve as the oversight committee on any governmental subsidizations. If we don't catch this, it could come crashing down on this department as a whole."

"I'll get on it. If there's something there to find, I'll find it. I hope you won't mind if I use more than financial records to investigate." Tristan's eyes brightened. Something smelled distinctly off. It didn't feel like a misappropriation of funds was the entire issue.

Tristan spent the next couple of weeks looking into Lado Pharmaceuticals with Riley. As Tristan wasn't truly a fully trained forensic accountant, he followed Riley's lead. They went through the records backward and forward. The evidence supported their claims of legitimacy. Something was still off, and Tristan could smell it. The records were too perfect. Tristan began to research the less direct financial aspects. He pulled their shipping and receiving reports to compare to the invoices and receipts. He started noticing minor discrepancies. As the number of discrepancies accumulated, he attempted to talk to people through trans-spatial comms. No one was willing to give him more than noncommittal responses.

Three weeks after starting the case, Riley was done investigating. He knew something wasn't right about the situation, but without evidence, there was little more that he could do.

"Riley, let's take what we've got to Leland. I think we should go to Stiliani III, do some in-person interviews, and look the situation over."

Riley shook his head. "We've got nothing concrete. A few discrepancies don't constitute illegal activity."

"There's something to this. You know there is."

Riley sighed. This young, impetuous investigator wasn't going to let this go. "If he says no, will you drop it?"

"I suppose I'll have to."

"That's what I thought. Let's go talk to him." Riley resigned himself to the fight.

The two walked into Leland's office. Seeing them together and a determined look on their faces, he scowled. "Oh, this can't be good."

Riley, as the lead investigator, began, "Leland, this Lado case has got us against a wall. We've found a few small—tiny even— inconsistencies. This resourceful young man has tried getting some additional first-hand information, and they're giving him the runaround. We would like your permission to go to Stiliani, conduct some personal interviews, and see the situation for ourselves."

Leland's eyes landed on Tristan. "Personal interviews, huh?"

Tristan knew exactly what Leland was thinking. "I'm not authorized for those kinds of interviews, sir."

Leland stared hard at the zealous young man. "You're right. You aren't. I wanted to be certain you know that. Riley, are you sure this is worth it? He didn't talk you into this, did he?"

"No, Leland, he didn't talk me into this. There's clearly something here. I don't have nearly enough to invoke charges or even sanctions against the company, but I have enough to warrant a more in-depth investigation. If you send both of us, I can continue training him and keep him in line. He would also be a valuable asset, because his background allows him to see things I might miss."

Leland leaned sideways in his chair and rested his chin on his fist. He looked back and forth between the two men. This trip would cost the department a significant number of credits. Stiliani was several light-years away. "Do you know how much this is going to cost?"

Tristan leaned forward. "I've already looked into it. There's a pacification ship leaving the area in two days. We could hitch a ride with them. It would get us there faster than commercial transport, and it wouldn't cost us a thing. There's another ship coming back a week later. If we can have things wrapped up by that time, we won't have to pay passage back, either. The only thing it will cost us is lodging, meals, and transportation while we're there."

"The trip out and back, even on a fleet ship, would be, what? Five days one way?"

"Six," Tristan confirmed.

"You would be gone for nearly three weeks. Are you both okay with that?"

The two affirmed they were. Leland looked directly at Tristan. "Are your handlers going to be okay with this?"

"I'm just protecting my cover." Tristan grinned impishly. "If I don't go on the occasional investigation, it might arouse suspicions."

"All right, you have my blessing. Do what you need to, and eat cheaply! This department is on a tight budget!"

"Yes sir, we'll get right on it," Riley answered. A fervor he hadn't felt in several years spurred him on. He had never done covert ops like Tristan, but he had been a criminal investigator in his earlier days.

Riley prepared his files, then went home to pack some clothes and spend time with his family, since he wouldn't see them for nearly three weeks. Tristan cemented their travel plans and headed home to pack as well. He had dinner with Jessica that night and told her about his plans. She was not happy with his sudden schedule change. Tristan teased her about breaking up with him over a simple business trip. She pouted until he pleaded with her to cheer up so that her fretful look wasn't the only thing in his memory for the next three weeks.

Jessica understood his request and did her best to cheer up. She insisted they keep in touch daily. He promised to call her as often as his schedule would allow. The two spent as much time together as they could the next day until Tristan had to catch his shuttle to the Pacification ship. Jessica went with him to see him off. Riley's wife also accompanied him to the CIF Shuttle Port. They had a few minutes of polite conversation before it was time to board the shuttle. Jessica clung to Tristan's neck and whispered, "Is it always going to be like this?"

"Trust me, it will get easier, and this is better than Covert Ops where I would be gone for months sometimes. I'm sorry I won't be there to help you move back home with your parents."

Tears formed in her eyes. "How is this supposed to get better?"

Tristan smiled and wiped the tears from her cheeks. "Once we're living together and you learn all my disgusting habits, you'll start wishing I had a case to get me out of your hair for a while."

"I'll never feel that way," Jessica claimed, her ignorance of her own circumstances clearly evident.

Tristan and Riley finished their goodbyes and left their loved ones behind.

They continued some light conversation while they settled into their bunks aboard the ship. Riley looked at the tiny room. "It's been a long time since I've been in one of these." Their bunks were rectangular cubicles built into the walls with a seating area and a foldout desk/table combination. The bathroom ran down the side of the seating area, and the bunks ran across the back of the room. There was a small refreshment area in the corner between the end of the bunks and the bathroom.

"I hope you brought something to do on this trip. This certainly isn't a standard commercial vessel, but there are a few options. There's a rec room three decks up, and a gymnasium complete with a Zone court and weight room. I could sign us up for a couple of games if you want."

"I wouldn't fare well against these young soldiers in a game of Zone. I'm too old for that," Riley said.

Tristan grinned. "I could always check with the ranking officers to see if they'd like to play. They aren't that young."

Riley gave Tristan a dirty look. "I'll pass." He decided it was time to change the subject. "That Jessica seems like a nice young woman—pretty, too. You did good picking her out."

"I didn't pick her. She's my assignment." Tristan wanted to set the record straight in case anything ever came up about his undercover operation. "And you are right about her being pretty and likable. It makes this job easier."

Riley stopped asking questions. He doubted Tristan would feel comfortable discussing his case. They unpacked their bags quietly for a moment until Riley's curiosity got the best of him. "Is this a protection detail or an investigation?"

"To be honest, there's a lot I don't know about this case. My job so far is to earn the family's trust, watch them for evidence of subversion, and saddle Jessica with a couple of kids." Tristan was no longer afraid of the wrath of his handlers. Leland had defended his right to run his own department his way. He didn't talk about it around the office, but he decided it was safe enough here. "I can't give you the details, but I have a list of names to pay attention to, and if there is sufficient reason, I may need to use extreme sanctions."

"Against Jessica or her family?" Riley's eyes widened.

Tristan glanced around at the devices capable of monitoring their conversation. Riley's eyes followed his, and he understood the significance immediately.

"Against Jessica or her children," Tristan said simply.

"These ships have lap pools, don't they?" Riley abruptly changed the subject again. "I may not be able to handle Zone, but I enjoy a nice long swim. Are you up for it?"

Tristan grinned. "Sure, I can handle it. You don't get claustrophobic, do you?"

"Uh—I'd better not if I'm stuck in this tiny bunk with you for a week. What does that have to do with swimming?"

"You've never been in a pool in space before, have you?" Tristan grinned.

"No, why?"

"The first time they put a pool on a ship, there was a malfunction in the artificial gravity. Three swimmers drowned four feet above the pool because they couldn't separate themselves from the floating bubble of water. The pools are only four and a half feet deep, and the ceiling is eight feet above the bottom of the pool. The lanes are divided with safety railings that you can grab onto if necessary. You are also required to swim with a tiny compressed air tank, shield generator, and mouthpiece with four hours' worth of air. It's almost like swimming in a tube."

"If you're a ground pounder, how do you know all this?" Riley scowled.

Tristan grinned. "Even ground pounders have to use spaceships to get where they're going."

"Why four hours' worth of air?" Riley wondered out loud as he grabbed his swim trunks.

"So you don't drown while waiting for a rescue." Tristan thought that part was obvious.

"You should be able to get out of the pool in a matter of minutes with the safety railings. Why four hours?" Riley was certain he was missing something.

"You're assuming no gravity, not increased gravity. Either one is a possibility. If the gravity increases drastically, you may be trapped on the bottom of the pool and unable to climb out. The shield generator is there to prevent the water from crushing you."

"Why would a ship have the ability to increase the gravity that much? People don't have to adjust to those extremes because we don't live on planets with that much gravity." Riley's face was pale at the thought.

"It's not there as a normal function. It's a safety buffer. You always want more than what you need. Say the artificial gravity generators are only working at partial capacity, you might have to increase the output far enough to counter the decreased capacity and bring it back to something near normal." Tristan saw Riley was still disconcerted. "I've never heard of it happening before, but when the first incident happened, they looked at other safety issues and planned for a worst-case scenario."

Riley glanced at the swimming trunks in his hand skeptically. He decided it was worth the risk. "Let's do this. I can tell the folks at the office how dangerous this trip was and how my life was hanging in the balance. I'll find a fun way to spin it so that they're all jealous." He grinned.

Tristan asked, "Do you ever bring your wife on trips like these?"

"What? No! Why would I do that?"

"I thought it would keep her from missing you when you're gone for so long. She would get to see new places and enjoy the sights while you work," Tristan volunteered. "Most of this stuff isn't dangerous."

"Nah, she's got a boyfriend or something on the side. She looks forward to the times when I'm gone so she can be with him." Riley was seemingly unaffected by the thought.

"What? Why haven't you ended your marriage contract? She seemed so loving and attentive when she left us at the terminal."

"She is loving and attentive when I'm with her. She keeps me happy, and he keeps her happy. It's an arrangement we're comfortable with," Riley lied.

"Your wife knows that you know about her affair?"

"I doubt it. She keeps things pretty well hidden. She forgets I'm a forensic accountant. I notice things where our finances are concerned. I was angry at first, but after I cooled off, I decided to let it go. For over a year, I traced the discrepancies. I also noticed she treated me better after it started. I think she feels guilty and tries to make it up to me." Riley changed into his swimsuit and grabbed a shirt and shoes to go to the pool.

Tristan thought about the situation. "Do you think she might not want the other guy if you brought her on some of these trips?"

"I don't know. I'll give it some thought."

The two tossed their bracelets into a drawer and headed to the pool. The bracelets were waterproof, but swimming was more enjoyable without the added encumbrance. They took an indirect route and wandered around, purposely looking lost so their circuitous route would prevent anyone from getting a lock on their whereabouts to record their conversation.

Riley got directly to the point. "Could you really kill your own kids? Or your wife? I know I wanted to kill mine for a little while, but that's pretty extreme."

"Riley, you really shouldn't ask me that question. If I said yes, I'm pretty sure it would scare you and affect our friendship. If I said no and my handlers learned about it, I would probably get pulled off this case. It also means they would bring in someone more capable to take my place. I will tell you what I told my handlers: I would need a well-documented dispensation and a good reason before taking such actions. I'm no assassin. I've killed in the line of duty, but my own life was in danger at the time." Tristan spoke softly while walking briskly and turning down the wrong hallways.

Riley knew what he was doing. He only questioned him to cover their conversation. "Are you sure this is the right way?" Riley asked loudly, then followed with a softer question. "What are you going to do if they demand that you take action?"

Tristan flashed an appreciative smile. "Are you kidding? Do you really expect a dumb ground pounder to know his way around these convoluted ships?" He turned the correct way and softly answered, "I don't know. I haven't figured this out yet."

A week later, the two arrived on Stiliani. They decided to talk to the families of the botched suicide victims.

The first family they approached was an older couple. John and Cheri Taft were in their sixties. John's father had chosen to have an assisted suicide when the elderly man was diagnosed with an incurable disease.

The couple sat down at the dining room table to discuss the matter. Cheri was polite and offered them something to drink as they talked. Despite her proper manners, it was clear she was nervous. Her husband took the lead in the discussion.

"Gentlemen, I appreciate that you're looking into this reprehensible situation, really I do, but I don't think there's anything we can say that would shed any light on this," John said bluntly.

Riley took a sip of his coffee as Tristan wandered about the room, casually drinking his own. Tristan was gathering his own intelligence as Riley questioned the family. Riley tried to keep the couple's attention fixed on him and the conversation. "You might not be able to shed any light on the matter at all, but you never know what details could slip through the cracks. Tell me exactly what happened."

Cheri looked nervously at her husband. "We—We aren't supposed to talk about it. We signed a non-disclosure agreement. It was a part of the settlement."

John nodded. "She's right. We did. We can't talk to you about this."

Riley didn't back down. "Those agreements are not legally binding where a criminal investigation is involved. It would actually be considered impeding an investigation and possibly even conspiracy, depending on your involvement. Those agreements were meant to prevent you from telling the press and putting the company in a bad light. Your names will never show up again if there isn't anything here. If we determine that Lado Pharmaceuticals is guilty of criminal activity, you might be entitled to a greater settlement if you cooperate. If you refuse to help us, we can't protect you."

"Protect us? From what?" Cheri had gone from nervous to frightened.

"Prosecution," Riley said.

Tristan picked up a holographic photo imager. "Mr. Taft, was this your father?"

"Yes, that's Dad," John admitted. His father's smiling face was hard to look at.

"Mr. Taft, they obviously did an injustice to your father. We want to see that this doesn't happen to any other families. Tell us what happened. We know Lado Pharmaceuticals did something wrong, but we don't know exactly what they did." Tristan held the imager so the smiling face pressured the son to set things right.

A voice from the doorway called out. "Put that down!"

Tristan turned to see the Tafts' oldest daughter, Karyn, who was in her late thirties, and her teenage daughter. It was the girl who had ordered him to put it down.

Tristan set the imager down gently while keeping eye contact with the girl. "My apologies. I meant no disrespect. You were very fond of him, weren't you?"

The girl glared at him. It was clear she was holding back her thoughts.

John stood up. "This is my daughter Karyn Bond from my second marriage, and her daughter Alicia. Karyn, why don't you take Alicia to the other room?"

Tristan stepped forward. "Would it be all right if Alicia and I went into the kitchen and fixed some more coffee? Perhaps Ms. Bond would be useful in this discussion."

Before anyone could object, Tristan took Alicia gently by the elbow. "I hope you know your way around your grandmother's kitchen. Do you suppose there might be some cookies or crackers and cheese? It's been a while since I ate last."

Alicia knew she was being manipulated, although she wasn't sure what to do about it. Karyn started to object when Riley let out an expletive. "That intern sure knows how to disappear when there's work to be done." He glanced at the others in the room. "Sorry, forget I said that. Where were we? You were going to explain exactly what happened to the senior Mr. Taft."

While Riley got the "official" story from the adults, Tristan programmed the coffee maker for an additional three cups of coffee. He glanced at Alicia. "You want a cup?"

Alicia's lip curled into a snarl. "No, don't be stupid. What do you really want?"

"I want to know what happened to your great-granddad."

"We're not supposed to talk about it." Alicia hopped onto the kitchen cabinet to sit.

"I know. Something went wrong. We're trying to fix it, so no one else goes through what your family went through. Cookies?" Tristan looked around the kitchen.

Alicia pointed at a cabinet near the coffeemaker.

Tristan opened the cabinet and found a package of cookies. He looked around for something to serve them on.

"Are you really going to go through this whole cookie charade?" Alicia snarked.

Tristan stopped what he was doing. He folded his arms across his chest and leaned against the nearest counter. "I have to maintain my credibility with the older set out there. I was trying to placate them, not you."

"So why did you ask me if I wanted coffee? Sounded like you were trying to put one over on me... unsuccessfully." Alicia retorted.

"No, I didn't want to patronize you by asking if you wanted a glass of milk. I just thought I'd ask while I was programming the machine. Now, is there a plate and serving tray around here? By the way, does your grandmother let you sit on her cabinets like that?" Tristan was good at adapting and overcoming whatever circumstances he was in, including dealing with obnoxious teens.

A guilty look crossed the girl's face. "No," she said as she slid off the countertop. She grabbed a plate from the cabinet and pulled a serving tray out a second later. "Nan and Pop keep fruit, cheese, and crackers around all the time for snacks. Would you like some of those?"

"We can make this as fancy or as simple as you want. They need time to talk about your great-grandfather's death."

"In that case, let's get the veggies out too. We can make this plate really awesome. I can make some veggie dip." Alicia sensed a kindred spirit in Tristan.

"Is your Nan going to expect us to wash the dishes?" Tristan teased.

"Nah, she doesn't want anybody in her kitchen. We wouldn't do it right."

"How do you know where stuff is, then?" Tristan quizzed the girl.

"She's not my real grandmother. She's Pop's wife. I do what I want when I come here. Nana lets me because she thinks it will make me like her more."

"Did she like your great-grandfather?"

"Not really. She tolerated him because he was old and needed help, and Pop wanted him to come here to live."

Tristan slowly arranged the food on the tray while Alicia mixed a vegetable dip. "I figured out real quick that you thought a lot of him. Can you tell me what happened? I know it dredges up pain from the past, but I need to know."

Alicia froze. Unwelcome tears welled up in her eyes as she held a half-stirred bowl of vegetable dip. "They weren't going to tell me. Granddaddy was sick, and he wasn't getting better. There were a lot of whispered conversations, and everybody was upset for days. Then things got quiet. It was a strange quiet. Mom sent me to stay with my dad for a couple of days. When I got back, we came straight over here. Mom said we needed to talk. I heard Granddaddy humming in Pop's workshop. Mom sat me down in the living room and told me Granddaddy died in his sleep the previous night. I thought she was nuts, and I laughed at her. I told her he was working in the workshop. She insisted he wasn't. She took me in there to prove it. Mom screamed and nearly passed out when she saw him. Nan and Pop came running when they heard her scream. Pop asked Granddaddy how he got there and what he was doing. He told us he decided it wasn't his time to go yet—there was something he needed to do first. He said he felt better than he had in a long time." Alicia started stirring again with greater force than before. She tried taking her frustrations out on the unsuspecting dip.

Tristan stopped what he was doing and waited for Alicia to continue. When she didn't, he quietly prodded. "I saw the death certificate. What happened?"

"I don't know exactly. I stayed with him in the workshop. He made me a wooden jewelry box. When he handed it to me, he told me he put a data crystal with a very special file in it. He said it was his way of saying how much he loved me." Alicia stopped talking, leaving an awkward silence.

"Was there something else?" Tristan prodded again.

There was one thing he had said, but she wasn't about to share this one thing. He had warned her not to let the authorities know she had heard it. As much as she was starting to like Tristan, he was still one of the authorities she had been warned about. "There were lots of arguments and people disappearing behind closed doors. Granddaddy kept interrupting them. He insisted he had changed his mind about dying. Late that night, I fell asleep on the couch. When I woke up, an ambulance was taking Granddaddy out. He grabbed my hand and told me not to forget what he said."

Tears welled up in her eyes again. Tristan put a reassuring hand on the girl's shoulder. Alicia whipped around and caught him in a desperate hug. Tristan returned the hug gently. When she calmed down and pulled away, she wiped the tears from her own eyes. "Sorry, I hate getting all blubbery like that."

Tristan patted her shoulder again. "It's okay. I don't have a granddad or even a dad to get blubbery over. Did you look at the data crystal?"

"No, I couldn't. It hurt too much. They told us the next morning that Granddaddy was gone. Something was different about him. He really didn't want to die. They said his mind was gone, and he had to be put down. It wasn't. He was just as alert as ever. He knew who I was and what he was doing. They killed him! He was old, and they killed him!" The girl's eyes flamed with anger.

Tristan attempted to distract her. "You know, we'd better come up with some coffee and snacks for those folks in the dining room before they start wondering what happened to us. The coffee's ready. Are you sure you don't want a cup?"

Alicia's anger melted, and she snickered. "No, I want a glass of milk."

Tristan stopped and laughed at the girl. "Let's get you a glass of milk, then."

Their laughter as they walked into the dining room with the tray of goodies was a stark contrast to the others' mood. Tristan glanced around. "So, who wants some fresh coffee?"

Tristan and Riley hit another few interviews over the next couple of days. The stories were similar, but not exactly the same. The morning of the third day, they made their presence known to the pharmaceutical company. Marguerite Bellamy, the CEO, met them with a polite, but cold greeting. She escorted the two to a boardroom and ordered her assistant to summon the other company executives to join them. She kept the conversation light and unrelated to the topic at hand until the others joined her. Riley and Tristan explained the nature of their visit and politely requested unrestricted access to the company.

Tristan was certain he felt a chill hit him after Riley made his request. "Gentlemen, I assure you this was merely a clinical error from a new employee who was insufficiently trained. We reassigned the employee in question to a less critical area and retrained him. I would have thought our financial records sufficed to answer your questions. Was there something in those records that I need to address?"

Tristan decided to play the renegade cop—not exactly the bad cop, but close. "I'm sorry, ma'am, but we can't discuss the particulars of an ongoing investigation. If you are refusing us access, we'll need to get the information through outside avenues. We've only been looking at the last two years. We may need to go through the last ten years of records to watch for trends. This could take months for us to get through. Don't you have a funding hearing coming up? We'll need to be involved in that as well. We may have to request that funding be suspended until we're satisfied."

Riley glanced at Tristan. The urge to laugh outright rose within him. They had no jurisdiction for half of what his junior partner suggested. Riley shifted in his seat and pinched his upper lip to appear to be in thought, although he was more interested in erasing the smirk from his face. "Chief Alexander, I think that's a bit premature. I think we can clear this matter if we walk through the entire process and do a few interviews with the employees involved."

Tristan started to argue, but the man promptly shut him down. The group finally agreed to start with Riley's suggestion. Marguerite invited the two to come back the next morning. She promised to provide an empty office if they needed it to conduct their interviews.

Ms. Bellamy smiled politely as the two left, followed by most of the board members. Two remained behind. Marguerite gave them one quick set of orders. "Find out everything you can about those two, particularly that young one. He's trouble. I need to find something we can use to manipulate them. They've got a weakness. Find it."

That night Tristan called Jessica as promised. "Are you done with your investigation yet? I'm ready for you to come home," she whined.

"No, not yet, maybe another couple of days."

She sighed and looked annoyed.

"Is everything going okay with your parents? I know moving back home can't be very easy."

"I have some news, and I wanted to share it with you in person," she complained.

Tristan smiled. "I'm sorry. Do you want to wait, or do you want to tell me now?"

"I can't wait—I got a job offer from a company called Lado Pharmaceuticals."

JEDREK AND SLAINA

Joren and Eston returned to Halyn's home, talking the entire way. Eston wasn't completely over his hard feelings, but now he was willing to listen. They arrived to find two new horses tied up outside. The young men looked around to see who the horses belonged to. Joren finally located Slaina and Jedrek walking on a hill behind the house. Pointing to the couple, Joren told Eston, "The horses belong to Jedrek. He and Slaina are near the fruit trees."

"Jedrek? Why is he here?"

"He wants your sister to forgive him and marry him." Joren drove the wagon to the barn. The second it came to a stop, Eston was out of it and racing up the hill. His anger rekindled at both of them.

Slaina was holding Jedrek's hand as they walked. The two stopped at the edge of the small orchard. Seeing Eston coming at them at a full run, Slaina released Jedrek's hand to see what was wrong.

Eston ran full force into Jedrek, taking him to the ground. Eston was tall and thin, but his anger and speed enabled him to knock the older, sturdier young man to the ground. Eston pummeled Jedrek. He screamed at him as he punched mercilessly. Jedrek's surprise quickly gave rise to shock, then anger. Recovering from his shock, Jedrek defended himself. He caught the young man's fists in his hands and rolled out from under Eston.

Finding himself now pinned to the ground, Eston continued his verbal assault. Slaina took a minute to recover from her own shock. Once she did, she took charge of the situation. "Eston, stop this! What are you doing?"

"He's the reason we had to leave home! He got Papa and Mama beaten in public! He's the reason everyone hates us! Get off me!" Eston writhed angrily. "Why are you with him?"

Slaina put her fists on her hips. "I thought this was supposed to be my fault, Eston. Which is it? Are you angry with me, or Jedrek?"

Eston continued to push against Jedrek's grip on his wrists. "Let go of me! Take your beating like a man!"

There were several more heated exchanges as Joren ran to the house to inform Halyn of the recent development. Halyn and Slaina's family raced outside and around the end of the house to see what was going on.

Luisa started to break up the altercation, but Halyn stopped her. "Give them a minute first. Eston's got a lot of anger he needs to deal with."

Luisa was torn between rescuing her son and listening to the advice of the elderly woman, who was also their host. She stayed put for as long as she could stand it.

Finding himself totally outmatched again, the fight finally left Eston and he stopped struggling. "Slaina, why would you consider taking him back after what he did to Papa and Mama?"

Jedrek finally spoke for himself. "I didn't do that. My uncle found out what happened and ordered it. I never asked for it. I wanted it all to go away quietly." Jedrek got off Eston and stepped away from him.

Eston rolled over to hide his tears. "Why? Why? Why did it have to happen? Why did they have to hurt them? Why did everybody hate us? We didn't do anything wrong!"

Slaina knelt beside her brother. She placed her hand gently on his back. "Eston... did I cause you to hurt like this?"

The teenage boy, caught between childhood and becoming a man, fought to find his emotional footing. His sobs slowed as all the pieces fell into place. He rolled onto his back to see a pained look on his sister's face. He looked at the slight bulge in her belly. "It's really the Promised One? You really didn't betray us?"

Slaina's pained look melted into peace and acceptance. "It is truly the Promised One, or I would have been dead by now. The only reason I am alive is because Pateras protected me. Nasha was seconds from killing me, but a messenger from Pateras stopped him. I never betrayed the teachings of the Ancient Texts or my engagement to Jedrek. Even Jedrek now knows that to be true."

"She's right. A messenger came to me in a dream and told me it was true. I was wrong to think she betrayed me. I think she might be getting close to forgiving me." Jedrek squatted beside Slaina to address the young man.

Eston wiped the tears from his eyes. "But Mama and Papa..."

Seeing the timbre had calmed, Luisa approached the group slowly and quietly. Hearing his question, she softly answered, "Are we to accept only good from Pateras? He holds all in his hands, and he has blessed us many times. Jedrek did not cause these things to happen. The Dark Lord seeks to destroy Slaina's child, and he will do whatever he can to stop the child from being born. If it protects that baby, I would take a hundred beatings. What are you willing to do?"

Eston looked at Slaina's belly again. This baby might need him? The thought had never occurred to him. He slowly nodded his head. He searched the faces of the growing number of people around him. They all seemed to be silently asking him to join them. "Mama, you forgave Jedrek... and Nasha?"

"Yes, my son. I have forgiven them all. It will take time for the memories to fade, but it will be done. Papa will forgive them as well when he arrives," Luisa assured him.

Eston sat up slowly and faced Slaina. New tears slipped down his cheeks. He quickly tried to wipe them away. It wasn't fitting for a man to cry in front of all these people. Halyn, Joren and the rest of his family were assembled around them. The men Danyl had posted at the top of the rise heard the commotion and were paying attention from a discreet distance.

Eston positioned himself on his knees and grabbed Slaina's hands. "Slaina, I'm so sorry I was mad at you. Please forgive me."

Slaina smiled. "Eston, I forgive you. I'm sorry you got hurt by this. I would still have done this, even knowing the cost. I'm sorry it cost all of you so much."

Jedrek glanced at Luisa. He had not formally apologized to her or her family. Even though, as he previously said, he hadn't orchestrated any of what happened to them. He felt an apology was in order and promptly corrected his omission.

Seeing the excitement was over, the assembly broke up. The unnerving sound of a sword returning to its scabbard got Eston's attention. Jedrek's bodyguard eyed him cautiously. The guard had sized up the situation and knew Jedrek was not in any serious trouble. He did, however, want to make his point with Eston and anyone else who entertained the thought of harming his charge, that any attempt on Jedrek's life would be dealt with.

The group ambled toward the house. Slaina hung on Eston's arm, finally able to tell him about all the adventures she had experienced while running for her life.

Jedrek pulled his guard aside. "Thank you for your discretion."

The guard was old enough to be Jedrek's father. "You're welcome, my lord. He's just an angry child trying to be a man. There was no reason to harm him."

That evening as the group dined at Halyn's table, Jedrek shared with everyone that the magistrate was allowing him to purchase a piece of property directly west of Halyn's farm. The land was an area known as the Western Cliffs. It was extremely rocky and wasn't good for farming, so the price was quite low. Since Jedrek was a builder and not a farmer, the rocky land was not a problem for him. He needed only enough good ground for a few cattle and his horses to graze on, as well as a small garden plot. He planned to start building a home in the next few days. He invited Slaina and her family to go see it in the morning.

Joren joined Jedrek's enthusiasm and boasted about his own plans to build storage buildings and silos to store crops and grain. He planned to help the area farmers with their crops in exchange for a small percentage, which he would store until spring, when food would be a little scarce. By storing more than he needed, he could sell off his excess while waiting for the new crops to come in. While working in the stables, the young man had listened quietly to the businessmen of Helia and learned from them. Halyn had given him permission to start his endeavors on her land.

Hearing the other two men talk, Eston threw his own entrepreneurial input into the mix. "If we're going to be staying in the Nazaran Province, I think it's time I found work as well. If I don't get started soon, I won't be able to afford a family either."

Luisa smiled at her son, who seemed to be adjusting to the new situation. Faris and Orun laughed outright at the thought of their brother starting a family.

Halyn smiled as she looked around her kitchen full of people and laughter. Her husband would have been so happy to have a family such as this. Luisa was the right age to be her daughter, making her five children like Halyn's grandchildren, and the Promised One would be like her great-grandchild. She often wondered why Pateras had never given her children. Perhaps if he had, she would never have become a traveling healer and might not have been there when Slaina needed her. She was certain Pateras would have sent someone to rescue Slaina, but it wouldn't have been her. She would have missed the greatest thing Pateras could offer.

The front door burst open, and the blast of cold air from outside blew Halyn's warm thoughts from her mind. Jedrek's guard rushed in to alert his master, "There are two riders coming in from the south, riding hard."

All eyes turned to Halyn, expecting her to know what to expect.

Halyn stood slowly. The cold wasn't helping the ache in her bones one bit. "I reckon I had better find out what they want."

Jedrek stepped in her way. "Let my guard find out."

Halyn picked up her walking stick and swatted Jedrek on the shin with it. "Out of my way, boy."

"Ow!" Jedrek yelped as he limped backward a step. The guard tried to look away so Jedrek wouldn't see his grin. His actions still earned him a dirty look.

"This is my house, and I'll tend to it. If they mean to harm anyone, let them start with me. I'll delay them while you get Slaina and the others to safety," Halyn continued.

The guard took a position inside the door where he could hear what was being said and intervene quickly if needed. Jedrek moved to back his guard, but was hastily rebuked. "Lord Jedrek, stay near the young woman. If they enter the house, get her to the city quickly."

The riders rode straight to the house. Neither was brandishing a weapon, which allayed some of Halyn's fear. Her next thought was that they were bringing bad news. The sun had set, and an overcast sky made the night extremely dark. The first rider was off his horse the second it stopped. He took two long steps to reach the porch but found himself at the point of Halyn's walking stick.

"Hold on there, young man! I don't know you. Who are you, and what do you want with me?" She raised her lamp to better see the man's face.

The man pulled his hood off his head. "My name is Garand. I was told my family is here."

Leesil quickly got off his horse and came up behind Garand. "Healer, it's Leesil. This is the girl's father."

Halyn wasted no more of the man's time. "Go inside. Your family is here, and they're safe."

Garand raced past her and into the house. Leesil started to follow, but Halyn stopped him with her stick. "Leesil, don't you know better than to ride in here like that? You could have gotten him hurt. There are guards all over the place."

As if to prove her point, the guards who had been watching the perimeter suddenly appeared on either side of the porch. They had ridden around the back of the house to protect Slaina's escape if needed. Hearing no sounds of distress, they worked their way around the side of the house to the front. Seeing Leesil and Halyn, they sheathed their weapons and returned to their posts.

Halyn invited Leesil to come inside. The two found a heartwarming reunion playing out in the kitchen. Garand took his time embracing each member of his family at length. Slaina held back, treasuring the sight of her reunited family. Garand finally reached for his firstborn daughter, the child he feared he had lost. "Slaina."

Slaina threw herself into her father's arms. "Papa, I didn't think I would ever see you again," she cried.

After a long embrace, Garand relaxed his grip on her. He lifted his head, and his eyes landed on Jedrek. An anger akin to Eston's, yet tempered by maturity and wisdom, rose within him. "Jedrek, why are you here?"

"Garand, I had nothing to do with the way you, Slaina, or the rest of your family were treated. My uncle did that against my wishes. I said some terrible things to Slaina, and I am here apologizing to her. I now believe she is carrying the Promised One of Pateras. My uncle has also sent his apologies to Slaina. He believes he overreacted and wants to make amends."

Garand glared at the young man. "You came here to apologize for your uncle? If he believes he did wrong, why didn't he come himself?"

Jedrek stood his ground. "I'm not here to apologize for my uncle. I came here because I wronged Slaina and I wanted to set things right. My uncle also asked me to send his apologies to her. I still love Slaina. I want her to be my wife."

Garand grabbed Jedrek and slammed him against the wall. "You aren't taking my daughter to Somi! Do you hear me? We're never going back there!"

Leesil, Joren, and Jedrek's bodyguard jumped in to separate the two. They held Garand at bay until Jedrek could speak. "I have no intention of taking her back to Somi. I purchased some land here. Nazar is my home. Pateras sent his messenger to me in a dream and told me not to be afraid to marry Slaina. I have accepted this. I want to raise the child as though he were my own. Garand, Slaina has forgiven me. The one thing I lack is your blessing to marry her."

"What makes you think I would ever give you my blessing?" he spat.

Halyn jumped in. "You know, I really don't want all this food to go to waste. This meal is already colder than dirt. Can we sit down and eat it before I find ice floating in the stew?"

Halyn's abrupt interruption broke a tiny hole through the tension. Seeing her father angry made Irana cling to her mother's tunic. Halyn's words and tone suggested to the four-year-old child that the fighting was over. Her small, impatient stomach cried out for satiation. "Mama, can we eat now?"

Garand relaxed enough for the men to release their grasp on him. Still, no one moved to sit at the table.

Halyn added another rebuke. "Everyone sit down and eat! We thanked Pateras for this food, and if we don't eat it, he'll start thinkin' we were lyin' to him." She thumped her walking stick on the table. "When we're done eatin' I think one of you menfolk should read to the rest of us from the Ancient Texts. It seems we need a good dose of Pateras' message. Now sit!"

Everyone moved slowly to their places. Luisa scooted over on the bench to make room for Garand. Faris was comfortable with Halyn's kitchen and quickly grabbed two more place settings for Leesil and her father. Leesil was eager to get home to his own family, but the long cold ride had left him stiff and drained. Halyn's warm fireplace and the aroma of a hearty stew beckoned him to stay longer.

The table was crowded now. For years, it had been used by only Halyn and her husband. Today it served eleven. Her husband had built a table big enough to host the large family they never had. Today, it was a perfect fit. Halyn marveled at how Pateras had provided for this day.

The conversation was strained for a time until the youngsters asked Leesil and Garand about their adventures. Leesil deferred to Garand to tell the tale of their escape from Somi. After Garand regaled the youngsters about scaling the wall and arrows flying at them, Leesil downplayed his own part in the adventure by stating, "I just held the horses and ran for the hills," though he had done far more than that by leading Garand away from trouble and keeping him from going too far, too fast.

Leesil asked the questions he knew Garand wanted to know the answers to. "Eston, how did Wintin get you out?"

The stories continued on for another hour as everyone caught up. Even Jedrek's comments and exclamations of amazement were welcomed into the conversation.

Jedrek finally stood to leave. "It's getting late. I should return to town. Marek will begin to worry if I don't return soon—he isn't a pleasant person to be around when he's worried."

Halyn wagged her crooked arthritic finger at him. "You sit yourself back down. We haven't read Pateras' words yet. Joren, fetch the texts. Leesil, would you do us the honor of reading to us this evening?"

Leesil looked surprised. "You have a copy of the texts?"

"Of course I do. My husband used to read them to me until his eyes went bad. Joren has been reading them to us since we returned. They've been handed down through several generations."

Joren reverently carried the large book wrapped in a leather binder to Leesil. The dingy cloth pages were bound by hand-sewn stitches, and the raw edges of each page were folded over twice, then sewn in place to secure them inside the cloth. The words on each page had been painstakingly scrawled with thick black ink.

Leesil placed his hands on the Holy Book and said a brief, heartfelt prayer. "Pateras, may the reader of this book be worthy to speak your words, and may they inspire the ears of the listener."

Leesil decided to read from the beginning of the large book. He laid it out on the table, untied the leather straps, and opened it to the first page. He recounted the story of the origins of mankind on a world of peace. Mankind flourished until the Dark Lord seduced one couple to drink from the Fountain of Understanding. Pateras knew of their crime and removed them from the world. He sent them to a new world and hid the one world of peace from the skies so they or their children could never return there. Pateras sadly told them, as a father disciplines a child, that their actions would cost them dearly. He promised them he was not abandoning them into the hands of the Dark Lord. He promised he would one day send a child to be born, a son who would pay for the crimes of all of mankind. Pateras would sacrifice his own life to save the lives of all who broke their covenant with Pateras. As Leesil read the next words, they struck chords among those present.

> *Pateras spoke to his wayward children: "As I have made a way to forgive your crimes, you must also forgive one another's crimes. Do not let the crime of unforgiveness keep you from my presence. I*

created you, and I love you. Love each other as I love you."

Garand was pained by the words as his eyes landed on Jedrek. Had the young man wronged them? Even if he had, Pateras expected him to forgive the young man.

Leesil reached the end of the section and reverently closed the book. He softly spoke another prayer, asking Pateras to bless the reading of his words. He tied the book in its leather binder and handed it carefully to Joren, who returned it to its protected wooden box.

The women collected the dirty dishes and put away what little food was left.

Jedrek pulled Slaina aside to speak privately to her. "Slaina, do not pester your father about forgiving me or accepting me. It is my responsibility to seek his forgiveness, not yours."

"But Jedrek, if I tell him I've forgiven you and that I love you, he'll listen."

"That's exactly why I don't want you to talk to him about this. I'm the one who should earn his forgiveness. He needs to believe me. He already believes you," Jedrek explained. "I need to know beyond a doubt that he trusts me before we can be married."

"All right, Jedrek, I will not mention it to him. I will answer him honestly if he asks, though."

Jedrek smiled at his strong-willed girlfriend. He stroked the side of her face lovingly and leaned down to kiss her forehead. She was petite but feisty. He wasn't sure, but he suspected Halyn was teaching her how to use her feisty nature.

Jedrek thanked Halyn for the food and her hospitality. He looked around for Garand, who was no longer in the room, then spoke briefly to Leesil to thank him for bringing Slaina's father safely from the city.

Leesil was ready to get to his own home and followed Jedrek and his bodyguard out onto the porch. The bodyguard was the first to step outside. He moved to untie the horses. Garand was standing on the far end of the porch, staring at the sky. A small hole punched in the clouds revealed a brilliant, nearly full moon.

Jedrek nodded to his companion to continue to the horses without him, then stepped to Garand's side. A glint of light caught his attention. Garand was standing there with a small dagger in his hand, his fingers gently tracing the flat side of the blade. He looked over at Jedrek guiltily.

Jedrek stiffened. Without moving his eyes off Garand, he ordered his bodyguard to ride out to the bend in the trail leaving Halyn's farm and wait for him there. Leesil joined the bodyguard, sensing the two needed their privacy.

The second the two rode away, Garand turned to face Jedrek. "You're comfortable remaining alone with me? Do you think you can best me?"

"I have no intention of fighting you. What is it you want from me? Revenge for what my uncle did to you?" Jedrek opened his arms wide, exposing his body and vital organs to an easy attack. "I didn't do this to you or your family. Perhaps I am guilty of not doing more to stop it. I should have found a way to stop it. My uncle is not a man to be crossed. Forgive my cowardice. If you believe nothing else, believe this: I love Slaina, and I want to raise this child as Pateras would want him raised. I wronged you by staying silent, and I am truly sorry for that."

Garand turned toward Jedrek. "Swear to me on your life that you are only here because you love my daughter. Swear that you will never put her in harm's way or take her back to Somi."

Jedrek raised his hands in the traditional posture to take an oath. His eyes locked on Garand's. "I swear on my life, I love Slaina, and I abhor the harm that was done to her and your family. I swear I will never take her even one step within the Somian Province, and I will never allow harm to come to her. May Pateras punish me ever so severely if I fail to fulfill this oath."

"And if I still desire revenge?" Garand stepped closer to Jedrek and pushed the tip of the blade forcefully against his belly.

"Then have your revenge." Jedrek didn't pull away. He closed his eyes to wait for the pain of his impending evisceration.

Garand saw what he wanted to see. Jedrek wasn't overconfident. He was genuinely afraid he was about to die.

Garand had no intention of harming the young man, at least not more than a possible fist across his face. He pulled the blade back, then inverted the dagger. "Jedrek, I need no revenge against you. I believe you. Forgive me for the harsh test."

"I believe I deserved worse." Jedrek wiped a bead of perspiration from his forehead. "Is it too soon to ask if I can have your blessing to marry Slaina?"

Garand gave the brash young man a disgruntled look. "Yes, it is. Where are you staying?"

"I'm staying at the inn in Nazar."

"Go back to the inn. You can ask me again another day."

"Yes, sir." Jedrek pulled his cloak tightly around himself and stepped off the porch. He untied his horse and mounted it quickly, feeling lucky to be leaving unscathed. This wasn't how he had expected his day to end.

Garand moved to the door to get in out of the cold. He stopped and called over his shoulder, "Jedrek, when you ask it again, the answer will be yes."

"Yes sir. Thank you, sir." Jedrek rode off fueled by adrenalin.

Garand walked inside and laid the dagger on the now empty kitchen table. He said simply, "I need to return this to Leesil."

Slaina looked nervously at the weapon. "Papa, what did you do?"

Halyn pulled the girl forward to give her a closer look at the weapon. "What do you see?"

Slaina gave Halyn a confused look. "Nothing. I don't understand. Papa, did you hurt Jedrek?"

Halyn grabbed Slaina's arm. "Girl, think. Look at the dagger. If he hurt anyone with that thing, what would you see?"

Slaina looked down at the blade. It was spotless. "There's no blood."

Garand approached his daughter. "As much as I wanted someone to pay for the harm done to us, Jedrek is not the one who owes us. I have forgiven him. He is unhurt."

The relief on Slaina's face told him how much she cared for Jedrek. If he had harmed the young man, Slaina would never have forgiven him.

Three weeks later, Jedrek and Slaina stood before the magistrate as he pronounced them husband and wife. They intended only a small family gathering. The news of the child brought the most ardent servants of Pateras forward to show their support for the girl and the wedding brought an entire day of celebration. The town hall was full to capacity.

Slaina's family was living inside the city gates. Slaina and Jedrek planned to live with Halyn and Joren until their new home could be built. As the day of celebration ended and everyone went their separate ways, Jedrek pulled his guards off to the side and dismissed them to return to Somi.

Marek objected. "My lord, we are under orders from Governor Pravin to protect you."

"I am no longer a Somian resident, and we are not on Somian soil. I cannot keep you from your families any longer. My safety is in the hands of the Nazarans now, and I have no enemies. My uncle has enemies, but they aren't here. Go home. Tell my uncle I am following his advice and I am happy. Leave first thing in the morning." Jedrek didn't give Marek a chance to argue. He rejoined his wife, who was surrounded by women giving her more advice and tips than she could possibly ever remember on how to be a wife and a mother. When Jedrek approached, the young women scampered away, giggling nervously.

Slaina looked at Jedrek. "The women were trying to tell me what to expect when we... uh..." She couldn't finish the sentence.

Jedrek took Slaina's hands in his. "Slaina, we cannot, and we will not, until after the child is born. To do so would be to blaspheme against the prophecies. I will not oppose the will of Pateras, not on this. We will return to Halyn's and occupy separate rooms until after the child is born. You have my word."

The two rode in the wagon back to Halyn's home. Halyn and Joren made the couple sit with her around the fireplace before the evening went any further. She sent Joren to fetch the Ancient Texts.

Joren carried them in to her and asked, "Do you want me to read them to you, Healer?"

"Not tonight, Joren. Tonight, I want to let you in on a secret. There are a number of things not right in all of creation, and more things go wrong every day. My dear husband sought to put one small thing right. I want all of you to swear to me that what you learn tonight, you will speak to no one about."

The young people looked at each other, wondering where she was headed with this. They each gave their vow of silence. Halyn opened the leather wrapping, flipped through numerous pages in the giant book, and read one of the prophetic passages about the Promised One.

> My beloved son will be lifted up and exalted by many and despised by those who serve only themselves or the Dark Lord. Those who do not serve me will seek to silence my son and all who follow him. He comes to bring mercy to all who will receive it. Although he is innocent of all wrong, he will give himself to pay for the crimes of all. The pain of death will be visited upon him twelve times. The pain and bruises of the Defender will become his. His death will save the lives of those he has chosen to be messengers and defenders of the followers of Pateras. He will give his life to spare the life of the Defender, who will lead the war against the Dark Lord. His words will be the words of life.

> You will know my son when you see the signs. The handmaiden chosen by Pateras will be with child yet untouched by any man. The stars will herald his coming. He will be the descendant of kings and will unite two kingdoms with his birth. Messengers from afar will see the newborn king.

Joren's eyes widened. "Healer, you can read?"

Halyn's eyes sparkled. "Yes, boy, I can read. My husband taught me many years ago. When his eyes started to fail, I read the texts to him. He believed women ought to know a little more than cooking, cleaning, and sewing. He believed everyone should be able to read the words of Pateras for themselves. Now, don't you forget your oath that you swore to me. Tell no one about this."

Jedrek looked nearly as startled. It wasn't the same thing as sending girls to school, but he couldn't argue with her logic. She no longer had a husband to read to her. It wouldn't be fair if she possessed the words of Pateras and still could not hear them. A woman reading still seemed unnatural. He had to admit he enjoyed listening to her read, though.

Jedrek felt Halyn's eyes on him and looked up. He didn't bother giving her time to ask. "I will keep your secret. I also enjoyed your choice in what to read this evening."

Slaina was quiet. Halyn closed the book and returned it to Jedrek, who carefully put it away. "Slaina, are you feelin' all right, girl?"

"Yes, Healer, I'm just tired. It has been an exhausting day, and my feet and ankles are swollen." Slaina wiggled and twisted her feet uncomfortably.

"Drink two full cups of water, then get yourself in the bed," Halyn instructed.

Slaina's face fell. "Do I have to? I hate getting up during the night to use the chamber pot."

Halyn put her hands on her hips. "You know you're going to be getting up anyway. You might as well make it worth your while. Do as I told you."

Slaina sighed and followed Halyn's instructions. Her belly was showing a distinct bulge now. The baby would be born in about four more months. Slaina was nervous about the upcoming event. She had gone with Halyn to help with the birth of two babies in the province now. Childbirth did not look pleasant.

Jedrek escorted Slaina to her room and stoked the fire in her fireplace to get it going again. He helped her get her shoes off. The young woman was so tired, she was nearly asleep the moment she sat on the bed. She hadn't even tried to change into her night clothes. Jedrek smiled at her. He lifted her feet onto the bed and covered her with the quilts. He kissed her forehead and softly whispered, "Goodnight, my love." His room was on the other side of the shared fireplace. He went to his side and continued to build the fire. As he stared into the flames, he wondered if the war with his uncle was truly over.

LADO PHARMACEUTICALS

"Tristan? Tristan, did you hear what I said?" Jessica stared at his face on the screen. His blank eyes stared back at her.

Realizing she had asked him something, he finally blinked twice to refocus his thoughts. "I'm sorry, Jessica. Did you say you got a job offer from Lado Pharmaceuticals?"

"Yes, isn't it exciting?" Jessica's smile nearly covered her entire face.

"Did you apply to Lado?" Tristan was hoping this was just an odd coincidence.

"Well, no, not specifically. I did put my resume in with a job marketing firm, and they may have shared it with them."

"Do they have an office on Juranta?"

"No, but that won't be a problem. They said whoever gets the job could work from home via the Interplanetary Communications Network. They said I might have to travel to the main office from time to time, but they would try to keep that to a minimum. Isn't this exciting?" The young woman was bouncing on the inside, but Tristan's lack of enthusiasm was putting a damper on her excitement.

"Who conducted your interview? Was it someone locally, or was it conducted via the IC Net?"

"It was an IC interview."

"When did this offer come in?" he persisted.

"A couple hours ago." Jessica wasn't sure this qualified as discussing or not. It was starting to feel more like an interrogation. She supposed this might be the norm for an investigator.

"Did you keep a record of the interview?" Tristan drilled.

"Of course I did. Why are you asking all these questions?" Jessica was becoming more troubled by the moment.

"Did you accept the offer?" Tristan leaned in anxiously.

"Well, no, not yet. I wanted to talk to you first. I've not really heard of this company."

Jessica had more to say, but Tristan cut her off. "Good. Don't. Don't accept it and don't turn it down, at least not yet."

"Tristan, what's wrong?"

"Do you remember when you thought I lied to you about Robert?"

"Yes..." Jessica's excitement level took a nosedive.

"I told you I would only lie to you for one reason. Please don't ask me any more questions about this and don't accept or reject this job offer. Also, don't go anyplace by yourself for the next few days. Don't even stay home alone. Most importantly, don't agree to meet with any representatives of Lado Pharmaceuticals. If they want to know why you haven't accepted the offer, tell them I am off-world and will return in a few days. You will give them your answer next week." Tristan's eyes had only looked like this a couple of times. Each time, there had been trouble.

"Tristan, you're scaring me. What's this about?"

"Jessica, you aren't listening to me. This may be a coincidence, and it may be nothing, but if it isn't, I want to be prepared."

"If you don't want me to be alone, what am I supposed to do while my parents are at work?"

"Go with them if you have to."

"Tristan, I haven't gone to work with them since I was a child. They're going to want to know why," Jessica argued.

"Then... go to my office. I'll contact security and tell them to expect you. I'll hail Leland and let him know what's going on. Order a private car, no driver, or get your parents to drop you off."

Jessica folded her arms resolutely across her chest. "When do you plan on telling me what's going on?"

"As soon as I can, I promise. I need to make some calls. I love you. Be careful." Tristan closed the comm channel and headed to Riley's hotel room. He punched the button, letting Riley know he was present. Riley didn't acknowledge his presence. Tristan pushed the button a second time. Two seconds later, he pushed it a third and a fourth.

By the time he got to the fifth, Riley was standing at the door. "What is so blasted important that you couldn't wait a minute?"

Tristan pushed past his superior into the room. Riley gave an annoyed, "Please… do come in. It's not like I wasn't relaxing for the evening."

Tristan glanced around the room. He reached into his pocket and pulled out a short-range jamming device, then scanned the area. The scan was negative for any active listening devices. Riley recognized his actions for what they were. His curiosity cut off his complaints. "You find a bug in your room or something?"

Tristan stepped closer to Riley. "No, but you might want to contact your family. Jessica got an unexpected job offer - from Lado Pharmaceuticals."

Riley jumped to the desk and attempted to hail his wife. Tristan's jammer hindered the call. "Shut that jammer off!" he barked.

Tristan shut it off. Moments later, Riley's wife was on the computer screen in front of him. Her eyes were bloodshot, and her face was puffy from crying. "Mia, what's wrong?"

Before she could respond, a flash of guilt and fear washed over her face. She clearly slowed her response, only give her husband the pertinent information. "I accidentally bumped into Kyle Amos, having breakfast in the coffee shop down from the office. You remember him, don't you?"

Riley knew exactly what she was trying to hide. If he had broken off their relationship, Riley doubted she would have even brought him up. He surmised she would have blamed the tears on having a bad hair day or something. So what was it about him that would make her cry and reveal it to him? "Yes, I think we met at an office party or something a couple of times. Did something happen to him?"

"He collapsed in the coffee shop. They think it was a heart attack. He's never had any history of heart problems. Riley, he's dead! I sat there and watched him die." Mia erupted into another round of crying.

Riley was now dealing with a flood of emotions of his own as he sat there staring at the screen, feeling helpless. Part of him was relieved his rival was out of the picture and this secret was gone. Another part of him was worried about his family's safety if this was truly no accident.

Mia interrupted his thoughts. "Riley, I need you to come home."

"I know you do, dear. Even if I left in the next hour, the trip would take me at least five days on the fastest ship in the galaxy, and I'm pretty sure that one's not currently available. Mia, I know you and Kyle were - good friends, and I am very sorry for your loss. If I could be there for you, I would. Listen carefully: pack a bag and go stay with your sister. Don't return home until I get planetside. Do it now."

Even through the haze of her grief, Mia knew something sounded off. "Riley, what's wrong?"

Riley glanced at Tristan. "Amelia, I'm concerned about a case I'm working on right now, and I want you out of harm's way. It's possible..." Riley paused to word his next sentence carefully. "It's possible the people I am currently investigating did something to your friend to send me a warning message." He paused again and took a deep breath. "Mia, it might have unwittingly been my fault he died. Again, I am really sorry if this case has hurt you. Please go stay with your sister and don't tell anyone where you're going. I'm going to bring Leland up to speed on this. We will look into his death very carefully."

Amelia's tears stopped flowing as she processed the information. "You think I'm in danger? If they were trying to hurt you, why kill Kyle? You barely knew him."

"Mia, they weren't trying to hurt me yet. They were trying to send me a message by hurting someone you cared about. I'm sorry this case has involved you and your friends. Don't tell your boss where you are going, just tell him you need to take a leave of absence after you are headed out the door. Get going now. I'll hail you again when I have more information for you. Don't even try to go to Kyle's funeral. I mean it, Mia. Do you understand?"

Mia nodded solemnly. She was quickly becoming numb.

Riley searched the air around him for the right words to say to comfort his wife. He was suddenly feeling guilty for colluding in hiding her secret and not confronting her sooner. "Amelia, we need to talk when I get back. I know I haven't been the husband I should have been, and I want to fix it. I promise to work on this. Promise me you'll do what I told you. I want you to be safe."

A new tear slid down her face. Mia nodded again. "Yes, dear, I promise."

"Good, get moving. I need to make some calls. I love you." Riley closed the call out quickly.

Tristan fully expected the representatives from Lado Pharmaceuticals would contact them soon. He sat down and hailed Leland to get some pieces in place before that happened.

Leland's face appeared on the screen. "Are you gentlemen ready to head home yet?"

Tristan didn't waste time on pleasantries. "This case is not as simple as it appears, not by a long shot. Leland, let security know Jessica may show up at the office and she needs to be protected. She got an unexpected job offer from Lado Pharmaceuticals. Let Agents Wallace and Gershom know there's a problem. Jessica, her family, and Riley's family need a protective detail assigned to them, covertly. Emphasize that last word to them. I also need you to see to it that a recently deceased man named Kyle Amos gets an extensive autopsy, looking for chemicals that one might not normally look for."

Leland leaned forward in his chair. His brow now wrinkled with concern. "Care to explain this a little more?"

Tristan's face turned toward the entrance as he heard an override code opening the door to Riley's room. The lights and power went out, leaving the room dark. Several shadowy figures rushed in, and the two felt a brief stinging sensation as tranquilizer darts hit them.

Tristan began to rouse. His mouth tasted like some of the smells he had encountered when working out in the gym. His arms and legs weighed ten times their normal weight. His head was spinning. Hearing muffled voices, he tried opening his eyes to see who was near him. Bright lights from overhead blinded him. People were standing over him talking, but their words weren't making sense. It finally dawned in on him they weren't speaking in Intergalactic Standard. They must be using a native language.

He forced himself to take a deep breath to try to clear his head. Things were beginning to be less fuzzy, but his head wouldn't lift. It was still far too heavy. He could roll it right or left, but not upward. He tried again to open his eyes, and this time they cooperated.

He heard one of the voices. It spoke in I.S. "This one is waking up."

Tristan tried again to raise his head to get a better look around.

CEO Marguerite Bellamy stepped into view. "Chief Alexander, good morning. You said you wanted to see our entire process from beginning to end. How's this for a start?"

Tristan tried to speak, but the drug in his system had dried his throat. It took a second for him to clear it and swallow, which was unusually difficult. "What are you doing? Why are you doing this?" His voice still sounded raspy.

Marguerite folded her arms across her chest. "To make a point. You and your partner have been meddling in an internal problem. I want it stopped now. I'm willing to work with one of you and I don't care which. Since you woke up first, you get first chance at my offer. I want one of you working for me."

"Doing what?" Tristan tried again to lift his head. He could move his body in short increments left and right, but he still felt extremely heavy.

One of the men in the room stepped up on Tristan's left. His voice was accented, as though he hadn't been speaking I.S. for very long. He was wearing a physician's attire. "You need to lie still. We are using an artificial gravity field in the bed. You will pull a muscle or give yourself a hernia if you move around too much."

"Dr. Sokolov is correct. We wouldn't want you to hurt yourself."

"Interesting. The artificial gravity could skew autopsy results," Tristan observed.

Ms. Bellamy glanced at Dr. Sokolov, who gave her an affirming nod. The corner of her mouth smiled slightly. "Well, that's a side benefit we hadn't considered. We use this, along with the sedatives, to ease our patients through their transition into death. Patients are given medications to slow their breathing, then the gravity is increased gradually, making it more difficult to breathe. It also prevents them from hurting anyone if they react badly. Sometimes, when people reach the point of transition, they have regrets and second thoughts. This prevents them from making a mistake and trying to go back to the misery they were living in."

"In other words, they decide they want to live, and you keep them here to finish the job," Tristan wryly replied.

Marguerite glared at Tristan. "They couldn't stand living, or they wouldn't be here. It's natural for them to want another way to fix whatever is wrong with their pitiful lives. Once they've received the first doses of medication, they aren't legally allowed to change their minds. Changing their minds is more likely an emotional reaction caused by an intolerance to a particular medication."

"Is that what happened to those who accidentally survived the process?"

"Uh-uh, that's all you get until you agree to work for me." Marguerite shook her head at him. "Do we have a deal?"

Tristan tried swallowing again. "I need a few more details before I agree to anything."

Two other men stepped up beside her. "Marguerite, I think the other man is a better choice. I don't trust this one."

"I agree with Mr. Nash," the second man said.

"Here's the arrangement, Mr. Alexander. I need you to make this investigation go away and steer any others away in the future. I also have, as I said, an internal problem that I need fixed. Find out who's sabotaging my business and *end* them."

Tristan had been in investigation and interrogation mode. He now switched to undercover officer mode. "Uh, I'm just an accountant, and a new one at that."

"Chief Alexander, this is my chief of security, Philip Henderson. He knows almost everything there is to know about you, former Covert Ops Agent Alexander."

Tristan didn't skip a beat. "There's a reason I got out of Covert Ops. I couldn't stomach it any longer. I'm no killer."

Kendall Nash, the chief of operations, shook his head. "Let's use the other guy and put this one down."

Tristan felt his heart skip a beat. He had trained himself to pick those tiny inflections of emotion and ride them into bigger displays of emotion. "Put down? How are you going to explain that to my superiors? They know where we are and what we're doing. You'll draw all kinds of attention if we disappear."

Chief Henderson grinned sadistically. "There was some confusion between you and some actual patients, and you were put down by accident. It was really tragic. Our sincerest apologies to the GFOD."

Marguerite glanced at Riley, who was finally showing signs of waking up. "Time's running out. Do we have a deal, or do I offer it to your partner? Only one of you walks out of here alive."

"What do I get out of this deal?" Tristan asked quickly. He knew his time to bargain was slipping away. He needed to stall for time. Leland had to get word to Agents Wallace and Gershom, and they would take steps that were more extreme than anything he had been authorized to do in Covert Ops. The only question was, how long would it take? Hours? Days?

"First, you get to live. Second, if you follow my orders and rid my company of this problem, you could see some bonus credits come your way. Dr. Sokolov can give you something to use on whoever is messing with my clinics. That way, you can put them down as humanely as possible. Will that satiate your delicate stomach, Mr. Alexander? Oh, and on a personal side of things, your fiancée gets the job of her dreams, which you will encourage her to accept."

"I'll do it on one condition."

Mr. Nash was ready to be done with this mess. "You're in no position to make demands. Dr. Sokolov, put him down."

Dr. Sokolov glanced at Marguerite before moving. "What is it you want?" she asked.

"I need Riley alive. I was the one who pushed to do this investigation. If he dies or disappears, it will still get too much attention. If we both go back empty-handed, he can lay the blame on me, and nobody will look at this investigation any further. It's also better to have two of us on the payroll. We can cover for each other."

Marguerite's eyes narrowed as she tried to size the young man up. Was he trying to stall for time until he could escape them?

Tristan knew she was weighing whether or not to trust him. "How about this? I can explain the situation to him and get him on board. I'll root out your problem and take care of it with your humane cure." He winced as he spoke the last part to emphasize his distaste for the task. "I'll provide you with proof the deed is done and who did it. You can always use it against me later if I am—less than cooperative."

Chief Henderson scowled. "I don't like it. That sounds too good to be true. He's up to something."

Marguerite folded her arms across her chest. "Like what? Explain it to me, and I'll deal with it."

"I don't know what, but nobody's going to hand us evidence to use against them," Chief Henderson argued.

"I'm not handing you evidence to use against me. I'm trading it to you for Riley's life and freedom. It keeps me from reporting you, and he won't report me because I've just saved his life. What's not to understand here?" Tristan looked at Riley in the bed behind Marguerite. His gut told him Riley was fully awake and listening to them.

"All right, Chief, we have a deal. In case you ever think about going back on our deal, know this. We have people on Juranta, among other places. That attractive young fiancée might suffer some unfortunate accident. Mr. Hardin's wife or children could suffer a bigger loss than an illicit lover," the cold CEO alluded.

Marguerite nodded to Dr. Sokolov. "Release him and give him what he needs to take care of our problem. Oh, yes, I almost forgot. Put a tracker in him so he doesn't get lost."

"Yes, ma'am."

The two executives and the security chief left the room. Tristan waited for the painful injection. The doctor did a quick scan and discovered Tristan already carried a tracking device. A look of fear crossed his face. Tristan watched the man walk quickly over to his computer panel and scramble the feed. He whipped around. "You already have a tracker. Why?"

"Because I never left Covert Ops. I'm on a mission that's much bigger than Lado Pharm. I have no real interest in your company. This investigation is to keep my cover story intact. You need to put that tracker in me now and unscramble that feed."

"Why did you tell me this and not them?" Dr. Sokolov asked.

"I had a hunch I could trust you. Now give me that tracker and unscramble the feed," Tristan ordered.

The doctor looked over at Riley, who was still lying motionless. "What about your friend?"

"My friend is on board with me, so get moving," Tristan ordered more emphatically.

The doctor jammed a hypo-sprayer against a shoulder muscle near the base of Tristan's neck and pressed the button. The device forced its massive payload into his tissues. "AH! OW! That stings." Tristan hated getting trackers put in. At least local anesthetics were used when removing the vile things.

Tristan was right to be concerned about the surveillance feed being scrambled. Chief Henderson came in to check on the situation. "Doc, is everything all right in here? Your computer is offline."

Dr. Sokolov looked at it blankly. "It is? I must have touched something by accident when I retrieved the tracker. Sorry. Are you sure you're ready to release these two?"

"I'm not, but the boss is. Turn this one loose, and I'll move that one to a secure location when he's able to move on his own." Chief Henderson got the computer back up as the doctor unobtrusively released the controls holding Tristan in his bed.

Tristan felt his weight return to normal. He pulled his head up, then sat up slowly, keeping a cautious eye on both men. He continued to play the part of the subjugated officer.

"Why's he still out?" Philip nodded at Riley.

Tristan grinned slightly. "He'd had a couple of drinks before you guys drugged us."

Riley moaned slightly but refused to open his eyes. His gravely voice finally addressed the others. "It was more than a couple. I don't suppose you could dim the lights—and the noise a bit?"

Tristan glanced at the doc to see if he would oblige. Dr. Sokolov turned out the exam lights directly over Riley's bed. He ordered the computer to lower the ambient lighting by twenty-five percent.

Riley did have a couple of drinks, as Tristan said, but they hadn't affected him as drastically as suggested. Riley was learning quickly from Tristan, although the younger man was the intern.

Tristan stood slowly and moved to his partner's bedside. "I'm assuming you were awake enough to catch most of that?"

Dr. Sokolov released the gravity field on Riley's bed. Riley reached up and grabbed his head when he felt his weight release. "Oh, that made me nauseous. I heard the important parts. You made some kind of deal to get us out of here alive. You're going to continue investigating this problem while I sit here on my backside doing nothing. I hope you get this right, kid. I'd really rather not go home in a tube. Don't take too long, I get bored easily."

Tristan turned to Chief Henderson. "I need Riley's help on this. Get him a place to work and computer access. I want my weapon back, the compound I need to handle the problem, access to your data files, and communications access to Riley."

The man stiffened and shook his head. "You don't make demands of me."

"What's the matter? You afraid some kid almost straight out of the Academy is going to show you up?"

"Show me up?" the seasoned security officer snarled. "You're dreaming if you think you're going to show me up."

"Look, I work for this company now. If you want me to get this job done, I need some tools to work with. If you're worried, give Riley view-only status, and I need access to Riley. He's going to feed me information so I'll know where to look. By the way, I also need a set of Lado Pharm security credentials."

Philip stood there, unresponsive for a moment, staring at the nearest security camera. His face revealed his annoyance at the voice speaking to him through his earpiece. His eyes finally focused again on Tristan. "Fine, wait here. I'll be back momentarily."

Riley continued to play the part of a man hungover and got up slowly. He glanced at the door and the security camera. "So what is it I need to look for? Hey Doc, can I get a little something for this hangover?"

Dr. Sokolov nodded and moved away to get the requested medication. Riley rubbed his head and looked away from the surveillance devices. "What's the plan?" he mumbled softly.

Tristan leaned against the wall as he waited for Philip to return with what he needed. He spoke in his normal tone. "I have some ideas about where to look, but the first thing I need is to know where each of the events and failed procedures has occurred. The next thing I need is to see all the video footage, and this is going to be a lot of footage of every person involved prior to each procedure." Tristan stopped leaning against the wall and stood to face the surveillance feed. "Give us an office, or someplace we can work on this."

The doc returned with the required medication and dosed Riley with it. He also handed Tristan a hypo-sprayer with a single dose of medication.

Tristan looked at the device. "Doc, I may need more than one dose if there's more than one person involved in this."

The man seemed oddly nervous and disturbed by the thought. He went back to his counter and prepared the additional doses. While he worked, Tristan glanced at Riley and whispered softly as he paced back and forth in front of the man. "I just need to wait for Gershom and Wallace to get a handle on this, and we'll be fine."

Chief Henderson returned and ordered the doctor to put a tracker in Riley as well. His was armed with an alarm that would go off if he got within twenty feet of a building exit. He then led them to a conference room where they could start working. Chief Henderson stayed with them and watched them work for a time. Tristan finally asked, "Chief Henderson, this is what we wanted to do the moment we arrived here. Why didn't you let us do this from the beginning? Why go to all the trouble to coerce us to work for you?"

"This wasn't my call, but Marguerite saw this as a chance to get a GFOD officer in her pocket to protect her interests. This also guarantees keeping a lid on this. The press, or her governmental contractors, won't have to know about it. Personally, I would have let you do the investigation. I think we could have spun it so we came out looking like heroes when we captured some bleeding-heart activist."

Several hours later, the three could not pin the botched procedures on any one person. No one individual was linked to all the procedures. It appeared this could well be a team effort.

Tristan stood to go talk to Dr. Sokolov. Mr. Henderson jumped to stop him from leaving the room.

"Chief Henderson, may I remind you, he's the hostage," Tristan said, pointing at Riley, "not me. I have an investigation to conduct, and I wouldn't mind some lunch, since we never actually got breakfast. Why don't you get Riley some food while I go ask Dr. Sokolov some questions about the clinical routines and procedures."

Philip wasn't amused, but he knew Tristan was technically correct. He was still not about to trust either of these men yet, though. He grudgingly allowed Tristan to leave the room, then escorted Riley to the company commissary.

Tristan caught up with Dr. Sokolov in his office. "Doctor, I was wondering if you could walk me through the procedures involved from beginning to end. What happens from the moment a potential patient walks through the door asking questions until he is laid to rest?"

"Can we do this later? I was about to go get some lunch," the man groused.

Tristan sensed something was off, although he had no idea what it was. "I haven't had breakfast or lunch. Perhaps we could both get something from the commissary and go someplace quiet to talk? I would rather our conversations not be overheard by the general public."

"Very well, if you insist." The man started to close his computer then asked Tristan if he minded waiting in the hall for a moment. "I have a personal call to make to my wife. It will only take a minute."

Tristan gave the man his privacy. He tapped into the security system from his bracelet and watched the man discreetly from the corridor. Dr. Sokolov called his wife, as he had indicated. He also pulled a weapon from a drawer and slid it into his pocket. Knowing his wife was at work, he left her a time-delayed message. "Natali, I must be brief. I'm afraid my time is coming to an end. I've done some things I never told you about, and only Pateras can help me now. Forgive me. I love you. Give my love to the children. Goodbye, Natali."

Pateras? That was one of the names on Tristan's watch list for Jessica, the one Riley said was a ghost.

Tristan shut off his bracelet as Dr. Sokolov closed his office. He had seen the man pick up the weapon, but he did nothing to acknowledge it as yet. The two men headed to the nearest commissary and chose some sandwiches and drinks. Dr. Sokolov led Tristan to a stairwell at the end of a hallway. Tristan knew whatever move the doctor was going to make, he would make it at any moment.

Dr. Sokolov didn't reach for the weapon he carried and led Tristan up one last flight of stairs and through a doorway onto the roof. The doctor had to go first, as he was the only one with access to release the door. Tristan saw the man go through the doorway and turn a sharp corner. He knew that when he stepped through the door, he would be facing the weapon he had seen Dr. Sokolov pick up in his office. Tristan kept his hands, which were occupied with his food, in plain sight. He stepped through the door and into the sights of the weapon as expected. The Tri-EMP could fire a pellet programmed with an electromagnetic charge. The weapon had three settings: a light stun, a heavy stun, and a lethal setting. Tristan raised his hands slowly. He was fairly certain the man wasn't a killer. He did expect he would defend himself if needed. Tristan did everything in his power to keep the man at ease. The man motioned for him to be silent. He moved around behind him and pushed Tristan against the outside wall. Tristan tensed as he found himself in a vulnerable position. He prepared to defend himself if needed. Dr. Sokolov pressed the weapon against Tristan's neck at the base of his skull, then reached over to remove his bracelet. He tossed the bracelet inside the stairwell. Pulling the weapon back, Dr. Sokolov closed the door and promptly scrambled the lock code. He stepped away from Tristan. "Now, we can talk."

Tristan turned around slowly. "Do you mind if I eat while we talk?"

"You still have an appetite, even when you are about to kill?"

"Considering you're the one with the weapon, I thought I was preparing to eat my last meal. Who am I about to kill?" Tristan tried to set the man at ease with a hint of levity and a dose of ignorance. His appetite radically diminished when faced with a weapon, but his actions served as a distraction, more for the doctor than for himself. He knew far more answers than he was letting on, but he wanted more. If he put the man at ease, he might be more forthcoming.

"You're about to kill me. You were looking for whoever was causing the failed suicides, and that led you to me. I know who and what you are. It's just a matter of time before you disarm me and kill me." The strain in Dr. Sokolov's voice thickened his accent.

"I came to you to ask you to walk me through the procedures. I didn't have any particular reason to suspect you until you pulled a weapon on me. Now I'm finding your behavior questionable." Tristan wasn't trying to toy with the man. He merely wanted to set the record straight. The man had given himself away.

"Once I filled you in on the procedures, you would have learned about my part in all of this. It's why I only gave you one dose of medication." Dr. Sokolov motioned for Tristan to sit on the ground along the roof ledge, while he sat on the ledge outside of Tristan's reach. "Eat your sandwich."

Tristan casually unwrapped his food and took small bites as he questioned the man. "Would you care to explain what's happening around here?"

"This world is new to the Commonwealth. We don't agree with certain things that the Commonwealth has enacted, and assisted suicides are one of them."

"We?" Tristan took another bite of his sandwich.

"Certain citizens of Stiliani. It doesn't matter who. We don't serve the Commonwealth the way others do. Certain people who come in for the assistance to cross over are being pressured by family or they are suffering from treatable depression. We put patients through a screening process, and those who agree with me do everything possible to stop them from making a mistake. Unfortunately, some were brought back in and put down with a secondary procedure, which may or may not have been as— humane. We got careless. I need you to do me one favor, stop your investigation with my death. Don't look for the others. I've already warned them to stop what they are doing and lie low for a time. They know you're looking for them. They're just trying to stop people from making tragic mistakes."

Tristan took another bite of his sandwich. "Is there evidence pointing to you as acting alone?"

"There's enough evidence to point to me in eighty to ninety percent of the cases. I suppose the other ten to twenty percent could be viewed as medical errors, which will go away for a time." Dr. Sokolov put his weapon on the ledge beside him and picked up his own sandwich. His confession made the flavors more delectable. He expected his stomach to be tied in knots. It wasn't. A sense of peace settled over him.

"So, there are others involved," Chief Alexander surmised.

"Yes, but please, just take my life and leave the others alone. If Ms. Bellamy and the others aren't satisfied, use those other doses I gave you. The medication simulates death for a few hours, long enough to fool a medical examiner. Get the bodies shipped out and then release them from stasis when the medication wears off. Please don't hurt them. They don't mean any harm," Dr. Sokolov begged.

Tristan took a large bite of his sandwich, buying him time to think. Alicia's great-grandfather had seemingly been forced into a premature death, and Alicia was robbed of a dearly loved grandfather. No, Dr. Sokolov was not the primary problem here. Marguerite Bellamy and her co-conspirators trying to put him and Riley in their pockets was a distinct problem. "What was the first dose of medication you gave me, then?"

"It is a deadly dose. It's designed to make a death look like a heart attack. The medication is untraceable if you don't know what to look for," the doctor explained.

"Why haven't you considered opening your own clinic to screen potential candidates?"

Dr. Sokolov took a bite of his own sandwich while he considered Tristan's suggestion. "I suppose that's not a bad idea. A little late, though. I doubt Ms. Bellamy would allow me to simply disappear. Opening a prescreening clinic would take money out of her pocket. She would find a way to shut us down."

Tristan glanced around. There were no signs of surveillance at all. He wolfed the last of his sandwich down and chased it with his drink. He cautiously got to his feet and meandered back and forth in front of the man. The doctor's behavior was atypical for a man who expected to be dead shortly.

"Let me make sure I understand this. You brought me out here so you could fall on your own sword, leaving me to present your corpse to the powers that be, along with proof that you were the sole party responsible for orchestrating all the botched procedures. If you're turning yourself in, why pull a weapon on me?"

"I needed to be sure we could talk privately."

"What about the monitoring capabilities of the tracker you put in me?"

A smirk crossed the doctor's face. "It monitors your location, not your conversations. I may have inadvertently misunderstood my instructions."

"What did you want me to know that they don't need to hear?"

"I want to know you won't pursue this any further. Something, or someone, told me to trust you."

Tristan latched onto the phrase the doctor tried to quietly slide past him. "Someone? Who?"

"It's not anyone you're familiar with, but one who knows you quite well."

Tristan's mind jumped back to the message Dr. Sokolov had left for his wife. Tristan had been living with someone higher up pulling the strings for a year now, or so he thought. In truth, it had been far longer. "Was it Pateras? I've heard his name—or her name—a couple of times recently. Who is Pateras?"

"It no longer matters. I have failed him."

Sensing this was a closed topic, Tristan moved on with his investigation. "You and your friends oppose merciful euthanasia, and you run interference in the Lado Clinics subversively by making it look like a botched procedure. Won't people repeat the procedure or use another clinic? If a person wants to die, they usually find a way to do it."

"If they get that far, it's usually pressure from family that gets them to that point. If they become combative, we know they don't truly want to die. We give them a dose of the medication I put in that second vial I gave you. They wake up hours later. If they want to go home, we get them home. If they want to disappear, we help them do that. If they truly want to die, we allow them to repeat the procedure with the correct drugs. We aren't monsters, Mr. Alexander."

Tristan glanced at Dr. Sokolov sitting on the ledge. If he went over it backward, it was a fall of several stories. The man would die. His weapon sat untouched on the ledge beside him. He didn't seem worried about Tristan at this point, as both his hands cradled his sandwich as though it were the best meal he had ever had.

"Dr. Sokolov, it doesn't sound like you and your friends are guilty of anything worse than maybe medical misconduct and a couple of misdemeanors. These are not capital offenses. Why are you so prepared to die?"

"Ms. Bellamy wants the perpetrator dead. She typically gets what she wants." The doctor stopped eating. His thoughts of the woman sickened him and ruined his appetite.

Tristan stood still. "Ms. Bellamy is trying to send a message to anyone who opposes her. She also wants me to kill someone so she has something other than a loved one to hold over my head and keep me loyal to her. Right now, all she has on me is a threat to harm someone I care about. If my fiancée and I go our separate ways, or if I find a way to hide her, Marguerite has nothing to keep me in line. If I kill unnecessarily, she can threaten to expose me and get me arrested. I could kill a janitor, and she'd be happy, although she would still want me to stop your operation."

Dr. Sokolov laid his sandwich on the wrapper beside him. "We're running out of time. They'll be here soon looking for us. Are you going to throw me off the roof, shoot me, or use the syringe to make it appear that I had a heart attack?"

Tristan knew the man would throw himself off the roof if he suspected what he really had planned. Tristan pulled the syringe out of his pocket, palming the secondary vial. He pulled the original vial out of the syringe as though to check its readiness. When he did, he secretly swapped the two vials. He pulled his weapon. "Toss your weapon on the ground away from you."

The man was suddenly nervous and pale. He picked the weapon up slowly and tossed it away.

"Stand up and turn around," Tristan ordered.

Dr. Sokolov stood shakily. His knees grew weak, and his movements became awkward. He swallowed hard. The doctor was confused about which method the young man planned to use on him. He hoped he wouldn't be pushed from the rooftop. To his relief, the young man ordered him to kneel on the ground.

Tristan pressed his weapon against the man's neck. "Dr. Sokolov, swear on the life of your wife and the life of this Pateras that the second vial of medication isn't deadly, only the first vial is."

"What? Why are you asking that?" The man panicked.

"I want the truth quickly. Is the second vial truly harmless, and the first one deadly? Tell me now, or I will use my own weapon to take out your wife and any other of your conspirators I find." Tristan pressed the weapon more firmly into his neck, putting him slightly off balance.

"Only the original vial is deadly! I swear it! Please don't hurt my wife! She did nothing wrong." Dr. Sokolov now feared he had made a mistake in trusting this man.

Tristan relaxed the pressure on the man's neck. "Dr. Sokolov, when this is over, I strongly suggest you find a new line of work. Thanks for trusting me."

The words weren't making sense. He started to ask what Tristan meant when he felt the hypo-sprayer press into his neck and a burning sensation as the medication entered his tissues. The light of the afternoon sun went dark. His heart thumped loudly and slowly in his ears. He felt himself falling. The last thing he could feel was Tristan catching his body and easing it onto the ground. Why would this young stranger grant him this kindness? His thoughts stopped.

MAREK

Marek returned to Somi and reported to Governor Pravin. "Governor, I don't believe your nephew intends to consummate his marriage until after the child is born. I suspect he does not intend to ever return to Somi. I know you didn't want me to start a war with Nazar. If I killed the young woman outright, it would certainly result in war. What would you like me to do?"

Governor Pravin stared into the flames in his fireplace as he pondered the situation. He finally came to a decision. "We will be patient. How did you find the province of Nazar? A pleasant place to settle, perhaps?"

Marek looked puzzled. "It wasn't much different from Somi. The terrain is rockier and more mountainous. There isn't as much land for grazing herds or farming. I suppose, if I were going to settle down, I would prefer Somi."

"If I asked you to settle in Nazar, could you?"

"Governor, I will do whatever you need of me. What do you want me to do?"

"I want you to betray me."

"Excuse me?" Marek scowled.

The governor took a hearty swig of wine from his goblet, then offered Marek a chair across from him in front of the fire.

He called out to a servant to bring the young soldier a goblet of wine. Marek took the seat and sipped the wine cautiously. Was the governor trying to poison him for some reason?

"Governor Pravin, exactly what is it you are asking of me?"

"Go back to Nazar. Tell Jedrek and the others you seek asylum in Nazar. Tell them I ordered you to kill or violate Slaina, and you refused to follow my orders. Get close to them as equals. Tell them you believe she carries the Promised One, and you want to serve him. Give them whatever drivel you feel they will believe. I'll even send a patrol after you. They'll issue a formal request to have you returned to Somi for prosecution. Danyl will refuse, and your story will be validated." The governor seemed pleased with himself.

"I can do that, but how does that help you?" Marek questioned.

"I will let you know when the time comes. I have another ally who can help me. I need to have whatever information I can when the time is right, and I need the Nazarans to trust you. Can you live the life of a retired soldier?"

Marek sighed, then grinned. "If I must. I rather enjoyed my life as a soldier."

"If all goes well, you can come out of retirement by the middle of spring. I suggest you ride out quickly. I will have to send a patrol after you, so ride hard and fast, in case Nasha still has friends here."

Marek gulped down the last of his wine. When he stood to leave, the governor grabbed his arm. "This is the only time you will be permitted to lay a hand on me. You must put a knot on my head with the butt of your sword."

Marek knew it would make his situation more plausible, but this was a hard request to grant. "Are you certain, my lord?"

"If you don't. you aren't worthy of this assignment." The governor didn't relish the idea of a headache, but he knew the story needed to be believable. "Do it!"

"Forgive me, my lord." Marek pulled his sword and raised it over the governor's head. He brought it down with enough force to give the man a large lump on his scalp.

The rotund man dropped to his hands and knees as his head spun from the blow. He shook his head, trying to clear it. He managed to issue one order: "Get moving."

Governor Pravin collapsed unconscious on the floor. Marek shook his head and sheathed his sword. This wasn't the way he imagined his day going. He grabbed a couple of pieces of fruit from the governor's table and raced from his residence. Mounting his horse, he rode for the nearest city gate, barely getting clear before the alarm was sounded.

The servants had stayed out of sight until called for, so the governor's unconscious body wasn't discovered until a dignitary sought an audience nearly thirty minutes after Marek's departure. Pravin purposefully took his time regaining perceived consciousness. His behavior bought Marek a four-hour head start.

Governor Pravin called for the ranking officer among his troops. Asa, Nasha's former friend, was that officer. He ordered Asa to pursue the man, but only to the border of Somian territory.

Pravin quickly hired a handful of local thugs. He sent them to find Slaina. "Your goal is to attempt to kill her. If you succeed, so much the better. Do not attack until Marek is in a position to defend her. Marek still works for me, but your attack and his defense must be believable."

Four days later, Asa reported to Governor Pravin. He regretfully informed him that Marek had made it safely to Nazaran territory. Governor Pravin ordered Asa to take a formal written request to the Nazaran magistrate requesting his assistance in returning Marek to Somi for prosecution. He allowed the man a night to rest from his most recent trip before he sent him out again. It was his intention to give Marek another few days in Nazar to cement his position. It appeared he was merely being gracious to his loyal soldiers.

Governor Pravin neglected to order Asa to bring Marek back in good shape, or even alive. He decided if the young man hadn't ingratiated himself to Jedrek and Danyl by the time Asa arrived, he didn't deserve to be returned in good condition.

A snowstorm blew in, slowing Asa's progress. Snow was not a regular occurrence for the region. It wasn't unheard of, but certainly not routine. The region was temperate, and snow came in small amounts, followed by days warm enough to melt the snow. Rain was equally present in winter in the area. The day started with rain, then freezing rain followed by a blinding snow.

It seemed the weather didn't want Asa's envoy to progress any faster than Pravin did.

Slaina spent numerous hours indoors sewing. Her only chances to get outside were when she accompanied Halyn to treat an illness or injury. Many times, those who needed treatment came to Halyn's home, again keeping Slaina indoors. Once every eight days, Halyn, Slaina, Jedrek, and Joren would go to town to attend the Holy Day Celebration. Slaina loved to listen to the men read from the Ancient Texts. The thing that made her uncomfortable was the way everyone treated her as an honored guest. She wasn't accustomed to being the center of attention, whether it was positive or negative. She tried to distract herself from the curious glances of the people around her by listening closely to the readings from the Ancient Texts.

One of the readings extolled the wondrous virtues of Pateras. The baby within her jumped about excitedly. In a few minutes, the baby had jumped so much, Slaina needed to step away to relieve herself. Her bladder seemed to be under frequent assault from her tiny baby.

She hesitated to go back inside. It was rather cold outside, but she enjoyed being outdoors for a few minutes. Slaina walked around until a voice called her name.

She turned around to see Marek approaching. She was accustomed to his presence with Jedrek, but he still made her nervous. Jedrek had sent him away. Why was he here now? Why had he returned? Was he here to harm her and her baby?

Slaina stepped nervously backward. "Marek, what are you doing here?" She held up her hand and ordered him to stop his approach.

Knowing it was his job to convince her and Jedrek his intentions were honorable, he stopped as she requested. "Slaina, I mean you no harm. I'm here seeking asylum from Governor Pravin. I disobeyed his orders, and he means to have my head for it."

"What orders?" she asked curiously.

"When I came here with Jedrek, Governor Pravin gave me orders in the event you rejected Jedrek. If you didn't accept him, my job was to kill you and your child. He... uh..." Marek couldn't make his eyes meet hers. "He gave me the option of violating you to destroy the veracity of your child. I couldn't do it. It was an order I couldn't follow."

Slaina took another frightened step backward. "Stay away from me, Marek!"

Marek held his arms spread out and his hands open, palms upward, in the traditional greeting indicating that one came in peace. "Slaina, I believe you are carrying the Promised One and Pateras has protected you. I'm not here to hurt you. I came back to serve you and your child. I could have gone anywhere." Marek pulled his sword from his sheath. Kneeling before her, he pointed his sword to the skies and swore. "I offer my sword and my life in the service of the one promised to rule over all."

Slaina touched her belly nervously. "I'm not sure… I don't think… please go away."

Marek sheathed his sword. He remained on his knee. "I have nowhere to go. Please don't send me away."

Slaina wrapped her cloak more tightly around her. She turned to run back to the meeting hall and plowed into Jedrek. Jedrek put his arm around his frightened new wife and glared at Marek in distrust. Jedrek sent Slaina to the meeting hall while he spoke to Marek.

"Marek, I sent you back to Somi. Why have you returned?"

"I came to serve the Promised One. I wish to protect you, Slaina, and the child. I can't do what Governor Pravin has asked of me."

Jedrek stepped closer to Marek. "What did my uncle ask of you?"

Marek forced himself to look away as though he were ashamed. "Jedrek, I believe now. Only Pateras could have kept Slaina safe."

"Answer my question, Soldier."

"He… ordered me to either kill her or to violate her." Marek raised his head in defiance. "I couldn't do that to her, the child, or you. I swear my allegiance to you and the Promised One. Please don't send me away."

When Jedrek heard about Marek's orders to harm Slaina, his face flushed and his heart pounded in anger. He nearly attacked the man himself. The one point he couldn't deny was that Marek had not harmed his wife, despite his orders. "Remove your weapons and drop them on the ground. We will speak to the magistrate. I can't grant you asylum. It will be his decision."

Marek did as he was told. Jedrek picked up the weapons and followed him into the meeting hall.

Slaina's panicked return to the meeting got the attention of everyone present. She ran straight to Halyn and whispered to her. Upon hearing what happened outside, Halyn's eyes landed on Nasha.

Nasha bolted for the nearest exit. He didn't know what was happening, but he knew he was needed. Marek and Jedrek met Nasha at the door, and the meeting came to an abrupt halt. Seeing the situation, Danyl put away the Ancient Texts and dismissed everyone. Many curious onlookers were hesitant to leave. Danyl sent everyone out except those directly involved. The town council and Slaina's family, which now included Jedrek, Halyn, Nasha, and Joren, remained.

Marek explained his purpose for being there and requested asylum. He apologized to Slaina for his original intention of harming her and again vowed his allegiance to her and to the child she carried.

Danyl stared intently at the man standing in front of the council, pleading his case. Nasha wanted nothing more than to ask the magistrate to deny his request and throw Marek out on his ear. What stopped him was that he was a refugee from Somi as well. He finally decided what he should do. "Magistrate, before you make your decision, allow me to return to Somi and make some discreet inquiries. If his story is true, I will find out."

Danyl crossed his arms and leaned back in his seat. "What do you propose I do with him in the meantime? Someone will need to take responsibility for him. I can't lock him up, because he's done nothing wrong."

Marek had been standing silently, offering no suggestions of his own, despite his desire to remain near Slaina. He finally volunteered, "Magistrate, wherever you determine I should stay, I would like to earn my keep. I don't have sufficient funds to stay at the inn for longer than a day or two. I wasn't able to collect my pay or anything from my home when I left. Allow me to work for you or anyone else who needs a laborer."

Jedrek felt a degree of responsibility for the man, but he wasn't inclined to bring him near Slaina since his loyalties were under such scrutiny.

Slaina finally positioned herself in front of Marek. "You tried to capture me—you wanted me dead. You had orders to harm me. Why did you disobey your orders?"

Marek glanced over at Nasha. "Nasha said we wouldn't be able to catch you if you were protected by Pateras. He was right. I have lived without fear until now. I have no desire to cross Pateras. He has protected you—from me. I believe all that Nasha told me. I do not want to make an enemy of Pateras. I want to serve his child."

Slaina looked the man in the eyes. She couldn't discern whether he spoke the truth or not. Slaina chose to trust him. "Jedrek, you need help building our home, don't you?"

Nasha was quickly on his feet. "Slaina, no! He can't be trusted!"

Several people expressed similar objections. Halyn wasn't one of them. Slaina looked over at Nasha. "Pateras stopped you from killing me. Is Marek more powerful than you... or Pateras?"

"There's something to be said for not testing the will of Pateras," Nasha argued.

"Girl, you ran in here scared to death just a bit ago. Why aren't you scared now?" Halyn finally asked. "You aren't getting overconfident, are you?"

"No, not overconfident. I'm learning that this is the will of Pateras, and my life is in his hands. Every night when the Ancient Texts were read to me, the words were about not being afraid. I'm ready to trust Pateras to protect my baby and me. Why would he spend so much time telling us not to be afraid? I'm not afraid of Marek anymore." Slaina spoke with a finality and confidence that no one dared challenge.

Jedrek approached the magistrate. "I believe he is my responsibility. Allow me to take him with us." It occurred to Jedrek that he was living in Halyn's home. He turned quickly to her. "If you will allow him into your home."

Halyn glanced around the room. Danyl's face reflected cynicism, as did the other council members'. Nasha's face looked as though he was ready to rid them all of the doubts by eliminating Marek. Slaina seemed calm and accepting of the situation. What had calmed the girl down? It had to be Pateras. Nothing else could have changed her so easily. She was nearly panicked earlier, and now she seemed to want Marek's presence. "I'll allow it, for now. Young man, you attempt to harm anyone in my household, I will see to it no healer in any province ever tends to your needs. Whatever you die from will be slow and painful. Do you understand?"

Marek nodded. "I've learned a lot in recent months. Never anger a healer is one of those lessons. I am here to learn and to serve the Promised One, nothing more."

Halyn took him home and gave him a room. Danyl sent troops again to watch Halyn's house from a distance.

Two days later, the thugs Pravin had hired arrived. Knowing this was a healer's home, three men brought a fourth man on horseback, claiming he was in pain. Jedrek and Marek were in the barn with Joren loading the wagon with supplies for the construction of Jedrek and Slaina's home when the men arrived. Jedrek and Marek helped his companions carry him in and get him settled in the area off the kitchen, then Jedrek and his companions returned to the barn to work.

Halyn instructed Slaina on what to look for to determine the cause of the man's pain. Halyn scowled as she examined the man, whose pain seemed to move around to unrelated places. She finally determined a course of treatment after deciding the man might be suffering from severe constipation. She mixed some herbs and other medicines together, handed the potion to the man, and ordered him to drink it.

The man was waiting for his friends to signal him to attack the women. The other three men had seen Jedrek and the others return to the barn. They wanted to wait until the men were gone.

The man gingerly sipped the drink. He felt perfectly fine and didn't know what she could possibly be giving him. She ordered him to drink it all quickly and set a pitcher of water beside him. "After you finish that, start drinking this water, all of it."

As Jedrek and Joren loaded the wagon, Marek was unusually quiet and distracted. Jedrek finally walked up behind Marek who was standing inside the barn staring toward the house. "Marek, is everything all right?"

"Something about those men doesn't feel right. Where did they come from, and why would three men bring a friend here? It only takes one man to transport a sick or injured man via horseback. Two of them looked familiar, but I haven't been able to place them yet."

Joren came up behind the two. "I agree with Marek. Somethin' was off about them. I didn't like the way they was lookin' at Ms. Slaina."

Anger flared on Jedrek's face. Before he could storm to the house, Marek pulled him back. "Jedrek, you can't go in there like that. There are four of them, and Slaina's in there with them. We've got to have a plan to get her out of there."

Marek cussed. "My sword is in the house. The only weapons here are farm implements."

Joren picked up a shovel and pitchfork. "I think we can take 'em."

Marek smiled. "Okay, here's the plan." He laid his idea out for the other two, and they arranged their new weapons carefully.

A moment later, Jedrek and Marek began yelling at each other. Joren bolted for the house yelling, "Ms. Halyn! Ms. Slaina! Come quick!"

Halyn looked over at Slaina. "Go see what that boy's hollering about."

Slaina opened the door and stepped onto the porch. She heard more yelling in the distance and saw Marek and Jedrek fighting. Slaina broke into a run and screamed for Halyn.

Hearing her cry, Halyn shook a crooked finger at the man on her treatment bed. "Drink that water, all of it! I'll be back in a minute." She hurried out the door, followed by two of the men.

The third one watched the activity for a moment, then decided it was a ruse. "Let's go. We need to take care of all of them."

Joren met Slaina halfway up the hill. He grabbed her arm and pulled her toward the fray. "Get in the wagon. They aren't really fighting. Those men are trouble!"

Joren finished conveying his message just as Marek slammed Jedrek into a wall in the barn. Instinctively, Slaina screamed, thinking Jedrek had been hurt.

"Ahh!" Jedrek let out a manufactured cry of pain.

Joren continued to pull Slaina past the fight and toward the wagon. "Get in, Ms. Slaina! Get in! You're not safe!"

Seeing Slaina's hesitation, Jedrek pushed Marek backward until they hit the back of the wagon and rolled to the ground. Jedrek grunted then hissed, "Do as Joren says!"

Marek rolled on top of Jedrek. "Slaina! Go!"

Hearing all three giving the same message, she climbed laboriously into the wagon. "Where's Halyn?" she asked.

"What in the world is goin' on out here?" Halyn's voice sounded behind her. Joren reached for the old woman and pulled her toward the wagon.

The two men who exited right behind Halyn pulled daggers from inside their cloaks and raced toward Slaina.

Marek rolled off Jedrek and onto his feet. He grabbed the pitchfork propped against the wall and hit the man nearest him on the back of the head. The man stumbled a step or two, then turned to face his adversary. He quickly found the business end of the pitchfork coming toward his neck. The man caught the blade of his dagger between the tines and swung the instrument away from him. Marek twisted his body around and pulled it away from the dagger. He pushed forward again and jabbed the man in the thigh. The man grabbed the base of the fork with his left hand and swung the dagger wildly with his right. Marek dodged two such swings and continued to push into the man's thigh. Seeing the pitchfork wouldn't advance, Marek twisted it violently. The man shrieked from the excruciating pain. He dropped his weapon to protect his wound. Marek pulled the pitchfork from the man's thigh, sending him to the ground in pain.

Jedrek was no soldier, but had received a little training, along with his cousins, in Pravin's house. He rolled to his feet nearly as neatly as Marek had and grabbed the shovel, also conveniently placed within easy reach. He swung it at the second man who was attempting to pull Halyn away from the wagon and hit the man squarely in the back of the head. The man caught himself on the wagon and turned to charge Jedrek. The two exchanged glancing blows as their weapons collided and slid off each other. Jedrek finally found an opening and shoved the head of the shovel roughly into the man's belly, doubling him over. Jedrek jerked back and cuffed him on the chin. He widened his swing and pummeled the man across the face, sending him to the ground.

Meanwhile, Joren helped Halyn into the wagon and climbed into the driver's seat. Grabbing the reins, he slapped the horses aggressively. The animals bolted out the backside of the barn. Joren directed them toward where he knew Danyl's men were camped out. The men had heard the yelling and were already charging down the hill toward the barn, but they were still a fair distance away.

The two men who had been last to leave the house now approached. Seeing their comrades in trouble, one grabbed a small crossbow from his saddle and raced to join the fight. The man who had been the patient mounted his horse and charged after the wagon, but the medications Halyn had given him began taking effect. With each bounce of the horse, his stomach churned. He tried to ignore it and focus on catching the wagon.

The man with the crossbow loaded his weapon and aimed it at Jedrek. Marek, seeing the man's intention, threw himself in front of Jedrek. The bolt flew from the bow and embedded in Marek's ribcage. Jedrek was startled to find Marek in his arms. Seeing the bolt protruding from his back, he eased the man to the ground. Marek tried reaching for the bolt to pull it out. Jedrek grabbed his arm. "Don't pull it out! Wait for Halyn!" Marek tried to find a comfortable position against the wall. There wasn't one. He pushed himself into a halfway seated position where he could watch out for his opponents as well as keep an eye on Jedrek.

The troops coming down the hill saw the bolt fly from the attacker's bow. One stopped where he was and loaded his own crossbow. He fired and dropped the man before he could reload.

The man pursuing the wagon caught it and forced Joren to stop. He jerked Joren out of the driver's seat, then ordered the women out.

Joren stepped toward the back to help the women down. Halyn's former patient reached down from his saddle and grabbed the young man by the collar. "Where do you think you're going?"

Joren jerked his cloak from the man's hand. "The Healer is a well-respected woman, and Slaina is pregnant. They both deserve to be helped down from the wagon."

The man allowed him to complete the task. He dismounted, pulled his dagger, and moved toward Slaina. Halyn stepped in front of her.

His bowels churned again and growled loudly. Halyn grinned at the sound. His stomach was also getting quite nauseated. Her smile grew larger as she watched the man's face turn colors. She reached behind her and squeezed Slaina's arm. "Don't worry, girl. If we wait long enough, this man won't survive to kill you."

The painful cramps began again, and nausea overcame him. He turned aside and vomited forcefully. "You poisoned me. Give me the antidote, or I'll run you through, Healer!"

"The antidote is in my house. You let those two young people go, and I'll get it for you."

"No! We'll all go there right now. Start walking!" he ordered.

"It'd be faster if we took the wagon," Halyn suggested.

The man scowled. It had taken them a long time to get out of the wagon. It would also take a long time for them to walk that far. He had an idea. "Send the boy to get the antidote."

"I'm no boy! I'm a man!" Joren retorted.

"Joren knows nothin' of my medicines and potions. He can't help you. I'm the only one who can. Pateras could also help you if he had a reason to," Halyn goaded.

The man doubled over and vomited again. He wiped his face, then reluctantly motioned for everyone to get into the wagon. He tied his horse to the back of it and forced Joren to drive to Halyn's home. The troops guarding Halyn's home now had the other three men subdued and collected in the yard. The man peered over the edge of the wagon and knew he was in trouble. He raised his sword to order Joren to turn the wagon around. Joren slapped the horses aggressively with the reins. The team bolted as ordered. The man tried to get his balance to stop Joren and the horses, but the wagon pitched and shook too roughly.

The wagon's haphazard, spirited approach got the attention of the troops in the hollow. Two of the men mounted their horses and met the wagon before it reached the house. Joren pulled on the reins until his arms ached. The man trying to stand in the back of the wagon was knocked over once again. He doubled over in pain. The two men jerked their prisoner out of the wagon and disarmed him.

Halyn got to her feet. "Gentlemen, you might want to stick that one in the outhouse and tie the door shut for a couple hours. He's gonna need to stay there awhile."

The man pushed himself partially off the ground. "Please help me. She poisoned me. Make her give me the cure."

Halyn grinned. "He'll be fine in a couple of hours. His bowels were full, and he needs a good cleaning out. Might want to get him to the outhouse pretty soon. That potion's about to kick in any minute," she warned.

Two of the troops grabbed the man by his arms and headed for the small structure. The man objected. "She said I was dying! Make her give me the cure!"

Halyn called after the man, "We're all dyin'. We just don't know how quickly. I doubt you'll die today, though."

Jedrek came running to Halyn. "Healer, Marek needs help. He jumped in front of a crossbow bolt and saved my life, but he's hurt. Can you help him?"

Halyn surveyed the situation. The man who had been shot had died instantly, and the other two were injured. One had little more than bruises, but the second had deep puncture wounds that would need treatment. "Put that one on a stretcher and don't let him walk. Slaina, bind that wound before he's moved. Take Marek to his room. I'll treat him there."

In a couple of hours, Halyn had everyone treated. The men who had attacked them and lived were taken to the jail in town. The one who died was buried in the town cemetery.

Slaina helped Halyn tend to Marek. She quietly thanked him for saving Jedrek's life.

Marek manufactured his most sincere face. "I'm glad I was there to protect him, as well as you and your baby."

Halyn forced Marek out of bed that evening and coerced him into reading to them from the Ancient Texts.

"Healer." He sighed deeply. "It's hard to breathe. Someone else should read."

"I want you to read so that you'll breathe deeply. It's good for you. Now read. I need some calmin' words to help me sleep tonight," Halyn ordered.

Four days later, the magistrate sent for Marek. The entire household accompanied him. In the town hall, they found Asa and a small contingent of troops, as well as Nasha.

Nasha reported that the stories of Marek's hasty escape appeared to be true. He had heard accounts of the governor being attacked and Marek running for his life. Nasha reiterated his distrust of Marek and stressed to the council that such a story could have been created to perpetuate a lie.

Asa affirmed that the stories of the attack and escape were true. He presented Danyl with the letter from Pravin requesting Marek's extradition for his treason.

Jedrek spoke on Marek's behalf. "Magistrate, Marek not only saved my life, but he saved Slaina, Halyn, and Joren. Marek has only been here for a few days, but his reasons for being here appear to be genuine."

The town council deliberated for several hours. Nasha and Asa were the only ones who had a negative perspective on the situation. The council decided Marek could be trusted, for now. Danyl issued an apology to Governor Pravin and hailed Marek as a hero of the province for saving Slaina's and her companions' lives. He informed the governor that he would not be able to return him to Somi at the present time.

Through the rest of the winter, Marek made himself useful by helping Jedrek build his new home. The winter was harsher than usual this year, and building the house took longer than expected. Through the long wintry nights, Marek sat with Halyn and the others, reading from the Ancient Texts. Halyn kept her secret about being able to read from Marek. She knew his days in her household would come to an end soon enough, and she didn't want her secret to spread beyond her own household.

Halyn considered Slaina to be her successor as Provincial Healer and treated her like the daughter she never had. She fully intended to leave her house and property to Joren. He had been like a son to her since he was around nine or ten years old. Jedrek had become her son-in-law. None of them were related by blood, but to her, they were family. Halyn looked forward to becoming a grandmother in the early spring.

FALL OF THE LADO EMPIRE

Tristan laid Dr. Sokolov down gently, then picked up the discarded weapon and the remains of their lunches. He headed to the stairwell to retrieve his bracelet when Philip Henderson and Riley came rushing through the door, accompanied by several other company security guards. Their weapons were drawn and actively seeking a target.

Tristan backed off and moved his hands away from his weapons. The entourage intended to "save" Tristan from Dr. Sokolov and moved past him to examine the doctor's corpse on the ground. One of the officers reported to Philip, "The Doc is dead, sir. How do you want us to handle this?"

"Get a trash bin and dump him in it. We can throw his body into the incinerator."

"No, get a stretcher and carry his body to the infirmary. Keep his face covered, but let word get out within the company. He didn't do this alone. His co-conspirators need to know what happens to people who interfere with the company. If he disappears, no one will learn anything. The information doesn't need to go outside the company. We need to start some substantiated rumors of our own." Tristan's youthful face was overshadowed by his coldness.

Philip glanced at Riley, who seemed more lost than concerned. He pulled himself together enough to ask, "Does this mean I can get this tracker out now? It's itching like crazy."

Philip turned his attention to the matter at hand. "You sure this is the best way to handle this? Marguerite doesn't want any adverse publicity over this."

"Definitely. I want him quietly displayed to teach his cohorts a lesson, then I will make his body disappear—permanently." Tristan folded his arms confidently across his chest and dared the man to challenge him again.

Philip looked at the waiting officer. "You heard the man. Get a stretcher and handle him with care."

"Yes, Chief Henderson." The man trotted off to handle the arrangements.

Philip walked over to survey the situation. "You laid him out rather neatly, like a man who had regrets about what he'd done. Is your conscience bothering you?"

Tristan smirked. "No, not a bit. I laid him out because I fully intended to use his death to send the message I mentioned earlier. I wanted every security officer who came out here to see him and understand the seriousness of the situation."

Philip noticed the handful of trash Tristan had collected. "What's that?"

"Our lunch. The doctor wanted to kill me, but he didn't have the stomach for it. We ate our lunch while he worked up his nerve. It bought me the time I needed to get his weapon away from him. I taught him several well-deserved lessons." Tristan offered Philip the trash. "You're welcome to examine it for evidence if you like."

Philip declined the offer. He stepped over the body and headed toward the door, then turned around. "I'll inform the others."

Tristan let him go, for the moment.

Riley looked at the body nervously. "Okay kid, now you're starting to scare me."

Tristan grinned. "Don't be scared now. It's not what it looks like. I didn't kill him."

Riley's eyes grew wide. "He committed suicide?"

"That was his goal. Listen, I need to check in with Leland, and we need to find out who their operatives are on Juranta.

Once those operatives are secured, we can take care of things here and go home. I also have some evidence to compare to Kyle's autopsy report." Tristan explained.

"How do you plan on learning who the operatives are?"

"That's why I need to talk to Leland. I'm going to the Infirmary with the doctor. Don't let them do anything to his body." Tristan leaned in close. "Don't let them do a scan or anything."

Riley's eyes widened. He nearly choked on his own saliva as he inhaled sharply.

The doctor wasn't dead.

Tristan made as big of a production as he could of transporting the doctor's body to the Infirmary. He pranced about looking pleased with himself so no one would doubt his responsibility for the event.

Now alone in the Infirmary with the doctor's so-called corpse, Tristan took the poisoned vial from his pocket and scanned it. While the scan was running, he put together several other files and programs. A few minutes later, he was ready to hail Leland. He accessed the comms to send the hail.

"Leland… oh, I forgot about the time difference. Did I wake you?"

"Yeah, kid, I haven't had much sleep since you disappeared yesterday morning. I finally fell asleep… an hour ago. Are you and Riley all right? What happened?"

"We were attacked by some radical extremists. The Lado Pharm security guys were a great help to us. They've been tracking these guys for weeks and caught them in the act of trying to end Riley and me. We ended up in the Infirmary here at Lado, but we're both fine. These extremists have people on Juranta. Were you able to call my good buddies Wallace and Gershom to ferret them out?"

Leland had taken the call from Tristan from his own bed. He sat upright when he learned who the call was from. His wife gave him an annoyed look as he kept the call going in their room. "Give me a second." He placed the call on hold, then moved to another room. "Your buddies are not the most forthcoming with information, but I do know they have full security details in place. They weren't happy though."

"I'm sending you a file. If you can trace this, it might help you find those extremists. Riley and I have a little more to do to wrap this up, but we got the ringleader. The top people here at Lado aren't guilty of any misappropriation of funds like I thought. They were just trapped in an internal problem which we're getting under control. There were some criminal activities, but nothing company driven."

Leland stared at the screen. Tristan was clearly painting a picture for him. It was vague and unlike Tristan's training. Leland slowly responded, "I've got the file. I'll see what I can do with it, and I'll give a copy to your good friends."

"Thanks. I'll hail you again when we're done here." Tristan closed the commlink and then hailed Chief Henderson.

Chief Henderson was monitoring the entire communication. Those had been his operatives on Juranta that Tristan was framing. "What are you doing? Do you think you can escape us by getting rid of a couple of our operatives?"

"No, Mr. Henderson, calm down. He already knew someone was pursuing our families. I gave him a little more to keep our cover story intact. I called you to give you a head's up. You need to alert your people to get them out of danger. I used to be Covert Ops, remember? I know what I'm doing."

Philip scowled. "I know you do. That's what worries me."

"Mr. Henderson, Dr. Sokolov was not guilty of any capital offenses, and even though he pulled a weapon on me, we both know he was incapable of hurting me. You have proof I executed him. I believe you are quite secure in retaining my loyalty." Tristan snapped. "Whether you pull your people out of there or not is still your call. You could replace them with new ones tomorrow if you feel the need. I'm just trying to cover both our backsides!" He slapped the computer controls, cutting off the conversation abruptly.

Tristan continued working until Riley walked in. "All right kid, what did you want me working on now?" Riley was accustomed to working on financial records. This investigation into accessory files was unfamiliar territory to him.

Leland continued to stare blankly at the files as his mind processed the verbal information Tristan had given him. His wife's voice came from the doorway. "Should I make you some tea to help you sleep?"

Leland rubbed his face with his hands. "No, you better make it coffee. I think I'm going to be up for a while."

While his wife was preparing the coffee, Leland stepped into his bedroom and put on a casual, yet simplistic outfit. He needed something at least one step above loungewear. Returning to the living room, he set to work. The first file was a list of Intergalactic Communications Network codes. The codes belonged to the CEO, COO and Security Chief for Lado Pharmaceuticals. Leland hailed the office for Agents Wallace and Gershom. Neither one was currently on-duty. He reached another agent who was familiar with the situation. He passed the codes to the man, along with Tristan's expectations that one code would hail operatives on Juranta at this very moment. The man quickly began tracing the access codes.

Leland forwarded the second file, which was the chemical composition of the mysterious drug to the coroner's office along with a memo. He informed the medical examiner's office that the drug may have been used to fake or induce a heart attack in the Kyle Amos death. He firmly requested a thorough investigation into the death and the drug, as well as a report on the findings as quickly as possible.

Leland accessed the third file. It was a request for a new identity packet for Dr. Sokolov and his wife. The man's children were grown and could need to be relocated as well. Tristan also warned Leland that he was about to take out the top leadership of Lado Pharmaceuticals, and not politely. His warning was cryptic and foreboding.

Capt. Barrett hailed the appropriate governmental agency to request the credentials for every member of the Sokolov family. Having this young man in his department was stirring up more excitement than that departmental remodel a few years back. The coffee dispenser was unavailable for three days and sent the coffee drinkers into a tailspin. Tempers ran rampant among the heavy coffee drinkers and among those who didn't, as their patience wore thin dealing with their decaffeinated coworkers.

The fourth file was far more important than the last one and more tedious. Leland set to work. It took well over an hour to complete this one requested task. Before he ran the program, he muttered under his breath. "Kid, you better know what you're doing."

Leland finished his tasks and stretched out on the sofa to catch a nap before the next leg of his impending adventure started. He awoke to a hail from Agent Wallace. "Capt. Barrett, I thought you should know, we took out four operatives. Two were watching the Deacons family, and two were watching Amelia Hardin's sister's home. Full re-education will be required if they make it beyond their extensive interrogation." The woman seemed quite pleased with herself and excited about the impending task of getting whatever answers she wanted from the men.

Leland interrupted her glee. "Do you still have protective details on both the Deacons family and the Hardin family?"

"We still have a detail on the Deacons family, just in case. We didn't see the need to continue the detail for the Hardin family."

Leland felt his blood pressure rising. "You asked for my cooperation in establishing Chief Alexander in my department with a viable cover story. I expect that when his case converges with the workings of my department, you will reciprocate in your cooperation. I want protection back on Riley's family immediately. If Tristan's family needs protection, then so does Riley's."

"Capt. Barrett, Mr. Hardin's family, is not our concern, and they aren't under our jurisdiction." Agent Wallace replied clinically.

"If something were to happen to his family, it could jeopardize Tristan's cover. The media might question why one family received protection, and the other didn't." Capt. Barrett stopped ranting to wait for Agent Wallace's response.

The cold-hearted woman gave him an icy stare before relenting. "The detail will be returned to duty within the hour."

Leland watched her angrily shut off the commlink. He muttered to himself as he went in search of his wife. He quickly discovered she had already left for work, which he should have done as well. She recorded a message for him before she left.

"Good morning Dear, at least I hope it's still morning when you get this message. I left your breakfast in the warmer, and I gave you a kiss before I left, though I think you were too tired to remember it. I called your secretary to let her know you wouldn't be in early this morning. I hope to see you for dinner tonight. If I don't, I'll put it in the warmer again for you. Love you, Dear. Bye."

Leland scowled for a moment. He should have been at work an hour ago. His wife's thoughtfulness softened his frustration. Picking up his food, he returned to the living room and hailed Tristan.

Tristan answered quickly. His demeanor told Leland they were still under surveillance. "Chief Alexander, I wanted to let you know we put a protection detail on Jessica's family and Riley's. I think we have everything tied up on this end. We're just waiting for you to finish on your end and head home."

"Understood, sir. I'm hoping to finish in the morning. I'll hail you again when we're done."

"I look forward to reading your full report." Leland finished the conversation by saying as little as possible. He closed out the commlink and finished his breakfast.

Tristan and Riley spent most of the night reviewing the company's records from an internal perspective since they were given access. They found a few more questionable practices. Tristan tried digging into Chief Henderson's files, but there wasn't anything incriminating in them. Tristan decided he must have more files kept some place else. Riley pushed a reluctant Tristan to get a brief nap. "Look, kid, I know you are the young, energetic one, but you aren't infallible or invincible. You're the one who needs to be on his toes in the morning. If I fall asleep on the job, it's no big deal. If you aren't thinking clearly, it could be catastrophic for both of us. Get some sleep!" Riley ordered, knowing the obstinate young man may or may not follow the order. He had to try, though.

Tristan trusted Riley implicitly. The thing that concerned him was whether Riley could be ready for anything. He decided to take the man's advice. He laid down and fell asleep quickly. Six a.m. rolled around far too soon. Riley roused Tristan. The two hadn't showered or changed clothes in two days. All of their personal belongings were still in their hotel rooms. This morning, the two were able to get an ion shower in the infirmary. The ion shower enabled them to keep their clothes on, which refreshed both them and their clothing. Neither one could shave or do much with their hair. Luckily, military specs required a short haircut needing little attention.

Dr. Sokolov's body was still lying peacefully in the stasis chamber. Tristan checked the computer and found several frantic hails from his wife. He decided the woman was quite distraught by now. He hated to keep her dangling like this. Almost as an afterthought, he hailed the woman. "Mrs. Sokolov, my name is Chief Alexander. I represent the Government Financial Oversight Department of the CIF."

Before he could explain the purpose of his call, the woman erupted in tears, pleading for reassurances. "Is my husband all right? Is he there? He didn't come home last night. Can I talk to him?"

"I apologize if we caused you unnecessary worry last night, ma'am. We had to detain your husband as part of our investigation. He's here, and he's fine." Tristan assured her.

"Could I speak to him, please?" She sniffled.

"No, I'm afraid that's not possible until we clear him of any wrongdoings in this case. Would you be able to come here later this morning to answer a few questions for us?"

The woman sniffled again. Her eyes were red and puffy from crying all night. "He's okay? And I can see him if I come there? I—I don't really know much about his work."

"After you answer our questions, we can let you see him and talk to him. If you can't confirm or dispute his claims, then you won't affect our case. We would no longer have a reason to keep you apart." Tristan explained.

"Exactly what is this about?" She asked.

"I would prefer to discuss it with you in person. Can you get here around ten a.m.?"

"I can make it by eight a.m. if you want." She eagerly volunteered.

"No, I can't meet you that early. I have some other meetings scheduled this morning. I'll contact you again if my schedule clears any earlier. Don't worry, I'm taking good care of your husband." Tristan smiled reassuringly. He gently ended the call in time to see Chief Henderson standing in the doorway with his mouth hanging open.

"Now what have you done? You know that woman can't talk to her husband."

Tristan smiled saucily, "Sure she can. He's not going to respond, but she can talk to him all she wants... after she answers my questions."

"What kind of information do you think you're going to get out of her? What exactly do you have planned, mister? You're up to something, and I know it." Philip got in Tristan's face. "Let me set the record straight for you right now. You work for me. You try anything, I will take you down so fast, you'll be dead before you hit the ground. Before your body is even cold, I will go after that pretty little girlfriend of yours. Maybe I'll even hang around and console her while she grieves for you." He grinned wickedly.

Tristan knew Jessica was protected and the man couldn't harm her, but he had a part to play in this drama. He reacted appropriately, shoving Philip away from him. "You're not going to touch her!" He belted.

Chief Henderson continued to smile sardonically. He had gotten under his adversary's skin—at least to all appearances he had. Riley feared for a moment he was going to have to separate the two.

Philip's smile faded as he tucked this important piece of information into the back of his mind and addressed the next issue. "What meetings do you have scheduled before Mrs. Sokolov arrives?"

"I need to meet with you, Ms. Bellamy, and Mr. Nash about some ties to Dr. Sokolov."

"Give me what you have, and my security people will round them up. I'm not going to bother the others with this."

"You better bother them with it. There are some top-level people involved. You go taking corporate-level employees out, it's going to get some attention from the local authorities and the media. I doubt Ms. Bellamy would like that. I have some ideas about how to handle it, but we need her input on it. This will be the last time I interrupt their schedules, I promise." Tristan argued.

"At least give me the names of the low-level people, and I'll start pulling them in," Philip demanded. He wanted to win at least one point.

"No. You do that, and the big guys will disappear along with any evidence. If we get the big guys, even if we miss some of the lower ones, the machine will grind to a halt. The common man doesn't have the skills or resources to disappear. We'll find everyone that matters if we get the big guys first. I'll give you everything at the meeting." Tristan argued resolutely.

Philip looked at the senior agent who was more even-tempered. "Can you talk some sense into him?"

Riley chortled. "Did you really just ask me that? I doubt his fiancée could do that."

Philip stormed out to make the arrangements. Tristan cast one more glance at Dr. Sokolov. They had put his "body" in stasis under the guise of preventing his body from decomposing. The field was set to its lowest level so that the drug in his body would slowly metabolize. Normally, his system would have cleared the drug from his system in eight to twelve hours. It had been approximately eighteen hours since the drug was introduced into his system. The displays indicating life signs were turned off. An override program was in place to prevent anyone from turning them on and discovering the doctor was still alive. He was quite vulnerable in his current state. Tristan programmed the security system in the room to alert him to anyone entering. Deciding everything was in order, he and Riley went to the commissary to get some breakfast.

Forty-five minutes later, the two walked casually into the boardroom. Riley loaded a file onto the computer. Five minutes later, Chief Henderson joined them. He sat down stiffly in a chair directly across from Tristan. His position kept him between Tristan and the only route in or out of the room. He was certain the young man would try to harm the others and escape. He pressed a button on his bracelet, notifying the other two executives they were assembled. Tristan noticed the man had wisely placed two additional security guards outside the door. He smiled and thought, "*Only two?*" He wiped the smile off his face when Ms. Bellamy and Mr. Nash blew into the room, along with an icy chill.

"All right, Mr. Alexander, what was so important?" Marguerite asked coldly.

Tristan raised the privacy screen, which caused Chief Henderson to tense up. Riley displayed a list of the euthanasia clinics, along with the potential participants in the botched procedures. He began to extrapolate and drone on about the participants being political activists and religious fanatics of sorts. He explained how hard it was to track these individuals because there was no money trail to follow, only social ties. He also pointed out that Dr. Sokolov was not alone in this endeavor.

Marguerite finally lost patience. "This is enough. Why are you bothering us with this drivel? I pay other people to deal with this so I can take care of more important issues."

Tristan sat unaffected by her explosion. He rested one arm on his armrest and the other he rested on the tabletop, swiveling his chair back and forth casually. "What you're telling me is you have no idea who works for you and who doesn't? You don't have records of the people who are on your payroll either officially or unofficially?"

"Human resources have official records. The others are paid as contract labor or consultants. Mr. Henderson pays some under the table. That's how you'll be paid, since we can't have any kind of professional connection." Marguerite suspected this conversation was headed some place unpleasant.

Tristan kept his hands relaxed and didn't move them around. "Mr. Henderson, do you have files with that information... including the financial information?"

"Of course I do, but not on the company's database. I keep it on my datapad which doesn't synchronize with the corporate computers. That isn't the kind of information you want on the company computers where some prying GFOD agent might find it." Philip snidely replied. "What kind of fool do you take me for?"

"We'll get to that question later," Tristan snarked before turning his attention back to his other two guests. "Ms. Bellamy, Mr. Nash, the reason I wanted to meet with you is because I didn't want to take action without your approval."

"What about me? You work for me, remember?" Mr. Henderson worked to re-establish his position in the room.

Tristan gave Philip an unenthusiastic glance. "You and I talked about this early this morning. You are an impatient hot-head who would miss investigatory opportunities—at least that's the appearance you give."

Kendall Nash leaned forward. His brow deeply furrowed. "What is that supposed to mean? Philip is a trusted employee.

He's been with us for fifteen years and with Lado Pharmaceuticals for seventeen years."

"If you've got an accusation, make it, so I can answer it and put this matter to rest right now!" Philip snapped. His hand stayed near his weapon. He wanted to pull it and use it on Tristan.

Tristan leaned back in his chair and looked at the ceiling. His chair continued to swivel, and this time, it had contracted an annoying squeak as it moved. "You know, I have to ask myself how two GFOD agents can waltz in here after two or three weeks of investigation and find something a trained security chief who knows this company from the inside out couldn't find."

Kendall gave Philip an annoyed look. "That's a good question, Henderson. How does a kid fresh out of school come in and find all of this from the outside when you haven't been able to track any of it down?"

Philip tried to swallow, but his mouth was suddenly dry. "Dr. Sokolov has been with Lado Pharmaceuticals nearly as long as I have. He knew my routines and procedures well enough to circumvent them." Philip wasn't guilty of any betrayal where the company was concerned, but his failure to bring this to an end was not doing him any favors. "This problem has been slowly growing. My primary focus has been on damage control. I wasn't able to investigate as much as I wanted. I do have people patiently watching specific individuals for suspicious activities. I have files on my investigation which will line up fairly close to the new golden boy's investigation."

Marguerite narrowed her eyes. Leaning forward, her gaze pierced the security chief like lasers through metal. "Perhaps you should bring the rest of us up to speed on your investigation, Chief Henderson."

Philip pulled his datapad out and interfaced it with the main computer. Kendall jumped on his actions. "I thought you were trying to keep those records off the company database."

"I'm not loading the payroll or insurance files, just the investigative files for this particular case," Philip explained.

Riley pressed a couple of buttons on his computer terminal, taking down his own display. Philip posted a table listing all the employees working greater than fifty percent of the incidents. He explained that for something this detailed, no one employee could have been present for every incident. In a moment, Riley gave Tristan a nod.

Philip noticed the exchange immediately. "What are you two up to?"

Tristan sat up in a defensible position. "Riley, put what you found on the screen."

Riley displayed a file showing the payments to various operatives on worlds across the galaxy where Lado Pharmaceuticals had offices. The thing that got everyone's attention were the deposits made into that same account. It was Philip's file, but Riley had run a program to update his ledger. The thing had been nudged to synchronize with Chief Henderson's personal bank account, which Leland padded a few hours earlier with backdated deposits corresponding to the dates of the botched suicides.

Philip stared at the file, trying to make sense of it. "What the-?" He realized he was being set up. He went for his weapon, but it was too little, too late. Tristan hit him with his Tri-EMP. Philip convulsed and collapsed on the floor.

Marguerite and Kendall were instantly on their feet, staring in shock. The two had several choice words for the unconscious man. Once the initial shock wore off, they turned their attention back to Tristan, who still held his weapon casually in his hand. "He's the one you wanted to know how to handle?" Marguerite asked angrily.

"Yes. My problem was that I suspected him, but I couldn't prove anything until I got access to his datapad. Once he connected it to the database, I had Mr. Hardin upload a program to search his files and send a copy to Riley. While Mr. Henderson has been trying to explain himself, Riley was looking at his financials." Tristan explained.

Kendall glanced at Riley and nervously asked, "How do we know he wasn't sitting here doctoring Philip's files? Nobody was watching him."

Riley spoke to his terminal. "Computer, display the surveillance footage of the boardroom for the last five minutes."

The logs revealed Riley sitting there staring at his screen with his arms folded across his chest. The only times he reached down was to open a new file. Tristan closed the video footage then pulled Philip's file back up. He scrolled through the history.

He went through the previous year. "Riley didn't have time to put in a batch of backdated entries."

Marguerite stepped forward, squinting. "Go back further than the last year."

Tristan scrolled further back, the amounts on the entries got smaller. He silently hoped she wouldn't ask him to go beyond two years.

Marguerite scowled. "Why are the amounts decreasing the further back you go?"

Riley jumped in. "My guess is the longer he did this, the more he felt he could get away with. The cost of looking the other way went up over time."

Marguerite wagged her finger at Kendall, pulling him to the back of the room. The two talked in hushed whispers for a moment while Tristan and Riley talked softly at the front of the room. In a moment, Marguerite and Kendall rejoined Riley and Tristan. "Mr. Nash and I are in agreement. We want this to go away quietly and permanently. Can you handle that for us?"

"Sure we can. We'll eliminate Mr. Henderson for you, but I want his job here. Riley will be our liaison in the GFOD. Here's the first installment on your investment. Riley, use this syringe and take care of Mr. Henderson." Tristan placed the hypo-sprayer in Riley's hand.

Riley looked at the instrument and turned slightly pale. "Tristan, I don't think I can do this."

"Sure, you can. We're partners. We share the work. Besides, it's an assisted suicide. It's perfectly legal. I'm sure we have the appropriate documentation around here somewhere." Tristan glanced at Ms. Bellamy.

"Yes, I'm sure we have it somewhere. Mr. Hardin, I need to know that I can trust you. You use that syringe on him, and we will have a healthy and lucrative arrangement." Marguerite assured the hesitant accountant.

"Tristan, you know this isn't my thing. I'm no killer." Riley hesitated.

"Riley, he's the worst of criminals. He exploited the dying. Besides, I negotiated to save your life. Don't make me regret that decision. He won't feel a thing. It's perfectly humane."

Riley got up slowly and stepped over to Chief Henderson's collapsed form on the floor. He knelt and fumbled nervously with the syringe. In a moment, the familiar hiss sounded. Riley angrily handed the thing back to Tristan and sat down in his chair. He looked like he was caught between the desire to vomit or cry.

"Computer, transfer all of Chief Henderson's privileges and security accesses to Chief Tristan Alexander. Notify all personnel that Chief Alexander has taken over the recently vacated position of Security Chief for Lado Pharmaceuticals. Congratulations, Mr. Alexander, you are our new Security Chief. Mr. Hardin, I will arrange to transfer a retainer fee for your consulting services before the day is out. I assume you will notify Mr. Alexander the second you learn of any further inquiries into our business."

Riley nodded sullenly. "Yeah, sure, no problem. Can we do something about him?" He pointed at the crumpled body on the floor.

Tristan poked his head out the door and called the two security guards into the room. The two men were quite disturbed to see their superior lying dead on the floor. Ms. Bellamy decisively put their concerns to rest. "Mr. Henderson betrayed the company and has resigned. He used his last company benefit to receive an assisted suicide. Mr. Alexander is your new security chief."

Tristan calmly asked the two security officers to retrieve a stretcher from the infirmary and place Chief Henderson's body in stasis next to Dr. Sokolov's. He knew they might not take kindly to any mistreatment of their former boss.

The security guards did as they were instructed. They said nothing, but eyed Tristan suspiciously as they carried the body to the infirmary.

The room's privacy screen was still in place. Tristan kept himself between Ms. Bellamy, Mr. Nash, and the only exit from the room. "Could we talk about one more thing before you return to your duties? It will only take a moment, I promise."

The two were anxious to leave but indulged their new security chief a moment longer. They sat in their chairs and Tristan moved around across the table from them. He drew his weapon as he took his seat. He wasn't aiming it at either of them, but its presence was making them nervous. "Ms. Bellamy, Mr. Nash, I am hereby placing you under arrest for extortion, murder, conspiracy, attempted murder, and a good many other charges. Stay in your seats and silent, or I will consider it resisting arrest."

Marguerite glanced uncertainly at Kendall. She was torn between laughter and anger. She chose to begin with laughter. "You're guilty of murder yourself, Mr. Alexander. We have the proof. Is this what you would call a hostile takeover?"

"Are you referring to the files Mr. Henderson kept on his personal datapad that we just got control of? Those will do nicely in proving the charges against you."

Marguerite now vacillated toward anger. "You killed Dr. Sokolov. You can't deny that, and you can't make it go away. All I have to do is revoke your security clearances and notify security. You'll never make it out of here alive. The operatives we have on Juranta will also take care of your families the second I give the word."

Tristan pressed a button on the computer terminal and displayed Dr. Sokolov's bed in the Infirmary. "Computer, activate life signs monitoring on Dr. Sokolov's bed."

The group watched the displays flash on and settle to a level indicating no life signs. Then there was a fluctuation. Tristan watched the two executives as they held their breath. A second fluctuation occurred, then a third. By this time, a full minute had passed. Marguerite's face turned blood red while Kendall's paled in inverse proportions.

"You'll never get away with this! You'll pay and pay dearly!"

Tristan glanced at Riley. "I think she's resisting arrest. Does it sound like she's resisting arrest to you?"

Riley nodded. "She is threatening you. That could be considered resisting."

Kendall stood slowly from his seat, attempting to diffuse the situation. "Perhaps there is some other agreement we could come to? Some arrangement to your liking?"

"Riley."

"Yes, Tristan?"

"Add bribery to the list of charges."

Kendall's hands balled up into fists, and he slammed one of them on the table.

Tristan reacted calmly. He fired his weapon at Kendall, then fired again at Marguerite. The two writhed and collapsed onto the table. Tristan pressed a control on the computer again. "All security officers, report to the security chief's office on the double. Computer secure all comm channels. No incoming or outgoing calls are to be made without my personal authorization. Change all override codes and send those codes to my bracelet. As soon as all security officers have entered the building, lock down all the entrances and exits, no one comes or goes without my authorization. Lock out the emergency fire override."

Tristan went to speak to the security guards to enlist their help while Riley secured some outside assistance. Riley hailed Leland and updated him on their situation. Leland moaned audibly. He was a desk jockey for a reason. This was not what desk jockeys did. "All right, I'll have the troops you need within the hour."

Riley closed the connection and did one last thing. He took the syringe Tristan had left behind and used it on Ms. Bellamy and Mr. Nash to be certain they didn't wake up any time soon.

A little over a week later, Riley and Tristan were standing in Capt. Barrett's office, giving a preliminary verbal report. Capt. Barrett swallowed a newly prescribed ulcer medication as he listened.

The three Lado executives were questioned at length and quickly hustled into a full re-education program to turn them into productive members of society. Once their reprogramming was completed, they would be given new identities and relocated to a new world. They would be assigned new jobs suited to their skills and personalities. The Sokolov family was relocated with minimal re-education, which amounted to nothing more than strong counseling on how to keep moral objections to themselves. For their own safety, they were also given new identities. Lado Pharmaceuticals was shut down for three months while all employees were investigated and either charged or returned to duty. A surprising number of the local authorities were faced with charges of their own resulting from the investigation.

Tristan added one last thing strictly for Leland's benefit. "I took the liberty of having one last discussion with Ms. Bellamy. I informed her that I wasn't simply a GFOD agent. I told her I worked for an unnamed government agency and her attempts at getting control of me threatened the security of the case I'm working on. I made sure she knew that if she had simply allowed me to conduct my investigation, we would have fixed the problem and moved on. She now knows she made three mistakes."

"Three?" Leland asked.

"She got greedy and made too much out of a simple situation that could have been easily rectified."

Leland nodded his understanding. Riley looked confused. "That's only two. What's the third thing she did wrong?"

A cold, hard look crossed Tristan's face. Leland interpreted the look for Riley. "She interfered with Tristan Alexander's case."

EVACUATION TO NAZAR

Winter was early and forceful. The rains quickly turned to ice and snow. The weather kept travel to a minimum. There were still concerns about Governor Pravin sending troops in to destroy Slaina and her child. Danyl entreated her and Jedrek to move their household within the city walls. Each time he asked, the couple politely declined.

Although winter never lasted long in the temperate climate, the severity of this season kept Jedrek from building their home as quickly as he wanted. Instead, he built a cradle for their son and crafted other furniture they would soon need.

Spring arrived as early as winter had. The days grew warmer and longer. The ground was still hard and not quite ready for Halyn to plant her garden, which would contain a number of her healing herbs.

Slaina was due to give birth any day. Jedrek, Marek, and Joren headed over to work on building their new house. Slaina's father and brothers came from town whenever they could to help. The warmer, sunnier days accelerated the construction.

One such day, Slaina's family came to help with the house. Her mother and sisters came to visit. They knew her time was getting close.

Slaina was exceptionally energetic when her family arrived. She packed a large lunch for the men and gave Jedrek a warm hug and a quiet kiss as he departed for the site of their future home.

Danyl, Nasha, and the captain of the Nazaran troops rode to Halyn's home once again. The women greeted Danyl from the porch. He and Nasha stood on the ground, putting them at eye level with Halyn and Slaina. Their serious looks set aside any pleasant greetings.

"Danyl, what's wrong?" the old woman asked.

"There have been raids among the farms along the outer edges of the province. Several families were slaughtered and their homes burned to the ground. Until those who are doing this are caught, Halyn, Slaina, we implore you to bring your households within the city walls," the magistrate pleaded.

The women looked at each other. Halyn stared at the ground for a moment. She knew everyone would depend on either her or Slaina to make such a decision. Slaina wasn't much beyond being a child herself. Halyn finally turned to the young woman. "Perhaps we should consider goin' into the city for a few days until they catch these raiders."

The tension forced Slaina's uterus to contract tightly for a moment, then relax. She absently rubbed her belly to ease the sensation. "This is your home, Halyn. We will do whatever you ask of us."

Halyn turned to the magistrate. "The men are out workin' on Jedrek's house. We'll talk to them when they return tonight and plan to come into the city tomorrow."

Danyl breathed a sigh of relief. "Thank you, Healer. I will leave a contingent of troops here with you for the night. I'm glad you're finally agreeing to accept my protection."

Nasha took another step forward. "Where is Marek?"

"He's with the other men." Halyn's eyes sparkled with an unexpected hope. She understood Nasha's paranoia where Marek was concerned. She also knew the young man had been exposed to potentially life-changing ideas. They treated him as an equal, not a subordinate to be ordered around. Over the winter months, he had learned the teachings of Pateras. After being shot with the arrow, Halyn had given Slaina a great deal of responsibility in treating his wound. He now owed the girl.

Nasha pushed further. "Has he remained here every night? Has he been alone even once?"

Halyn kept her tongue in check. "He's not been out of sight except when he retires to his room for the evening or steps away to relieve himself." Her inclination was to inform Nasha that Marek was not a child requiring such supervision.

"I'm concerned he and Governor Pravin have something to do with the attacks in the province. You don't seem worried about him, Healer. Has he fooled you into thinking he's an ally? You know I don't trust him."

"Nasha, he has fooled no one but himself. He'll surprise you one of these days. Mark my words. Pateras has his hand on that one." Halyn smiled slyly.

"If Pateras has his hand on him, it would be around Marek's throat, I assure you," Nasha remonstrated.

Danyl assigned some of his troops to watch the perimeter, then rode toward Jedrek's homestead. The men discussed the situation at length. Learning of Halyn's choice, Jedrek didn't balk, even though he wanted to. Relocating into the city would slow their progress even further on the house. It spurred Jedrek on to get as much done as he could, knowing they wouldn't be working tomorrow. He and the others pressed on until late in the day. Garand and Eston were using the horses to haul lumber to the homestead, less than a mile up the road.

Marek sat down to take a break. He was fully recovered from his injury but still tired more quickly than normal.

A few minutes after the other two left him, Marek heard a twig snap behind him. With his left hand, he picked up a rag and wiped the sweat from the back of his neck. His right hand reached slowly toward his ax.

Before his hand touched the ax, the point of a sword pressed firmly against his back. "Stand down, soldier," a voice ordered.

Marek raised his hands slowly in surrender. He stood and cautiously turned to face whoever had confronted him. The man keeping him at bay was Clovis, a high-ranking official in Governor Pravin's army. "Clovis, why are you here?"

"You seem nervous, Marek. I'm just here to get your report. Governor Pravin told me your attack on him was a ruse to allow you to insert yourself into the young woman's life. It appears you've done a good job at that. We've been watching you for several weeks. What do you have to report?"

Marek kept his hands up in case Garand or one of the others returned. "Governor Pravin didn't give me any instructions other than to get close to the family and wait for orders. That's what I've done, and it nearly cost me my life when I took an arrow in the ribs. Did you bring me new orders?"

"Your orders are to get the woman to retreat to the city. Volunteer to stay in the Healer's home to guard it in her absence. Don't go with them. Governor Pravin has a plan to destroy the entire place. He wants to expand his territory to include the Nazaran Province, subdue its occupants, and rid himself of the Promised One in one quick move. The gods have sent men from the stars, and they promised to help the governor in exchange for mining rights in Nazar," Clovis explained.

"Men from the stars? How is that possible?"

"I don't know. What I do know is that they have homes that fly like birds and they are incredibly powerful. You would do well to heed my warning about not entering the city."

"You have my word, I'll stay clear of it."

"Why do you still have your hands up?"

"You have a sword pointed at me, and it would seem better to appear to be at your mercy if the others return unexpectedly. I also know Nasha still doesn't trust me. He was here earlier. It wouldn't surprise me to find out he remained behind to watch me. Are you responsible for the attacks on the locals?" Marek was doing a little investigating of his own.

"Not specifically. Pravin's new allies fly in from the skies at night and destroy the people without setting foot on the ground. We just ride around the area and take the blame. We're here to scare people enough to send them cowering behind the city walls. With a majority of the people in the city, the governor's allies can come in and destroy the people and the city at one time." Clovis' explanation was hard to swallow. "Do you think you can get them to move?"

Marek's thoughts lingered on the men from the stars. "People from the skies? Like gods?"

"No, they're men like us. They eat, bleed, and enjoy the pleasure of women like we do. Can you get Slaina and the others into the city?" Clovis persisted.

"Yes, we're supposed to go tomorrow morning," Marek answered. The second he answered the question, a twinge of guilt pulled at his gut. "Is there anything else you need to know? Anything I should know?"

"I don't think so. Just stay out of the city if you want to live. If they're going to be in the city tomorrow, we'll attack tomorrow night. Governor Pravin wants this over quickly. If I were you, I'd head straight back to Somi. The Sky People will hit houses that are still occupied, too. We can meet you at the bridge tomorrow night if you want to travel together."

"I'll consider it. Don't wait on me, though. If I don't see you at the bridge, I will see you in Somi. You'd better get going before the others return." Marek glanced up the road, expecting them to be back soon.

Clovis nodded then backed away before returning his sword to its sheath. The man darted into the woods. Moments later, Marek heard a horse galloping away.

Marek slowly retrieved his ax and moved to the next tree he had chosen to cut down. He pounded away at the tree as the conversation replayed in his head. He struck with such force, he failed to realize how close it was to falling until he heard the telltale popping sound as the tree twisted and fell. He barely had time to step away from it before the thing landed with an impressive crash. Marek, drenched with sweat, stood there staring at the fallen tree as Garand and Eston returned with the horses.

Garand was equally surprised. "I didn't think we were gone long enough for you to take down another tree alone."

Marek took a drink of water and wiped sweat from his brow. "I didn't either."

That evening, the men arrived at Halyn's home as the sun was setting. Supper was ready and sitting on the table. Faris and Irana had water ready for the men to wash up prior to eating. The chatter was strangely laden with worry and concern. Slaina didn't want to go into the city any more than anyone else did. She seemed to accept it, though. Slaina's mother wanted Slaina and Jedrek inside the safety of the city's walls. Garand was in agreement. Joren, being young, wanted to stay and fight off the offenders. Jedrek wanted to move Slaina to safety yet remain at Halyn's home so he could return to his own homestead to continue working on the house.

Marek was strangely silent until Jedrek began to discuss staying outside the city. "Forgive me, Lord Jedrek, but your place is at Slaina's side. Her child will be born any day. You can't leave her right now."

Jedrek gave Marek an annoyed look. "Why is it you have to refer to me as Lord Jedrek every time you're going to disagree with me? I'm no longer a lord over anything. I'm a poor working man, like you. We are equals. If you want to disagree with me, then disagree with me as an equal, not as your superior."

Marek grinned disarmingly. "Yes, my lord."

A round of laughter erupted from everyone at the table as Jedrek looked around for something to throw at Marek. Orun pulled at Jedrek's sleeve. Jedrek looked down to see what he wanted. The boy opened his hand to reveal a pebble he had pulled from his pocket. Jedrek smiled and took the pebble from the boy. He promptly pegged Marek's left collarbone with the small rock.

"Ow! You're asking for it, LORD Jedrek!"

"Not at my table or in my kitchen!" Halyn barked. "No more of that in here. You men are worse than a bunch of children."

The two men apologized for their rambunctious behavior. Marek got serious again. "Jedrek, allow me to stay here. I can look after the farm and perhaps get some work done on your home. I doubt there is much I could do inside the city anyway. The city could run short of space if everyone leaves the outlying areas for the protection of the city walls. I will leave the space for those who need it. I have no family."

Orun piped up. "We're your family, aren't we?"

Slaina smiled at the young man. "Yes, Marek, you are part of our family."

Marek scowled at Orun. "He's not. He gave Jedrek a rock to throw at me."

Orun grinned and pulled another handful of pebbles from his pocket. "I can share some of these with you."

Garand scowled. "Orun, put those away."

"Yes, Papa. I was just trying to even things up."

Halyn rolled her eyes. "You two, don't encourage that boy. He'll turn into an armaments peddler."

After dinner that evening, Halyn invited Slaina's family to stay the night. The group gathered around the table to listen to the nightly reading of the Ancient Texts. Joren brought them out as usual and started to hand the texts to Garand, the oldest male member present. Halyn quietly redirected him to hand the texts to Marek.

Marek was surprised, but didn't resist. He opened to the next scheduled passage to read.

This sign is given so that you will know when my beloved son is to come. The son of Pateras will not be born among the wealthy. You will find my son in the lowliest of places. In the valley of Efrath, the child will be born to the untouched woman chosen by Pateras. The stars will welcome the blessed one who comes to bring justice and mercy to all of creation. His hand will strike out at the evil reigning and remove the Dark Lord and those who follow him from their thrones. My son will reign supreme.

Warriors from the heavens will descend, bringing destruction and death. Their hands will smite the city that offers refuge to the Promised One. The war on my name will descend from the stars and visit the land twice. Weep for the lost. There will be silence in every land. Silence will be carried across the stars. My son will mourn for those who are lost and whose names are never known. He will appoint one to follow in his steps and defend the names of those who are lost.

Mourn for the lost but rejoice for those who are found. The Promised One will give up his life to free everyone who desires from the price of his crimes against Pateras. Pateras loved his creation and all of mankind so much, he sent his Promised One to give back the life that was lost. His blood is the pardon for the crimes against me. He will be guilty of nothing.

Marek stopped reading. The section moved on to another topic, but this topic was enough to occupy his thoughts. "Halyn, don't you think this is enough for tonight?"

"I suppose it is. Leave the texts open there for now. With the birth of the child so close, there's a lot to consider. Someone may want to read that part again." Halyn glanced at Slaina.

Marek's eyes followed hers. Slaina was sitting in a rocking chair, touching the child that filled her belly. The child looked as though he was turning somersaults. Jedrek was seated on the floor by Slaina. He reached out to touch the baby. Despite the child not being his, he already loved him as his own. His mind couldn't comprehend the magnitude of what this tiny baby was coming to do.

Garand and Luisa ushered their children off to bed. Joren pulled more firewood inside. Despite the warm spring weather, the nights were still nippy. Halyn began going through her medicines and potions. Marek wasn't entirely sure what to do with himself. He approached Halyn. "Healer, is there something I can help you with?"

"No, not tonight. I'm just lookin' over my supplies to see what I needed to take with me tomorrow. There is one thing you can do. Fetch me a cup of water. Slaina looks tired. I'm goin' to mix some herbs for her."

Marek grabbed a cup of water and brought it to Halyn, who stirred a few herbs into it. "There. Take that to her and make sure she drinks all of it."

Marek did as he was told. "Ms. Halyn says to drink all of this. I would like for you to drink all of it as well. I don't want to get into more trouble with the Healer, or she'll have me sleeping in the barn tonight."

Slaina smiled. "We can't have that." She drank the herb water promptly and returned it to him. Jedrek helped her out of the rocking chair and escorted her to her room. Faris was already curled up in Slaina's bed. Jedrek helped Slaina lie down. He tucked her in quietly before returning to his own room.

Joren put his last load of firewood down and headed to his bed. Halyn had several extra rooms in her home, but Slaina's family, along with Jedrek, Joren, and now Marek, pushed the limits of occupancy. Marek volunteered to sleep in the bed off the kitchen that Halyn used to treat patients.

Halyn sat down in the rocking chair and stared into the fire as she rocked. She waited patiently for the questions brewing in Marek's mind to surface.

"Halyn, how do you know Pateras is real?"

"I've spoken to him many times, and he's answered me, not audibly, but in my soul. I've seen his hand at work in too many matters to doubt him. Most recently, in the life of that girl in there. If he weren't workin', she'd been dead several times over by now. Think about it. What if you had been in charge of that patrol when we first met? You would have stripped my wagon down, found that girl, and probably killed us both. Pateras put Nasha over that patrol for a reason.

"The weather's been downright odd this past year. The rain washed away Slaina's tracks. The winter weather has kept Pravin's men from slipping into Nazar. There's lots of reasons to know Pateras is real."

"The weather's warm now. How's Pateras going to protect her now? Does he plan to keep her safe in the city?"

"No, not right now he doesn't." Halyn continued to stare into the fire as she spoke.

"How do you know?" Marek pressed.

"Two reasons. First, that girl is about to deliver in the next day or two. Second, the city of Nazar is outside of the Efrath valley. We are in the middle of the valley right here. That passage in the texts is makin' me think we are not leavin' here tomorrow." Halyn stopped speaking and rocked, deep in thought.

Marek watched her for a time before cautiously asking, "Do you think the attacks on the outlying farms were meant to drive everyone to the city?"

Halyn stopped watching the fire. Her eyes pierced the dim lighting to peer into Marek's soul. "The only way that would be an advantage is if somebody could destroy the city walls."

"I suppose you're right. It would take an army and several catapults to do that." Fearing he'd said too much, Marek rolled away from Halyn and closed his eyes.

That night his mind was filled with harrowing dreams of the city on fire and people screaming. He woke in the middle of one such dream where a large fiery figure stood before him. The figure said one sentence to him: "My Lord knows your name."

Marek bolted upright in bed, his body drenched in a cold sweat. Who, or what, was the creature that spoke to him, and what did he mean? Who was his lord? Marek knew the answer, but he refused to admit it to himself.

Marek splashed some water on his face. The texts were still sitting open on the table. He lit a candle and reread the passage. The words were written hundreds of years before. Why did they really matter?

Marek woke the next morning to Joren shaking him. "Wake up, Marek. The sun's already up. Are you sick or something?"

Marek rolled over stiffly. "No, I just didn't sleep well. I'm coming."

The household wasn't moving very quickly this morning. No one wanted to move into the city. There was little else they could do, though.

Marek wasn't the only one getting up late. Slaina was still sleeping as well. Jedrek came to Halyn and asked if he should wake her. Halyn told him to let her sleep.

The extended family finished eating and began to clean up. Halyn left some breakfast out for Slaina, who finally roused. She came into the kitchen grousing. "Jedrek, why didn't you wake me? There's work to be done if we're going into town to stay."

Jedrek promptly rerouted her complaint. "Halyn told me to let you sleep."

Irana, sensing the moodiness in the air, went back and forth from person to person, seeking attention. She ran straight into Slaina's belly. "Irana! Stop it! Go away!"

The little girl's feelings were clearly offended. She ran to Luisa for comfort. Luisa was busy trying to help Halyn pack. The child clung to her mother's tunic, crying and complaining loudly that Slaina had yelled at her.

Slaina was still griping to Jedrek about the decision not to wake her. Jedrek defended the decision as being correct, given her current mood. Luisa and Halyn were trying to give directions about what should be packed and in what order. Orun, having no directions, played with the pebbles in his pocket and flicked them at things as well as people.

Luisa made an executive decision. "Orun, take Irana outside, away from the house, to play."

Orun perked up. "You mean I don't have to work?"

Garand stepped behind Orun and placed his hand on the boy's shoulder. "No, son, you have the most important job of all. Your sister is in need of care and attention. This is a job for an adult, and your mother is busy with this tedious work. We need you to care for her until your mother is free. Can you handle that responsibility?"

"Yes, Papa. Come on, Irana, let's go outside." The boy led his sister outside and began to play.

Slaina continued to complain that the bench was too hard, her back was hurting, and her food was cold. Everyone tried to stay out of her way, but Halyn and Luisa seemed to stay closer than ever.

It took Slaina a long time to eat her breakfast. She kept stopping to massage her tight belly. "Halyn, what kind of herbs did you give me last night?"

"They were to help you sleep."

"I don't think they worked very well. I kept waking up, and my back hurt all night," Slaina complained.

Halyn laid her hand on Slaina's belly. It was tight again. "Has your belly been doing that all night?"

"Some. It woke me up several times last night." Slaina's heart raced as she realized why Halyn was asking. "Is the baby coming?"

"If I were to guess, I would say by this time tomorrow you will be holding your son in your arms. I can't say for certain. Babies often have a mind of their own."

"What should I do?" Slaina asked. She was both nervous and excited.

"You and Jedrek should go for a walk and talk all you want to. It'll probably be the last uninterrupted conversation you ever have." Halyn grinned. Although she had no children of her own, she was familiar with the impetuousness of childhood.

"But what about the packing?" Slaina watched the hustle and bustle around her.

"There's not that much to do, and the rest of us can handle it. We'll have it done before long, and then we'll have lunch before we head to town. Now go spend some time alone with Jedrek while you can. After today, there'll be a baby demanding your attention."

Slaina nodded. She finished her food, and the two went for a walk.

The couple walked toward the house Jedrek was building for them. Slaina hadn't been there recently, so she didn't know how much had been done on it. It was a bit of a walk, and Slaina had to stop several times as the contractions increased. She and Jedrek didn't know that Orun and Irana were sneaking behind them the entire way.

The couple toured the small house and talked about where Slaina wanted to place certain pieces of furniture. Finally, Slaina could concentrate on their plans no longer. The contractions were coming harder and faster. The walk had been longer and harder than she anticipated.

She sat down on the porch out front and asked Jedrek for some water. Jedrek grabbed a bucket and headed for a nearby spring. He moved quickly, and it only took a few minutes for him to retrieve the water for her. Slaina drank liberally and splashed some on her face and neck. Taking another couple deep breaths, she waited for yet another contraction to pass. They had been gone for a couple of hours already. She suspected Halyn would be cross with her for going so far, and there was a good chance lunch was ready.

Jedrek and Slaina walked toward Halyn's home. Orun and Irana waited until the couple were out of sight then jumped up excitedly to explore the new house. The two occupied themselves long enough for Jedrek and Slaina to get totally out of view even from the nearest rise.

The walk back took longer than the walk to the house. Slaina took more frequent rests, and her stops lasted longer than before. She finally sat down, insisting she didn't want to walk anymore. Jedrek was torn. He couldn't leave her out here alone while he went to fetch a wagon, and he was afraid to push her to keep moving.

Frustrated, Jedrek looked to the skies. "Pateras, I need help. What should I do?"

The sound of horses reached his ears. Jedrek spotted Nasha leading a patrol up a nearby rise. "Wait here. I'll be right back." He took off running toward Nasha, yelling, before she could respond.

Nasha and his patrol turned aside to answer Jedrek's call. When Nasha saw the situation, he was hesitant to put Slaina on a horse. He sent one of his men to Halyn's home to bring the healer and a wagon back. The men waited nervously at her side for the wagon to return.

It felt like an eternity before Halyn arrived with the wagon. Jedrek carefully lifted Slaina into it. Halyn sat in the back with Slaina while Jedrek took over driving. Halyn warned the young man to drive slowly and carefully.

Presently, the wagon returned to Halyn's home. Jedrek carried Slaina inside and laid her on the bed off the kitchen. Halyn pulled a curtain closed, giving the girl a little privacy.

Jedrek stood by nervously. "Halyn, is the baby coming?"

"Oh, it will still be awhile." Halyn sat down to finish her lunch.

Garand's wagon was the one used to retrieve Slaina. Halyn's wagon was packed and ready to go to the city. The only thing they still had to do was to finish eating and clean the dishes.

Luisa came inside. "Jedrek, were Irana and Orun with you?"

Jedrek was distracted. He hardly knew Luisa had spoken to him. He heard Slaina moan softly from behind the curtain. When he looked up and saw Luisa waiting for an answer to her question, he replayed the memory in his mind to recall what she had asked. "No, I haven't seen them since before we left the farm. They were playing outside when Slaina and I left. Halyn, I'm really sorry I let her talk me into walking so far. Why didn't you yell at us for that?"

"I certainly would have preferred you to stay closer, but the walk was good for her. It will help the baby come faster. My only worry right now is those young'uns. Is Nasha still here?"

Luisa was moving from aggravated to worried. "He said he would stay with us to see that Slaina got safely into the city."

Halyn stepped outside and motioned to Nasha. The man wasted no time coming to her side. "Can Slaina be moved to the city?"

"Slaina isn't the problem. The two little ones are missing. I'm gonna have Joren unhitch the horses and send all the men out to look for the young'uns. I'll keep Jedrek here with Slaina. Do you still have men on the rise?"

"Yes, but if you unhitch the horses, you can't get Slaina into the city. At least keep two of the horses so you can move her. She needs to get to safety," Nasha insisted.

"No, Nasha, she doesn't. The Ancient Texts say that baby is supposed to be born here, not in Nazar, and it's comin' tonight. The Ancient Texts also say the city's not safe. We read the prophecy last night. It's all happenin' accordin' to the prophecy," Halyn mused.

Nasha badly wanted to object, but Halyn had not been wrong yet. He had nothing but his own common sense to rest on, and that had failed him before. His best option was to find those children and get back to protect Slaina and the others. "Where were the children last seen?"

"Jedrek says they were playing here in the yard when he and Slaina walked out to their own house. I'll go get the menfolk."

Nasha jumped to unhitch the horses from the wagons by the door. Moments later, the other men came out to help. Nasha split his troops and sent everyone in different directions in groups of twos and threes. He wanted someone considered family with each search team in case something had frightened the children.

The group made a thorough search of the farm before branching outward. They had difficulty searching for the children's tracks because of the recent traffic in and out of the area.

Nasha brought Marek and one other man with him. The three stopped to update the patrol keeping an eye on things from the top of the rise. They questioned the men, who had paid little attention to the children. One man vaguely remembered the children following Jedrek and Slaina for a bit, but he couldn't remember how far they had gone.

The patrol rode west toward Jedrek's new place. They spread out to cover a little more territory. Marek got separated from the others. He spotted Clovis in the distance and rode toward him.

"Clovis, what are you doing here? I thought you would be preparing to attack the city."

"We aren't attacking the city. The men from the skies will attack it. We're just rounding up any stragglers who escape or come in from the outer areas late. Has the girl gone to the city?"

"No, not yet. She's ready to go, but her youngest brother and sister have disappeared. They can't leave without them. You haven't rounded them up, have you?" Marek asked.

"No, I've been keeping my distance from the locals. The others and I are camping further up the mountainside. I saw you coming this way and came to see what you needed."

Marek looked aggravated. "I need those two noisy brats to get home so we can get moving. Slaina's baby is coming."

"If you can't get her into the city, at least keep yourself out of the house. The men from the skies are going to be attacking houses around the province all night. They'll attack the city first then the farms. Stay outside or in the barn. I need to go before Nasha sees me."

Marek nodded. "If you see those kids, send them home right away."

Clovis acknowledged the instruction as he rode up the mountainside as Marek guided his steed away from the mountain. He rejoined Nasha a little ways ahead.

The men searched for another couple of hours, then headed back to Halyn's. It was getting late. They hoped one of the others had found the children, but upon returning, they learned the children still hadn't been located.

The group discussed what they should do next. From the yard, they heard Slaina's moans of pain increase.

Marek wandered away from the group. He stood there, listening to Slaina's cries. His conscience had been pricking him for months. Now it was stabbing him outright. His pain coincided with each of Slaina's contractions.

"Marek? Marek! Marek, are you with us?"

Marek realized Nasha was calling his name. He turned around and asked, "Nasha, do you really believe in Pateras? Do you really think the prophecies are true?"

Nasha gave Marek a befuddled look. "What does that have to do with anything?"

"I need to know. Do you really believe in the prophecies? Are they ever wrong?" Marek demanded.

"I've only seen a handful come true so far. Most speak of days we haven't seen yet, but no, I've never known them to be wrong. Why is this important?" Nasha persisted.

"The prophecy we read last night spoke of the birth of Slaina's baby and the destruction of Nazar. The prophecy mentioned men coming from the skies to destroy the city and a war from the heavens brought down," Marek explained. His eyes clearly revealed his distress over the thought.

Nasha sensed there was more. "We have no way of knowing when that will happen."

"It's happening tonight. Clovis is here. He told me to stay out of the city and to get out of Halyn's house. He said warriors from the skies had allied themselves with Pravin. They're coming tonight to destroy the city and hit any houses outside that are still occupied. We have to get Slaina into the barn and empty the city before nightfall."

Nasha stared at Marek as he digested the man's words. Nasha took two long steps then broke into a run to reach Marek. He promptly belted him across the face, knocking the man to the ground.

Marek shook his head to clear it then rolled over onto his back. He started to sit up and found Nasha's sword at his throat.

"The only reason Clovis would have given you that information is because he thought you still worked for Governor Pravin." Nasha's anger was stayed only because he feared the reason the children were missing had something to do with Marek. "Where are those children? Tell me now, or I'll run you through!" Nasha seethed with anger.

"I don't know! I had nothing to do with their disappearance. I even asked Clovis if he had seen them. I told him they were the reason we hadn't gone into the city. He's supposed to send them back here if he sees them. Nasha, I was helping load the wagons when they disappeared! Ask the others!" Marek looked nervously over at the others, who were frozen in shock.

Nasha refused to take his eyes off Marek. He watched his face carefully for signs of lies. He could see none, but he didn't know how good of a liar Marek was.

Garand finally found his voice. "He's telling the truth—about loading the wagon. He never left us until after the children disappeared."

Nasha backed off a moment. Marek eased into a sitting position and started to stand, but a pointed look from Nasha kept him on his knees.

A rider came charging in. The men anxiously waited for what they knew would be bad news. The rider pulled the reins hard to bring his steed to a rough stop. A cloud of dust kicked into the air, adding the dry acrid taste to match their mood. "Nasha! The magistrate needs you! Somian soldiers are headed this way! They'll be here by nightfall. He says to get the mother of the Promised One inside the city walls immediately."

Nasha's blood ran cold. He turned and took two fast steps toward Marek, grabbed the man by the collar, and reared back with his sword, prepared to run him through. "If it's war Governor Pravin wants, it's war he will get. Starting with Marek!"

Slaina had a particularly violent contraction and cried outright.

Nasha hesitated on hearing her cry. It was a normal part of labor, but not something he was accustomed to hearing.

Marek took advantage of Nasha's hesitation. "Nasha, please, if you must kill me, at least wait until after the baby is born. I would like to see the face of the Promised One. Just one time. Please."

Nasha looked up to see Halyn standing on the porch watching. He called out so she could hear him. "This is what you were talking about, isn't it? Has Pateras really changed him?"

"I have reasons to believe he has. Ask him whatever you like. If Pateras has changed him, he will answer you fully and quickly," Halyn responded calmly.

Marek couldn't see Halyn's face behind him, but he heard her words. He didn't struggle or even attempt to fight back. The man feared for his life, but accepted that it was about to end.

Nasha saw Marek swallow hard before attempting to speak. "Ask me whatever you wish. I will answer truthfully." He gave no oath. They both knew his word was virtually useless now.

Nasha lowered his sword for the moment. "What do you know about this army?"

"Nothing. Clovis said he and his group were to take out any stragglers who managed to get away from the city. Perhaps Governor Pravin is sending the army to destroy all who survive the city or even wipe out anyone they find. Clovis never mentioned the army to me."

Nasha ordered Joren to fetch some rope from the barn to tie Marek with. Once the boy was on his way, Nasha looked toward Halyn. "Can Slaina be moved to the city?"

Halyn had left the porch and ventured closer to the men. "She could be, but we can't do that."

Nasha shook his head. "I don't understand. Can she be moved, or can't she?"

"She can. It won't hurt her. It won't be an easy or comfortable ride for her, but it could be done. I'm not going to do that, though. The prophecies say that the child will be born here in the valley. We aren't supposed to go anywhere." Halyn repeated the prophecies they had read the previous night to Nasha. "The city will be attacked from the skies. Marek is right. We need to get as many out of the city as we can."

"But the city is the safest place for her and the child," Nasha argued.

"Safe according to whom? Do you doubt the words of Pateras?" Halyn challenged. She knew he didn't, but his faith was colliding with his fear.

Nasha wanted nothing more than to find a safe way to disagree with her. The things he had seen over the last few months flashed through his mind. Pateras had protected Slaina from impossible situations as far as man could see. It was Pateras that saved her from certain death at his own hand. Nasha glanced at the messenger. "Where is the magistrate?"

"He's with the town council in the town hall."

Marek took this opportunity to make a suggestion. "Nasha, let me ride to Clovis and bring them out of hiding. The town council may want to get rid of both of us if we don't have proof of our allegiance. We're both Somian."

"All I have to do is hand him your confession, and he'll have no doubts about my loyalties. These witnesses are all the proof I need. I don't even need to bring you back alive." Nasha spoke with a chill in his voice.

"Let's take one of the wagons, cover it, and drive it through the Iguptos ravine. I can go to Clovis and tell him you're taking Slaina out of the province to the west. He'll chase after you. We can take him and the men with him, so no one will find out where Slaina actually is." Marek stood slowly, despite Nasha's threatening glare.

Joren returned with the rope. "Bind him!" Nasha ordered as he stepped back, giving Joren room to tie Marek's hands.

Marek eyed the rope nervously. "Nasha, I don't want to work for Governor Pravin any longer. Please let me help."

"You've used all the grace I had left. The magistrate can pronounce sentence, and I will gladly carry it out." The man didn't care to waste another thought on the enemy soldier. He moved on to the task of addressing Halyn. "Get Slaina ready to move. We've got to get her to the city."

"We're not going unless Pateras himself says so. You can forget it." Halyn turned and went inside to tend to her patient.

Nasha cussed under his breath. "Stubborn old woman is going to get a lot of people killed."

Joren wasn't accustomed to tying people, only horses. He struggled to bind Marek. Marek balled up his fists and flexed his muscles tightly. When Joren lost his grip on the rope, Marek relaxed his muscles and the ropes slipped neatly off his wrists. Marek grabbed the slack, wrapped it around Joren's neck, and twisted him around to face the others. Joren cried out in surprise.

"Joren!" Eston cried out. The young man had become like an older brother to him. Seeing him at Marek's mercy elevated his feelings to near panic.

Nasha spun about and returned his sword to a position of readiness. "Marek, let him go!"

"Keep your distance if you don't want him harmed."

"You know it takes time and a great deal of strength to strangle a man, don't you?" Nasha attempted to edge forward.

"You've seen me in battle. You know I have the strength. I could snap his neck easily enough." Marek's warning forced Nasha to back off.

Marek stepped backward, pulling Joren with him. His first order of business was to level the playing field. The messenger was the only one on a horse. The other horses were tied by the watering trough.

"You—off the horse. Don't touch that crossbow or your sword!" The man's sword and crossbow both hung on his saddle.

Marek watched the man's every move while gripping the rope around Joren's neck. The messenger obeyed, waiting for the opportunity to rescue the young man from Marek's grasp.

Marek secured the rope around Joren's neck in one hand, then grabbed the saddle with his free hand. He climbed carefully into the saddle. With the reins securely in one hand and the rope in the other, Marek looked back at the others he had begun to think of as family. His formerly cold, hard heart was completely melted, despite its current appearance.

"Nasha! Get the wagon and hide some troops at the mouth of the Iguptos Ravine. I'll have Clovis there in two hours. If you don't get there and take him down, you won't have to worry about me. He'll handle it for you. I didn't know about the army, and I don't know where the children are. I don't work for Pravin any more. I serve Pateras." Marek leaned down to softly address Joren. "I'm sorry if I hurt you or embarrassed you. I would never have purposely harmed you. I just needed to prove a point. Forgive me." He loosened the rope and released Joren.

Despite his anger and the desire to fight back, Joren pulled the rope from his neck and backed away from Marek. He stared at the man, weighing whether he really spoke the truth this time or not. Marek allowed him a glimpse into his soul before riding away.

Joren rubbed the burns on his neck from the rope. The men gathered around him to check on the young man. Assured that he was in good condition, they rehashed this set of circumstances.

Nasha pulled Joren aside for a moment. "What did he say to you before he rode off?"

"He apologized to me. He said he wouldn't have hurt me, and he just needed to prove his point." Joren looked confused for a moment.

"What is it?" Nasha asked.

"I know this don't sound right, but I believe him," Joren offered. "There was somethin' in his eyes."

Nasha dismissed Joren as being young and naïve. He began to ponder his options. If he took a wagon and troops to the ravine, that would leave Slaina unguarded. It seemed like a valid way for Clovis and the others to get at her. Halyn and Joren both seemed to think Marek had changed. If he had, this was the perfect opportunity to catch Clovis and his men, otherwise there would be rogue troops behind their lines when facing the army coming from Somi. His head told him to get Slaina and the others into the city. His gut told him something very different.

Every time he had ignored his gut, things went wrong. He marched up to the house. "Halyn, we need to move Slaina!"

GENESIS
CONVERGENCE

The CIF SS *Deliverance* under the command of Capt. Ibrahim Imani was testing out a new engine technology. The ship was a Pacification-class ship designed to "keep the peace." Its basic layout and appearance were the same as every other ship in the Pacification Fleet. The most noticeable difference was a network of thin conduits interwoven across the hull. The matter/antimatter engines produced tachyons, which, when pushed through the net on the hull, created a wormhole-like field that pulled the ship through space at speeds significantly faster than light. The engines had been developed by Saul and Kay Deacons, among others. Their son, Robert, now had the privilege of serving as a senior officer on the first Pacification ship to use this technology.

Robert didn't discuss his parents' contribution to the new engines. Inwardly, he was still proud of their accomplishment. The first part of their tour of duty had been a shakedown cruise to test out the engines and their capabilities. They covered a great deal of the galaxy on the first leg of their trip and their fuel reserves were getting a little lower than anticipated. Lt. Cmdr. Deacons' current assignment was to locate a supply of tetrabradium or tetratachium. Planets containing the elements had a very specific profile. Robert ran the profile through the planetary database. Once he had the information he needed, he reported to his superior.

"Capt. Imani, I have three possibilities for finding the ore we need. There's a system a little off our current course. We can be there in a few hours at our current speed. There are two possibilities for finding ore in that system. The system is known as the Galatan solar system. They have an asteroid belt we could mine for the ore. It would take a bit of time in artificial environment suits and utility pods, not to mention the risks for collisions. The shields will protect us, and the pods, but those in the AE suits would be at risk."

Capt. Imani scowled. He wasn't inclined to risk losing people for such trivial reasons. "What's the next option?"

"The third planet is a Level II on the tech scale. It shows high levels of tetratachium and tetrabradium on one continent in particular. I don't show that any contact has been made previously, only scans from space."

The captain sighed. New contact situations with primitive cultures could be dangerous. "Third option?"

"The third option is technically outside our range. We might have to travel at sub-light speeds until we reach the mining colony at Basaan III. It's a Commonwealth colony, and they will have ore available, no mining needed." The new Lt. Commander knew the captain wouldn't care for this option either. He had no idea which option he might choose.

Capt. Imani took a sip of his coffee as he contemplated his options. "Lt. Commander, how about you start earning that new pay grade of yours? Which one would you choose, and why?"

Robert stopped and thought a moment. "I'd go to the Galatan asteroid belt and mine enough using the pods to get us safely to the mining colony."

Capt. Imani took a sip of his coffee again as he weighed Robert's suggestion. It was a decent suggestion, one he had already been considering. This young man had potential. "Set course for the Galatan asteroid belt and start preparing the equipment we'll need. Don't put anybody outside in AE suits. I'm not willing to risk lives over this."

Robert passed the orders to the helm and navigation. He went over the equipment and staffing requirements to mine the ore, compiled a list and had the ship's first officer review it to be certain he hadn't overlooked anything. When he was satisfied, he went off duty. After some sleep and a hot meal, Robert was ready to put the mining operation into action.

The ship put itself along a path parallel to the asteroid belt and began scanning the area for a rich supply that would be easily accessible. However, the belt wasn't as rich as they had hoped. They were halfway around the star system when one of the officers scanning the area interrupted their search. "Lt. Commander, I have bradyon emissions leading through the asteroid belt." There was a pause as he continued to study the readout. "The trail appears to head toward the third planet in the system."

Robert scowled. "Commander, we may have Lo-Tech Raiders in the system. Do you want to track the bradyon trail?"

The commander queried the captain to learn his preference. The captain made the unexpected call of bypassing the Commander. "Lt. Cmdr. Deacons, leave your mining op plan with Lt. Cmdr. Johnson, then assemble a well-armed team and hunt those raiders down. Use whatever force you feel is necessary. These raiders need to understand that we will not tolerate them violating Commonwealth restrictions and harassing those incapable of defending themselves."

Robert nodded. "Yes Captain." He hailed Lt. Cmdr. Miles Johnson to request his presence on the bridge and prepared his new team for this new project. He updated Miles on the mining operation and assembled a team to meet him in the launch bay.

The captain pulled him aside before departure to check on his progress. "Who are you taking, and what're your goals?"

"I'm taking six fighters and a shuttle with one doctor, two field medics, and nine additional ground troops. My goals are to track the ship or ships present and place their crews under arrest if possible, shoot them down if necessary," Robert replied.

"Why the medical personnel instead of more troops?" his captain asked.

"If they have attacked the planet in any way, there may be civilian casualties. It would go a long way in preventing future hostilities if we helped repair any damage the raiders caused. It could prevent future contact problems. We're a peacekeeping ship. It's what we do. We just need to make sure the press hears about it."

"I take it you enjoy playing politics?"

"No sir, I don't. They are, unfortunately, a necessary evil," Robert replied honestly. "I have a friend, Lt. Cmdr. Edgardo Garcia. He does enjoy playing politics. He, Lt. Cmdr. Johnson, and I worked well together because our strengths and weaknesses overlap in the right places."

"Hmm, interesting." The man was clearly thinking more than he was saying. "Again, your plan seems sound. Hail the commander if you have any issues."

"Yes Captain."

Robert loaded his supplies and personnel aboard the shuttle. He had the co-pilot relay the flight plan to the accompanying fighters. The group launched toward Galat III.

Nasha drove the wagon as hard as he dared. He really didn't like this plan—he didn't really care for any of the plans. He was feeling defeated, and the battle hadn't even started yet. He couldn't believe Halyn and the others had talked him into this.

He looked behind him and caught sight of torches bouncing in pursuit of the wagon. Riders were advancing on them. Nasha hollered to his passengers, "We've got company!" He slapped the reins, driving the horses harder.

The laden wagon was no match for the horses pursuing them. The riders got close enough that one of them tossed a torch onto the canopy covering the wagon. A voice from the rear of the wagon called out, "We're on fire! We've got to stop!"

Nasha pulled on the reins. The wagon slowed, and he turned it toward their pursuers, intending to charge and lead them toward Halyn's farm. If they didn't get the fire off the wagon, the horses would bolt. Nasha's passengers threw off the burning cover, revealing the contents of the wagon.

They were hastily surrounded by a dozen men. Clovis and Marek were the first to approach. The band of ruffians were met with angry glares from Nasha, Garand, and a couple of other men, along with the stares of a frightened young woman.

"Marek, I knew you weren't to be trusted!" Nasha drew his sword and pointed it at the man. For the first time, he didn't mean the words he spoke. Marek had surprised him.

"Nasha, give Slaina to us, and no one else needs to get hurt," Marek countered.

Clovis jumped in to interrupt. "Everyone out of the wagon, including Slaina."

Garand moved to help a small woman wrapped in a heavy cloak out of the wagon. On the ground, the frightened young woman nestled under Garand's arm. The men in the wagon climbed out slowly. The men drew their swords and surrounded their precious cargo, shielding her with their bodies. Nasha kept the high ground by staying in the front of the wagon.

"Clovis, let this one go. Pateras has his hand of protection on Slaina. You won't win this fight," Nasha warned.

Clovis and his men raised their crossbows and pointed them at the men surrounding their prey. "Put your swords down and move away from her."

A party of Nazaran soldiers was coming behind them, and the group knew they merely needed to keep these troops at bay until the others arrived. The men didn't respond immediately to the threat, so Clovis placed a warning shot into the back of the wagon, nicking the arm of one man. The man cried out in pain. Seeing his plight, the young woman pulled away from Garand and jumped out in front of the men. Garand reached to pull her to him, but the girl stayed beyond his reach. She pleaded, "Please don't hurt them."

Marek looked down at the girl, and a lump entered his throat. He had to get her to safety. He dismounted and approached the brave young woman, who was now offering her life to save the surrounding soldiers. Looking into her eyes, he reached his hand out to her. "Slaina, give me your hand."

The young woman extended her hand to Marek. She didn't know what would happen or whose side he was on. She did know terrible things would happen if she didn't go with him.

Garand leapt after the girl. The soldiers held him back, fearing he would get himself shot by a crossbow bolt. Garand knew there was one thing he could say that might protect his daughter, but if he did, it could cost him far more. He cried out, "She's just a child. Let her go!"

Marek turned around and walked the two steps to Garand. He backhanded the man with the hilt of his sword. "I suggest you hold your tongue. I know exactly who and what she is. Keep still if you know what's good for you."

Garand landed on the ground with a bloody nose and blurred vision. Marek squatted beside him. "I promise, this will be over quickly, and you won't see any of it."

Marek grabbed the girl and pulled her toward his horse. He set her petite frame into the saddle then climbed up after her.

Nasha still gripped his sword tightly. "Marek, don't hurt her. Touch her and I will take you apart one piece at a time."

"I told you, if you gave us Slaina, no one else would get hurt. I am a man of my word." Marek started to ride off into the dark with the young woman.

Clovis called out, "Where are you going with her?"

"If I do this in front of them, they'll fight back. I'm going to take her up the trail and handle it. Don't worry, I'll bring proof back." Marek urged his horse forward. He trotted around the bend in the ravine then stopped. He got down from his horse and helped the girl down from the saddle. "Faris, why did Nasha let you come? Is he insane? You know they expect me to kill you and bring back a bloody sword—don't you?"

Faris' eyes teared up. "I know, but everyone else is working so hard to protect Slaina, I had to do something too. Will it hurt much?"

"Will what hurt much?" Marek was confused by her question.

"They want you to kill Slaina. They think I'm her. You have to kill me, or they'll go after her and her baby."

"Faris, I'm not going to kill you. I do need you to take your cloak off. I'm going to need it and some blood that isn't mine," Marek hastily explained.

Faris took her cloak off. She hadn't realized the one thing he was trying to warn her about. If he returned with a gash of his own, they would know the blood on the cloak was his. He needed blood from some other source. He didn't want to injure the twelve-year-old girl. "Faris, I'm going to need to cut your arm to get the blood I need. I don't want to hurt you, and I'm not going to kill you, but I don't see any other way around this."

No sooner had the words left his mouth than a rustling sound reached his ears. Marek reacted without thinking and stabbed at whatever was moving near him. His actions were rewarded with a loud squeal. A wild boar had been sleeping near them, and their noise disturbed its rest.

The boar went down with a single blow. Marek stood there a moment, staring at the beast.

Faris stepped forward and touched Marek's arm lightly. "See, Pateras provides for our needs."

Marek acted quickly. He placed the cloak around the beast and stabbed it a second time through the cloak. He let it sit there to soak up the blood that was oozing from the gashes. With the beast's heart no longer beating, the blood was doing little more than flowing downhill.

Once he had enough blood on the garment, he grabbed Faris by the shoulders. "Stay here and out of sight no matter what you hear, no matter how scared you might be. Do you understand?"

Faris nodded. She found a niche in the rocks along the ravine wall and scooted into it. It was starting to get cool out. Her mother had wrapped a blanket around her waist to add to the appearance of looking like the pregnant Slaina. Faris pulled the blanket from her waist and covered herself with it.

Marek cleaned the blood from his sword with the bottom of the cloak then sheathed it. He gave one last glance at the young woman. This child had taken her first real steps toward becoming an adult. He shook his head in disbelief at what she had tried to do for her sister.

When Marek rode off with the young woman, Garand struggled to get to his feet. The men around him held him back. He yelled after Marek. Nasha glanced toward the road behind them. Without their reinforcements, they were severely outnumbered.

Although Clovis and his men had the tactical advantage, he knew if the men heard the girl cry out, they might riot. "Nasha, get down from the wagon and drop your sword, or my men will drop you where you stand."

Nasha placed his sword on the wagon seat. He hoisted himself onto the ground. Clovis urged him to move to the back of the wagon. Nasha stepped slowly, keeping his eyes glued to Clovis. He walked to a spot close to Garand, who was shaking with tears running down his face. "I should never have agreed to this. I'm going to lose my daughter."

Nasha answered softly, "Trust Pateras to take care of this. He knows what he's doing."

A distant squeal reached their ears. Garand sobbed openly. "My daughter, my daughter."

Nasha's heart ached. Had he been wrong to trust Marek? Marek knew the girls apart, but he had called Slaina's name. Would he have harmed Faris? Nasha looked at the surrounding men. "We wait to find out the truth and for our reinforcements. Stay calm." The stress of the moment was evident on each of their faces.

Marek came riding back. He approached Clovis and tossed the bloody cloak to him. Clovis held the garment up. The garment was pierced with a large opening in the front and a smaller tear in the back as expected from a victim who had been run through. There was blood around each opening. The bottom of the cloak had bloody smears and smudges. Clovis pointed at the unexpected stain. "What's this?"

Marek held his hands out to his sides innocently. "What? I needed to clean my sword before I sheathed it."

Clovis got down from his horse and carried the garment over to Garand. He shoved the cloak into his arms. Garand grabbed onto the cloak and hugged it tightly. He sank to his knees in open sobs. "No, my baby. My precious child."

A bolt from a crossbow flew silently through the air and into the back of one of Clovis' men. The man cried out in pain and surprise. His own crossbow fired wildly, and the man tumbled from his saddle. It only took a second for Clovis to realize he was caught in a trap, but whose? Had Nasha done this, or was Marek somehow responsible? He decided Nasha was the most likely candidate. He loaded his crossbow as he shouted, "Spread out! Kill all of them!"

Nasha shoved Garand under the wagon. He moved around to the side and pulled a crossbow of his own from under the supplies in the wagon and fired at another enemy soldier.

Clovis raised his crossbow to fire at Nasha. Marek rode up beside the man, knife in hand. Before Clovis could fire, Marek cut the sinew of the bow. Realizing Marek's betrayal, Clovis swung the disabled crossbow at him. Marek dodged the blow and swung his knife, earning him the reward of drawing first blood. It also resulted in getting an elbow to the face as Clovis grabbed the hand with the knife to redirect the weapon away from him.

Garand knew Nasha had shoved him under the wagon for his own safety. He was not a warrior. But this was a fight for his children's lives, and he wanted to join the fray, despite being outmatched. Realizing Marek was now fighting Clovis, Garand looked at the blood on the cloak Faris had been wearing. Faris could still be alive. He had to get to her.

Garand bolted from under the wagon. He disappeared down the dark path where he had last seen his daughter alive. Spotting the carcass of the boar, he knew this was where they had stopped, and the girl must be nearby. "Faris… are you here? Are you safe?"

Hearing the welcome sound of her father's voice, the girl scurried out of her niche and threw herself into his arms. "Papa, I'm glad you're safe. Is it over? Can we go home now?"

In the struggle for control of the weapon, Clovis maneuvered himself into a position to throw Marek from his horse. Seeing Garand head down the road, Clovis concluded, as Garand had, that the girl was still alive. He rode after Garand to find her.

Clovis spotted the two, still in their embrace, and rode straight at them. The sound of hooves pounding the ground behind him warned him of the danger. Garand peeled Faris away from him, grabbed her hand, and tried to escape into the darkness. Clovis rode past the two, landing a booted foot in the center of Garand's back.

The blow sent father and daughter rolling on the ground. Clovis pivoted his horse. He caught Garand before he could get to his feet again and shoved him back onto the ground.

Garand attempted to roll away from his pursuer but found himself trapped, like a turtle on its back. The heavy foot on his chest and the sword at his throat inclined him to believe turtle soup was in his future.

Garand braced himself and tended to one last piece of business. "FARIS! RUN TO NASHA!"

The girl scampered away as ordered, but she hadn't gotten very far when she heard Clovis call out to her. "Get back here, girl, or your papa dies!"

Faris froze at the warning. Clovis lured her back despite her father's orders to the contrary. When he got his hands on her, he jerked her forward. "How old are you?"

"T-twelve."

"You're Slaina's sister, aren't you?"

"Yes."

"Where's your sister?"

"Someplace safe!" the girl replied defiantly.

"Tell me where she is, or I will hurt your papa!" Clovis shook the girl roughly with his left hand. His foot was no longer on Garand. He had changed the grip on his sword so that it rested on Garand's chest, directly above his heart. The movement, to convince Faris to answer, caused the sword to dig into Garand's skin. Garand grunted, then clenched his jaw shut. If he cried out in pain even a little, it might push Faris into revealing the information he was trying to protect. "Faris, run! Now, no matter what he does to me!" Garand yelled again through gritted teeth.

Marek recovered his horse and rode full speed toward Clovis. He stopped short of where he left the girl. Sliding off his horse, he pulled the crossbow from his saddle and led the horse toward the others. When he got within sight, he slapped the horse across his hindquarters. The horse bolted but swung wide, away from Clovis and his prisoners.

The sound of the horse got Clovis' attention. He released Garand and pulled Faris close to him. Faris and Slaina were the same height despite the four-year difference in their ages. Both were only shoulder height to Clovis. Before he could pull Faris directly in front of him, the bolt from Marek's crossbow grazed his right arm. Clovis grabbed Faris and lifted the lightweight young woman easily in front of him. Holding the blade of his sword near her throat, he ordered, "Marek! Stay put! Girl, tell me where your sister is, right now!"

"Clovis, you coward! Why do you hide behind a child? Fight me for the information! You beat me, and I'll tell you where the woman is," Marek challenged.

"No, Marek, tell me now, or I kill her."

"Last I knew, Nasha was sending her to the city," Marek replied honestly. He didn't know for certain that was where she was, though.

"Thank you, Marek. Now throw down your weapons."

Marek dropped the crossbow, then removed his dagger and sword and tossed them in front of him. He wanted the blades clearly between himself and Clovis in order to retrieve them quickly. "Let her go, Clovis. She's just a child."

An icy stare from Clovis said the things Marek didn't want to hear. "Marek, I know she isn't the one we're looking for, but you still should have taken care of her. When did you change sides? What did they say to convince you to join them?"

"They said nothing. You're the one who convinced me to change. You told me what was about to happen to the city. Pateras foretold those events in the Ancient Texts. Governor Pravin is afraid and he should be—he can't defeat Pateras." Marek inched closer as he spoke. His sword was directly at his feet. "Clovis, you can't defeat Pateras either. He's too big for anyone to defeat him."

"This farm life has made you soft!" Clovis' anger at Marek's betrayal clouded his judgment. He knew his best options logistically were to kill the girl first, then her father, leaving only Marek to contend with. The fiery eagerness to pass judgment on a fellow soldier burned more hotly than the desire to obey the strategies he had been taught. Clovis tossed the terrified Faris toward her father, who was now crouched on the ground, waiting for the opportunity to charge the man holding his daughter captive. Garand caught the girl, who collapsed into tears.

Marek dropped to grab his sword and charged Clovis. Their swords scraped and clanged noisily. Marek drew Clovis away from Garand and Faris. "Garand, get her out of here!"

Clovis stopped his advance momentarily. The two weren't worth his time right now. Slaina was the one he really wanted. If he didn't finish Marek off, Slaina would no longer be his concern. If he did slay Marek, he could quietly follow them back to Slaina.

The brief respite ended with Marek charging Clovis, knocking him off balance. The two resumed their scuffle.

Nasha and his men subdued the dozen men who chased them into the ravine. With the fighting ended and the enemy soldiers captured, Nasha assessed the damage of the men from both sides of the conflict. His own men had suffered no casualties and only minor injuries. Three of Clovis' men were dead, and several others were injured.

Nasha glanced around again. "Where are Clovis, Marek, and Garand?"

"We're here," came Garand's breathless reply.

Nasha was still gripping his sword. "Where are Clovis and Marek?"

"They're fighting further down the ravine."

Nasha glanced at the others. "Get the prisoners tied up and the wounded into the wagon. Fashion a sling to put the bodies on and drag them back. Give Faris and Garand horses for the trip back. I'm going after Clovis and Marek!"

"I'm here," came Marek's weak reply. He limped toward Nasha, leading his horse. Clovis' body was thrown across the saddle.

The Nazaran soldiers escorted the prisoners toward the bridge. The others returned to Halyn's farm. Shrill noises could be heard echoing through the hills. Nasha glanced around at his companions. "Something evil is in the air this night."

The group crested a hill and caught sight of eerie lights flying above the capital city of Nazar. Marek had been near the back of the small caravan. Nasha presumed his battle with Clovis had worn him down. With a burst of energy, Marek pushed his horse forward. "Nasha, did you send word to the magistrate? Did he clear the city?"

Nasha's brow was knit tightly together, and the lines on his face seemed deeper than usual. "I sent word. I only hope he listened." He nudged his horse forward, anxious to check on Slaina and the others. The closer they got, the faster he rode. Nasha left the caravan behind and raced for Halyn's farm. He rode straight into the barn and climbed out of his saddle before the horse even stopped. He stood in the doorway to the stall where Jedrek, Slaina, Halyn, and Luisa were staying. Joren was standing guard from the loft.

Slaina was covered in sweat, biting down on a stick of wood to prevent crying out in pain. She rocked back and forth on a bed of straw, clinging to Jedrek's and Luisa's hands. Tears rolled down her face as she tried not to worry about the events going on around her. Luisa and Halyn decided it was best to keep the information about her missing siblings from her.

Halyn glanced up at Nasha. Her questioning look pierced the darkness.

Nasha answered the unspoken question. "Marek spoke the truth. We got the raiders and suffered no casualties." He wanted to add that the children had not been found yet either, but he knew Slaina was unaware of the situation. He knew his silence on the matter would convey what he couldn't say.

Marek had ridden closely behind Nasha. "I–I wouldn't say n– no casualties," Marek disputed.

Nasha scowled. "What do you mean? No one has died from our party."

"No one has d–died… yet." Marek attempted to dismount slowly and deliberately. Instead, he fell to the stable floor.

Marek's rapid pursuit of Nasha had gotten Joren's attention. He dutifully watched until Marek collapsed on the floor. There was no doubt in his mind the man had legitimately collapsed. Joren abandoned his post and scrambled down the ladder to help Nasha pick Marek up from the ground. The two rolled him over and discovered a rough bandage tied tightly around his waist.

Halyn stepped away from Slaina to investigate and untied the bandage. Halyn's expression was already serious, and she flinched at the sight of his wound. Marek broke out in a cold sweat. He was slowly losing blood, but the worst thing he would suffer was an infection. The wound was large and deep. His time was clearly limited.

Marek laughed at the look on Halyn's face. "At least I know the healer truly cares what happens to me. She tried to hide it, but I've seen th–this before. She can't fix this."

Halyn glanced at Slaina and Luisa. Luisa had served as a midwife, and having given birth five times, she could help Slaina if needed. "I don't know if I can fix this or not, but I intend to try. Bring him in here."

Nasha and Joren lifted Marek gently and moved him into the opposite corner of the stall from Slaina. Halyn grabbed Joren and sent him to the house for supplies.

Marek grabbed Halyn's arm. "See to Slaina, not me. I just want to see the child once before I die. Please—don't be concerned with me."

Nasha moved around beside Marek and gently removed Marek's hand from Halyn's arm. "I'll stay with him. Tend to Slaina."

Joren met Garand and Faris as he reached the barn door and pointed them to Slaina's stall. The two stopped in the doorway. Luisa and Slaina relaxed, seeing that they had returned safely. They were happy to see they hadn't missed the baby's birth until they noticed Marek collapsed in the corner.

Garand jumped to his side. He was indebted to Marek for saving his and Faris' lives. "What happened?"

"He was injured in the fight with Clovis. Garand, can you stay with him? I need to stand watch from the..." A noise overhead interrupted Nasha, like the noise reverberating through the hills, only louder.

Joren called his name in alarm. Nasha raced out of the stall. He grabbed Faris and hoisted her halfway up the ladder to the loft. "Hide! Now!"

Faris scampered up as she was told. Nasha met Joren at the barn door. Joren's face paled. "I–I saw a giant wagon. It was flying around Halyn's house. I'm not lying. I swear it! It had lanterns brighter than the moon. It went down behind the house."

Nasha caught sight of movement around the side of Halyn's home. He jerked Joren inside and stepped out of sight. A group of men were advancing on the house. Nasha had very few weapons at his disposal right now. He grabbed his crossbow, pulled the sinew back, and strapped a quiver of bolts around his waist. Nasha drew his sword and ordered, "Joren, get back in the loft. Use the crossbow I gave you to keep anyone from entering the barn. Don't fire unless you have no other choice. Right now, they don't know we're in here."

"Are they demons? Or evil spirits? Evil spirits can't be killed!" Joren argued.

Nasha pointed at the men entering the front door of Halyn's house. "I don't believe demons use doors. They are men like us. Shoot them if they get near the barn. Don't waste your shots."

The sight coupled with his wild imagination shook Joren. Scrambling up the ladder, he missed a rung and nearly fell down. He reached the top and bravely prepared to defend them all.

Nasha stealthily worked his way toward the house. The sounds of voices and footsteps grew louder as the mysterious men abandoned the empty structure. Their target hadn't been located. Nasha heard them talking, but their language was foreign to him. The men carried torches that projected the light in only one direction. Nasha noticed other oddities about their torches: they were small, and the light never flickered. He wondered how they could carry such a small flame on their wrists and helmets without getting burned. The men's weapons looked like tiny crossbows, easily held in one hand. Nasha reasoned they must fire only darts. He had heard of distant civilizations that used poisonous darts, though he hadn't heard of men riding large birds. Surely these men were practicing witchcraft, which was forbidden by the Ancient Texts.

Joren watched as best he could through the darkness. He saw Nasha move close to the porch. The soldier took cover behind the loaded wagon intended to carry Halyn's household to the city earlier in the day.

The first man emerged from the front door. Nasha shot the man in the chest. The man was wearing protective body armor, and the bolt startled him as it bounced off his chest. Instinctively, he jumped backward, tripping over the man behind him.

Shouts of alarm and confusion went up. Nasha knew he had startled them by the tone of their voices. He had time to reload the crossbow one more time as the men reorganized themselves. Seeing the ineffectiveness of his first shot, Nasha chose a less protected target. The bolt found its way into a chink in the second man's armor and lodged in his neck. The first man who had been startled by Nasha's bolt caught his companion and lowered him to the floor of the porch. Keeping an eye on Nasha's position, he rendered medical aid to his fallen companion.

The third man stayed undercover for a moment inside the door, surveying his target. Nasha ducked to prepare his crossbow to fire a third bolt. He moved to a new spot behind the wagon, hoping to get a better angle. He had no way of knowing that his adversaries' helmets contained advanced night-vision technology, along with short-range heat sensors. They could see Nasha, but he couldn't see them nearly as well. Nasha rose to fire again and was hit by a poison dart from his enemy's crossbow. He convulsed violently. His bolt fired wildly from the bow, and he dropped unconscious to the ground.

The men looked at the next large structure on the property. The barn was too far away for the weak helmet scanners to pick up clear heat signatures. They could pick up fluctuations, but nothing definitive.

The men regrouped and headed toward the building. They surrounded the structure from a distance, then moved in.

Six men entered Halyn's house. Four of the remaining five were closing in on the barn. Joren's heart pounded in his ears. He raised his crossbow and aimed at the one nearest to his position, but his bolt missed the man completely. The man caught sight of Joren and fired his own weapon. Joren writhed and collapsed onto the floor.

The men worked their way inside. Their sensors found heat signatures belonging to various farm animals until they reached the stall where Slaina and the others were.

Slaina was at the point of delivery. The baby's head was seconds from emerging when a dark figure stepped into the doorway. A glowing red dot appeared on Slaina's chest. Slaina saw nothing of it. She was drenched in sweat, and her eyes closed tightly as she attempted to push the baby out with each contraction.

Luisa followed the mysterious dot to its source and screamed in terror at the frightening creature in the doorway. Marek struggled unsuccessfully to get off the floor and draw his sword. Garand pulled Marek's sword from its scabbard and charged the mysterious figure.

The man turned his attention to Garand. The glowing red dot moved with the stranger toward his new target. His finger tightened on the trigger, and then a second dark figure tackled the first one, forcing the weapon off its target. The two man-like creatures struggled, bouncing off the walls of the stalls.

Garand moved to the edge of the doorway, brandishing the sword he only vaguely knew how to use. His eyes darted from the two men fighting to the sounds of similar scuffles and shouting from several directions. Brilliant flashes of light danced all around him. Those he protected glanced nervously at him. They were too involved in the task of delivering the baby to look for themselves.

Marek was the only one capable of interacting with Garand. He hollered instructions, hoping to keep the man alive and capable of wielding a sword.

Faris was terrified beyond anything she had felt earlier that evening. "Papa? What's happening?" She started crawling out of her hiding place.

"Stay out of sight, Faris!" he ordered.

Faris slipped back into her hiding place and curled into a ball, staying as small as she could. She closed her eyes and shook with every flash of light that crossed her eyelids and every vibration that shook the loft when the monsters below her rammed into the walls. The torches these creatures carried were as bright as daylight, and she could see glimpses of the light through closed eyes.

In a moment, the fighting stopped. The five men who had attacked them were lined up outside. Two of the men were unconscious, and three were on their knees. Lt. Cmdr. Robert Deacons ordered his troops to secure the prisoners and strip them of their gear. He hailed the rest of his team. "Status report! What's the situation with those renegade shuttles?"

A voice came back. "All shuttles have either been destroyed or forced down and their crews captured. We've got significant casualties among the local population. It looks like they attempted to evacuate the city before the attack, or this would have been a total bloodbath. The city walls and numerous buildings are destroyed. We need medics here on the double. Sir, if we're to clean this up, we'll have to have more help. There's one more thing you should know—an army is attempting to cross the river via a bridge to the southeast and another group is coming through a mountain pass."

Robert contemplated the possibilities. Were these other troops enemies or allies coming to help?

Before he could issue orders, the voice came back. "Sir, fighting has broken out at the bridge."

Decision made. "Fire some warning shots, then use a low-level beam to burn the bridge down slowly. Give that army a chance to withdraw. Fire some warning shots ahead of those coming through the mountain pass. Convince them to turn back. Let me do a check for injuries here, then I'll release the medical team to your location. Keep me informed."

Robert sent for the medical team to check on the injured near the house, then he returned to the barn. Garand met him, swinging a sword. Robert raised his hands to let the man know he meant no harm and spoke calmly to him. The man couldn't understand his words, but Robert's tone seemed to stop his wild swings and advances.

Robert hailed the security chief, who was outside guarding the prisoners. "Chief, see if one of the prisoners has a language file."

A moment later, the security chief hailed the commander back. "Sir, the files are locked, and no one seems eager to release the lockout."

"Fine. Put me on an open channel." Robert stepped back from Garand to put the man further at ease.

"You're on."

Robert moved to the doorway of the barn and broadcast his message to the conscious prisoners. "I need those files unlocked. There is a man with a sword in the barn eager to take someone's head off. I'm willing to let him take the head of any man not willing to cooperate, and my report will read that we found the prisoners already dead at the local population's hands. Who wants to go first?"

The men looked at each other nervously. No one volunteered. Seeing a lack of cooperation, Robert ordered the nearest man brought to him. The security chief grabbed the man and jerked him to his feet.

The man laughed. "He's bluffing. He can't do this to us. It's not legal. The penalty for interfering with a low-tech world is a fine and re-education."

Robert took the man from his security chief. "Wait out here, Chief. I would prefer not to have any witnesses."

The chief returned a serious nod. He looked past the two at Garand, who gave the appearance he would rather die than allow anyone entry into the stall. "Yes Commander."

The chief trotted back to the other prisoners. He and the other security officers and medics discussed the situation. They speculated whether the Lt. Commander would indeed sacrifice his prisoner to the angry native. The one thing they were concerned about was that Lt. Cmdr. Deacons was new to them. They really didn't know what he was capable of. Their conversation only aggravated their prisoners' fears.

Robert pushed his prisoner to his knees in front of Garand. The man looked back at the young Lt. Commander. "You can't do this. I have rights! I'm a Commonwealth citizen!"

Robert grinned. "This isn't a Commonwealth world. We don't have a treaty with these people. They have absolute jurisdiction here."

The man inched away from Garand on his knees. "But he's not the legal authority here. Take me to Governor Pravin in the Somian Province! He'll vouch for me! He requested our help."

The man's words were gibberish to Garand until he heard the words "Pravin" and "Somian." Garand shouted, "Governor Pravin sent you? He sent you to kill my daughter? My family?" He raised the sword again and came toward the man.

Robert grinned. He had gotten part of the information he wanted. He looked at the terrified prisoner. "It appears he knows your boss." Robert didn't know the specifics of his message, but he understood the anger and recognition.

Garand swung his sword, and the prisoner screamed in terror. Robert stunned his prisoner with his Tri-EMP, then grabbed a nearby pitchfork and blocked Garand's sword from striking the unconscious prisoner. He nodded his thanks to Garand, who was starting to understand what had transpired. He had never killed a man before and was relieved to still be free of such a burden. Hearing Slaina's muffled cries behind him fueled his protective nature.

The man injured by Nasha's bolt could not currently speak, but hearing the scream of terror, he motioned frantically at his wrist where his bracelet had been. The doctor got the bracelet for him. He and one of the security officers watched him closely as he input the code to release the lockout.

The second the data on the bracelet was available, the security chief began an information dump onto his own datapad. He located the language translation files and hailed his

Lt. Commander. "Sir, we have access to the files. There is a translation file present. I'm transferring the file to all personnel. Is everything okay in there, sir?"

"Everything is fine. We may need the doc and medics in here. We have a woman about to give birth and others with possible injuries. Oh, and the prisoner is unconscious." Something told him his men were nervous about the status of the one prisoner and what their commander had or not done to him.

The language files loaded and initialized. Robert introduced himself and assured Garand he was here to help. Once Robert spoke the words, the program translated his message verbally using Robert's voice in the native language.

Garand stepped back and looked nervously at the bracelet. "What sort of witchcraft is this?"

The translation came through into Robert's earpiece. He breathed a sigh of relief as he realized they could at least communicate now. The next goal was to convince the man he wasn't casting spells. "I am not using witchcraft. This is a tool, an excellent tool. It can help us speak together."

Garand insisted tools did not speak, but Robert didn't want to get into a long argument with the man. People were dying. "Do you have books or tablets that tell stories from long ago?"

"Yes, of course we do."

"As your books speak words to your eyes, my bracelet speaks words to the ears. I am not here to endanger anyone. We are here to help. We captured those who intended to harm you, and we want to offer treatment to the injured. We have healing that surpasses your own. I know the woman is about to bear a child. Does she need a doctor?"

Robert's bracelet beeped a warning at him. The term doctor had no direct equivalent. It suggested healer instead. Robert corrected his error.

Halyn, though actively delivering the Promised Child, heard the question and irately responded. "I am a healer! I've delivered most of the folk in this province, and I will deliver this one. Nobody's takin' my place for this one. Marek could use a healer, but I think only Pateras can help him now. Garand, if he means to help, let him through."

Garand lowered his sword and allowed the man to pass. He glanced at Slaina, yet kept his attention focused on the stranger.

Robert entered the stall cautiously. The healer seemed to have things well in hand. The baby's head was out, and the body was soon to follow.

Robert took one look at Marek and knew the man needed serious help. He signaled his doctor for immediate assistance. Halyn's comment that only Pateras could help Marek hung in Robert's thoughts. In his mind, Pateras was too cold, uncaring, and self-absorbed to care about the problems of humanity. This man was in better hands with Commonwealth medicine.

The doctor left the men he was currently caring for in the hands of the two medics. When he investigated Marek's injury, he scowled. "Lt. Commander, I can save him, but I need a medical shuttle. I can only stabilize him for now. He needs surgery. To be honest, from what I saw before we landed, we need the medical shuttle and a full complement of medical staff to treat the host of injuries we're going to find."

Robert acknowledged the information and told the doctor to do what he could. He hailed his ship, which was still mining ore in the asteroid belt, and informed the captain of the situation. Robert requested a fully staffed medical shuttle.

Capt. Imani was not happy to learn the raiders had somehow allied themselves with one of the powers on the planet. The captain agreed to his request, although it would be a couple of hours before help could arrive.

Hearing the discussion, the doctor gave Marek a reassuring smile and stepped away, pulling Robert with him. "Commander, a couple of hours may be longer than this one has. He's going into shock. Perhaps we could put him in the shuttle and meet the medical shuttle in route?"

Robert made the tough call. "No, we can't do that. I can't send you away while so many other lives are at stake. Do everything that you can for him, then move on. We can't save everyone."

"I can put him in a portable stasis field until the shuttle gets here," the doctor offered.

"How many fields do we have?"

"I have four. Even if I have to take it off him to use it on someone else, it would at least slow the deterioration of his condition and buy him some time for the shuttle to arrive. Lt. Commander, do you know what's so special about these people? Why would these raiders focus on the city and this one farm?"

"I don't know, but I want to find out."

The answer to the question began to cry with the voice of an infant. Robert turned to see the young mother cradling her newborn baby, adoring the tiny child. The man behind her, presumably the infant's father, reached around her and stroked the baby's face. His smile was equally big.

Robert saw the injured man in the corner struggling to see as well. A feeling of warmth filled the chilly room. Robert supposed this feeling was pervasive in any room where a child was born. He scowled. Too bad he would never experience this personally. No, he would never give in to the weakness of having children who could be used against him. His mind reinforced the wall inside him.

The doctor returned to Marek's side. Switching his translator back on, he explained his intention of putting the man to sleep until more help could arrive. It was easier than explaining a stasis field. Marek grew agitated at the suggestion. The doctor tried to explain that it was the only way to save his life.

Sensing the struggle, Robert joined the two. "This sleep could save your life. Why do you refuse?"

"Please—Healer, may I see the child?" Marek begged. There were tears in his eyes.

Halyn stood wearily. "Slaina, may I take him to Marek for a moment?"

Slaina glanced nervously at the two strangers and clasped her baby. Garand wanted nothing more than to hold his first grandchild, but he delayed his desire to accommodate Marek's deteriorating condition. "These men are helping us, and Marek saved Faris and me. He will be safe." Garand added softly, "Marek is dying."

Slaina nodded and handed the child to Halyn, who carried him to Marek. She laid the baby gently in his arms.

Marek looked at the tiny child. Powerful emotions overtook him, and his weakened condition prevented him from keeping them in check. He knew he was dying. The cause and solution for all his problems now rested here in his arms.

The tiny eyes looked up at him, and the baby grunted softly and nestled himself in more comfortably. Marek rocked the tiny child and sobbed openly. "I'm so sorry. Please forgive me."

Robert shook his head. The man was obviously delirious and probably shouldn't be trusted to hold an infant.

A security officer brought a cuffed, belligerent Nasha to the door of the stall. "Sir, I can't get this one to calm down without stunning him again. He keeps demanding to see a baby and its mother."

Robert nodded. "I'll handle him." Robert grabbed Nasha firmly by the arm and pulled him forward. He looked at Garand. "Is this man an ally or an enemy?"

Garand joined the two near the door. "He is an ally. He has protected my daughter and my family many times. He serves Pateras and would give his own life to protect Slaina's child."

Robert bristled for a moment at hearing the name of Pateras again. He glanced at the baby and stories about the Promised One of Pateras from years ago flashed through his memory. Knowing it wasn't supposed to have meaning for him, he snapped himself out of his stupor. "Before I release him, would you kindly reassure him we're here to help?"

Garand complied. He pointed Marek's direction. "The child is here. These men are helping us. This one saved Slaina and the baby. Faris is hiding. Everyone is safe except... I don't know what's happened to Joren. Orun and Irana are still missing, and I don't know where Eston disappeared to."

A quick search found Joren unconscious in the loft from the Tri-EMP blast. Faris gladly left her hiding place to see Slaina and the baby.

Halyn stepped over to Marek to reclaim the child. Before she took him from the dying soldier, Marek placed his hand on the baby's head and blessed him. He was a seasoned and dying soldier, not a man of piety, and his words were rough but heartfelt. "May Pateras forgive me for the harm I intended for you, and may he bless and protect you for the entirety of your life."

He released the child into Halyn's arms and gasped, frozen in place for a moment, staring into nothing. Robert sneered. If the man had allowed them to get him into stasis, this wouldn't have happened. Pateras had allowed yet another helpless soul to die.

The doctor gave the scanner a confused look. He had learned his patient's name in the few minutes the two were together. "Marek?"

Marek wasn't dead, as they suspected. His head turned toward the doctor who had called his name. His eyes focused again. In a flurry of activity, Marek scrambled to his knees and clawed at the tight bandages around his waist. The doctor was equally eager.

Robert was curious about what was transpiring, but he still had a prisoner to free. He released the binders. Nasha, seeing no one else in danger or concerned, merely rubbed his wrists and watched Marek.

The bandages, which were strips of cloth cut from Clovis' cloak, finally gave up the secret they were hiding. Clovis had gotten in one deep gash to Marek's abdomen as Marek struck a more decisive blow into Clovis. Marek had nearly been disemboweled until now. His abdomen and the bandages were covered in damp blood, but the gash was gone. He was completely healed. The doctor ran numerous scans. He found no further signs of injury, no hint of infection, nothing to indicate the man was dying. His scans from minutes earlier still indicated a potentially deadly injury, but his current scans did not concur. The doctor gave Robert a stunned look. He had no explanation for whatever had happened.

The baby, once again in Slaina's arms, whimpered. Slaina looked at Halyn questioningly.

"What is it, girl? You look like you got somethin' on your mind."

"He looks like a regular baby."

"What were you expectin'? A baby with two heads, or somethin'? You know why he was sent here. He has to be a normal baby and the son of Pateras. I think he's ready to eat now."

Halyn chased everyone from the stall so the new family could have some time alone together. With Slaina settled, Halyn looked at Marek's injury. She was aghast at what she saw. She asked the strange healer, "Did you do this?"

The doctor shook his head. "I wish I could claim credit, but I can't. I don't know how that happened. That man was dying, and now he isn't."

Robert was uncomfortable. He looked to Garand and Nasha for some answers. "Why were you attacked? What were these men after?"

Nasha pointed toward the stall. "They were trying to destroy that child."

"Why?"

"He will one day rule all of creation. He is the Promised One from the Ancient Text prophecies. He has come to unite mankind with Pateras. Governor Pravin doesn't want to lose his rule to anyone but his own son. He believes the child threatens his rulership."

Robert's eyes glazed over slightly. The words Promised One and Pateras reverberated in his mind. The prophecies spoken of in the Ancient Texts from his own homeworld echoed in his memory. He nodded. "I see." Robert shoved the memories back into a dark corner of his mind and changed the subject. "What did the mother name him?"

Luisa stepped forward and gently wrapped her hand around Garand's arm as she answered the stranger. "She named him Arni Sotaeras Liontari."

Robert burned the infant's name into his memory: Arni Sotaeras Liontari. Was this really the child of the one who allowed his sister to die and his family to be stolen away from their homes? Maybe the chance to pay Pateras back would present itself someday, but it wouldn't be today. Robert wasn't the type to harm an infant, and he didn't want this young mother to face the same pain his own parents had, but someday.

Robert was immersed in his own thoughts when he realized Luisa was speaking. "Garand, we still haven't found the children, and now Eston is missing. With all the strange things that have happened this night, I'm afraid for them."

"Mama! Papa!"

The cry echoed from the top of the rise. The strangers had produced several bright lanterns, lighting the area well. The group looked up to see Eston walking down the hill carrying Irana on his back with Orun walking beside him. Luisa and Garand took off to greet their returning children.

Robert turned back to Nasha. He switched off his translator a moment. He had to be sure of something he had heard. The two were reasonably alone, as everyone else was focused on the returning children. Robert asked Nasha a question that was not quite a question. "Pateras? Pateras El Liontari?"

Nasha had accepted the translators at face value, but he was confused when Robert deactivated his to speak.

Nasha wasn't sure what he meant. He nodded, then repeated the same words, "Pateras El Liontari." Their languages were different, but Pateras' name was the same in both languages.

Robert rubbed his pale face. What had he stumbled into? He marveled the words were identical to those he had learned in his own childhood on a planet light-years from here. Was this a coincidence, or were these events connected to the stories he'd heard as a boy? He looked up at the stars and mentally compared them to star charts of this part of the galaxy. Yes, it was visible from this world. The Drean sun. Its light grew brighter. This one star seemed to be directly overhead. Robert surmised the atmosphere was somehow amplifying the light. It shone more brightly than other, closer stars. Why just the one star? Why not all of them? Drea was special, that was certain.

The sky had an odd light coming from nowhere in particular, and music seemed to reverberate through the hills.

Nasha also noticed the star and the strange light. He spoke an unintelligible sentence. The only word Robert caught was Pateras. Robert shook his head again in disbelief, and a wave of anger washed over him. Pateras was the reason he could never return to Drea. He was the reason Abigail was dead. Now he was the reason many in this province were injured or dying. Robert realized his life was probably going to be spent cleaning up Pateras' messes.

He turned his translator back on. "If this child is the reason for the attacks by the neighboring territory, I suggest you send him away until things settle down."

Garand and Luisa returned to Nasha's side with their three missing children in time to hear the translation of Robert's last suggestion. Nasha echoed his sentiment and added, "Garand, you and your family should go with them. If things settle down soon, you can return in a few weeks."

"I will send the women and children away tomorrow morning. Jedrek and I can join them in a few days. I have not decided whether Eston should stay or go."

Eston balked. "I'm no child! I brought Irana and Orun back by myself! It's what a man would have done!"

"Where were the children?" Nasha asked.

"They were at the house we've been helping Jedrek build," Eston explained. "They said they followed Slaina and Jedrek out there. They went into the house after Jedrek and Slaina left. Orun says a wild dog wouldn't let them leave. He said the dog ran off after sunset, but they were scared to come back after dark."

"What made you go there to look for them?"

"I don't know. Something just told me to look there." Eston had no better explanation. Everyone sensed Pateras had guided Eston, and that Pateras had been the one who kept the children in the house.

As morning drew near, the medical shuttle arrived. Large groups of people who had fled the city began congregating at Halyn's farm with incredible stories of celestial figures appearing to them and singing Pateras' praises as they announced the birth of the Promised One. Considering the large number of wounded coming to see Halyn, Nasha advised locating the medical shuttle between Halyn's farm and Jedrek and Slaina's future home. The area was rocky, and the heavy shuttle would not be likely to sink into the ground there.

Nasha was not familiar with a number of the concepts regarding the shuttle, but he learned quickly that it was heavy, and like a heavily laden wagon, it should not be placed on soft ground.

The soldiers on the eastern borders of the Nazaran province retreated, seeing their plans to invade Nazar had gone awry. Governor Pravin drank himself into a stupor when he learned what had happened. The day after, he began to construct his next plan.

The SS *Deliverance* spent several more days in the system. The crew aided in search-and-rescue missions for victims trapped in the city, mined the hills for ore, and cleaned up after the raiders. They left a small data module with Danyl so his people could contact the Commonwealth if any more raiders visited them. Lt. Cmdr. Deacons also explained the data module's capability to teach his people the Commonwealth language, Intergalactic Standard.

Robert met with Danyl and Jedrek to explain the need for a landing pad and a rough explanation of how to construct one. Capt. Imani decided early on that since there had already been a breach in protocol, it would be best to establish a presence of protection over this planet, which was rich in tetrabradium and tetratachium. He supposed that was the reason for the raiders' presence. What he didn't know was that someone rapidly climbing the political ladder in the Commonwealth government had sent the raiders. Capt. Imani made an agreement with Danyl to trade for ore occasionally.

The raider shuttles were taken back to the *Deliverance* along with the prisoners. The raiders were charged with multiple crimes, in addition to murder and attempted murder, which came as a shock to them. It was obvious they didn't consider low-tech inhabitants to be people. Their crimes fell under the jurisdiction of deep space law, which meant Capt. Imani could render whatever punishment he deemed appropriate.

He called each surviving prisoner into his office one at a time and gave them the chance to redeem themselves. He asked each one to reveal who hired them to destroy Nazar. They all pointed an accusing finger at Governor Pravin, but none would reveal who told them to seek Governor Pravin.

Capt. Imani grew tired of the refusal to cooperate. "I will give each of you one last chance to tell me who sent you to Galat, or I will space you."

Most claimed total ignorance and begged Capt. Imani not to space them. Two of those captured remained tight-lipped. It was clear they had information. The first one refused to speak and accepted his punishment without argument. The second appeared scared of both living and dying. In his last meeting with Capt. Imani, Robert was also present.

The man pleaded for his life. "I can't tell you. He'll kill me, and it would be a death far worse than spacing. Please, I can't."

"Space the two of them. Do this one the small mercy of stunning him first." Capt. Imani was ready to be done with this. The security officer escorted the man out. Sweat poured off his brow as he stumbled weakly out the door.

The second the door closed, Robert soberly asked, "Are you really going to space them?"

Capt. Imani shook his head, "No, I'll stun him, stick him in stasis, and we can make a side trip to a penal colony a few light-years from here. He'll never wake up as himself. The next time he's conscious, he'll have a new name, a new personality, and a new home. I don't like spacing. It's an ugly death. The one thing we can't do is allow that governor another opportunity to make deals with raiders. Lt. Commander, do whatever you must to see that never happens again."

"Yes sir."

Robert took one last trip to the planet with a security detail to talk to Governor Pravin. "Governor, our government has laws about interfering with less developed societies. Who offered to help you conquer the Nazarans?"

"This is not your jurisdiction, and therefore not your concern."

"I have no grievance with you. Once we are gone, if you conquer the Nazarans on your own, so be it. My concern is who came here against our regulations. Give me his name, and I will be on my way."

"I will not betray my allies. Go away now."

Robert grew tired of being nice. "Governor Pravin, does anyone else in your household or government know who you've been conspiring with?"

Pravin grinned. "Do you think you can pressure my family or my servants to get that information? I'm the only one who knows. Now get out. I want everyone out of here now!"

Robert nodded. "Gentlemen, let's leave and allow this man to rest in peace."

The room cleared. Prior to leaving the governor's chamber, Robert stopped. "Governor Pravin, by refusing to reveal your co-conspirator, you have allied yourself with criminals and enemies of the Commonwealth, which now makes it our business. Last chance to tell me what I want to know."

Governor Pravin harrumphed. He was unconcerned. "I assume you know about the baby?"

Robert nodded and added, "I know more than you realize."

"That baby will die by my hand. It's only a matter of time." Pravin raised his stein of beer in a defiant gesture, then took a large gulp.

"You can't fight Pateras and win." Robert didn't really believe what he was saying, but this man angered him.

The group climbed into their shuttle, and Robert took the co-pilot's chair. He ordered the pilot to circle the governor's home. The man did as ordered. The pilot watched as the Lt. Commander did some scans.

The shuttle made one more pass and powered up its weapons. Governor Pravin stepped out onto his balcony to see what the shuttle was up to. Robert launched two small explosive torpedoes. The governor's mansion exploded and crumbled into a pile of rubble. In the city streets below them, people scrambled for shelter, fearing the monstrous beast in the sky was coming for them next.

Asa stood on duty on top of the wall. He smiled to himself. The governor had finally gotten what he deserved.

The shuttle pilot glanced nervously at the higher-ranking co-pilot. "Sir, I assume we had orders to do that?"

"I was ordered to do whatever was necessary to stop Governor Pravin from making deals with raiders again. I felt this was necessary. Shall we go? I have a wedding to get to."

"Yes sir."

Hearing of Pravin's death, Jedrek and Slaina didn't stay long in the Western Province. They returned to Nazar, where Jedrek completed the building of their home. Slaina continued to study under the tutelage of Halyn and became an accomplished healer. The one person neither of them could heal was Jedrek. He took ill one winter shortly before Arni turned sixteen. Arni had healed no one since the day he healed Marek. Slaina asked Arni why he wouldn't heal Jedrek. His answers always seemed cryptic. This day was no exception. "It is not my time yet. It is his."

Her reunion with Jedrek would come all too soon.

MARRIAGE

The day of Tristan and Jessica's wedding was coming both slowly and quickly. In the working out of the matrimonial details, there never seemed to be enough time to get it all done. Their eagerness to finally live in the same household and an eternity of waiting tortured the young couple. The day Robert's ship returned to orbit around Juranta yielded twice the excitement as it otherwise would because it heralded the imminence of the wedding.

A few days after Robert's return, with the wedding only five days away, Tristan was greeted by a surprise visit from Agents Gershom and Wallace in Leland's office. Sensing there was a problem, Tristan played things casually. "To what do I owe the pleasure of this visit?"

Agent Wallace was quick to jump in. "2nd Lt. Alexander, you're coming with us."

"Would you mind telling me where we're going and why?"

Knowing the ongoing tension between the two agents, Agent Gershom stepped in quickly. "We need to escort you to the Psych Division for an evaluation. It's just routine. We thought it best to do this before the wedding."

"What sort of evaluation is it that would make you feel the need to escort me there in person?"

Agent Wallace smiled sadistically. "It's a full-spectrum loyalty and motivational analysis probe."

"Are you accusing me of something?" Tristan demanded.

Leland knew Tristan was attempting to get along professionally with Agent Wallace, but she was making no such attempts. "Calm down, Tristan—they aren't accusing you of anything. They're concerned you may be getting too personally involved. They thought it would be best to do an evaluation before you get married."

"I understand that part. It's their concern that I can't get myself there that bothers me. As I recall, getting myself there is part of the evaluation."

Agent Wallace stood resolutely and placed herself between Tristan and the door to Leland's office. "I don't trust you to do that." She flexed her hands as if to dare Tristan to object. She was eager to draw her weapon and drop this insubordinate young man. Her desire to see him writhing on the floor was obvious.

Tristan had been through these evaluations twice before. The first time was after he declared his specialty of Covert Ops. It was merely a taste of what his class could expect in deep cover assignments. The second time was after his first deep-cover mission, which lasted ten months. It took him a little time to regain his composure as an Infantry officer. He had grown accustomed to the violent behavior of the criminals he worked around, and shutting the violence off was difficult.

Tristan shook his head slowly. "You're determined to sabotage my mission, aren't you?"

"Sabotage your mission? Agent Wallace isn't trying to do that. How would this sabotage your mission?" Agent Gershom's brows knit themselves together. Tristan's evaluation would just take a few hours. If they started this morning, he would be done by the end of the business day. His fiancée would never have to know about it.

"You want the entire list? Have you ever been through one of those evaluations? I'm in the middle of planning my wedding, and those drugs can mess you up for a day or two. Jessica's going to have a million questions about the wedding and honeymoon. If I'm suddenly unavailable, she's going to freak out. On top of that, if she's got prewedding jitters and the groom disappears, then reappears in a foul mood, what's she going to think? What if she sees you escorting me there? Or her family does? Do you really want to risk her calling off the wedding? I'm not refusing to go—I'm saying I need an hour or so to get over there and to give Jessica a story to cover my absence."

Agent Wallace opened her mouth to object. Agent Gershom held up his hand, motioning her to wait. "Might I suggest a compromise? You do whatever you need to keep your cover intact. We will stay discreetly near you until you check yourself into the clinic. If you make any attempts to run or evade us, Jessica and her family will be arrested. Are we clear?"

Tristan wasn't accustomed to Agent Gershom agreeing this closely with Agent Wallace. He suspected there was a reason for their concerns, and his objections would only make matters worse. "What happens if I don't pass this evaluation?"

"You don't get married. We'll have to arrange an accident and break the news to your fiancée. You'll be relocated to another world and given a new assignment," Agent Gershom explained with far less malice, although his tone was still not warm or friendly.

"New identity too, or just moving to the other side of the galaxy?"

"Does it matter?" Agent Wallace wryly asked.

"No, I suppose not. I was just comfortable with my name. Let me grab a cup of coffee and call Jessica, then I should be ready to go. Keep your distance. If you lose me somehow, I will be registered in that clinic within the hour. I have nothing to hide and no reason to run. Are we done here?"

The agents reluctantly allowed him to leave Leland's office, but they tracked his every move.

Tristan did exactly what he said he would. He entered the break room and programmed the dispenser for a cup of coffee dressed differently than normal.

Riley quietly entered the room behind him. He prepared a cup for himself and watched Tristan. The young man usually greeted him with at least a polite nod, if not with a friendly salutation. Riley finally asked, "Everything all right?"

"Yeah, I'm fine."

His answer wasn't convincing. "Want to talk about it?"

"What makes you think something is wrong?" Tristan realized he needed to know. If his behavior was askew, he had better know it and have an answer for it.

"You seem to be brooding about something and distracted. Your coffee isn't giving you the same pleasure as normal." Riley sat down at a table, letting Tristan know he wasn't leaving without some answers. Riley had seen Tristan's coffee choice. He normally ordered a plain black coffee—today's order had extra caffeine with cream and sugar. Tristan was wincing with every sip.

"You have some keen observation skills."

"If you want to hide your thoughts, you might want to disconnect them from your face," Riley suggested. "And maybe add a little more cream and sugar to your coffee."

Tristan nodded. He added the additional cream and sugar as he briefly explained his plight. Knowing his handlers were probably listening to him, he complained loudly for their benefit. "I know I'm young and don't have years of experience, but every time I turn around, they're questioning me, second-guessing me, and screwing my job up. This evaluation isn't pleasant, and it can mess with a person's head. I really don't need my head screwed up right now. If Jessica gets prewedding jitters and starts to back out, I've got to have my head in the game to calm her down. I know my job. I wish they would quit doubting me and let me do it."

Riley smiled and sipped his coffee. "I assume they're monitoring you."

Tristan grinned incriminatingly. "What? I know they're watching me, but I didn't think about them actually listening to me. Do you think they heard what I said?"

Riley stifled a laugh and nearly spat his coffee out of his mouth. He set the cup down and grabbed a napkin to wipe the dribble from his chin. After coughing and sputtering for a moment, he regained his composure. He grinned at Tristan. "You really are distracted, aren't you?"

Tristan looked around the room at the various computer terminals that were present everywhere except the restrooms. He glanced at his own bracelet, then spoke aloud to anyone listening from outside the room. "Sorry guys, just venting. It's nothing personal." He grinned just as guiltily as before. He knew exactly what he was doing. Even Riley knew that much, and it still caught him off guard when Tristan feigned innocence.

Riley wished Tristan luck as the two headed back to their respective offices. Tristan paused at his computer terminal. Getting himself into the appropriate frame of mind, he found himself nearly convinced of the lie he was about to give Jessica. He surmised it was partially due to the odd coffee concoction he was drinking. When his story was firmly imprinted on his mind, he hailed his future bride.

"Hey beautiful. How are you this morning?"

"I'm fine. What's up? You don't usually call me until lunchtime."

"Leland told me if I could close out my cases today, he would give me the rest of the week off to get ready for the wedding." Tristan winced and rubbed his stomach, which was offering some resistance to the foreign coffee choice.

Jessica immediately spotted his aberrant behavior. "Are you okay?"

"You know how my stomach gets when I'm nervous." His nervous stomach had become part of his cover since the day the couple got engaged.

"What are you nervous about? You aren't having second thoughts about getting married, are you?"

"No, absolutely not. You know I get nervous when I want things to be perfect for you. I only get nervous about pleasing you." Tristan smiled warmly to smooth her ruffled feathers. "Which is the reason I called. I won't be able to make it to dinner tonight. Wrapping up all my cases is going to make me late getting out of here. I might also stop by a clinic to get something to calm my stomach down a bit. I'm afraid I won't be able to see you tonight, but you will have me for the rest of the week and for the rest of our married lives."

Jessica pouted for a moment, then brightened as Tristan finished speaking. "I suppose I can handle missing you for one night if it means I get to have you for two extra days before the wedding. It's okay. This gives me one last night alone with Mom, Dad, and Robbie. Robbie's girlfriend, Hannah, won't be able to make it tonight either."

The two chatted for another minute before they got back to work. Tristan didn't really have any cases pending, as his job was only a cover. Despite the rough beginning, his co-workers had come to depend on him for troubleshooting their own projects. He had uncovered some rather well hidden criminal activity in the sixteen months he had been there. He gave the credit for the discoveries to others in his department, but no one forgot his help.

Tristan left his office and stopped by Leland's. He grinned the same guilty grin he had given Riley earlier. "Hey Boss, just wanted you to know the cover story I gave Jessica. I told her you said if I worked late today and got all my cases closed out, I could have the rest of the week off."

Leland sat back in his chair and folded his arms across his chest. He scowled at Tristan. "I really said that? I must be a really nice boss."

Tristan sipped his coffee again. "Yes sir. Jessica is thrilled. She's looking forward to thanking you personally at the wedding."

Leland shook his head at the brash young man. "Yeah, I bet. Thanks for the heads up. I'll see you at the wedding. Go get your head descrambled."

Tristan turned to leave when Leland hollered one more time. "Hey kid, don't mess this up. Our fraud apprehension rate is at an all-time high because of you. I'd hate to lose you."

Tristan smiled and nodded. "No sir, I won't." He knew Leland was thinking of more than his own departmental approval rating. It just wasn't appropriate to say anything more.

Agents Wallace and Gershom, as promised, discreetly followed Tristan to the clinic. Tristan checked himself in and polished off his cup of coffee. They forced him to sit in the waiting area for several minutes before his name was called. The area was busy at first, then quiet, as the others were called in before him. Tristan smirked. Being observed in the waiting area was part of the evaluation, and he knew it. They wanted to know exactly how nervous he was. If the waiting drove him up the wall, it would not be a point in his favor. The extra strong cup of coffee was not helping him through this part of the evaluation.

Someone finally escorted Tristan to a large, nearly empty room. They instructed him to change into the clothing lying on a small table then to lie down on the bed provided.

Tristan did as he was instructed. The outfit was made of a stretchy material, with neural fibers and microcircuits interwoven into the fabric. It would measure his vital signs, perspiration, and muscle tension.

Tristan made himself as comfortable as possible on the bed. His chest was already pounding from the overdose of caffeine and sugar. A technician came in and strapped him to the bed with restraints. His heart rate increased yet again. A display on the wall revealed his elevated heart rate and blood pressure. The technician took notice and asked, "Are you nervous, Mr. Alexander?"

"A little." Tristan didn't want to spill too much information too quickly.

"There's nothing to be nervous about. This evaluation is for your own good. We want to be sure you don't get lost in a fantasy world," the technician blandly replied.

"If you say so," Tristan responded with equal fervor.

"Mr. Alexander, I need to ask you a few questions. Then I will administer some medication, and I will repeat those questions. After we're done with this part of the evaluation, we will begin the simulation portion. Are you ready to begin?"

"Yeah, let's get this over with so I can go home and detox."

"That answers my first question. So, you've had one of these evaluations before. When was your last evaluation?"

"About two years ago." Tristan flexed his muscles against the restraints. He didn't like feeling helpless.

The technician went through a long list of questions about his assignment, his state of mind, his thoughts about his assignment, and lastly, an image of himself finishing a cup of coffee in the waiting room appeared on the wall. "How many cups of coffee have you had today, Mr. Alexander?"

"Two, one before I left my apartment, and a second after I got to work."

"How many cups do you normally have in a day?"

"I guess around four? Three in the morning and one in the mid-afternoon? Probably more in the winter."

The technician looked at a wall monitor behind Tristan's head. A green light blinked, conferring a subtle message to the technician, who pulled a tiny boxlike instrument from his pocket. He placed it on Tristan's neck and activated it. The box attached itself painfully to the skin on his neck, then dosed Tristan with a relaxing serum. A warmth traveled through his body. His thoughts began to get fuzzy.

Tristan searched for some external stimulus to focus on. The stinging in his neck was numbed by the mechanism's numbing feature. One of the sensors in his clothing was under his shoulder blade. It was a small sensor and didn't bother him any more than a seam in his clothing. He forced himself to focus on it. It kept his mind from losing all control and relaxing too far. He knew his motives in Jessica's case were not pure. Had he really gone native? If he had, there was no way to protect her.

The technician went through the list of questions again. Tristan's mind remained foggy for a time, then he drifted off to sleep. He woke as the door to the room opened and a psych officer entered. The doctor released the binders on his wrists and ankles. His medication box was no longer on his neck. The doctor helped Tristan into a sitting position and dosed him with a stimulant to rid him of the final effects of the sedative. "As soon as your head is clear, you can get dressed and return home. You're free to go. Your handlers will contact you shortly about your new assignment, if they're willing to give you another one after this fiasco."

"Excuse me? What are you talking about?"

"You're truly in love with Miss Deacons. You've let your emotions get in the way, and we can no longer trust you with this assignment."

Tristan took a deep breath. He mustn't look overzealous. He shook his head to clear it. "Doc, I'll admit she's a beautiful woman, and I've thoroughly enjoyed seducing her to marry me, but come on. Don't take me off this assignment before the honeymoon. I've worked on this for sixteen long months."

"Sorry, the results are pretty obvious. You can't be trusted to handle her if needed."

"What happened to the simulation portion of the evaluation?"

"We didn't need it. You are clearly incapable of using extreme measures on her."

Tristan scowled. "That's because I'm not an assassin. I use my emotions to handle whatever situations I'm in. I suppose I am emotionally involved to a degree, but that's how I operate in any case." Tristan cursed. "Doc, if you don't let me do the simulation portion of the evaluation, it's going to kill my career in Covert Ops. Nobody's going to trust me with a deep cover operation again if I get pulled off this one."

"Tristan, what are you talking about? You said you weren't spying on me or my family." Jessica's voice came from the doorway.

Tristan looked over at her and forced himself to remain calm. "Sorry, Jess. I told you I would only lie to you where my job was concerned. You are my job. Just about everything I've said to you has been a lie. Doc, why is she here? How did she get in here?"

Two security officers escorted Jessica into the room and forced her into the chair near his bed. The doctor turned his attention to Tristan. "She followed you in here. We detained her until we could determine what to do with her. I guess we can definitely dispense with the simulation now. She knows who and what you are. The case is closed, whether you like it or not."

"Maybe not. Jessica, we only have one way out of this. We have to go through with the wedding and start a family." Tristan stood slowly and carefully. He knelt on one knee in front of her. "Jess, you can never tell anyone who or what I am. Would you still consider marrying me?"

A myriad of emotions crossed her face, anger being the most obvious. Jessica slapped Tristan. "I'd rather die than marry you."

Tristan stood up. He had the information he needed. He nodded. "I was afraid you were going to pick that option. Jessica, that's the only option they're going to give you. You know too much. You can live with me, albeit as a hostage, or they will force me to kill you."

Jessica's face paled, and her anger drained away with the blood from her face. "You wouldn't... you couldn't..." Tears slipped down her face. "Tristan, I'll marry you... and I promise... I won't say a word to anyone, not to my mom or dad—or Robbie."

Tristan held a hand out to one of the security guards. The man pulled his weapon from its holster and handed it butt-first to Tristan. The second security guard watched Tristan carefully.

Jessica jumped out of her chair and threw herself into Tristan's arms. "Please, Tristan, don't do this. I swear, I won't say a thing to anyone."

Tristan laid the weapon on the bed beside him, then grabbed her arms and pushed her back into the chair. He held her wrists tightly. "Jessica, I'm sorry, but your family would notice if we treated each other differently. I could pull off my part in our relationship, but you're far too emotional, and your family is very observant. They'll notice the difference in you. You aren't capable of faking loving me. I wish I didn't have to do this, really I do."

Tristan released her arms and stepped back. He picked up the weapon and powered it to a lethal setting. Amid her cries for mercy and desperate pleas, he raised the weapon and fired.

The young woman writhed violently in the chair, then slipped to the floor. Tristan handed his weapon to the guard. He looked at the body on the floor. "What a waste." He shook his head, then looked at the doc. "Do I need to play the grieving fiancé, or am I totally out of this? If I don't go back in, things could get rough for Hannah."

The doctor squinted at him. "I don't know what your handlers want from you at this point. You'll need to check in with them. They're waiting in the lobby for you. Are you not upset at all by this?"

"I wasted sixteen months of my life taking accounting classes and pretending to be an average guy looking to start a family. Personally, I'm going to go a few rounds with a sparring bot before I go home tonight. At least I got an early promotion out of this deal." Tristan grabbed his clothes off the small table he had lain them on at the beginning of his evaluation. "Are we done? Can I change clothes someplace?"

Tristan knew his profile didn't show him to be a cold-blooded killer. Changing in the same room with the body of his dead fiancée would not be believable. The woman on the floor wasn't Jessica, and Tristan knew it. This was the simulation portion of the evaluation. They presented it in different ways. Sometimes you were placed in the holographic chamber and told it was a simulation. Since he had done this before, they didn't present the scenario as a simulation. They presented it as a live situation.

Tristan squatted next to the body of his fiancée. "Jess, I'm really sorry things happened like this. We could've had some good times together." He stroked her hair, then looked sharply at the doctor. "This isn't Jessica."

The doctor nodded at the two security officers. The two men carried her limp body out of the room. "What gave it away?"

"The texture of her hair is wrong. A hologram can change the appearance. It doesn't change the touch. If I didn't kill Jessica, whom did I kill?"

"You didn't kill anyone. The pellet contained a charge limiter and a poison to drop her vital signs to nearly nothing. She'll make a full recovery. I'm going to let you get dressed, and we can discuss your test results. After you get dressed, go to the reception desk in the hall and they'll direct you to me."

Tristan caught up to the Psych Officer in a conference room with Agents Wallace and Gershom. Their discussion of his case was already well in progress. Tristan came in and sat down quietly. The group stopped discussing the results and waited for Tristan's response.

He glanced at the looks on each face. Agent Gershom was his usual stoic self, although a hint of annoyance haunted him. The doctor seemed genuinely irritated, and his attention was focused on Agent Wallace, whose venom had saturated the room.

Tristan grinned. "I passed the test, didn't I?"

The doctor took his attention off Agent Wallace and tried to focus on Tristan. "Yes, as far as I'm concerned, you did, with flying colors. Your handlers seem to believe you've managed to put one over on me. I won't say that's impossible, but if you really are that good, there's no way to stop you from going native until it's too late. It also means when you get caught, you're in for a full reprogramming job." ·

Tristan winced. "I would prefer to stay on the right side of the law and keep my job."

"My recommendation is to put you back to work and let you do your job. Your answers before and after the medications lined up within acceptable parameters. I have no substantial reservations." The doctor laced his fingers together and rested his hands on top of the table.

All three were ready to jump on the one point. Tristan got there first. "What reservations do you have?"

"You seem more able to kill than your records indicated. I think you could be an assassin if you wanted to. It also indicates a slight propensity for violence."

Tristan grinned and looked at Agent Wallace. "Did you document that? I wouldn't want to be held accountable if someone were to push me too far."

Agent Wallace glared at Tristan yet remained silent.

The doctor watched the exchange, his attitude mirroring Tristan's. He took his eyes off Agent Wallace and focused on Tristan. "Of course it's noted. I'm a professional. If amply provoked by a knowing individual, you would not be guilty of using undue force. If you used it on Miss Deacons, for instance, you would be guilty."

Tristan glanced at his handlers. "Can I get back to work now?"

Agent Wallace gave Agent Gershom a grudging nod. Agent Gershom gave Tristan his blessing to return to his role. The two agents left without hesitation.

Tristan moved more slowly and timed his departure to match the doctor's. They walked to the door together. Tristan stopped and asked, "Doc, has Agent Wallace ever had an eval?"

"I doubt it. She doesn't do undercover work."

"Any chance you could arrange one? I think she needs some help."

The doctor laughed. "I agree. I'll look into it."

"By the way, I told my fiancée I might stop by a clinic to get something to settle my stomach. Do you suppose you could send me home with a week's supply of something, so she doesn't get suspicious?"

The doctor frowned. "What's wrong with your stomach?" He was now concerned he had come to an incorrect conclusion about this young man's stability.

"Nothing, it's part of my cover story, and I've spent six months suggesting that I've developed a nervous stomach. She believes it's part of the reason I left Covert Ops."

The two discussed the different aspects of a nervous stomach and what would be the easiest things to fake and hardest to prove. The doctor sent him away with a prescription for a medication and a refill on it. What he neglected to mention was if Tristan refilled that prescription in the next month, it would notify the doctor immediately. The doctor would know Tristan was lying to him and possibly covering his weaknesses. He didn't need to worry, though. Tristan was still in complete control, mentally and physically.

Tristan hadn't expected to be done with his evaluation this early. He headed to the gym available in the building where he worked. It wasn't as extensive as the one he normally used, but he couldn't afford to get caught at the gym after telling Jessica he was working late.

He stopped in long enough to tell Leland he had passed his evaluation. Leland was tied up with other matters and couldn't do more than acknowledge the information, but he sent Riley a message to check on Tristan in an hour.

Riley found the young man laying waste to a punching bag and sweating profusely. He talked Tristan into putting his boxing gloves down and going out onto the rooftop garden for some fresh air. It was the one place in the building aside from the restrooms that wasn't easily monitored.

The two discussed Tristan's frustrations at being questioned and doubted at every turn. Tristan wondered how much he could trust Riley. He chose to trust him fully. "Riley, I knew it was part of the simulation. I knew the woman wasn't Jessica. It was still the hardest thing I've ever done. I shot her like she meant nothing. I've never had this kind of connection with anyone before. I'm not sure when it happened, but I fell in love with her. If they ask me to, I can't do it. I can't kill her. I really hope you aren't going to betray me. If you report what I said, I'll be off the assignment and potentially reprogrammed."

"Kid, don't you know me better than that by now?"

"I make a living by lying and distrusting others. Trust isn't easy for me. I just put my life in your hands. That should tell you something."

"I've never done undercover work, and it's not my thing. I believe in being straightforward. Your secret is safe with me. Keep something in mind, though. At some point, they may tell you it's time to walk away from her. You need to be ready for that moment, however you intend to handle it. It's okay to fall apart tonight, but get your head back in the game tomorrow. Lives depend on it, yours and hers."

Tristan nodded and polished off his water. He and Riley talked for another few minutes. The mixture of medications, caffeine, and sugar in his system, followed by vigorous exercise, had drained him.

With everyone leaving for the day, Tristan showered and returned to his office. He grabbed another bottle of water and a bite to eat from the food dispenser, put the privacy screen up, turned on some light music, and propped his feet up on his desk. In less than five minutes, he was sound asleep.

He was so exhausted he slept for three hours. His feet roughly fell off the desk as he tried to reposition himself to get comfortable. Deciding the hour was late enough, he headed home and crawled into bed. His sleep was filled with strange images of things that he couldn't make sense of. The last thing he dreamed about was shooting Jessica. Instead of falling to the floor, she simply looked at him with displeasure and asked, "Why did you do that?"

Tristan woke with a start. It was slightly after midnight. He got up, poured himself a glass of water, and moved over to his desk to drink it. He stared at the computer screen for a minute, then hailed Jessica.

Jessica answered with a tired but happy smile. "Are you just now getting home from work?"

"No, I was exhausted when I got home and fell asleep. I probably shouldn't have called, but I missed you."

"I'm glad you called. I missed you too."

The two talked softly until Tristan was more at ease after his unsettling dream.

The next few days went by quickly. Tristan stayed busy getting ready for the wedding. He knew Jessica wanted it to be magical. The wedding was a combination of ceremony and party. Tristan arranged for the ceremony to be held at Lachland Falls Park and Observatory, the place Jessica mentioned as being the most magical place she had ever seen. The resort had a glass-domed enclosure on a polar continent, which allowed the polar aurora lights to dance across the ceiling for everyone to see. The lights inside the dome were on brightly in the early part of the evening, but as it got later, they were dimmed, so the display from outside was more clearly visible.

The first part of the ceremony was the signing of the legal documents. Tristan arranged to have Jessica's father ceremonially give his daughter to him and officiate the wedding. The lawyers were the true officiates, but her father was the one she admired. The lawyers simply watched the proceedings curiously.

Tristan stood near the table where the lawyers and the wedding document awaited their final signatures of acceptance. Riley stood with him as his official witness. Both wore their formal dress uniforms. The guests sat at tables near them, waiting for Saul Deacons to escort his daughter in. When all was ready, Robert escorted his mother to the head table and sat down beside her. Saul escorted Jessica in, followed by Maddy, Jessica's former roommate and best friend. Jessica wore a bright blue gown that accented the blue in her eyes. She was the most beautiful woman Tristan had seen, and he took a step back in awe. Riley gently nudged him forward again and softly said, "Easy, boy. It's too late to run."

Tristan stared at the goddess in front of him. The urge to kneel in her presence settled on him. Jessica was smiling nervously from ear to ear. She knew Tristan had worked hard on these unusual arrangements. She didn't want to spoil it for him by saying or doing the wrong thing.

Saul faced the couple, with Tristan on his left and Jessica on his right, and addressed the crowd. "Ladies and gentlemen, we are all here to celebrate the union of Tristan Alexander and Jessica Deacons. The documents for their marriage have been drawn up and are ready to be signed, but there is more to marriage than documents. Marriages involve the doldrums of everyday living, the illnesses, the bad moods, the birthday parties, the broken food dispensers or heat and air units. I am very protective of my family and want only the best for my daughter. Tristan Alexander, what do you bring to this marriage that a document cannot provide for?"

Tristan smiled and cleared his throat. He promised to love Jessica, to protect her with his own life if necessary, to care for her through the smooth times and the rough ones.

Jessica, in turn, promised similar things. The two signed the agreement. The lawyers placed the appropriate holographic stamp on their hands and the couple stepped back into their places. Saul took Jessica's newly stamped hand and placed it in Tristan's stamped hand. "It's official. You are husband and wife for the contracted period of two years. You may kiss your bride."

The couple kissed and were cheered by the guests. Tristan offered his hand of gratitude to Saul. Saul shook Tristan's hand, pulled him in close for a hug, and whispered, "Remember what we talked about. Marriage isn't something you take lightly. You hurt my daughter—I'll come after you."

"Understood, sir. You have my word. No harm will come to her as long as I'm alive."

The witnesses signed the agreement, allowing the lawyers to go on their way—then the party portion of the ceremony began. The newly married couple made the rounds to greet each of their guests. They took breaks from the meet-and-greet portion of the evening to dance together under the stars and polar lights. Jessica stared at the dancing aurora. "Tristan, I never imagined a night so magical. Thank you."

Tristan grinned. "I hope I didn't set the bar too high."

"What do you mean?"

"After the honeymoon, we go back to being our normal selves and moving into my tiny apartment."

"Well, I guess there's only one way to fix that."

"How?"

"You'll have to buy me a big house in the country." Jessica grinned.

"Oh, is that all?"

"It's a start."

Tristan stopped dancing and let go of Jessica. He looked around the room conspicuously.

"What are you doing?"

"I was looking for those lawyers. I want to reread our marriage contract."

His comment earned him an elbow in the ribcage.

Late that night, the couple escaped the party to their own room. The facility was a hotel with the party being held in the main hotel enclosure. Jessica and Tristan's suite was a peripheral room with its own glass-domed roof.

Jessica was in awe of the scenic view and the beautiful accommodations. She stared up at the sky. Tristan approached from behind and wrapped his arms around her. He looked at the lights dancing above them. The whole day had gone perfectly. Now they reached the moment both desired, but each had denied themselves until now. Still staring at the sky, Jessica whispered. "Tristan, thank you for waiting for me."

"You're welcome. You're worth the wait."

Jessica turned and looked at him oddly. "How do you know? We haven't done anything yet."

"That doesn't matter. You're still worth it."

Six months later, the couple was settled into a pleasant routine. The apartment was small but cozy for them. Tristan had suggested they increase their savings before buying their first home.

Tonight was supposed to be extra special. It was Tristan's twenty-sixth birthday. They planned to meet Jessica's parents, along with Maddy and her fiancé and Riley and Mia.

Jessica left work to stop by a clinic. She was feeling a little under the weather and didn't want it to spoil their evening. She returned to the apartment and sat down, stunned. The diagnosis was not what she expected. She expected it down the road, but not now—not this soon. She stared straight ahead, then called Maddy.

Maddy had just gotten home as well and was getting ready for the birthday dinner. "Hey, Jess, what's up? We are still on for tonight, aren't we?"

"Huh? Oh, yeah, we're still having the party."

"Jess, what's bothering you?"

"I'm nervous. No, I'm scared silly."

Maddy tossed clothes and shoes around as she tried to decide what to wear. She stopped moving and sat down in front of the computer screen. "Scared? What are you scared about? Did you get fired or something?"

Jessica's eyes widened. "No—I got pregnant."

Maddy squealed with excitement. "Really? Congratulations! That's awesome news! Wait... why does that make you scared? Doesn't Tristan want children?"

"Yes, he does, but he didn't want them so soon. He wanted us to save up to buy a house before we started a family. He's very meticulous about these things, you know. He's going to be so upset."

"No, he's not. Is it a boy or a girl? When are you due? Is the baby healthy?"

"It's a boy, and yes, he's fine. Maybe I should go back and have the baby removed and placed in stasis until we're ready to start our family."

"Don't you dare! You tell Tristan first. The two of you should talk it over before you make that kind of decision. It's not fair to Tristan to do that without telling him. The baby is half his, you know."

Jessica knew that more than she cared to admit. "Okay, okay. I'll talk to him first. I just..." A noise at the door got Jessica's attention. "I gotta go. He's home. I'll see you in a couple of hours. Oh, and wear the purple. You look good in purple."

Jessica saw Maddy scramble for the purple dress as she closed the computer. Tristan came in nonchalantly and looked surprised to see Jessica. "You're home early. Everything okay?"

"Yeah, I left a little early to get ready for your birthday party."

Tristan shook his head at her. "It's not a party. It's just dinner with friends. I really wish you hadn't gone to all this trouble. I'm not used to people making a fuss over me or my birthdays."

Jessica wrapped her arms around his neck. "That's why I'm doing this. I know you didn't have a family life when you were growing up, and if we're going to start a family someday, you need to know how to be a family man."

Tristan sighed. "I suppose you're right." He kissed Jessica's nose gently. "It may take a while for me to learn how to do that, though. It's a novel concept for me. I need a shower." He kissed her again and pulled away to undress.

Jessica watched him a moment, unable to interpret his comments as favorable or not. Maybe she and Maddy would have time to talk more later.

The group settled in at the restaurant. Maddy jumped to sit next to Jessica so they could sneak in a few private discussions any chance they got. Maddy was bubbling with excitement and full of questions.

Tristan ordered a bottle of wine and poured Jessica a glass along with everyone else at the table. He stood to offer a toast.

Jessica stared at the glass of wine. She knew drinking and pregnancy were contraindicated. She wasn't sure what to do. She supposed one small sip wouldn't be detrimental. Perhaps she could simply place it to her lips feigning a sip. She couldn't keep that up all night, though. Someone would notice if her wineglass didn't slowly empty, but she wasn't sure she was ready to make her situation public.

Maddy called the waiter over, ordered a glass of water for herself, and asked if anyone else would like one. Kay asked for one, and Jessica quickly joined them in their requests. One hurdle handled. Now, how to get rid of the wine in the glass?

Tristan offered his toast. "My beautiful bride wants me to get used to having a family to fuss over me on birthdays. A toast, to me and having a family for the first time to celebrate a birthday with."

"Hear, hear!" Riley chimed in.

"To Tristan," came Saul's agreement.

Everyone raised their glasses and toasted.

The rest of the meal went by pleasantly enough. Maddy pulled Jessica away to the restroom to grill her about the baby and Tristan. Jessica got frustrated with her. "Maddy, I've got more important things to worry about right now. Somebody's going to notice that I'm not drinking my wine and they're going to want to know why."

"It's okay. I can cover you on that. Just keep your glass near mine, and I can switch them or drink from yours. Whatever it takes."

When the time came to order dessert, Jessica had prearranged to have a special birthday cake brought to the table. The cake came out looking scrumptious with two tiers drizzled in various tasty syrups.

Tristan sat back in his chair with his mouth hanging open. "Wow. That looks amazing." He started to cut the cake, but Maddy stopped him.

"Uh-uh, you can't cut the cake until you give us twenty-six things you're thankful for."

Tristan set the knife down, looking pained. "Are you kidding? I've never done that before. Where am I supposed to start?"

Riley snickered. "You might try starting at number one, Mister Forensic Accountant."

Tristan gave a perfunctory evil glare at Riley. "Thanks, Riley. I think I got that part."

Tristan stood again and began his soliloquy with expressing his gratitude at having an adoring wife, a father, mother, and brother for the first time in his life, a place to call home, and friends to celebrate with. Tristan looked around the table at Riley. "I am thankful Riley and I got off Stiliani alive and that Lado Pharmaceuticals didn't harm Jessica or Mia. Mia, I'm glad you were able to be here tonight." Knowing what he did about Riley and Mia's relationship, he was glad the two had gotten closer than they had been in years. It wasn't something he could acknowledge, but he was thankful, nonetheless.

Tristan managed, with a great deal of coaching, to get twenty-four. "That's it. That's all I got."

Sensing the moment had come, Jessica guardedly whispered something in Tristan's ear. The only tell-tale sign of his surprise was a heavy blink. Jessica paused and whispered one last thing. Tristan smiled broadly. "Really?"

"Yes, really. You aren't mad, are you?"

"Mad? No, why would I be mad?"

Seeing the exchange, Maddy knew instantly what she had done and gasped. "Twenty-five?" she prodded.

Kay Deacons' eyes teared up as she realized what had probably transpired in the whispered conversation. Saul was beginning to suspect the same thing when Kay grabbed his hand.

Tristan put his arm around Jessica's waist. "Twenty-five, we're having a baby, and twenty-six, it's a boy!"

A great deal more celebration ensued.

Tristan and Jessica moved out of their apartment and into Saul and Kay's home for a time. Tristan wanted to save as many credits on rent as he possibly could to put toward a home of their own. They both earned good money, but Tristan was being extra cautious as Riley's warning still hung in the back of his mind to be prepared for the day he was told it was time to leave

Jessica. He wasn't just putting money away for a house. He was saving untraceable credits, in case they needed to run someday.

A few months later, they had their own home, complete with a fully supplied and decorated nursery. The months spent waiting for their baby to arrive abounded with preparations. The couple settled into their new home a full month before the baby's arrival.

The day the newest member of the Alexander family arrived was a chilly spring day. Jessica went to work as usual, but by lunchtime, she knew the repeated tightness in her abdomen was true labor. She headed home, got her bag ready for the birthing center, and tried to rest while she could. Jessica attempted to fix dinner for Tristan, but the contractions were growing so strong, she began to struggle. She finally called her mother. Kay and Saul rushed over to Jessica and Tristan's house immediately.

Kay was frustrated with her daughter for not heading to the birthing center or calling Tristan sooner. Saul put in the call but caught Tristan already heading home. The second he arrived, the three of them whisked Jessica out the door to the birthing center. Jessica kept assuring everyone she was fine. She attempted to persuade her mother to finish preparing supper for Tristan. The anxious father insisted he was no longer hungry and preferred to go to the clinic. The group's anxiety level made them feel like a circus act as they struggled to get everyone into the vehicle, along with Jessica's bag for herself and Tristan, a bag for the baby, her favorite pillow, and every last-minute item she had forgotten to pack.

The clinic was accustomed to handling family circuses like this. They easily got Jessica settled into a room. Her scan revealed the baby was still several hours from delivery. A neural inhibitor patch was placed across Jessica's back, allowing her to catch a brief nap.

Robert's ship was back from its most recent adventures. He was granted some leave time to visit Tristan and Jessica. The group waited anxiously into the night for the baby to make his appearance.

A little before five a.m., the stubborn young man finally arrived. After the new little family had some time to bond, Tristan invited Jessica's parents and brother in to meet the new arrival. Tristan took the baby from Jessica and handed him gently to Kay Deacons. Calling her by her intended title, he introduced them. "Gramma, I would like you to meet David Liam Alexander. He was born at 4:54 and weighed in at seven pounds, three ounces."

The family took turns holding and loving the precious baby. By mid-morning everyone was ready for some sleep, except Jessica, who had enjoyed medically assisted rest through a good portion of her labor. Tristan and Robert headed to the cafeteria to grab a late breakfast. The two talked very little, as both were too tired. Robert finished his breakfast and headed home to get some sleep.

Tristan went back to Jessica's room. Despite her claims not to need any more rest, she was very much asleep with her hand resting on the baby's bassinet. He stood over the tiny infant and watched him sleep.

The door opened quietly, and Agent Gershom motioned him to step outside. Tristan slipped out the door to talk to the man. Per usual, he was accompanied by the not-so-friendly Agent Wallace.

"What are you two doing here? Do you want me to get caught?" Tristan snapped. He was tired and not in the mood to put up with their banter.

Agent Wallace talked more calmly and quietly than Tristan had ever heard her do. "Agent Alexander, just a polite reminder and word of warning. Don't get overly attached to that baby. If it's decided this mission calls for extreme measures, he'll be the first one to go. I know you passed your evaluation, and you are capable of executing your wife, but you need to maintain the same level of professionalism where her son is concerned. I know he is your son as well, but you can always have another with someone else. This one is our insurance policy. Do you understand?"

Agent Gershom started to jump in to defuse the ongoing antagonism. Tristan waved him off. "I know. I figured that out a long time ago. If you want me to continue the charade of being a good husband and father, I'm going to have to look like I care. Do you understand that? When it comes time for our marriage to break up, let me know in plenty of time to sprinkle in some marital discord. I will need an appropriate amount of time to become the bad guy, so she doesn't try to stick me with visitation privileges or joint custody or something."

Agent Wallace smiled genuinely for the first time, although it could be contributed to sadistic glee. "You do understand. Good. We just came to be certain you still had a grip on reality. Agent Gershom, I believe we are done here."

Agent Gershom looked back and forth between the two. Something felt off about the situation. "Agent Alexander, are you all right with this?"

Tristan rubbed his tired eyes. "I've been up all night, and I'm exhausted. I'm doing my best not to cop an attitude with you or anyone else. I'm as all right as I can be. I would like to remind you that I'm no assassin and I don't kill innocent people, especially not helpless infants—that part I'm not fine with. I will do my best not to get attached to the baby but don't ask me to hurt him, or any other baby for that matter. I can't do that. Give me a heads up so I can be someplace else if and when the issue arises. I would prefer not to witness it. Can I get some sleep now?"

Agent Gershom nodded. "We understand. If anything has to happen, we'll take care of it. I'm not expecting anything, but I did want you to be prepared."

"I appreciate that."

The two agents left him alone, and Tristan stepped back into his wife's room. A medical technician was in the room perusing the readings on the monitors and making notations on a datapad. Tristan was puzzled by his presence. He didn't remember the man being in the room when the agents called him outside, and he had been standing near the door the entire time in the corridor.

He decided he must have been too tired to notice the man. The oversight reinforced his desire to get some sleep.

The technician looked at him. "Morning. My name is Gabe, and I'll be taking care of your wife and baby. You look tired. Can I get you anything?"

"No, I just need some sleep. I never even saw you come in here."

"Most people don't see me. Part of my job is to remain invisible. You have a fine-looking boy here. Congratulations."

"Thanks." Tristan stepped over to the crib and looked down at the sleeping baby. The baby seemed to feel his father's eyes on him. He squirmed and grunted. Tristan picked him up gently. He had never been around children before, but somehow, this came naturally. The thought of someone harming his son sent a wave of near panic through him.

Gabe put his hand on Tristan's shoulder. "Just don't panic. Kids can smell fear. He'll be fine, and so will you. I guarantee it."

Tristan smiled at the tiny face in front of him. "Don't panic, huh? It's funny you should use that particular choice of words." Tristan turned around. Gabe was gone. Tristan shook his head. His need for sleep was becoming more obvious. Placing his newborn son back in the crib, Tristan stretched out on the guest couch in the room and was out in seconds.

Saul and Kay crawled into their bed. They were exhausted yet exhilarated at the birth of their first grandchild. The two snuggled together and talked for several minutes to allow the adrenalin rush to settle before trying to sleep.

Their discussion was light as they discussed who David looked like. Kay finally asked, "Do you think Tristan will make a good father? He's never had a family or been around children."

"I don't know. He didn't seem uncomfortable holding David. My concern is we had to stop teaching Jessica about the things she really needed to know. How will David learn—about Pateras? Jessica was only seven when we stopped teaching her. Does she even remember Pateras? I mean, really remember. We should have found a way to teach them." Saul blinked back tears of regret.

Kay placed her hand gently on his cheek, her heart aching equally. "I know. Perhaps now that she's grown and has a baby of her own, we could find a way to tell her. Tristan's helped us get more privacy."

"I still don't trust that. They can slip monitors back in here at any time. I also don't trust he did that out of the goodness of his heart. He's up to something. I know he has to be. Pateras will have to find a way to reveal himself to them if we can't."

A bright light appeared at the foot of their bed. The couple scrambled to sit up. Their first thought was that the light was a police searchlight and they had been caught in a conversation they shouldn't have been having. As their eyes refocused, they realized, it was definitely not the police. A single man stood in front of them. The couple were terrified at first, thinking they were about to be arrested again. Now they were terrified at the magnificent figure in front of them who was clearly not human.

"Don't be afraid." The man spoke in Drean, Saul and Kay's native language.

"Th-they keep us monitored. They'll notice if they hear you speaking in Drean," Saul warned the figure nervously.

"Don't be afraid," the man repeated in Drean. "Pateras holds all things in his hands. They will hear nothing. Pateras has seen and heard all that you have suffered for him. He has heard the cry of your hearts. Your family is not lost to him. Your son, Richard, has seen the birth of the Promised One, the one who will intercede for all of mankind."

The man continued calling each one by their Drean names instead of their Commonwealth names. "Richard does not understand what he has seen yet, and his anger will cost him a great deal before he understands, but his day will come. Your grandson is spoken of in the prophecies. He will carry the message of Pateras to all who will listen. He is one of the twelve twelves. Do not lose heart. Elliot, your family will once again call Drea home. Tyra, a day will come when you will be tempted to give up. Do not let the loneliness and separation rule you. Fight for your life. Fight for Pateras. A great light now shines in the darkness, and your family will be counted among those who carry the light. Even Tristan will eventually come to see and understand the light. This is not his time, though. Be wary of him for now. Vanessa will return to Pateras as well. Hope is alive."

The figure disappeared from the room, and darkness closed in on them again. Tyra Paulson threw herself into Elliot's arms. Elliot could feel her trembling, and his own body seemed to tremble equally. Tyra cried tears of joy, sorrow, and relief. The message they had been given was full of hope and excitement. Sleep was again far from the couple.

After many tears, Elliot finally whispered, "Pateras, please give us some privacy for a little while longer."

It was mid-morning on an overcast day. A good day for one to be able to catch a long nap. The sun moved out from behind a cloud at the precise moment of Elliot's prayer for privacy. The room lightened again and grew slightly warmer. Sensing his prayer was answered, the two discussed what the messenger had told them. It was another hour before they could rest. Their biggest questions were how was this going to come about, and when would it happen.

EPILOGUE 1 - THIRTY YEARS LATER

Admiral Robert Deacons summoned his nephew, David Alexander, to his office. David had just made captain. The impending Explorer Mission had advanced several people to the rank of captain earlier than normally expected. His nephew was an exceptionally bright young man, and he truly deserved the promotion.

Robert was concerned about a conversation he'd had with his parents thirty years ago. Just after the birth of this young man, his parents claimed a celestial being had visited them.

Robert shook his head as he tried to shake off the eerie feeling brought on by the thought. Twelve ships manned this mission with twelve crew members each, the twelve twelves mentioned in the ridiculous prophecies of the Ancient Texts. Fairy tales! The prophecies were a joke. Still, something about this continued to eat at him. It was quite a coincidence to be sending out twelve twelves. He had to shake his nephew up, to do something to be certain David didn't fall for Pateras' lies. Was it just another coincidence? A celestial visitor had spoken to Robert's parents about David's participation in Pateras El Liontari's mission and now his nephew had been accepted on this mission to hunt Pateras' followers? Robert knew Jessica had never taught David about Pateras, his father never heard of him, and Robert's own parents had only mentioned Pateras on two occasions since Abigail's death. The second time had cost his father his life.

A twinge of guilt pricked Robert's conscience at the thought of the part he had played in his father's death. He hadn't intended for anything to happen. Robert was drunk and said more than he should. There was no proof that it was anything more than an accident. But deep down, Robert knew differently.

He couldn't let the same thing happen to David. He had to push him and push him hard. He had to stay strong and fight against Pateras. Robert's parents told him he had witnessed the birth of the Promised One. Robert remembered the baby he saw born on Galat III. He clearly remembered the event and the names ingrained in his mind that day, Pateras El Liontari and Arni Sotaeras Liontari.

That had been on a low-tech world. If that was where the man was, there was only one way to stop him. Robert would send David there to see to the end of this resurrection of a following of Pateras. It would also prove the prophecies to be what they were—a fairy tale. Galat III and Drea were all within the territory assigned to David and his crew. If the Admirals' Board sequestered the planets or destroyed them, the problem would be contained. His family could never again call Drea home. The Dreans had not protected them from the Commonwealth anymore than Pateras had. Now Robert would see to it the Commonwealth stopped Pateras from deceiving anyone else.

Admiral Deacons' door chimed. Robert opened the door to admit the handsome young captain.

"Capt. Alexander, reporting as ordered, sir."

Robert proudly smiled inwardly at the young man. He would end this prophecy, Pateras, Galat, and Drea in one swoop, and David was the key.

EPILOGUE 2 - THE YEAR AFTER

Tristan woke up and blinked at the bright lights above him. His blurred vision cleared in a moment. This wasn't good, he thought, as he faced two stern-looking SS *Evangeline* security officers. If things were going well, it should have been his son, the former Capt. David Alexander, who retrieved him from the stasis chamber. After all, he was the one who put him in there. He wasn't sure how long David had left him in stasis, nor what he intended to do with him now.

This lifetime of lying had finally caught up to him. Jessica had found him out, and now his fate lay in the hands of their son. He had secretly sworn to protect them, despite warnings from his superiors. How did things end up this way? Tristan had been an officer of the law and a Commonwealth soldier all his life. He got paid to lie. Now his lies might well cost him his life. At the very least, they had cost him his family.

With a heavy heart, Tristan climbed out of the chamber. He had always kept his emotions in check, but the heaviness would not lift.

The security officers placed binders on his wrists. He thought back to the days when he and Jessica had just married and David was born. Agents Wallace and Gershom's repeated warnings not to get attached to his family and the potential requirement of using extreme measures against them echoed in his thoughts.

Cmdr. Braxton Flint and Security Chief Jake Holden escorted Tristan to the primary airlock. Seeing sunshine streaming in from outside, Tristan sighed with relief. He wasn't being spaced. He had no idea what planet they were on, but he would at least survive. He paused at the top of the steps. The entire crew was assembled on the ground. His eyes caught Lt. Marissa Holden cradling her newborn baby. He had just seen the baby born, so his time in stasis had been only days at most, hours at least. Tristan's escorts pushed him to keep moving. They stepped slowly down the stairs to the ground. The crew's faces were serious, and some were even angry. The ship's doctor refused to make eye contact.

Tristan had never thought things would come to this when he took on that assignment thirty years ago. He hadn't really had a choice at the time. He wasn't given a choice when the Commonwealth ordered him to hunt down his own renegade son. He was tired of never being given a choice. The one choice he did have was how he felt about his family. No matter what he had been warned about, he had loved Jessica and their two children.

Tristan approached the baby boy the agents had warned him not to get too attached to. Being forced to divorce Jessica and leave his family behind when David was only twelve, he was uncertain of his son's limits or motivations. What kind of man had his son become? He was about to find out. Was he capable of executing his own father? "So, I guess this is goodbye?"

David had his feet planted firmly and his arms folded across his chest. "That's entirely up to you."

THE DEFENDER
SERIES

CONTINUES WITH

THE MISSION (BOOK 1)

PICK IT UP TODAY
FROM YOUR FAVORITE
BOOKSTORE!

The newly promoted captain, David Alexander, takes command of his first crew and starship on a multifaceted mission of diplomacy, intelligence gathering, and dangerous first contacts. He and his crew are searching out a dangerous and subversive new enemy to the Commonwealth, the ruling power in the galaxy. After finding and eluding the enemy on the ship's first contact, David discovers the enemy is now stalking him and his crew with warnings of impending doom.

A loyal Commonwealth soldier, David resists his enemies' attempts to seduce him to change sides. On his second mission, David finds himself at the mercy of a primitive group of savages intent on killing him. His only hope is his sworn enemy, but what is the price for saving his life?

David learns that his enemy, Arni Liontari, has gone out of his way to protect him and his crew. Could the Commonwealth's Intel be wrong or is the enemy more dangerous than he realized? Get on board the *Evangeline*, now, before it's too late.

DEFENDED

THE DEFENDER SERIES BOOK 2

REGGI BROACH

Captain Alexander and the crew of the *Evangeline* continue their Commonwealth mission to make allies of the non-space-faring planets in the galaxy. Drea III is a technologically advanced world shrouded by a dark and bloody history with the Commonwealth.

Drean officials politely agree to hear the crew's proposal of an alliance with the Commonwealth. A series of heinous discoveries land the crew in jail, charged with several capital crimes. Captain Alexander finds himself torn between his Commonwealth mandates and protecting an entire planet from annihilation.

David throws himself on the mercy of the courts, defending his crew to his last breath. More unexpected revelations cause the Captain and crew to question everything they've been taught.

The Commonwealth groomed Capt. David Alexander from birth for this mission. David rejects his Commonwealth upbringing and joins Pateras El Liontari and his son Arni. His actions create a rift among the crew, particularly for Security Chief Jake Holden.

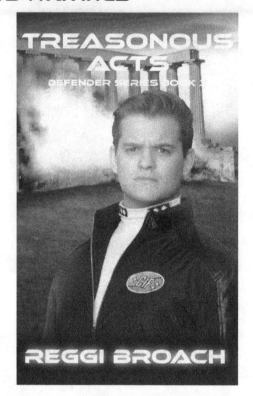

Jake's job is to protect the crew from Pateras and the primitive planetary locals. He can handle the locals, but Pateras proves to be too much. It's his job to execute his captain or arrest him. Capt. Alexander saves the life of Jake and Marissa's unborn baby, adding to Jake's conundrum.

The lives of David, his crew, and the local citizens hang in the balance when David challenges a power-hungry High Priest. The crew struggles to trust Arni as the priest's followers rise up against the local chancellor. An unexpected visit from David's uncle, Admiral Deacons, puts a heavily armed Pacification Ship in orbit. If Jake reports David's treason, the Admiral will be forced to arrest or execute his traitorous nephew. Can Pateras protect them from the Admiral and the powerful ship in orbit?

Captain David Alexander and his crew are guilty of treason against the Commonwealth. Security Chief Jake Holden openly opposes the crew's treason. Arni, the superior being who now holds David's loyalty, warns him that Jake will betray him. David knows the cost and the benefits of willingly stepping into Jake's trap.

Alone, imprisoned, beaten, and drugged, David struggles to remain loyal to Pateras and to resist the urge to surrender to Supreme Executor Hale's enticing offers. David is pushed to his limits when his crew is led to believe he betrayed them, and his wife told about a contrived relationship between him and another woman.

Tortured mercilessly, Jake offers him a way out, a syringe with a lethal sedative. The drugs forced on him by his captors wreak havoc with his thoughts. Did Pateras abandon him? Was this the only way out?

Capt. Alexander and the crew of the *Evangeline* are running for their lives. The Supreme Executor of the Commonwealth, Luciano Hale, has framed the treasonous crew for mass murder and terrorism, making them the most hunted individuals in space.

The crew has only one chance, get the truth out to the other eleven Explorer ships. David's best chance is his old friends from his academy days, Nate and Stephanie Weiseman. David tracks down the SS *Emissary*, hoping his friends will listen. To his disappointment, Nate attempts to place him under arrest. In an effort to get the crew to trust Jake again, Capt. Alexander puts his life in Jake's hands, the one who initially betrayed them all.

Difficult losses among both crews and the planetary natives wreak havoc as David attempts to win back his best friends' trust. Time runs out when a ship of super soldiers arrives to inflict the death penalty on the crew of the *Evangeline* and the crew of the *Emissary*.

BIRTH OF A REVOLUTION

DEFENDER SERIES BOOK 6

REGGI BROACH

Hunted for treason and haunted by his past, Captain David Alexander attempts to unite the Explorer Fleet against the Commonwealth. The belief that Captain Alexander mercilessly destroyed an entire military base fuels his comrades' desire to turn him in. David has evidence against Supreme Executor Luciano Hale, but it's subjective. Will it be enough to convince the other crews to join him?

The tenuous agreement reached by the Fleet is put in danger when four ruffians, hungry for revenge, kidnap Captain Alexander and Lt. Marissa Holden who is about to give birth. The two are forced into an empty mine tunnel. The odds are not good with four against one and the young lieutenant in heavy labor.

Can Security Chief Jake Holden reach the Captain and Marissa in time? Who is the mysterious stranger stalking them? Can they get off Zulimar before their enemies arrive? Get onboard before the enemy catches you!

UNDER DEVELOPMENT